Freda Lightfoot

Freda Lightfoot was born in Lancashire but lived in the
Lake District for many years where she was a teacher,
bookseller and smallholder. She is married with two
grown-up daughters and still visits the Lakes as often
as she can. Her first Lakeland saga, *Luckpenny Land*,
is also available from Coronet.

Writing as Freda Lightfoot

Luckpenny Land

Writing as Marion Carr

Madeiran Legacy
A Proud Alliance
Outrageous Fortune
Hester
Whispering Shadows

Wishing Water

Freda Lightfoot

CORONET BOOKS
Hodder and Stoughton

First published in 1995 by Hodder & Stoughton
First published in paperback in 1995 by Hodder & Stoughton
A division of Hodder Headline PLC

A Coronet paperback

British Library Cataloguing in Publication Data

Lightfoot, Freda
Wishing Water
I. Title
823.914 [F]

ISBN 0 340 63508 8

Printed and bound in Great Britain by
Cox & Wyman Ltd, Reading, Berkshire

Hodder and Stoughton
A division of Hodder Headline PLC
338 Euston Road
London NW1 3BH

To Debbie and Anna, who have never expected me
to be the perfect mother

Acknowledgements

I would like to offer my thanks to North West Water Group PLC, to Lakeland Knitwear, and to Kendal Public Library for their help in the research for this book.

1951

1

Lissa Turner kilted her thin cotton skirts and slid from the sheep-cropped turf into the icy waters of Allenbeck, squealing with delight as it foamed against her bare legs. She swivelled her head round to look up at the boy, still standing on dry land, very nearly over-toppling herself in the process.

'Come in, it's wonderful.'

She wriggled her toes, the stones grinding and slipping beneath her feet, and tried another step. Above her head a lapwing climbed on lazily beating wings, finishing in a dizzying display of joy in the May sky. Not always so blue in these Lakeland hills, it came as no surprise to Lissa to find it sun-filled and blue. For today was a special day.

Today she was to see her mother.

All around them grew alder and silver birch, pale slender stems crowding the edge of the small gushing stream, eager perhaps to cool their own feet in the exhilarating flow from the rocky depths of the high mountains. Over the low hump of Gimmer bridge, built a century or more ago with painstaking care and not a scrap of mortar, as was the way in this part of Westmorland, she could see right along the rough track to the stile where the road divided. If she took one twisting path she would come to Broombank, her home, and where Meg and Tam lived. The other climbed up over Larkrigg Fell to the place she should live, Larkrigg Hall. The place where her mother would be preparing a special tea this afternoon for their first meeting in years. Four years to be exact, not since just after the war when Lissa had been only seven and too young to understand anything.

But she understood now. In Lissa's pansy eyes was more knowledge than she admitted to, certainly more than was considered good for her. Her stomach tightened into a knot of excitement. Lissa meant to enjoy this day, to wring from it every drop of pleasure she could.

'What if you fall in?' grumbled the boy, pausing in the act of unlacing one boot as he wondered if he would get the blame, if she did.

Lissa gave a gurgle of laughter. 'Then I'd get wet.' The idea at once took root and she wanted nothing more than to feel the icy water flowing and stinging over every part of her young flesh. Something tickled her toes and she wriggled them, seeing darting slivers of dark shadows race away as she did so.

'Oh, look, there are millions of minnows here,' she cried.

'Don't talk daft. Millions, my foot,' he scoffed.

'There are.'

'Catch some then, clever clogs.'

Lissa lifted off the jam jar that had been hanging on a string about her neck and, still holding her dress with one hand, dipped it with the other into the gushing waters. The tiny fish fled. Not one was to be seen. The water that gushed into the jar was quite empty of life.

'Oh.' She sighed her disappointment.

'You're ignorant, Lissa Turner. All girls are ignorant. Can't catch fish to save your life.'

She stopped caring about her dress and the sharp stones and swivelled about to splash him with a spray of the foaming water. 'Yes I can!'

'Here, give over,' he protested and taking up a flat stone, tossed it carelessly into the beck, missing her bare feet by inches. The water splashed in great wet globs over her clean print frock and up into her face, making her gasp at its coldness.

'Oh, you *rat*!' But the imp of mischief in her could not resist retaliation, so she dipped her hands in the cold water and scooped up great washes of it. But though she aimed at the boy, laughing on the shore, she soaked herself more than him.

'Nick, we could go for a swim. A real one. Why don't we?' She was breathless suddenly with the unexpectedness of her idea, eyes shining with excitement. Why hadn't she thought of it before? The perfect way to celebrate a special day.

2

'We can't go for a swim.' The boy sounded contemptuous, as if she was wrong in the head. 'You know we're not allowed to go alone up to the tarn.'

'Oh, phooey.'

'And our Daniel can't swim proper yet.'

'I can too,' came a piping voice from some yards away but neither of them took any notice of the smaller boy, knee-deep in water and mud, engrossed in his hunt for wild creatures, as per usual.

'Anyroad, Miss Clever-Clogs is going out to tea.' The boy spoke with a lilting mockery in his tone. 'With the witch up at the big house.'

'She's not a witch,' Lissa hotly protested, uncertainty in her voice. 'She's my grandmother so how can she be?'

Nick put on his superior expression. 'If she is, how come you've niver been to see her afore?'

Lissa desperately searched her mind for a reasonable excuse. Not for the world would she admit the truth, that her grandmother would have nothing to do with her. Any story was better than that. 'She's not been well.'

The boy grunted his disbelief and Lissa wished she could stamp her foot at him but the water hampered her.

'If you want to know, she's been waiting for my mother to come home. She couldn't get here for my birthday but she'll be here today.'

'Huh! Rather you than me then. She's a witch I tell you,' Nick insisted. 'You'd best come out of that beck, afore our Meg catches you.'

Lissa had been thinking exactly the same thing but she hated to be told so. 'I'll please myself what I do, Nick Turner.'

'I'm your cousin and you're just a girl. I'm responsible for you, like I am for our Daniel here.'

Lissa was incensed. Though she had gladly slipped down to the beck at Nick's suggestion, bringing her jam jar to catch a few minnows, that was only because she hated to be confined, even for a minute, while the adults chattered on about the Festival of Britain Tea Party in the village hall, how good Betty Hutton had been in 'Annie Get Your Gun' at the pictures last week, and other matters which were of no importance at all.

'I'm three months older than you so how can you be responsible for me? Nor are you any cousin of mine, so there.'

3

The boy's lip curled with superior mockery. 'No one believes that old chestnut Aunty Meg tells, about her finding you in a Liverpool orphanage.'

'Believe what you like, you odious toad, it's true.' She slapped more water at him in her fury but he only laughed the louder. 'But I *do* know who my mother is. And she's flying all the way from Canada to see me. *Today*.' The joy of it sang in her heart like a hymn.

Nick Turner couldn't help but admire the defiant challenge in the glittering violet eyes that glared back at him. And the way Lissa tossed her head, as pettishly as a young colt riding recklessly against the north-east wind that battered these fells, as she would too, given half a chance. They'd grown up together, Lissa, Daniel and himself, like a litter of puppies. They'd learned to swim together, ride their bikes, walk miles over the fells without getting lost, help with the sheep and the harvest. Lissa was always determined not to be outshone by anyone, for all she was a mere girl. That's why he'd taunted her to take off her best shoes and paddle in the beck. Lissa never could resist a challenge. And damming up the stream was a favourite occupation.

They'd also fought, squabbled, competed at every game they could devise, joked and teased and had fun. She was a part of his life. Now all she could think about, all she ever talked about, was that big house. She wasn't fun any more.

'Meet your mother? Looking like that? Oh, aye, you *will* be popular.'

Now, when it was too late, Lissa did look at herself and was appalled. Her heart gave a little jump of fear. She couldn't meet her mother looking a sight. Katherine was beautiful, everyone said so.

'It's all your fault,' she cried, tears pricking the back of her eyes. But Nick only laughed, quite without sympathy for her plight.

She was coming slowly back to him now, her movements as liquid and graceful as the swirling waters that washed about her white slender limbs, hair ribbons slipping loose in the wild tumble of glossy black curls. For all she was still a child, it was abundantly clear to anyone with eyes to see that Lissa Turner would grow into a beauty. A wilful, high-spirited beauty, very much with a mind of her own. She tilted her head up to him and pouted her lips, unconsciously flirting with a naturalness that might one day lead her into any amount of trouble – as it was about to do today.

4

Then flouncing up her skirts, heedless of revealing a grand view of her drawers, she stepped on to the bank beside him. They were of a height still. Though one day soon he would outstrip her, for now she could look him straight in the eye, as equals, and Lissa revelled in that fact.

She untucked the cotton frock and it clung damply to her legs, the rows of pretty white daisies that a short time ago had given her so much pleasure now spotted with mud. Her feet had gone into little red and blue blotches with the cold and there were bits of grass and shale stuck between the toes. How could she possibly dress them in the bright white socks and shining black patent shoes that stood so neatly on the bank beside her?

'It's all your fault,' she said again, mischief gone from her now, swamped by misery at what Meg would say at the wreck of the so carefully prepared appearance. For weeks Lissa had watched as the dress had been painstakingly stitched, anxiously waiting for the day when she could wear it. Now this boy, who dared insult her by insisting he was her cousin, had made her dip her feet in the frothing water and she had ruined it. 'I didn't think,' she mourned. 'Oh, Nick, what shall I do?' Lissa began to weep then slanted her eyes sideways at him, begging him to apologise, to take the blame as she felt by rights that he should, and spare her from a scolding. The sunlight flashed on the rush of tears, making them shine like royal velvet.

Nick felt a sudden rush of interest that was startlingly new to him. Perhaps something to do with the odd dreams he experienced sometimes at night, dreams that woke him up, all in a sweat. His eyes narrowed, moving over the loose tumble of glossy curls where they hung damply against the rise and fall of her skinny chest and fastened upon two pert buttons straining against the fabric. One day he supposed these would grow into breasts and he had a sudden vision of how they would look on her. He experienced an intense urge to touch one now with the tip of his finger, to see how it would feel. Would it be soft, or springy like rubber? The very thought brought a rush of blood beneath his fair skin.

Then he remembered how she always liked to imagine herself better than him, showing off, denying she was the bastard they all knew her to be. He enjoyed using that word in his head. It made him feel daring and grown up. Nick remembered how she went boring on about Larkrigg Hall and how she really belonged there.

He gave a loud snort of derision, glad of her discomfiture. 'You don't look so fine a lady now,' he said. 'Your ma, if you have one, will mistake you for a tadpole, or a bit of chick weed.'

'You rotten . . .'

Ten-year-old Daniel chose this moment to interrupt, which was perhaps just as well. 'See Lissa, see what I've found. A baby bird. I think it's dying.'

All else was forgotten in the heat of discovery. The two children scrambled along the grass banking to where Daniel knelt in the water, a tiny form cradled in his palm.

'It fell into the water, down the mud bank,' he explained in his serious way.

'What is it?' Lissa wanted to know. She could see its tiny heart beating and its eyes wide open and frightened.

'It might be a young kingfisher. They dig long tunnels in the bank here and lay their eggs at the end. Perhaps this one came last and was forgotten.'

'Throw it away,' said Nick. 'You might catch something nasty from it.'

Lissa was appalled by this heartless suggestion. 'No, no, you mustn't. Give it to me.' She held out her hand for the bird but Daniel looked doubtful.

'You couldn't keep it,' he warned.

'Yes, I could. Why not?'

'It'll need feeding.'

'I can feed it.'

'You'd have to catch fish every day. It needs dozens, hundreds of live fish.'

'Then I'll do that. I can catch fish. Give it to me.' Her heart was beating hard against her thin chest with the fervour of her words, desperate to hold the bird but knowing if she revealed how much, these careless boys could as easily toss it away simply to provoke her. Boys were like that. 'It'll die anyway if I don't try.'

Daniel hesitated then looked as if he was about to hand the bird over. Nick stopped him. 'Catch the fish first,' he ordered.

'If you're so good at it, why don't you catch some for me?' The taunting challenge in her eyes caused him to hesitate, torn between proving how able he was at catching minnows and at not letting her think he would willingly carry out her every whim. Which they both knew he would.

'I'll start you off with a few,' he said, with just the right amount of airy unconcern, and picking up his jar, swaggered off along the bank to where he could climb down into the water.

In seconds his jar was teeming with fish and he was grinning from ear to ear. Didn't I tell you? his expression said.

'Oh, thank you, Nick,' and she reached for the jar. But a stubborn spirit of new independence glowed in the boy today. He tipped the jar up and poured the fish back into the free-flowing beck. 'Now you do it.'

'What?'

'Now you catch some tiddlers, prove you're as good as me and can feed this bird every day.'

'Oh, *drat* you.' Knowing it was a reasonable request somehow made it worse. Lissa slapped at him with the flat of her hand, smiling as the laughter on his round face began to fade into surprise as he lost his footing, arms flailed round and round like a windmill in the wind, and almost in slow motion, he fell backwards into the water. Fortunately it was more wide than deep at this point and he was as much winded as wet. But for Nick, surprisingly angry.

'Now you've done it,' he shouted.

But he looked so funny sitting there on the pebbles with his bony knees poking up out of the frothing water that Lissa curled up on the bank and laughed till the tears rolled down her cheeks. And after glowering his fury for several more minutes Nick joined in too while Daniel rolled on the grass and waved his feet in the air with delight.

But the baby kingfisher still had to be fed.

Too late now to argue. Too late to complain she was in her best dress and she really mustn't risk spoiling it. Lissa desperately wanted to prove she could look after that poor bird. 'Keep still,' she said. 'Don't frighten the fish away with your cackling.'

Going to the small shale beach she once more kilted her skirts, pulling them between her legs and tucking the hem into her waist band at the front, stuffing the trailing bits up the lace trimmed-elastic of her best knickers.

She waded slowly out into the fast-flowing stream, close to the bridge where there were fewer stones and the water spread out wide and deep and dark beneath a tunnel of greenery. When it was above her knees she stopped. For what seemed an age she waited until the tiny minnows had grown used to the pale trunks of her legs and brushed against them with casual ease. Very slowly she bent down, holding the jar in the flow of the river. At first there was nothing and her heart fluttered with despair. If she didn't catch any fish, Daniel would never give her the baby kingfisher and the poor thing would die.

Then she saw it, a great fat black cloud of darting fish. In seconds her jar was crowded with them and she swooped it out of the water with a cry of triumph.

'I've done it. See.'

But her delight was short lived, for the swift movement rocked a stone beneath her foot and the heavy water took instant advantage, pushing resolutely against her. Even as she struggled to find her balance she knew herself lost. Holding the jar high in her hand to save her precious fish, she sat with infuriated dignity, but nonetheless very damply, in the water.

Meg stared at Lissa with growing horror in her grey eyes. 'How could you? How *could* you?' Then she widened her gaze to encompass the two muddy boys, unusually subdued. 'How could any of you behave so badly, today of all days?'

They all stared miserably at the pools they were making on the slate floor, deeming it prudent not to reply.

'Upstairs with you, Lissa.' Meg jerked a thumb at her two nephews. 'You two had best go to the outhouse, clean that mud off and get out of those wet things. I'll find you something dry to wear, though I can't promise it'll fit, nor save you from trouble when you get home.'

She felt a jolt of pity for their sad faces as they trailed off to do her bidding. At any other time Meg would have laughed at their predicament. It was no more than childish fun after all. She could remember she and her brother Charlie being in exactly the same predicament on any number of occasions. But she was short on humour today. Kath's letters always seemed to put her in a temper, even now, after all these years. There was still the gnawing fear that she would come for Lissa and take her back with her, and Meg would never see her lovely girl again. Canada was the other side of the world, after all.

She could remember, as clearly as if it were yesterday, the time Kath had come for her daughter. Lissa had been seven years old by then. Seven *years* in Meg's care, and Kath had imagined she could simply collect her, like a parcel, and ship her away. But Meg had refused to allow it.

'Lissa stays here with me, at Broombank, where she belongs,' she had said, and that had been that.

Surprisingly Kath had made no protest. She had merely smiled her beautiful smile, shrugged slender shoulders and walked out of Meg's life with that elegant swinging sway to her hips, to start life in Canada with her new husband.

She had written once or twice a year since then, often claiming that she would visit soon, but nothing had ever come of these promises.

Until today.

A soft touch at her elbow brought her back to the present. 'Here,' said Tam, handing her a steaming bowl. 'Sponge her down quickly with some warm water and she'll be right enough. Did you never get mud in your own eye, Meg O'Cleary?'

Meg looked lovingly into her husband's face and her lips lifted into a smile. How could they resist when she loved him so much? Tam leaned over the bowl and dropped a kiss upon her nose.

''Tis a lovely woman you are, Meg, when you're thinking with your heart. I'll go and deal with them two tearaways and take 'em back meself. See if I can stop your father tanning their hides. He is staying at Ashlea again, is he not?'

'Yes,' Meg sighed. 'Poor Sally Ann.'

'She gets on with him better than you do. I'll see these lads don't suffer his wrath.' Taciturn and dour to a fault, the boys' grandfather Joe was supposed to be retired in Grange-Over-Sands but spent every moment he could at his old home, Ashlea, using the excuse that he was helping his daughter-in-law, Sally Ann, widowed by the war and never remarried. He'd remarried himself, at the end of the war, but the marriage hadn't prospered.

'Thanks.' Meg gave Tam a warm smile of gratitude, drew in a deep breath and started up the stairs. Lissa could be as troublesome to deal with in her own way as Joe, but there were no arguments from her now as Meg stripped off the sodden dress. No tantrums or tears as the dripping, best white underwear with the lace trim was replaced by everyday interlock vest and knickers.

'You'll have to wear your yellow cotton frock,' Meg said and smiled to herself as she saw the pretty nose wrinkle in disgust.

'Don't like it.'

9

Meg sighed, biting back the retort that perhaps Lissa should have thought of that before she decided to go fishing for minnows but managed, with difficulty, to hold her tongue. The young kingfisher, now installed in a box in the barn, would only be brought forth yet again as an excuse, or means of eliciting her sympathy. 'Which then?' thinking over Lissa's wardrobe which shrank daily as the child grew. Soon, all too soon in Meg's opinion, she would be a child no longer. Budding womanhood would take over. It was certainly long past time they had a talk about it.

'I shall wear my jersey skirt and blue embroidered blouse,' Lissa said, deciding on what she considered to be her most sophisticated items.

'Isn't it rather warm for jersey?'

'You're wearing a skirt and blouse.'

So the blue jersey it was. The tangled dark locks were brushed and fresh ribbons found to put them back into their tidy bunches, one at each side of the rosy, scrubbed cheeks. The sparkle was back in the arresting eyes, the tongue loosened once more into chatter. 'Oh do let's hurry, Meg. We mustn't be late. What will she be like? I don't remember her. Will she like me?'

The questions came thick and fast as they set off to walk the two miles up to Larkrigg Hall. Meg's heart went out to the child, for didn't her own anxiety match Lissa's?

'Of course you will recognise her, once you see her. But she will be surprised how much you have grown.' Meg didn't like to talk about the love aspect. She couldn't. She found it impossible to credit Kath with the ability to love a daughter she'd abandoned so soon after her birth. Not even a war would have persuaded Meg to do such a thing. But then there had been other, more pressing reasons, she supposed. Reasons best not remembered.

The slopes of Larkrigg Fell rose gently ahead of them, with the steep crag of Dundale Knott at their backs, its comical lop-sided appearance belying the very real dangers to be found on the crags and crevices that scarred its surface. As her beloved dog, Rust, had once discovered to his cost. He was at her heels now, as always. Battle-scarred and not so spry as he'd once been, yet fit enough to walk the fells with her every day tending the sheep, despite his thirteen years.

'Come on, old boy,' she urged, a softness to her voice these days whenever she addressed him. 'He's panting a bit more than he should, Lissa. Maybe I'd best retire him.'

Lissa rubbed the dog's ears, one brown, one black. 'You know he couldn't take to that. Where you are, so must he be.'

Funny thing, loyalty, Meg mused. It could cement a friendship or, misplaced, just as easily ruin one. Hadn't she learned so herself once? 'Dogs are so much less complicated than people,' she said.

To their left was Allenbeck. It began high on Larkrigg Fell where it gathered its strength to burst out as a waterfall, known locally as a force, and tumbled onwards through Whinstone Gill, a deep cleft cut into the rocks forming a wooded ravine, till it ran out of power and passed under Gimmer bridge at a more sedate pace.

Now they climbed the sheep trods through Brockbarrow wood which in its turn flanked the southern shores of the tarn.

Brockbarrow wood. The place for a lover's tryst.

'What shall I say to her?' Lissa worried. 'What can we talk about? She doesn't know me or any of my friends.'

Anxious dark blue eyes gazed up at Meg. Jack's eyes. She swallowed. 'Tell her all about yourself. About how you like to help on the farm, how you're learning to play the harmonium. How you are changing schools this year and mean to go to the High School.'

'If I pass my certificate.'

'Of course you'll pass.'

'I'm so nervous. Isn't it silly?' A small hand crept into Meg's and she squeezed it encouragingly.

'I'm pretty nervous myself as a matter of fact.'

'Are you?' An odd relief in the voice. They looked at each other and grinned. 'What ninnies we are. She can't eat us.'

Meg shook her head. 'She's not managed it yet.'

A companionable silence fell as they trudged on. Somewhere high above a curlew mewed its plaintive, lonely cry, but Meg was aware only of Lissa's deep thoughts. The worst part of Kath's letters were her promises to visit, the way they unsettled the child, made her think and ask endless questions.

'Tell me again how you came to Liverpool to find me,' Lissa asked, wriggling close, and Meg stifled a sigh.

'I've told you a dozen times. Kath couldn't keep you. She was going into the WAAFS, because of the war. She gave you to me to keep safe, at Broombank.'

11

'Did she come to see me a lot? Did she miss me?' Lissa frowned. 'I can't seem to remember.'

'It was difficult, with the war and everything.'

'I suppose so.' More deep thoughts, Lissa wishing she could understand it all properly. She wished and wished so hard sometimes that it hurt, deep in her tummy. If *only* her mother would come, just once. Her child's faith in the goodness of life made her certain that it would somehow change everything, that Kath would be kind and beautiful and tell her that she loved her, and Lissa would learn all about that secret part of herself she couldn't quite discover.

She worried sometimes that perhaps it was her fault that Kath had left. Perhaps she'd been a terrible disappointment and her mother had been glad to give her up. Today, at last, all those fears could be swept away.

They stopped for a breather by a stone cairn. Perhaps a place marked for burials in ancient times, now used by the weary traveller as an indication he was on the right route. They sat in the bracken with their backs against it to shield themselves from the wind and Lissa sighed with pleasure. She knew her childhood here had been happy. She loved these high places, the rocky narrow ridge of Rough Crag, the rounded shoulder of Kidsty Pike away in the distance, and the sweeping grandeur of mountains all around. But she couldn't help wondering what lay beyond them. All she had ever seen of the world was this dale, these familiar mountains. She ached to see the rest of it, live the life she felt was her due. She adored Meg and Tam, loved them as if they were her real parents, but what kind of life might she have had if she'd been Lissa Ellis instead of Lissa Turner? How would she have been different? It was hard to work it out.

A tall Scots pine stood like a sentinel on a small rise before her. Beyond that, Lissa knew, was the last sheep trod they needed to climb. This would join on to the long sweeping drive that led up to Larkrigg Hall through a pair of stone gate posts. It was a fine, nineteenth-century house, set high on a ridge as its name implied, surrounded on all sides by strangely shaped rocks and crags that poked out of the thin soil like old bones. A house that might have been her home, if things had been different. Or she might, even now, have been in Canada, seeing other mountains, visiting rich cities, riding the ponies on her mother's ranch. These dreams and wishes had filled her head for years, keeping her awake at night. Now, she was sure they were about to be realised.

'Will she tell me who my father is, do you think?' Her voice was soft, robbed of breath by the wind and the intensity of her excitement.

Meg and Kath had both avoided this part of the story. How they had both loved the same man, Kath had borne his child and Meg had loved her and brought her up. It hurt and embarrassed them both still, to think of it.

Meg drew the child into the circle of her arms. 'One day we'll talk about it,' she said with a smile. 'When you are older, old enough to understand.'

'I hate it when you say that. I am older. I'm eleven. Not a baby any more, Meg.'

No, more's the pity of it, she thought, and tightened the ribbons that were, as usual, slipping down the glossy curls. 'It isn't important, you know, not really. You have me and Tam. Remember that we love you. You are our own darling child so far as we are concerned.'

'I know.' Lissa wished that it was enough. But somehow it wasn't.

Larkrigg Hall, a rectangular, solid house, bigger than it looked at first glance, with a plain, protestant look to it, stood at last before them. Only its tall trefoiled windows and great arched storm porch relieved the austerity of the grey stone walls. Meg pushed Lissa forward and politely rattled the knocker, for the inhabitants of Larkrigg Hall did not follow the more usual country custom of using the back door for callers. Meg could feel her heart start to thump uncomfortably at the thought of Kath waiting within.

The door creaked open and Amy Stanton, Rosemary Ellis's housekeeper, stood four-square on the slate step. Solid and forbidding, taking her pleasures where she could find them in ill health and local disasters, she almost smiled upon them now.

'She hasn't come,' she told them with happy bluntness. 'Mrs Wadeson sent a telegram this morning. She says she's sorry but she won't be here after all.'

The door had almost closed before Meg came out of her shock. Slamming her hand against the polished panels she stopped it most effectively, but then she hadn't spent years lifting and managing sheep to be put off by an old door, solid oak or no. 'What did you say?'

If Amy Stanton answered, Lissa did not hear. She could only stand, unmoving, as if turned to cold stone like one of those littered about Larkrigg Fell said to mark the grave of a giant. She watched, bemused, as Meg lifted her chin in that stubborn way she had and the high-cheekboned face took on a dignified beauty that had melted stouter hearts than Amy Stanton's. But there was no sign of a thaw in this one.

Even to Lissa's miserable observation it was clear that Meg was wasting her time.

'Amy?' A stentorian voice from within settled the matter and the door shut fast with a solid clunk. Meg muttered something unpleasant under her breath that Lissa didn't quite catch then, spinning on her heel, took her hand in a firm grasp, grey eyes sparkling with a rare anger.

'Come along, sweetheart. Let's go home.'

2

The little kingfisher thrived, which helped to soothe Lissa's disappointment at being let down yet again by her mother. Each afternoon, when she returned from school she ran down to the beck to dip her jam jar in the cool waters and catch tiny minnows for its dinner. Then she would lie among the pools of gentian bluebells, drawing in their heady scent, watching grey clouds swell and burst and scud across the sky.

But the day came when Lissa knew the bird must be released. It had responded well to her care; its blue-green feathers were glossy and smooth as silk, strong enough to fly. Sorry as she was to lose it, she hated the idea of any creature being held against its will. Carrying it carefully in its mud-caked shoe box, Lissa took it down to the beck.

'It won't survive,' Nick said, in his loftiest tones. 'Don't let it go. You're protecting it, aren't you?'

'I've given it a good start. It's tough. It'll survive.' Like me, she thought.

First she waded into the water and caught a jarful of minnows. An expert now, it took her no more than a moment. Slipping her hand inside the box, she captured the bird quite easily, holding it firmly but gently in one hand as she was used to doing. She placed it carefully on a projecting branch and offered the little kingfisher a minnow but for once it ignored the fish, being too busy blinking and gazing about itself with interest.

'Keep your hand on it. Don't let it go,' Nick warned.

'No. I would hate to be kept a prisoner, and so does he.' The

15

kingfisher flew up suddenly into the air, fluttering its wings in a frenzy of astonished grace. Wondering what to do next and where to go it continued to hover, crying out its distinctive piping call. Then like an arrow of blue light it flew across the stream, dived into the water and caught a fish as if it had been doing so for years. Lissa watched in amazed wonder as it landed on another branch, banged the fish against a twig, and swallowed it head first.

'Oh,' she breathed. 'Isn't it clever? I wish I could fly.' Lissa tried to smother the feeling of sadness she felt at its departure. It was free and healthy because she had reared it from a baby. But it was as if she had lost her only friend, an orphan like herself, though she didn't say as much out loud as Nick would only laugh at her fancies.

Lissa thought of the last letter she had written to her mother, asking if Kath had another date in mind. It had not been answered. Not that she cared, she told herself. What did it matter if Katherine Ellis, now Mrs Wadeson, did not love her?

Yet somehow she knew that it did. It mattered very much. Lissa felt full of curiosity, ached to meet her. Not because she felt herself unloved by Meg, far from it. Meg had been the best mother anyone could wish for. It was simply a need to fill in the whole picture, to know who, exactly, she was. She couldn't explain it any better than that, not even to herself. It made her feel all uncomfortable inside to know she'd been dumped.

And then there was the house. Since that awful day she had several times asked Nick to go with her up to Larkrigg but he always refused.

That was the closest she'd ever come to it in all her life. She'd seen it many times from a distance when she was out walking, watched the sun glinting on its casement windows. It reminded her of a fairy palace and she would not have been surprised had it sprouted turrets, and a magic dragon had roared out from the porch. But she had never, until that moment, walked up to its door. So it was a great disappointment to be turned away.

'Just to peep through the windows,' she pleaded. 'I want to know what it's like inside.'

'What your grandmother is like, you mean.'

'Why shouldn't I be curious? I know why you won't go, you're scared.'

'I'm not.'

'Yes, you are.'

16

'Not.'

'Are.'

But no matter what she said, however much she wheedled and argued, he flatly refused to take her. He would shake his tousled head and sulk for hours, going on and on about how he and Daniel weren't good enough for her any more. And though she protested vehemently, Lissa was aware that the criticism was partly justified.

She might very well have ventured across the fells by herself had not Nick sworn to tell on her if she did. She punished him by not speaking to him for a whole week.

But Lissa was determined. Kath must come one day, she simply must. The question was, how to make her?

It was Grandfather Joe, surprisingly, who offered a solution.

'What's up wi' thee, moping about with a face like a wet fortneet?'

And because he was her special friend, Lissa told him of her disappointment.

'Stop frettin',' he said, shaking out his newspaper as if to remind her that the worries of the world, such as the progress of the Korean War which he followed with care, were far more important than any a young girl might have. 'It'll all be t' same in hundred years.'

'I suppose it will,' said Lissa sadly, though this was not a philosophy she could warm to. 'Do you believe in wishes, Grandfather?'

Joe pondered the question a moment then chuckled. 'I remember doing some wishing as a child, by the watter every spring. Eeh, what daft 'eads we were,' and laughing softly at his own foolishness, perplexingly returned to the paper. 'Will thee look at the price of wool?' he said. 'Fair wicked. Might as well work for nowt.'

'Grandfather.' Lissa's voice was coaxing, her smile bewitching. Aware he had a soft spot for her she knew she never got anything out of him by being miserable, for all he put on such a dour face himself. She leaned against the arm of Joe's chair and gazed up into his face. 'Tell me about the wishing.'

Joe regarded the child he'd come to think of as his granddaughter with a serious eye. 'It's not to be taken lightly,' he warned.

'Oh, no,' Lissa assured him. 'I wouldn't.'

He glanced around, as if he was about to impart a great secret, or preferred Meg not to know what he said. 'Watter has special powers, tha knows. Whether it be mere, beck or tarn, each has its own sprite or fairy and it don't do to cross 'em.'

Lissa solemnly shook her head, not daring to speak. Would this be the answer she so badly needed?

Satisfied he was not about to be mocked, Joe continued, 'Hm, well when we was no more 'n bairns we'd go every Maytime to the well or some other special watering place and fill our hands wi' watter. Sometimes we'd use a bottle and add a drap of sugar or a twist o' liquorice and drink some oop, then gie the rest back to the watter sprite. Or we'd drink from us hands and gie a gift instead, like a flower or a penny. You ask Meg aboot Luckpennies. Carry the luck for you they do.'

'Why do they?'

'Why?' Joe looked confused. 'Nay, lass, how should I know? We did it 'cause it were joost thing to do. Summat we'd allus done.'

'But did you make a wish? And did it ever come true?'

Joe was now anxious to return to the latest figures from the auction mart. 'Course we did. But I'm too old to remember what we wished for let alone if it ever coom true. It's all a lot o' nonsense anyroad. You have to drink it oop quick, afore it leaks out of your hand, and say your wish wi' your een closed.' And thinking of Meg's possible reaction he added for good measure, 'And you must believe in the Good Lord and say your prayers every neet,' nodding wisely, recklessly mixing Christian and pagan traditions. 'And you'll get what's good for you and no more.'

Lissa felt excited. She said her prayers every night already, but she thought she'd try the wishing as well, just in case. It could do no harm to try.

Nick had one or two wishes of his own which he could do with having answered, concerning learning to play football and getting a new bicycle, so he was ready enough to share the experiment with Lissa. It seemed harmless enough.

The beck was considered too mundane and the water too gushing for any sprite to survive in, they decided. There was nothing for it but to try the tarn. Strictly forbidden, tucked darkly behind Brockbarrow wood, they chose an afternoon when Daniel had been taken, protesting, to the dentist, since they didn't trust him to keep their secret. And he couldn't even swim. It was June by this time but Lissa hoped the fairies wouldn't mind, this being their first visit.

'We mustn't get wet or fall in this time,' she warned and Nick gravely agreed. The tarn might be small and round, a sheet of water innocently sparkling in the sun on a beautiful day like this, but it was bitterly cold, had been trapped in this cup of land since the Ice Age and nobody knew quite how deep it was. It was not a place to mess about with. Both children gazed on the ruffled waters and shuddered. They could well believe that sprites lurked beneath its glittering surface, perhaps even devils.

The small ceremony took no more than moments to complete. There was no time to waste as they were fully aware they risked the wrath of their respective parents should their trip be discovered.

'I'll go first,' Lissa said, dipping the small Tizer bottle in the clear water.

As she drank the sweet liquorice water she closed her eyes and wished with all her might that one day soon her mother would come. She sent her thoughts winging far across water, mountains and sea to a distant, unknown mass of land painted red on her geography atlas and known as Canada.

Send my mother home, her inner voice begged.

Then it was Nick's turn. They glanced sideways at each other and giggled.

'It's a bit daft is this,' he said.

'Go on. Get on with it.'

When he had done they emptied the rest of the brown liquid into the tarn and watched the wind sweep the sunlight like a shower of diamonds across the small lake. It seemed, to her lively imagination, like an answer, and a great sense of peace and certainty came upon her. It would work out all right in the end, she felt sure somehow, deep in her heart.

Time passed quickly for Lissa. She tried not to think of Kath and was happy enough in the dale, and though she found no more orphan birds, there was much to keep her amused. And each spring she and Nick continued to make their wishes though neither revealed them or owned up to whether they ever came true. That was far too risky and might spoil their chances, though Nick did boast one day that he'd got picked for the school football team.

Lissa continued to write regularly to Canada and twice a year, on her birthday and at Christmas, she received a reply. These were always a disappointment, telling her little, closing with the promise that one day Kath would come but never offering any definite date.

And then on her thirteenth birthday a different sort of letter arrived.

19

Meg handed it to her, frowning. 'It's from Mrs Ellis. She's declared herself ready to receive us.'

'Oh.' Lissa was stunned. Was this good news or bad? She couldn't quite make out from Meg's attitude. 'Why? Why suddenly now?'

'Perhaps a bout of conscience? Though I very much doubt it. Have you been writing to Canada?'

Lissa nodded, saying no more when she saw how Meg's face tightened in that odd way she had whenever Kath or Canada were mentioned.

'We are to call next Wednesday, at three o'clock precisely. You must put on your best frock, I suppose. Only I would prefer you not to fall in the beck this time. Let us try to present a civilised image, shall we?' Meg gave a wry smile and Lissa giggled with relief.

'I'll do my best.'

Lissa knew, the moment she stepped into the house, that she hated it, which was deeply disappointing.

They passed through a dark hall where a glassy-eyed stag's head glared down at them, causing her to shiver. Then they were shown into a small, oak-panelled room of faded gentility, dark and depressing. Where was the pretty turquoise and gold drawing room Meg had spoken of? Lissa had imagined a shining palace of a place, with delicate, tasteful furniture. Instead, most of the house seemed shut up, judging by the number of forbiddingly closed doors.

At first sight everything in the room appeared to be draped in some sort of covering. It seemed to be filled with mats, runners, tablecloths, even the piano was shrouded in an Indian rug. A single, rose-shaded lamp bloomed in the window embrasure. It should have given a cosy feel but it only cast gloomy shadows across the walls.

Lissa's small nose wrinkled with distaste at the stale smell that met her nostrils. The room was as unaccustomed to fresh air as it was to visitors.

A figure rose from the shadows by the empty fireplace and Lissa started, stepping back in sudden fright as she recalled Nick's constant teasing about a witch. What nonsense, she was a child no longer to be scared by fairy tales, but she felt glad suddenly of Meg's warm reassuring hand as it slipped over hers.

'Miss Turner.' The voice sounded cold and disembodied.

Glancing anxiously up at Meg, Lissa caught the ghost of a

knowing smile and knew instinctively that these two were old adversaries.

'Mrs O'Cleary, if you recall. But you always used to call me Meg.'

A pause, during which Lissa received the decided impression that she was being scrutinised from head to foot, though since the room was so dim and the woman was in shadow, she could not be sure.

'I see you have brought the – ah – child.'

Meg smiled again. Quite brilliantly. 'Of course. This is Lissa. My foster daughter.'

Lissa felt as if she were expected to curtsey, the moment so crackled with tension. Instead, she screwed up her courage, took a step forward and held out her hand, remembering her manners. 'Good afternoon . . .' she began, smiling politely, and stopped. How to address this woman whom she knew to be her grandmother but had never been acknowledged as such? She bit on her lower lip and waited. The rose-coloured light flickered across the thin, unsmiling face, showing up the whiskers on her chin.

Ignoring the small outstretched hand, Rosemary Ellis turned away, leaving Lissa feeling empty and foolish, forced to retreat to Meg's side.

'Pray be seated.' A regal gesture indicated a roomy sofa. It too was so swathed in paisley shawls, arm shields, antimacassars and cushions, that Lissa dared hardly sit upon it for fear of disturbing the arrangement. 'Amy, tea, if you please. For our guests.'

'Very good, madam.' Amy quietly withdrew, closing the double mahogany doors as she went.

Lissa sat gingerly next to Meg and fixed her eyes upon a display of dried leaves in a copper bowl that sat incongruously upon an upturned seed box in the wide, marble hearth. A spider hung from a thread on one leaf and Lissa watched it, fascinated.

They sat in silence in the cold room for what seemed an eternity. Somewhere a clock chimed and she counted out three strokes. Lissa's back started to ache and her legs to fidget. Meg cast her a warning glance, then clearing her throat, turned to Mrs Ellis with a smile.

'I trust you are keeping well? I haven't seen Jeff . . . Mr Ellis for some time. How is he?'

'Much the same. Never goes out these days.'

'Might we see him?'

'I do not think that would be wise.'

21

It was a relief when the double doors opened again and Amy wheeled in the tea on a clattering tea trolley that had seen better days. Meg touched Lissa's hand. 'Go and help Mrs Stanton serve the tea, sweetheart.' But as Lissa rose to do so, a stern voice bade her remain where she was.

'Amy is perfectly capable of managing. I hope we have better manners here at Larkrigg than to permit guests to serve themselves.'

Lissa sat down again, accepting the china cup and saucer with the first flutter of nervousness. Misery was sharp within her. This was not at all how she had imagined her first meeting with her grandmother would be.

She had so longed to see her, and the inside of the old house where her mother had lived as a girl.

It had confused and intrigued her to think that a member of her own family whom she didn't even know lived behind these grey stone walls. Now here she was at last, and nothing was as she had hoped. Perhaps Lissa hadn't quite expected words of love. But a smile, a word of welcome would have warmed her. There was none.

The only consolation was that through the tall, trefoiled windows she could see the friendly mountains that she loved so much, their dark faces streaked with snow-filled gullies for April had only recently come in. The house stood so grandly on its ridge that its face looked beyond Larkrigg Fell to the majesty of Kentmere Pike with the dark sentinel of Dundale Knot closer to hand.

Perversely Lissa wished herself out amongst them, where she might find the peace and sanctuary they offered; instead of here, where she felt an outcast. Unwanted.

She realised with a startled jerk that Rosemary Ellis was addressing her with some question and she had missed it. In horror, Lissa glanced at Meg for help who, sensing her predicament, attempted to breach the gap.

'Lissa attends the High School. She goes into Kendal each day by bus.'

'The High School?' The words were spoken with contempt, as if the idea were unthinkable. 'How very utilitarian.'

'It's a very good school as a matter of fact.'

'Katherine was educated privately. Only the very best of everything, naturally. Still, a local establishment is probably more appropriate in the circumstances.' Rosemary Ellis fixed her cold gaze upon Lissa who went quite pale, as if she were about to be sick.

She hated the increasing tension in the room and watched in dismay as Meg attempted to laugh away the implied criticism, though it seemed to be through gritted teeth.

'How is Katherine? She is well, I hope?'

'Perfectly. My daughter leads an exceedingly busy social life. Her husband, Ewan Maximillian Wadeson III, has quite a position to keep up. A property owner of some renown.'

'Then she shouldn't make promises that she intends to visit when she clearly hasn't time,' Meg daringly stated, making Lissa jump.

Rosemary stiffened and gazed down her long nose at Meg. 'She can't simply drop everything. On a whim.'

'It was always her idea to visit. We did not request it.'

'Well, I certainly did not, Mrs O'Cleary. For my part, I believe the past is best left buried.'

Lissa gazed perplexed at her grandmother. What did that mean? Best left buried. She couldn't be buried, could she? She was here, alive and well, a physical reality. Lissa felt a bit guilty suddenly, for though Meg might not have made any requests to Kath, she certainly had. Constantly. She thought it best not to mention it since now, at last, was her opportunity to get a few questions of her own answered. She edged forward in her seat.

'What is she like, my mother? Does she look like me? Or like you?' Here, Lissa's young mind quailed at this dreadful possibility, and she hurried on without stopping. 'You still haven't told us, Grandmother, why she keeps letting me down. Is it my fault? Will she be coming soon? She did promise, really she did. "I'll come as soon as I can", she said. When do you think that will be?'

Rosemary stared as if shocked that the girl owned a tongue, let alone a mind churning with questions. 'I really couldn't say, and I am not your grandmother.' And she turned away to sip her tea with patrician disdain, the subject closed so far as she was concerned. But not for Lissa.

'Why can't you say? Perhaps she would prefer it if I were to visit her in Canada?' Lissa strove to keep the eagerness from her voice. The thought of crossing half the world in a huge ship in search of this elusive, beautiful mother excited her, but she hated to show how much in front of Meg.

'That would be most unsuitable,' Rosemary said, shock evident in her voice. 'The very idea!'

'Why? Doesn't she want to see me?'

Cold, pale eyes raked Lissa from head to foot then turned chillingly to Meg. 'You have taught the child no manners, I see. Which does not surprise me, brought up as she has been with farming stock.'

Lissa saw Meg flinch as if Rosemary Ellis had struck her. Her own head was starting to ache and disappointment made her reckless. She decided she might as well be hung for a sheep as a lamb.

'Is he my father then? This Ewan Maximillian Wadeson III? Or is it because I'm a bastard that you don't like me?'

'*Lissa*!'

The effect was astonishingly gratifying. For one terrible moment she thought her grandmother was about to faint. She saw at once there would be no denial and felt a wicked surge of gladness that someone else could suffer hurt, as she had suffered so many times. Lissa watched, intrigued, as the whiskered chin and palid cheeks went stark white, grew wine red, then changed to brilliant purple.

'I must apologise for her behaviour,' Meg was hastily saying, frowning grimly at Lissa.

'The child is out of control. You clearly allow her to run wild. Spoil her, without doubt.'

'I don't think it possible to spoil a child. Where else would she find the love she needs, if not from me and from Tam?' Brave, reckless words, chillingly received.

'Enough of this. Do you take me for a fool?' Icicles dripped from the thin voice. 'I know why you persist in keeping up this contact with Katherine. Which is why I have called you here today, to inform you that it must stop. There will be no more contact between you. I am not too foolish to recognise a clever ruse when I see one.'

'Clever ruse?' Meg's eyes widened.

'Indeed. To get money out of me. Or my husband, as no doubt you have cleverly done in the past on many occasions, gullible fool that he is.'

'I beg your pardon?'

'Come, come, Mrs O'Cleary, do not pretend with me. But you will not succeed. I do not acknowledge *your* illegitimate child as any responsibility of mine.' She turned away and pulled on a bell pull. 'I think this interview is over.'

Meg looked as if someone had punched her in the face. Her voice shook. 'How dare you? How dare you suggest such things? And in front of the child.'

'It's all right,' Lissa said, anxious to calm Meg. 'I understand, and

24

I really don't mind about being a bastard, only I would've liked to know why I wasn't wanted.'

The shock waves of this little speech almost knocked Lissa off her seat. Rosemary Ellis shot to her feet, clasping and unclasping her hands in agitation. 'If that child uses that word again . . .' A tall, angular figure with good bone structure, any beauty she might once have possessed had been dissipated long since by a sour mouth which thinned perceptibly, even as Lissa gazed wonderingly upon it.

'Stern discipline and control is what this little madam needs. Though I can think of no respectable establishment which would admit her, and you seem quite unable to provide them.'

It was a long moment before Meg answered, concerned as she was about Lissa, seeing the tears brim in the violet eyes, young ears taking in every nuance of the argument. Very quietly she got to her feet. 'We need no help to bring up our own daughter, Mrs Ellis. And you are the last person I would ask, if we did.' It was plain that she was trembling but no one remarked upon it. 'Had I known you were going to attack us with your nasty insinuations, I would have left Lissa at home.'

Lissa was, in fact, paying less attention than Meg realised. The whole scene had made her feel distinctly odd. A pain started deep in her belly and she wanted, very suddenly, to be sick. She clamped her teeth tightly together in desperation as the room began to swim about her.

Meg was speaking now in that quiet, controlled voice Lissa knew so well, the voice that said she was angry but refused to lose her temper. It seemed to come from a long way off.

'If you had not been so hard-hearted as to throw your daughter out all those years ago, you might have found a bit more love in your own life. Which might have spared you this warped view of the world, Rosemary Ellis. And certainly would have benefitted Kath and her child, as well as your poor husband. Yes, Jeffrey was kind to me in the past, but I asked him for nothing and he gave me nothing but his advice and support. No more. I *never* took any money from him. Ever. Though I always valued his friendship. I will not stay and bandy insults with you. I want nothing from you, not now, nor in the future. But I agree with you about the letters. I too would prefer it if they were stopped. Please ask Katherine to refrain from making promises to Lissa which she has no intention of keeping. It is thoughtless and unkind and causes nothing but hurt and upset for the child.'

Lissa groaned as the pain shot deeper, like a great weight between her legs. Neither woman heard her.

'My daughter is not at all thoughtless. You have clearly read too much into her words. She responds as best she can only because the child insists on writing the embarrassing things.' The older woman was almost spitting her contempt now as the two stood facing each other, determined adversaries across a beautiful persian rug. Meg held to her point.

'Kath inspired and now encourages this fantasy of Lissa's that they might meet. It does greater damage than you might think. When Kath lets her down the child feels rejected all over again.'

'What utter rubbish!' The whiskered chin shook. 'Rejected indeed. You cannot believe that Katherine or I owe any responsibility to a child who readily admits herself to – to be what she is. Ours is a respectable family. She is no fault of ours.'

Meg dropped her chin and drew in a long, shuddering breath, steadying herself, fighting the urge to tear this unfeeling, cruel woman to shreds. How dare she deny Lissa's parentage? So concerned was she with her efforts that she did not notice Lissa's reaction to these callous remarks. She did not see the colour drain away and the pretty cheeks sink visibly beneath the violet bruises of her eyes. She only heard a stifled moan and then the air seemed to be filled with a piercing scream, bringing both women whirling.

'Look what you've done. Both of you,' Lissa screamed, terror in her voice. 'You've killed me. I'm dying, Meg. I'm dying.'

The blood of womanhood was running down the young girl's legs, soaking into the bright white ankle socks and dripping down to the ancient, prized carpet.

'Dear Lord,' cried Meg, horrified.

'As I said, Mrs O'Cleary. Discipline and control. Entirely lacking, you see.'

3

Meg sat on the edge of the big bed she shared with Tam, wring-
ing her hands in anguish. 'I should have told her long since.
I've failed her, leaving it so late. She was scared out of her
wits, poor lamb. And I should have explained all about Jack too,
then she mightn't have felt the need to shock with that dreadful word.'

'You've told her now?'

'Yes, everything.'

Tam slipped an arm about her to pull her close. 'Don't worry over
it. You wouldn't be the Meg we all know and love if you were
mooning about the house fussing over us all the time.'

'Even so, it was a mistake. And that dreadful woman. Discipline
and control, my Aunt Fanny!' Meg's hands clenched tight, as if
she would have punched Rosemary Ellis on the nose were she
present. 'You wouldn't believe the things she said to me, what she
accused me of.'

Tam stroked the golden curls away and tucked them behind her
ears, kissing the lobes as he did so. 'Haven't you told me, sweetheart,
a dozen times already? You mustn't let the woman get to you. She is
a vicious, bad-mouthed old besom and not to be listened to. I forbid
you to take Lissa to see her again.'

Meg turned to gaze into his moss green eyes, startled for a moment
by the unusual vehemence in his lilting voice. 'Forbid?'

'Aye. Why should our little girl be subjected to such an attack?
'Tis not her fault if she was born on the wrong side of the blanket,
now is it? So keep her away in future. We'll show Lissa how she is

27

loved. We'll go to Appleby Fair come June and buy that pony we've always promised her.'

'You can't buy Lissa's love with a pony.'

Tam looked shocked. 'Did I suggest such a thing? We have her love, we've no need to buy it.'

'I'm not so sure.'

Tam took her chin between finger and thumb and turned Meg's face to his. She tried to avoid his eyes. 'Why do you say that?'

'Because she has this desire to see Kath. Why? *Why*? After all these years.'

'Because Kath is the child's mother,' said Tam quietly. 'It doesn't mean anything. No more than natural curiosity.'

'How can you say that?' Meg's gaze was piercing now, begging him to convince her there was nothing to fear. 'If she was happy with us, she would never think of Kath.'

'The human spirit is far too complicated a thing for me to understand.' He drew aside a curl so he could kiss the curve of her neck. Meg brushed him aside.

'How will buying a pony solve anything? You know you spoil her.'

'Do not we both? Since she is the only child we have.' A shadow flickered briefly across his face and Meg's heart clenched. She loved him so much, his quiet strength, the way his mahogany dark hair fell into heedless curls upon his broad forehead. She loved his teasing manner and his effortless good humour. So why could she not give him what he most wanted in all the world? A child of their own.

'There is still time for us . . .' she began. 'Perhaps you're right and I should go to the doctor again. It's only that I've been so busy, what with buying the new tractor, getting used to it, and . . .'

'I've no wish to talk of tractors this night, Meg.' His voice grated in her ear. ' 'Tis Lissa who matters right now. The only way to deal with this obsession with her mother is to give her something else to think about. A pony may be the very thing.'

And so Meg allowed Tam to stop her protests with his lips and his loving hands. But as she willingly surrendered herself to his love making, she knew the problem would not be so easily solved. Lissa never let go, once she had set her heart on something.

The day of Appleby Fair turned out fine and warm, a perfect June day for a picnic, and the entire family piled into two cars and set off early with anticipation and excitement. Lissa sat with Daniel on the black leather seat with Meg and Tam in front. The second car held Sally Ann, Nick, and of course Joe was driving.

He had protested when Meg first broached the idea. 'I've nae time to be gallivanting off to no fair.'

'Oh, Father, what an old misery boots you are. With the lambing finished and the first dipping not due for another few weeks, a day out will do us all good. We'll make it a family picnic.'

'And wouldn't that be grand?' Tam had agreed. 'If we can't watch the coronation on the wonders of television, we can at least celebrate the dawn of a new Elizabethan age with a trip to Appleby Fair, eh?'

'Naebody listens to my opinion so I'll not give it,' the old man mourned.

'Well, that's settled then,' said Meg drily, and Lissa almost choked with laughter. She was very fond of Joe but his dour way of looking at life often made her laugh. As he said himself, he was on the back row when St Peter handed out jokers.

It was slow going over Shap Fell, the road so steep it made Lissa's ears pop, but the sun was shining, lighting the smooth humps of the fells to a radiant green. Daniel was bouncing up and down with excitement.

'See those folded hills. They look like an elephant lying down,' he said.

'When did you ever see an elephant?'

'I've seen pictures. In my *Arthur Mee Encyclopedia*. You're not the only one with brains, our Lissa.'

She looked to where he pointed and despite her efforts to prove she was older and more sophisticated, burst out laughing. 'You're right, they do look like an elephant.'

'The mountains are quite smooth here where they reach over to the pennines, not like in the Langdales where the peaks are sharp and pointed,' Meg said. 'But don't be fooled into thinking these are any less dangerous. And in my view they're every bit as beautiful.'

Lissa wondered where the Langdales were and wished she could see them.

They crossed High Borrow Bridge, and the gears in the small Ford car crashed as Tam prepared for the steep climb up over Crookdale Crag and on to Wasdale Fell. At the top they stopped the two vehicles to let the engines cool down. There was a small caravan selling tea, but since they hadn't been travelling long, none of them wanted any.

Another car pulled in by the tea van and a horde of children scrambled out shrieking with delight while the driver opened up the bonnet from where a hiss of hot steam escaped.

'Just look at that,' said Joe in disgust. 'I blame this National Park affair. Trippers, motor traffic, charabancs, all sorts o' dross we're getting now. Ramblers and campers too, I shouldn't wonder.'

'What's a National Park?' asked Daniel. 'Does it have swings?'

'Don't be silly.' Lissa had learned all about the new National Park at school and decided that now was as good a time as any to air her views and superior knowledge. 'We're driving right along the boundary of it now, as a matter of fact. I think a National Park is an excellent way of protecting the land. It was started last year and covers more than eight hundred and sixty square miles. It's the largest National Park in the country and known as the "Playground of the Nation". People will be able to start all sorts of businesses, offer bed and breakfast, make money out of the visitors. My teacher says it creates jobs. I think it's exciting.'

Joe snorted. 'Thoo would. "Playground of the Nation" indeed. Naebody's cooming playing in my yard, I'll tell thee that.'

'It's not as if this is Windermere, is it, all busy and crowded? It would be difficult, ever, to spoil this part of Lakeland, it's too wild and open,' Lissa persisted.

'And what does thee know about owt, madam?'

She giggled. 'I know the helm wind would blow a tent away.' And they all started to laugh at the thought of the trippers chasing their tents across the high fells.

'Thoo can laugh but see what it's done to our rates bill. Put another twopence or threepence a pound on. We had enough trouble with Manchester Water Board,' Joe warned, nodding sagely.

'What sort of trouble?'

'Weel, look what they did to Thirlmere. Ruined it, they did.'

'That was last century, Father,' Meg pointed out, with a look at Lissa that plainly said, Now look what you've started.

'Aye, and Mardale was only in the thirties. A whole village drowned.'

'What, people and all?' asked Daniel, wide-eyed, and his grandfather turned upon him, outrage on his round face.

'Thoo can mock but a bonny, secluded dale and a whole way of life were destroyed.' He prodded a blunt finger at the landscape. 'O'er there it were. Near Naddle forest and Burnbanks. Been there for centuries. Had its own king, Mardale did.'

'King?' Even Lissa was round eyed at this.

'Hugh Holme, his forebears coom over wi' William the Conquerer, he did,' Joe explained, as if it were only yesterday. 'Got into trouble with King John and landed up in Mardale. Liked it so much he stopped on, and his family after him. The last King o' Mardale died in 1885.'

'Do you remember him?' Nick asked, and got a clip round his ears for his cheek.

'I were nobbut a bairn at the time you young sprat, but it's not all that long ago if you want to know. The men kept sheep and the women knitted. Only time folk ever left Mardale was when they were dead and had to be carried up the corpse road on't back of a pack horse, to be buried at Shap cemetery. Ground were too stony to dig deep in Mardale. The animal was known to bolt on occasions, then it would roam these fells for weeks, still carrying the coffin on its back, before anybody found it.'

The three children exchanged horrified glances.

'Is it still there?' Daniel asked in a small voice.

'Don't be daft,' scorned Nick, 'it'd be a skeleton by now,' and sobered instantly at the thought.

Lissa giggled. 'You're teasing us, aren't you, Grandad?'

'Nay, I'm not. It's true, sure as I'm standing here. It happened once or twice. There's some weird goings on we know nowt about on them fells.'

'You shouldn't frighten the children with talk of corpses, Father. They'll be imagining ghosts in their beds tonight.'

'Aye, weel, then they flooded the valley, so that were that.'

'Why was it flooded?' Lissa wanted to know.

'Because Lancashire industries needed more watter. Farms, church, school, all had to be tekken down, stone by stone. Then they built a dam, flooded the valley and turned it into a reservoir. Mortal shame it were.'

'Oh.' Lissa and Daniel looked contrite, sorry now that they'd upset him, an old man living in the past, wanting to hear more of this doomed valley that had once had its own king.

'Can we go and see it?' Daniel started to jump up and down,

31

suddenly more interested in dams and floods and corpses that got lost than in ponies and fairs.

'No, you can't,' said Meg sternly. 'Can we get going or it'll all be over by the time we get there.'

They drove on past the quarries where Shap's famous pink granite was worked, then just before the village they turned right and headed over the wide open fells to Appleby.

'Are we there yet?' asked Daniel, and everyone laughed, the tension easing.

The small town of Appleby was packed on this, one of the busiest days of the year. Not at this fair could one find roundabouts or coconut shies. Perhaps once, long ago, there had been dice games, shooting galleries and wheels of fortune. Times when young maids, dressed in their finest muslin, kid boots and bonnets, came to the fair to find a job or even a lover. Lissa had heard all about the old days of the fair from Hetty Davies, who had looked after her when Meg was busy. The drovers used to come from as far away as Scotland to sell their black cattle, fighting for space with the gypsies and horse buyers, potters and pickpockets.

Nowadays it was mainly the travelling folk who came in their vardoes and vans, looking to fetch a good price for their blood-stock.

The smell of horses was strong in the air as they parked the cars by the castle and walked down the wide street, jostled by the crowds. There were several market stalls eagerly doing good business and Lissa bought some cinder toffee and Nick a toffee apple while Daniel bought a huge gobstopper that he stuck in the pouch of his cheek.

'That'll keep him quiet,' said Sally Ann with a laugh.

By the time they reached the bridge, getting through the crowds was a near impossibility. Then suddenly the people drew back and Lissa gained a clear view of what was happening ahead. Young, bare-chested men ran their horses up and down the street, showing off their beautiful animals.

'That's the only way to prove a horse,' whispered Tam at her ear. 'By galloping it. The fairground proper is up at Gallows Hill and we'll watch the racing up there later, but we'll go down by the river first. Come on, Lissa.' And pulling her with him, he pushed his way through the crowd. Breathless with excitement, Lissa found herself out on the towpath.

Here, more bare-chested young men were riding their ponies in the river, laughing and splashing and shouting as they made the slick coats shine in the sun from constant washing and grooming.

Then she saw it, the most beautiful pony she had ever seen in her life. It was golden pale with long curling lashes over huge dark eyes. And as Lissa pulled some grass and held it out, the pony nuzzled her flat hand with the softest nose imaginable.

'Oh,' she breathed. 'Isn't she wonderful?'

'A fine creature,' Tam agreed, grinning, and began at once to examine it, lifting up the pony's feet one by one, opening its mouth to check its teeth. Lissa watched, breathless with excitement, hoping he would find no fault with it. This was the most wonderful day of her life.

The pony's owner stepped forward and Lissa caught her breath. If the pony had been beautiful, this young man was more so. As bare-chested as all the rest, except that where the others were dark and tanned, he was fair-skinned with hair the colour of butter. It fell carelessly forward over his thin face and as he shook it back, he tilted his head to one side and stared quite openly at her, a smile curving his wide, pale pink lips. Lissa felt her heart flutter with a strange excitement. A boldness in the cornflower blue eyes made her feel oddly disturbed yet drawn to him, all at the same time.

A few years older than herself, seventeen or eighteen, perhaps it was because he was the nearest she'd ever been to a half-naked man that her mind started to replay all that Meg had said the other night about men and babies. The memory brought a painful flush to her cheeks and a shiver ran down her spine as he laughed at her, just as if he could read her thoughts.

'She's a fine wee mare,' he said, sliding his gaze from her face to Tam's, and then swiftly back again.

He must think her pretty. That was why he stared, she decided, and her cheeks flushed to an even rosier hue.

Tam, deeply engrossed with the pony's fetlocks, made a non-committal grunt and did not even glance up as the gypsy moved closer to Lissa. He was so close now she could feel the warmth emanating from his body, smell the earthy tang of him. Then before she realised what he was about he reached out one hand and stroked her cheek with the tip of one finger. She was shocked by the intimacy of the touch and filled with a strange sensation, part alarm, part electric excitement.

His gaze slid down over her child-woman body, perhaps coming into its most delectable stage in a young woman's life, and she felt as if he had actually touched her. She became embarrassingly aware of her burgeoning breasts and wished they didn't strain quite so blatantly against the cheap cotton fabric of her dress.

But he liked her, she could tell. Lissa tilted her head and slanted a smile at him, just to let him know that she quite liked him too and was amused to see a stain of colour flow up his neck and over his pale cheeks. It was the first time in her life that she had ever felt a power over a male and it was intoxicating.

He turned back to Tam. 'She'd not let you down. Steady she is, not traffic shy like some these days. Never thrown a body in her life and certainly wouldn't toss the little mistress here.'

'She seems exactly what we're looking for,' Tam agreed. 'Certainly if I don't find a better one this afternoon, I'll come back.'

'Might be too late by then, squire. She's young and healthy, easy to shoe. A sweet-natured little thing. Very biddable.' He half smiled at Lissa. 'I'll have no trouble getting my price but if you want to think about it, anyone will tell you where I am. Kenyon, is the name. Kenyon Parker.'

'What do you think, Lissa?'

Lissa had no doubts. 'Oh, I love her already, Tam. Please can I have her? *Please*. She is exactly right.'

A price was mentioned, dismissed, adjusted, considered again. Tam chewed on a stem of grass. Walked away. Came back. Lissa waited breathlessly throughout the performance but in the end a deal was struck. Hands were shaken and Kenyon Parker promised to deliver the little pony in a few days time.

'What is she called?' Lissa shyly asked.

'Goldie, what else? But you can call her whatever you like.'

'Oh, no, I think Goldie is perfect.'

'Is she your first pony? Have you learned to ride yet, little miss?' Blue eyes were mocking her now and Lissa straightened, standing as tall as she could.

'I can ride very well as a matter of fact.' She rubbed her cheek against the pony. 'She really is beautiful.'

'Come along, Lissa. Meg is on the bridge, and cross with us for deserting her, I shouldn't wonder. What'll she say when we tell her?'

But Meg was not cross. She and Sally Ann had taken the time to have their fortunes told and Meg, with shining eyes, announced to them all that she'd been told she was pregnant.

'It might be true,' she said, unable to control the excitement in her voice. 'I have felt sick lately, and I am late.'

'Oh, Meg,' breathed Sally Ann while Tam put his arms about her and hugged her.

'We mustn't hope too much,' he said. 'She's only a gypsy. You'll have to see a doctor first.'

'It's too soon yet, but I will, I will.' She turned to Lissa. 'Wouldn't it be wonderful?'

Lissa, hugging Meg, agreed that it would be, but deep inside was a sharp pang of disquiet. If Meg had a baby of her own everything would change. She'd have no one then.

Goldie was delivered the following week, as promised. Lissa was coming home from school when she saw the pony's coat glistening like honey in the June sunshine. She ran and flung her arms about the animal's neck.

'Oh, you are lovely.' She had to be tacked up right away, of course, ready for a first ride. 'I don't want to waste a moment,' Lissa cried, stroking the pony with delight.

'We'll keep her on a leading rein till you get used to her,' Tam said, in his steady way. 'Once we're certain the pony is safe I'll take the rein off.' And he refused to budge from this decision, for all Lissa considered it perfectly degrading, particularly since she was aware of being watched by the boy who had sold them the pony. She could see him out of the corner of her eyes, sitting on a gate, fair hair shining, blue eyes watching with an intentness that thrilled and alarmed her.

But it made her even more determined not to make a fool of herself, and indeed the pony proved such a joy to mount and ride that it took only a few laps of the farmyard before Tam relented and slipped the leading rein off.

'No galloping or cantering, mind,' he warned. 'Keep her at a walk till she's used to you. I'll come a little way down the lane with you.'

'Stop fretting, Tam. I know what I'm doing.' And with her chin held high, he had to confess the child sat a horse well. Watching from the farmhouse door, Meg thought it might have been Kath sitting there, so beautiful and proud was she.

*   *   *

35

The days now were nowhere near long enough for Lissa. She was up at six to groom Goldie, feed her with pony nuts and then ride her for an hour before hurrying in to grab a hasty breakfast and reluctantly go off to school. The same regime was repeated each evening. It was wonderful. She couldn't wait for the school holidays to come when she could ride the pony all day. Soon Lissa meant to venture further out on to the fells. Not that she had managed to persuade Meg to allow this privilege yet but she was sure she'd succeed in the end. The pony represented freedom, and a steadfast, loyal friend.

And Kenyon Parker stayed too. To check the pony was settling in, he told her.

Goldie developed an annoying habit of turning and heading off home whenever she took the fancy. Lissa could have asked Tam of course. Instead she chose to get the gypsy's advice.

'Being a bit nappy, is she?' he said. 'Confuse her then.'

'Confuse her?'

Kenyon Parker came to stand close by her leg as Lissa sat on the pony, then reached out a rather grubby hand to rub Goldie beneath one pointed ear. The ear flickered as he whispered secrets into it and Lissa felt a shaft of envy for the attention he gave to the animal. 'Next time she sets off home, circle her a few times,' he explained. 'By the time you've done she won't know which direction home lies. Never fails.'

He turned to go but Lissa wanted desperately for him not to leave her.

'Are you really a gypsy?' she asked, but he only laughed.

'Most folk call us tinkers. Not Romanies, do y'see?'

Gypsy or tinker, what did it matter? She wanted him for a friend, someone besides Nick and Daniel.

The gypsies camped close by and he would often come to visit. Goldie's ears would twitch when she sensed his approach and Lissa held her breath with excitement, hoping he would also talk to her.

She plied him with questions, gave him her most winning smiles, cast lingering glances from beneath lowered lashes, anything to attract and hold his attention. It frustrated her that despite the long hours they spent together working with the pony, he remained withdrawn, aloof even, saying little, volunteering no information that she hadn't prised from him with difficulty.

'Do you go often to Appleby Fair?'

'Every year. Sell our horses there.'

'Do you have a home?'

'I live in a vardo. A wagon to you.'

'And do you have a family?'

'Not like yours.'

'I don't have one really,' she said, stretching the truth to gain his interest. But he only gave that odd little smile and walked away. Still, she thought, she had made some progress. He must care about her a little to spend so much time with her.

If he didn't come to her, Lissa went to the camp. She couldn't let a day pass without seeing him. She loved it there and the tinkers seemed to enjoy her company, singing their songs to her, letting her share their food. But they also smiled at her avid curiosity and secretly laughed at the calf's eyes she made at their handsome Kenyon.

Not that Lissa noticed their amusement. She was too happy. It no longer mattered that Nick and Daniel had abandoned her for more boyish pursuits on the football field. She didn't care that Meg was anxiously waiting for her next visit to the doctor. She was too busy with Goldie, too thrilled to have found so many new friends. For hours now she could even manage not to think about her mother. Kenyon was an orphan too. It gave them something special in common. As with the little kingfisher, they were kindred spirits.

She often discovered him sitting on a wall or leaning against a tree. Watching? Waiting for her? The thought thrilled her and she would sit higher on her pony, preening herself for making such a handsome conquest. Her eyes sparkled and her skin glowed as she proudly rode out, taking every opportunity to speak to him, though he remained quiet, seemingly content to let her chatter.

And all the while Meg watched with growing concern.

As Lissa's confidence with the pony grew, she begged to be allowed to ride further up the fellside.

'Only as far as Brockbarrow wood mind, or along Coppergill Pass,' Meg warned.

Once or twice Lissa longed to break these rules, resenting the confinement when she was so bursting with life and curiosity. Kenyon rode bareback on a piebald pony. He liked to ride it right along the escarpment to where you could overlook the pitted remains of the old slate quarries. And wherever he went, Lissa wanted to go too.

'Coming?' he asked her one day.

He still hadn't kissed her, and Lissa knew that she wanted him to, more than anything. She worried a bit about this. Why didn't he kiss her? Wasn't she appealing enough? But much as she might long to go with him, not even Lissa at her most reckless dare risk going right along the quarry road, a full two miles or more, nor out on to Larkrigg Fell. Goldie might injure herself on one of the scattered boulders.

But not for the world would she allow him to guess how confined she was. He was free as air and she envied him that freedom. So she tossed her curls and flashed her most impudent smile.

'No. Who wants to poke about in dirty old mine workings? I'll race you over Coppergill Pass. That's much more fun. Then you promised to show me how to skin a rabbit.' And he lifted his finely sculpted head, flicked back his shock of butter fair hair and smiled, as if he knew something she didn't.

Sometimes his silences gave her a prickle of disquiet but she always dismissed this as fancy. He was different from ordinary people. He was special. Oh, yes, life was good at last. And if she could only persuade him to kiss her, it would be even better.

And then the day came when Meg suddenly announced that she truly was pregnant. The gypsy's prediction had been correct. Tam gathered her in his arms and whirled her about with delight.

'Isn't that fine news, Lissa?'

'Yes,' she said, very quietly. 'It is.'

38

4

Lissa felt dreadful. It shamed her to admit it, even to herself, but the thought of a baby in the house appalled her. It would take all Meg's time and attention. It seemed to prove how unimportant she was, for why should Meg want a baby at all when she'd always claimed Lissa was the only child she needed?

And her fears seemed at once to be justified. Meg withdrew into a world of her own, rarely hearing when Lissa spoke to her so that she had to say everything twice.

Mealtimes were changed to suit Meg's new delicate stomach. She went to bed early instead of sitting chatting by the fire, and left Lissa to make her own supper. Even iron her own clothes. It was quite incredible how much life changed. To Lissa's increasing dismay Meg became perfectly obsessed with making plans for the baby, took to having weird food fancies, morning sickness and back ache. And Tam's loving preoccupation with her grated every bit as much.

There seemed nothing else for it but to play the martyr or how would they ever remember she lived here too? If they saw she was unhappy, Lissa decided, then they would pay her proper attention. So she refused to speak to either of them, took to spending hours alone in her room, hoping someone would notice she was missing and come and look for her. Yet if they did, she would sulk and say she wasn't hungry. They even asked if she was sickening for anything, much to Lissa's disgust, though she made sure she ate very little. Except at night when they were both asleep, when she would secretly raid the larder for cuts of meat and slices of apple pie. It made her feel wickedly decadent.

Lissa chose to ignore many of the chores which Meg left for her to do, or pretend she hadn't heard the necessary instructions. She came home late when she was told to be early, left her clothes on the floor instead of picking them up, and generally managed, in her clumsy adolescent way, to be as uncooperative as possible. It gave her great satisfaction and made her thoroughly miserable.

She broke every rule she could think of, even to riding beyond the strict boundaries set her, but the ploy failed to bring forth the desired result. Neither Meg nor Tam showed the least sign of guilt. They kept saying how the new baby would make no difference, and how they loved her, but Lissa could see that wasn't true. It was making a difference already.

Then one morning when Meg insisted she come down to breakfast, Lissa felt sure she could see signs of strain upon Meg's face, perhaps even contrition. Her pallor was deathly and there were worried creases about her eyes, as if she wasn't sleeping much.

'How's Goldie?' she asked, as politely as if she were addressing a stranger.

But Lissa didn't intend to make things easy for her. 'She's fine. I'm surprised you're interested.'

The expression of pain on Meg's face intensified but she persisted with her interrogation in a falsely bright voice. She pushed the kettle on to the hot part of the Aga. 'Did I see you heading for the quarry road the other day?'

'I have a friend lives down there,' Lissa lied, trying for a casual air. She'd never told a lie before.

'Who? You've never mentioned any friend to me.'

Lissa could feel her stomach tightening with the heightened tension. 'Don't sound so surprised. I do have friends, you know.'

'I'm sure you do,' said Meg, spooning far too much tea rapidly into the big brown tea pot, then stopping to rub the small of her back. She felt so desperately tired these days she was almost beginning to regret this pregnancy. Perhaps she had left it too late. Thirty-five was old for a first baby and she was sounding as crotchety with Lissa as her own father had once been with her. Yet the child troubled her. She obviously felt threatened by the coming baby but Meg felt her own efforts to reassure Lissa being met by an obstinate brick wall. 'You know I don't like you wandering too far. Those old quarries are full of pot holes that a pony might easily catch a foot in.'

The point was valid, one that Lissa would have accepted gracefully at one time, but she was thirteen, well on the way to being a woman, and needed advice from no one, least of all Meg.

In any case she knew that Meg was talking about gypsies, not potholes. Just as Lissa was looking for Kenyon Parker and not some imaginary friend. But then it wasn't her fault, was it, if all her school friends lived miles away? It wasn't her fault Meg was having a baby and couldn't be bothered to spend time with her any more. It wasn't her fault her own mother had abandoned her. Lissa told herself that she'd always felt an outsider with Meg and Tam; now she had proof that they really didn't care for her. They no longer even pretended. Self-pity rose hot and bittersweet in her throat.

'You don't care what I do,' she said, sulking furiously. 'Nobody does. I must be a very unlovable person. No wonder my mother deserted me.'

Meg's look of horror brought a burst of sweet delight into Lissa's rebellious heart. 'What a thing to say. Of course I care. I love you dearly, Lissa. And so does Tam.' The kettle started gently to steam.

'You brought me up. That's not quite the same, is it?' The tone was cruelly mocking but Lissa didn't care. She wanted to hurt Meg as she was hurting, deep inside.

'Of course it's the same. You are very special to us and always will be.'

Hot tears pricked her eyelids and Lissa blinked them angrily away. 'That was only duty. You had no choice. You didn't even choose me. I was dumped on you.' With tremulous pleasure she watched the terrible effect of these words dawn on Meg's face. Instantly the feeling drained away and she was drenched in guilt. She wanted to run to Meg and smooth away the stricken look, to beg her forgiveness and say she hadn't meant it.

'Oh, Lissa,' was all Meg said, which made her feel worse than ever. Desperately she tried to put matters right.

'Come with me for a ride. I'm bored with Brockbarrow wood. I want to explore further.'

Meg looked distressed. 'I can't. Not today, love. Why don't you ask Tam to go with you?'

Lissa pouted. 'Tam says he has to do all your jobs as well as his own these days. He's too busy.'

'It's a difficult time.'

'Stop saying that. Come and meet the gypsies.'

41

Meg's face seemed to sharpen. 'I thought I told you to stay away from those tinkers? They bring naught but trouble. Besides, they've gone.'

Lissa was appalled. 'Gone? Gone where? Why have they gone? They weren't doing any harm.' Violet eyes glazed with anger as she fiercely defended them.

'Their horses eat our grass and we've little enough up here. I told them to leave.'

'You told my friends to *leave*?'

'They are not your friends. Keep away from them, Lissa, there's a good girl.'

Above everything, Lissa hated to be called a 'good girl' as if she were a child still, instead of a young woman.

'I like them. They sing and laugh a lot. They make me happy. Don't you want me to be happy?'

'Of course I do.' Meg reached for the knitted kettle holder that hung on a brass hook beside the mantleshelf. 'But I'd prefer it if you left them alone. And that boy . . .'

'Kenyon?'

'I don't like you spending so much time with him.'

Lissa gasped. 'He's my *friend*.'

The kettle was rattling furiously on the stove and Meg quickly lifted it and poured the scalding water into the teapot. There was so much she wanted to explain, about life, about trust, about love, but she couldn't seem to find the right words, the right approach to get through to Lissa any more. The huge farm kitchen filled with the comforting aroma of hot tea but when she turned back to the table, loving words of caution on her lips, Lissa was on her feet, knocking back her chair with a fierce hand.

'I knew it was a waste of time to talk to you. You don't want me to have any friends. You don't want me to be happy. You don't want *me* any more.'

Meg set the milk jug on the table with a steady calm she did not feel. A dull ache had started low in her back and she felt very slightly sick. Perhaps a cup of tea would make her feel better. 'If I've been preoccupied lately it's only this baby. It's important to me, to us both.'

'More important than me?'

'Now you're being silly.'

'Silly? Is that all you can say? Oh, forget it.' Lissa turned from the table, pushed aside the untouched porridge and flounced to the door. 'Fuss, fuss, fuss, over a stupid baby. That's what's silly. You can't even see any sign of it yet. God knows what you'll be like when it's actually here.'

She pulled back the door and marched from the room, back rigid, head held high. Lissa heard Meg call out to her but did not pause or look back.

The next morning, shortly after dawn, Lissa set out. She intended to ride defiantly right down the quarry road and find the gypsies. The triumph she felt at breaking Meg's strictest rule made her hum with pleasure.

It promised to be a beautiful autumn day. The sun was shining brilliantly by the time she'd ridden Goldie through Brockbarrow wood and onwards to the tarn. It glittered on the rippled surface, wrinkled as an old man's bald head.

She reined in the pony and let it take a drink at the water. A picture of herself and Nick, shaking their bottles of liquorice water, came to mind. What a childish thing to do. What innocent babes they had been. As if a stretch of water could answer their wishes. As if wishing could find a mother, or make Meg still love her. There was a tight feeling in her throat but she ignored it. It wasn't her fault if no one understood or cared for her? Or was it? A bleak thought.

'What will I do when I'm grown up, Goldie? Where will I go? I can't stay here where I'm not wanted.' Lissa thought about this for a moment. It was very slightly worrying, for how would she know when it was the right time to leave? What would it feel like to be a woman? What was she now? Not a child, surely. She almost felt invisible.

'Perhaps I am invisible, Goldie. Perhaps that's why Meg doesn't notice me and Kath forgot all about me. I don't really exist at all.'

Lissa rode on past the stand of mountain ash, flushed scarlet with their winter berries, and paid no attention to a red fox resting in the dry leaves at their foot. The fox did no more than raise a lazy eyelid as he watched her go by, sensing no danger here.

There was a sharpness to the air that filled her with a sudden rush of exhilaration. The morning mists lifted like a bride's veil, revealing the purple mountain tops, making her give an involuntary gasp of pleasure. How beautiful they were. How magnificent.

'No, Goldie, I must be visible because I feel so alive suddenly. I can see a stone cairn on the summit, a ridge of sharp rock over

43

there, a slither of loose scree.' Energy flooded into her, as if she could go on riding and riding and reach out to the whole world from these smooth mountain tops.

What did it matter if Meg and Tam didn't love her? She was young and they were old. This was her time. If she did not know exactly who she was or where she belonged she could at least be free, as the beautiful kingfisher had been free, and Kenyon too of course. Kenyon Parker liked her, she knew that he did, and he wanted to kiss her. And now Meg had sent him away. How she hated her for doing that! Kenyon might have kissed her today and then she would have had a special, secret sort of friend, all of her own.

She did not see him at first. The dark figure rose slowly, breaking away from a grey boulder against which he must have been leaning.

Lissa's heart gave a jolt, the sound echoing in her ears. She was barely able to contain her delight at seeing him. He hadn't gone at all. He'd stayed. Especially for her.

He made no move towards her, simply stood, waited, and watched. She was used to his stillness but still found it slightly unnerving. It seemed to echo the silence, like a presence on the fellside.

There was no movement. Not a creature stirred. A cloudless, wide blue sky hung above, empty even of birdsong. As if the whole world were holding its breath.

For a moment longer she stayed in the saddle, feeling the keenness of her pleasure in finding him, giving him ample time to enjoy looking at her, since that was what he seemed to want to do. Was this how it felt to be a woman? Exhilarating? Powerful?

She looked, had she but known it, much as her mother had done before her when Katherine Ellis had gone to call upon Jack. Only Kath had been older, and far more experienced. And when Meg had explained about them, she'd said they'd often gone out in a threesome. But Lissa was glad she was alone with Kenyon. At last.

'Hey there! Hello!' She lifted her arm and waved to him, afraid he might not wait for her.

She'd forgotten how pale his hair was. It shone in the sun like pale silk and she longed, suddenly, to smooth her fingers over it.

Goldie refused to be hurried and Lissa was slightly breathless from bumping her feet against the pony's flanks by the time she reached him. She slid down quickly from the pony's back, and swamped by a sudden attack of shyness, slanted her eyes up at him and smiled.

He still hadn't spoken, or returned her greeting, but the pale pink lips curved upwards into an answering smile and Lissa sighed with pleasure. How lovely he was.

'I thought you'd gone.' She looped up the reins so that Goldie could come to no harm, then left the pony to crop grass while she walked boldly up to him. This would show Meg that she really did have a friend, one who cared enough not to leave when ordered to do so. 'I'm so glad you came back. Have you brought a pony? We could ride out together. Right over the quarry road.' She offered this treat to him almost as a sacrifice.

'Your ma says she don't like you being with us gyppoes,' he said, one corner of his mouth curling in distaste. Despite this, in Lissa's eyes his beauty remained unmarred.

She laughed, trying to appear unconcerned. 'She isn't my mother as a matter of fact.' A prickle of contrition niggled at this rejection of Meg but Lissa pushed the feeling away. 'You really shouldn't let her bother you.'

'Told us she didn't want us on her land. Made us leave.'

'It's the grass, d'you see? We have to look after it for the sheep in the winter. Or they would die.'

'Folks don't like us around much.'

'I like you, Kenyon. I want you to stay.'

He took a step towards her as if he would argue the toss but then his eyes kindled with a different expression as he came closer. Lissa held her breath expectant, happy, smiling, thrilled at last to find her friend. He was going to kiss her this time, she could sense it, and swayed slightly towards him in anticipation. He stood casually with his hands in his pockets, and looked so delightfully serious that she tilted her chin, arching her neck enticingly as she slanted a teasing glance up at him, blinking in the sunlight. A bubble of laughter erupted from her throat. 'Do smile. You always seem so serious. And so quiet. Why do you talk so little? Are you shy?'

'Are you laughing at me?'

'No, of course not.'

'What do you want me to say then?'

Lissa shrugged her shoulders and giggled, feeling again that sense of power and wild excitement growing inside her. 'I don't know. Whatever comes into your head. I want to know all about you.'

'So you can have a good laugh with your family after we're gone?'

'No.'

'Do you want to touch me?'

Lissa remembered how she had longed to stroke the butter silk locks of his hair and felt her fingers itch with longing still. 'I might,' she said, teasing, more provocative than she realised.

'You can if you want to.' He withdrew his hand from within his coat, but was still holding something in it. The morning sun glinted upon it, white and smooth. Curious, Lissa looked, wondering what it was.

Cold terror seeped with deadly slowness through her veins. Horrified, she couldn't tear her eyes away from it.

'Go on,' he was saying. 'I don't mind.' He was coming closer, too close, his hand making strange jerking movements as he did so. She wanted to turn and run but her legs had turned to jelly and her feet seemed glued to the ground. A low keening sound filled the air. It surprised her to find it came from her own mouth.

She didn't need to look about her to confirm what she already knew, that no one had followed her down to the old quarries. Not even Meg or Tam would guess that her rebellion would take her this far.

A primeval instinct warned her not to panic. Lissa screwed tight her eyes, trying to shut out the awful sight, but could not shut out the sound of his grunting. For the rest of her life she knew she would remember that sound. And the cloying scent of sweet heather. It made her want to be sick.

Then a voice in her ear, low and hissing, laughing at her. 'I could rape you if I wanted. Only I don't. I don't want a kid like you hanging round me at all. D'you hear?' Whimpering and shivering with fright she tried to nod her head as she sank to the ground, no longer in control of her limbs. Then astonishingly she heard again his laugh. A hard, brittle sound this time, as if he were unaccustomed to making it.

'It's your own fault,' he said.

And when she risked opening her eyes again, expecting at any moment he would touch her with that . . . that thing, she saw to her profound relief that he had gone. Her shaking body collapsed as she vomited into the heather.

She did not, for one minute, doubt that he was right.

Hours later, Lissa lifted her head and was astonished to find the sun was still shining. The savage face of Dundale Knot smiled almost

46

benignly upon her. Lissa knew she could move now that he had gone but her limbs were stiff with fright, as if they'd been immersed in deep water where the sun couldn't reach them. She wanted to stay curled up, hidden away from the awful sight, from the fear that still crawled on her skin and beat with a hollow pulse in her stomach.

After an achingly long time she found herself back at the tarn, carved out centuries ago like a deep cup beside the small copse. Lissa wished she could make time stand still as the tarn had done. She wished there was no need ever to grow into a woman, that she could go back to that time of happy childhood where problems did not exist.

Forgetting the last of Meg's rules, Lissa pulled off her clothes and sank beneath the icy surface, cleansing every part of her body as if he had touched her as certainly as he had defiled her mind. She couldn't risk more than a minute in the water but it felt good. Cleansing every part of her.

She had wanted him for a friend and he had rejected that need in her and used her like an object. Lissa supposed she should feel glad he had done no worse but his cruel disregard of her sensitivity bit deep into her soul. It seemed that too many people had too little regard for her feelings.

Did no one recognise her as a person? A real human being? She hadn't asked to be born, or dumped when she'd become an inconvenience. A sob caught in her throat. She hadn't asked Meg to bring her up as her own child. And though Meg said she had come to love her, it couldn't always have been that way, not when Kath had betrayed her with Jack, the man Meg was meant to marry. Now she was to have a child of her own, even that love had faded and gone. Did everyone hate her? Why? Oh why?

Out on the grassy bank Lissa doubled over with the cramps, wishing she could be sick again but knowing her stomach to be quite empty. Then she pulled her clothes on over her damp body and lay supine on the prickly grass, staring at nothing.

It was only when a cooling breeze sent the silvered waters rippling back and forth in a noisy tide over the slippery shale that she became aware that the sun had gone, replaced by gathering gloom and a creeping mist. Lissa shivered with a new fear. The fells were not at all the place to be in a mist, let alone the cold dark of night.

There was a bothy at the far end of the tarn, a small hut used by shepherds if they were caught out on the fells overnight.

47

She crept within its stone walls and folded herself into a tight, protective ball.

The leaves of the rowan whispered to her, calming her as they always had. Familiar, normal, peaceful. But she had no wishing left in her, and the magic was quite gone. It was then that she wept for her lost innocence.

How could you tell, she wondered, as sleep weighted her eyelids and the tears dried in dark patches on her cheeks, when people wanted you for yourself and not as an object to be used for their own selfish needs?

She dozed a little, a troubled unsettled sort of sleep filled with gypsy laughter, a silent beautiful face and butter yellow hair. And pack ponies that roamed the fells at night loaded with a full coffin. She cried out and would have jumped from the bothy but the sound of rain on the corrugated roof soothed her, calming her thumping heartbeats, and she slept at last, deeply and well, no other sounds disturbing her exhaustion.

Lissa woke to find the blinding sun filling the open square of the entrance and her young heart lifted at the sight.

Again she swam in the tarn, unable to resist the sparkling water, and this time she splashed and even laughed, a natural youthful optimism starting to grow inside her. She would survive this. She must survive.

When she had done, Lissa lay on the grass to dry in the sun. Then she put on her clothes and set off for home.

Of course Meg would be cross with her for staying away all night and make her feel worse than ever. Lissa tried to work out how best to explain. Her first, natural instinct had been to rush to Meg with her troubles. Now that she was calmer, Lissa was having second thoughts. It would only prove that Meg's rules had been necessary. She would say it was Lissa's own fault. As she knew, in her heart, that it was. Nor did it help her case that Goldie had disappeared. It wasn't hard to work out where the pony had gone.

Oh, but she longed for some of Meg's loving comfort.

Lissa still hadn't decided what to do when she pushed open the heavy door and walked into a kitchen alive with activity.

'Where have you been?' These sharp words came unexpectedly from Sally Ann, who was dashing about in a frenetic sort of way quite unlike her usual placid self. 'Meg has been worried sick. Been out all night looking for you,' she said. 'We all have.' And grabbing a towel she ran off into the living room. Lissa followed, frowning as she struggled to find an answer. But she never did find one.

There was Tam who should have been out on the fells at this time of the day. Nick and Daniel, in muddy boots not usually allowed in the kitchen, standing about looking helpless and goggle-eyed. And a strange man she didn't even recognise. And in the midst of all of this pandemonium, Meg, quietly sobbing as her life blood spread out on the rush matting, rather as Lissa's had once done at Larkrigg. Only this was worse, far far worse. This meant there was to be no baby and Lissa knew that that was her fault too.

When Meg came back from hospital she was not the same. A light seemed to have been switched off behind her face and Lissa could not bear to look at her. Tam had warmed the bed with a stone hot water bottle and now she was installed in it, her hair scraped back like a child's, grey eyes translucent and sad.

Lissa knew she had to speak. 'Am I very wicked?'

'No, of course not. What a thing to say.'

'My mother was.'

Meg took a deep breath and plucked at the bedclothes, as if she really was too tired to be bothered with all of this now but knew she must put Lissa's mind at rest. 'Kath is different from you. And she wasn't wicked. You mustn't take any notice of your grandmother's warped view of things.'

But Lissa felt compelled to purge her soul.

'I didn't want that baby. I was jealous of it.'

Meg's eyes pricked with tears. 'I know. There was no need to be. Anyway, that was my last chance. I'm too old to try again.'

A terrible silence as Lissa shouldered the guilt of this bleak reality. 'Are you sad?'

'I have you.' Meg managed a smile. Her lips were trembling.

Lissa wanted to ask if that would be enough but dare not, for fear of the answer, and Meg turned her head away so did not notice her need. Was it possible to will a baby to die? She had never meant that to happen. Never, never. Lissa turned from the bed, unable to witness Meg's distress.

Confessing about the gypsy, Lissa decided, was quite out of the question. It would have to wait. She daren't risk adding to Meg's misery by mentioning something that was again her own fault. Meg

49

would say she had constantly warned her not to stray too far from the farm, not to talk to the tinkers, Kenyon Parker in particular. And Lissa knew that she had willed him to come to her. Just as she had wanted Meg not to be pregnant. And as a result these terrible things had happened.

But she could not escape Tam's hot Irish fury over the lost pony.

'How could you be so careless? Did she bolt? Did you leave her to wander free? How could you lose her?'

Lissa admitted to allowing Goldie to roam free since a reason had to be given. 'The sun was shining. I lay down and then I fell asleep. I'm sorry.'

They all knew why the pony had not wandered back to Broombank. The gypsies too had vanished from the fell. It wasn't hard to work out the connection.

'Were you looking for Goldie? Is that why you stayed out all night?' Meg's eyes were haunted, wanting to believe that the fault was not hers, that she hadn't failed Lissa in some way. 'We were frantic. We combed the fells all night long calling for you. Where were you?'

Lissa hung her head, not able to meet Meg's gaze. 'When I woke up I was caught in a mist, so I stayed in the bothy. I'm sorry,' she said again, rather pathetically.

'Well, that's it,' Tam said, green eyes flashing with unusual anger. 'No more ponies.'

And no more babies, Lissa thought, not daring to argue. She did not even cry. It seemed to her a just punishment, to lose her most precious possession, for hadn't she stolen Meg's?

5

In the days and weeks following, Lissa fell into a kind of malaise. At first they attributed her behaviour to the loss of the pony and Tam almost capitulated and bought her another, only Meg would not hear of it.

'No, she must be made to bear some responsibility for her actions. We should never have bought the pony in the first place. She was too young.'

Tam frowned. 'Are you saying it's all my fault?'

'No. I'm saying Lissa must learn to take care of her things. She so often has her head in the clouds, dreaming of unreachable things like ranches in Canada. This is Westmorland. This is reality. Money doesn't grow on trees.'

'Isn't that your own sense of inferiority to Kath speaking? Because she could have given the child all kinds of things we cannot.'

'We give her love.'

'Perhaps she doesn't see it that way. She says we didn't choose to adopt her, she was thrust upon us. You can see her point of view. That might give her a certain insecurity, don't you think?'

Meg pricked the spicy coil of Cumberland sausage with furious, stabbing thrusts of the fork then pulled open the oven door and almost flung the dish inside. 'What rubbish you do talk. I'm not bothered by Kath these days. Lissa is suffering from adolescence, that's all. She will be fine. You'll see.'

But she wasn't fine. She grew ever more moody and depressed. Lost weight, stopped walking on the fells, rarely went out. Sometimes she woke in the night in the grip of a nightmare, screaming

51

with terror, and Meg would come to her bed and soothe her till she slept again.

'She should go away for a while. It's people of her own age she needs,' Tam said, but Meg was heartbroken. She could feel Lissa slipping away from her and could not bear it.

'I know we haven't been getting on too well lately, but the house will be so empty without her. I can't bear to think of her going away.'

'It is the child we must think of, not ourselves.'

'We can't afford school fees.'

'Grandmother Ellis can,' said Tam. And Meg stared at him, dumbstruck. 'I can't ask her. I won't ask her. Not ever.'

'Not even for Lissa?'

It was the hardest thing Meg had ever done to walk back up to Larkrigg, sit in the shrouded room and eat her words. Rosemary Ellis folded her hands on her tweed-skirted lap and for the first time in years actually smiled.

'I knew you would come, in the end.'

Meg ground her teeth together, wanting to protest and walk away from this cruel, unfeeling woman who had caused so much damage. But there was no room now for her own feelings. Something was wrong with Lissa and she needed help. Help that Meg herself seemed unable to give.

'Lissa is still your granddaughter, Mrs Ellis, whether you like it or not. I dare say Kath would want her well educated and cared for, were she here.'

'Which she is not so that is mere supposition. I have seen the child wandering the fells, though not for some time I'll admit. And I agree you have a problem if she is not to turn into a hoyden like her mother, but I dispute the necessity for me to become involved. It really isn't my problem.'

Meg smoothed the backs of her gloved hands as she held on to her temper, wishing she had not come, glad at least that she had not brought Lissa to face this final humiliation. 'Are you saying you will not help Lissa out of her trouble?'

The lip curled. 'The Ellis family cannot be seen to acknowledge this – particular situation.'

Meg stared at the older woman, at the thin, withered cheeks, the sprout of whiskers on the blunt chin and the iron grey hair scraped back and fastened with a grip. Not one ounce of softness. So Lissa was not to be publicly recognised as Rosemary Ellis's granddaughter. Not now. Not ever. And if that rejection hurt the child, so be it. Family pride was all.

Meg stood up, stiff-backed, tight-lipped. 'I'm sorry to have taken up so much of your time.'

Rosemary Ellis did not move. 'Amy will show you out.'

'May she at least see Jeffrey? He was very good to her as a child.'

This concession too was refused on the grounds that the poor man was not long for this world and Rosemary had no wish for him to be 'inconvenienced at this difficult time'.

Meg inclined her head, biting hard on her lower lip, and left Larkrigg Hall without another word.

It was decided that Lissa should stay in Kendal during the week at a friend's house while she continued to attend the High School. It was the best compromise they could devise and at least gave her the opportunity to mix with more young people of her own age. Not that she did very much. She found it difficult to make friends and knew the teachers thought her too withdrawn and unforthcoming, but she always diligently handed in her work on time, neatly and tidily done, while failing to shine in any of her subjects.

There she stayed for the next two and a half years. For Lissa it was a relief to be away from the blank despair in Meg's eyes, from the terrible gnawing guilt. She went home at weekends but though she loved sometimes to walk on her beloved fells and sit beside Allenbeck, she found her pleasure in them had quite gone.

Meg knew only that on the day she had lost her baby, and Lissa her pony, there had been another, greater loss, one she did not understand. Perhaps in time, when these difficult days of adolescence were over, they might regain it. She could only hope so.

Jeffrey Ellis died, as expected, and Lissa attended the funeral with Meg as was only right and proper. Larkrigg Hall seemed even more gloomy than usual and her grandmother's glare only marginally less frozen than the stag's head in the hall.

Meg informed her that her grandfather had not forgotten her, as she had imagined. 'When you were small, he gave me a sum of money to invest for you. Not great, Lissa, but it will provide a nest egg for you when you come of age.'

Lissa wasn't interested in nest eggs. She wanted life to happen. She wanted action, to lift the gloom that had grown to be a part of her. She hurried back to school where everyone was singing 'Cherry Pink and Apple Blossom White' and tried not to think of her witch of a grandmother who lived alone high on the fell.

When she turned sixteen she left without taking her exams, despite all advice to the contrary.

There was pressure from Meg for Lissa to stay at Broombank. And, surprisingly enough, from Nick too.

No longer a boy, he was broad and strong now, a grown man with a shock of red-blond hair. She could tell by the glances he gave her that he did not see her as a little nuisance any longer. Nor did she miss the looks exchanged between Meg and Sally Ann. Lissa knew that if she stayed at Broombank, in no time at all they would have her married off and settled at Ashlea with Nick, her life decided for her. And that would not be right. Not for her, nor for Nick.

The trouble was, she didn't know what she did want and that made her feel unsettled and inadequate. In the end Lissa decided she could only find whatever it was outside the dale. When she told Meg of her decision to leave, her face seemed to crumple.

'Leave? Why? Where would you go?'

'To find a job.'

'But you're too young to leave home. You've only just come back. We can work together. Get to know each other again. Won't that be fun?' Meg's hands were red raw with the salt she'd been rubbing into some freshly killed pork and Lissa looked at them with distaste.

'There's no work for me here, Meg. You have your sheep and Tam. I don't belong.'

'Of course you belong.' Meg again felt the grip of loss around her heart. She reached for a cloth and wiped her hands upon it, then rested them on Lissa's shoulders, drawing her close. 'How lucky I am to have you,' she said. 'No woman could have had a better daughter.'

'Nor I a better mother,' mumbled Lissa, realising it was probably true, wishing it could be enough. The two exchanged tentative smiles.

'We've had our differences, our difficult times, but what mother and daughter doesn't? I want us to be friends. And Broombank to be your home.'

'Broombank is your home, not mine. Turner was your name before you married Tam, not mine. Who am I? Not Lissa Turner. Not Lissa Ellis. Who? Where do I belong? I have to build a new life and find my own place in it. Don't you see?'

A small silence then Meg blinked and gave a tiny nod. 'Yes, I do see.' She wanted to talk about the baby, to say that she didn't blame Lissa for what had happened, but couldn't trust herself to say the words without crying. Perhaps a part of her still did blame Lissa for so thoughtlessly staying out that night, causing them so much worry and anguish. She could not offer the forgiveness Lissa so desperately needed so the breach between them was not entirely healed.

It came as a great relief to Meg that Lissa decided not to go to Canada. She'd been almost sure that she would. But Lissa had been adamant.

'I won't go where I'm not wanted,' she said, with such bitterness in her firm young voice it cut Meg to the heart.

'Are you sure this is what you want?' She had agreed to drive Lissa into central Lakeland to look for a summer job, with many provisos of course, and words of caution.

Lissa had not spoken all the way through Staveley and Windermere, nor as they drove the long road that followed the lake as far as Waterhead at Ambleside.

Meg changed gear and eased her way out of the traffic and into Borrans Road, driving past the steamer pier, closed at this time of year, and on past the open field wherein lay the Roman Camp of Galava, her mind full of worries instead of the magnificent view.

As they turned left and headed out towards Clappersgate and Skelwith Bridge, the mountains of the Langdales rising ahead of them against an unusually blue sky, Lissa said, 'Yes, this is what I want,' and left it at that.

Birdsong filled the air, and the scent of new grass, but neither remarked upon it. Spears of pink and green were about to unfurl on the oak and horse chestnut and for a moment Lissa's heart lifted. Her life was not over. She could begin again. She was sixteen years old and could make of her life whatever she wished.

Having been rejected by her mother, and heedlessly damaged her relationship with Meg by trusting in a new friendship that had proved as corrupt as it was unreliable, she found it hard to believe anyone could ever truly love her.

55

But it didn't matter any more. She wouldn't let it matter. She never intended to risk rejection ever again.

Jan Colwith stood on a box behind the huge glass drapery counter and adopted the pleasant expression of polite enquiry necessary for a difficult customer.

'I'm sorry, madam, these are the only kid gloves we have in at present. Would you wish me to order a particular size or colour for you?'

Jan could hear the hiccuping sounds of her brother's deep voice trying to imitate Bill Haley issuing from the stockroom. The woman raised finely arched brows and Jan smiled apologetically, vowing to kick him the moment this dreadful woman had gone.

'I see little point,' the customer said tartly. 'I shall call again when you have more time to attend to me, or perhaps I shall wait until I go into Kendal. I am sure they will have a much better selection there. Good day to you.'

'Good day, madam, and thank you for calling.'

Derek Colwith erupted through the curtain behind her, snorting with laughter. 'How can you be so polite to that dragon?'

'The hideous noise you were making didn't help one bit.' Jan pushed back her straight brown hair, hooking it behind her ears with agitated fingers, brown eyes narrowing short-sightedly at her brother. 'Are you quite mad, Derry? You shouldn't even be here. Miss Stevens will have my scalp if she spots you.' She glanced nervously about the shop, expecting her employer to emerge from among the dusty mannequins which stood, arms raised in silent appeal, in the wide window.

'Oh, stop fussing. If I can't call in at lunch-time and talk to my own sister it's a poor do. Anyway, I might be buying something, mightn't I?' He swaggered outrageously, making Jan giggle as he strolled into the centre of the floor, hands in pockets, to gaze about him with a fine display of urbane assurance. They both knew he didn't feel half so brave as he appeared but that was all part of the joke. If the last customer had been a dragon, Miss Stevens was a dinosaur.

'What a sight you do look, Derry. Where did you get those socks?'

'Don't you like them?' He hitched up his trouser legs an inch or two, which was no mean feat judging by their narrowness, to reveal bright, lime green socks. He grinned. 'Cool, eh? They're luminous.

I've got some shocking pink ones too.' He pulled out a comb and started to slick back his already neat quiff which made Jan laugh all the more.

'No wonder Miss Stevens calls you a Teddy Boy.'

She looked again at the socks and the thick crêpe soles of his shoes. Her gaze slid over his long grey jacket, only an inch or two short of Teddy Boy length. Admittedly the lapels were not velvet but they tapered narrowly and hooked with a double link button at the waist. The most conventional garments he wore were a pristine white shirt and a slim grey tie. At weekends he was fond of a rather dashing silk waistcoat or a leather jacket and skintight jeans. But today was Friday, a work day.

'Sorry to disappoint you, sis, but I'm not really a Ted. Get as near to it as I dare but haven't quite got the nerve to go all the way. Besides, old Brandon would never permit any of his clerks to dress so outlandishly, even in their free time. Old fuddy-duddy, that's what he is.'

'And what does he think of your socks?'

'Er, he hasn't seen them.'

'Make sure he doesn't then or you may be forced to apply to Miss Stevens for a job.'

Derry rolled his eyes heavenwards with exaggerated charm. 'I'd rather chew nails for a living.'

Jan started tidying away gloves. It had been a long morning, starting shortly after eight, and she was tired. Her legs were aching, she was hungry and not really in the mood for her brother's jokiness so she spoke more sharply than she intended. 'What did you want anyway?'

'Ooh, sorry to bother you.' He fingered the net on a hat that dangled on a T-shaped counter stand and Jan slapped his hand away. 'Only to tell you I won't be home this evening. I'm going over to Tony's.' His apparent nonchalance did not sit easily with the glance he slanted sideways at her.

Jan pursed her lips then let them burst open in a tiny explosion. 'Oh, that's so unfair. So I'm to cope with things on my own again, am I?'

'You do it so well.'

'Dad will be hurt.'

'Let him be. He should have thought of us before he brought that – that creature home.'

'You didn't think she was a creature once.'

'I've learned different.'

Jan's eyes were pleading. 'I know you're hurting but don't make trouble, Derry. Please. We have to live with the situation whether we like it or not. There's nothing else we can do.'

'I don't have to sit there watching them bill and coo. Where my mother used to sit,' Derry said, a fierce brightness in his brown eyes.

Jan fell silent, knowing how to answer but unable to find the courage to do so. After a moment she said, 'Mum's gone, Derry. Dead and buried. And life goes on.'

He flung himself away from the counter and started circling the shop again, running his hands over the glass counters, flicking the ribbons that hung in brightly coloured rows from their reels, spinning a stand of buttons round like a whirligig.

'Stop it, you'll do some damage.' Jan studiously gave her attention to smoothing out the gloves, slipping each one into its appointed place in the drawer, a sick feeling settling in her stomach at the prospect of the difficult evening ahead.

'Had any applicants for the vacancy yet?'

Jan shook her head. 'Most of Carreckwater are wary of Stevens Drapery.'

'Except you.' Derry raised enquiring eyebrows at her, but his smile was conciliatory.

'Except me. But then I don't have much choice, do I? I like to eat.'

'Where is she now, the old harridan?'

'At lunch.'

'It's nearly two. What about your lunch?'

'I get half an hour. When she comes back. Just time for a quick sandwich and to powder my nose.' Jan wrinkled it ruefully as she stowed the glove drawers back under the counter. 'Speaking of lunch, hadn't you better go and eat yours?' She glanced up at him, anxious suddenly. 'You did remember to pick it up from the kitchen dresser, didn't you?'

He sighed and propped one elbow on the counter, cupping his chin in his hand while he grinned at her. 'Yes, sister dear, don't fuss over me. I'm a big boy now.'

'I sometimes wonder.'

'I've eaten my corned beef sandwiches and very good they were too though a touch more pickle would be appreciated. And perhaps a little more butter, if we can run to it?' He didn't tell her that he had also popped into the pub for a meat pie and half a pint of bitter.

'Cheek! Do them yourself in future. I'm not your servant.' She aimed a swipe at him and laughed as he ducked. Then, as wickedly spry as if he were still a boy of ten instead of seventeen, he leapt up into the window and positioned himself among the mannequins.

Jan squealed her dismay, jumping down from the box and running round the counter to grab for his coat. 'Derry, stop it. You mustn't play your silly games here, especially not in the window. You'll cause mayhem. Miss Stevens may be back at any moment. Do behave.' She had grown quite breathless with anxiety as her words fell upon deaf ears. Her brother simply grinned, sticking his arms out in imitation of the mannequins.

'Why do they have to stand in this silly way?' he asked.

'Because they do.'

'Don't you think I add a touch of class? Perhaps people will like my socks and come in and buy them.' He glanced out through the window as if expecting a queue of people to have formed already and found himself looking down into an oval, pale face with wide, dark blue eyes.

He was startled for a moment, as apparently, were the eyes. Then a wide mouth broke into the prettiest smile he had ever seen and he stared at it, entranced for what might have been eternity.

'*Mr* Colwith. Have you quite taken leave of your senses? Get out of my window this instant.'

The dinosaur had returned, via the back door, which was most unsporting of her in Derry's opinion. The stentorian voice made him jump so violently he knocked his head on the low ceiling. Turning too quickly he sent one mannequin in a smart apple green two-piece flying. Instinctively he tried to catch it but that only made matters worse as he elbowed the stomach of the one behind him and his thick crepe soles got caught up with another. The mannequins came down like dominoes, arms and legs flying free in a kind of celebratory *danse macabre*. And all he could do was helplessly watch them fall, a bright blonde wig dangling from the link button of his jacket.

He stepped down into the shop considerably chastened. 'I'll put them all back . . .' he began, but Miss Stevens took his ear in a pincerlike grip and marched him to the door.

'*Out!*' she barked. He cast an agonised glance at his sister but Jan

59

was beyond words, her face as white as the sheets that were used to drape the precious models in the stockroom.

'Look, I'm sorry . . .'

'Hello!' The pansy-eyed girl stood in the doorway. 'The card in your window says that you need a new assistant. I don't mind hard work, and I could start right away if you like, by fixing the accident you seem to have had.'

Lissa had fallen in love with Carreckwater the moment they drove into it. She thought it a delightful little village, situated as it was in a wooded valley in the heart of Lakeland with its very own small lake. To the north was Rydal and Grasmere, to the south Ambleside and Windermere. The jagged, snow-tipped peaks of the Langdales stood proudly to the west, and in the east Kentmere. Beyond that came Broombank and her own beloved fells.

She knew that it was her cheek that had got her this job, and best of all, the other girl shop assistant had quickly offered accommodation in her own home.

'If you don't mind sharing, that is?'

'Not at all.'

Lissa had raced off at once to collect her suitcase from the car and tell Meg she could go home without her. It had been hard, suddenly, saying goodbye to Meg, despite the friction that had grown between them recently but at the same time Lissa was excited, looking forward to a new beginning.

'You'll write regularly, and come home to see us from time to time?'

'Of course I will. I'm not a million miles away, am I?'

They stood facing each other, uncertain, awkward, then Meg put out her arms and wrapped them about Lissa's shoulders. The gesture felt strange to two people who had touched each other so little in recent years and Lissa experienced a great urge to put her head on her foster mother's shoulder and beg her forgiveness, to tell her all that was in her heart and somehow make her understand. But Meg was stepping back from her, moving to the car, smiling a distant smile of dismissal as if she couldn't wait to get away.

Lissa didn't see Meg's tears as she drove away.

'It'll have to be a camp bed in my room,' Jan apologised as they walked home that evening.

60

Lissa assured her that would be fine. 'I'm so thrilled to have got the first job I've applied for. Did many people apply for it?'

'Er, well, as a matter of fact, you were the only one.'

Lissa looked startled for a moment then both girls burst out laughing.

What did it matter? She knew she would enjoy working with Jan. Lissa liked her friendly smile, her practical, no nonsense way of doing things, and her brisk petiteness. And she already loved the rows of dark Lakeland stone cottages that seemed to huddle convivially along narrow streets or gossip together in ancient courtyards.

The two girls chatted freely as they made their way down a crooked flight of stone steps by the old stone church.

Lissa wanted to keep stopping to gaze in the shop windows, one selling jewellery, another clocks and ornaments made from slate. Here was a tiny gallery hung with lovely pictures to please the tourists while yet another sold more practical items of paraphernalia needed for climbing the beautiful mountains that surrounded the village.

She was beginning to feel quite buoyant about the future. She might even come to think that Carreckwater was as exciting as Canada in the end. Carrec, Jan told her, was an old Celt word for rock, which rose precipitously all around the lake.

The small cottages gave way to larger Victorian villas strung out around the perimeter of the lake. The kind of houses, she guessed, that had been built by the rich cotton magnates in the last century.

'Sorry to disappoint you but we don't live in one of those,' Jan told her.

'That's a pity. I thought you might be offering a butler and maidservice to go with the camp bed?'

Jan grinned then frowned, looking oddly uncomfortable as if suddenly regretting her hasty offer. Lissa, thinking she'd offended her new friend, hastened to reassure her.

'I'm not serious. I live in an old farmhouse. Big, admittedly, but draughty, freezing cold actually much of the time, and desperately quiet.' A wave of homesickness struck her right between the ribs as a vision of Meg and Tam seated within the warmth of the great inglenook rose in her mind's eye and she had to hold her breath. Jan didn't notice, she was too wrapped up in her own thoughts as they turned left, away from the villas and entered a labyrinth of cobbled streets beyond.

'You can catch a glimpse of the lake from the attic window and

61

that's about it. Not that anyone lives in the attic, it's full of junk,' she warned, then rushing on in one breath, 'I'd best warn you that things aren't exactly what you might call – normal, in our house at the moment.'

'Oh?'

Jan flicked a half glance at her new friend, wondering how much she should divulge of the Colwith family problems.

Lissa must be about the same age as herself, Jan decided, a year younger than Derry who was just turned seventeen. But there was an odd stillness about the girl that troubled her. As if she had known great sadness or was afraid to reveal any part of her real self. Jan wondered what had brought her to Carreckwater. Only the retired and the holidaymakers came voluntarily as a rule. She didn't want to put her off or make things sound worse than they were. Life was tricky enough. Thanks to Derry as much as anyone.

She came to a quick decision to take a leaf out of her brother's book. Whenever Derry didn't want anyone to probe too deeply into his feelings, he hid behind a shield of jokiness. 'Let's face it,' she said, laughing, 'no one would willingly come to live with my family. What a shower!'

'I'm sure they're not as bad as all that.'

'Don't you believe it.' Jan pushed back a swathe of dark hair and her small pointed face broke into one of her infectious grins. 'You'll probably be glad to leave after only a day, and who would blame you? Though I confess it'd be a great help to me if you did stay. Keep me sane. Oh dear, that sounds awful.'

Lissa found herself responding to the ready smile even as her mind thought, no, it didn't sound awful at all. It sounded about right. People generally thought only of themselves in her experience, thrusting from her memory all Meg's selfless acts of generosity over the years. 'I don't care what your reasons for asking me are, I'm grateful for the offer.' But she did care, she cared very much. How she would love someone to invite her into their life simply because they liked her and wanted her for herself.

Jan tucked her arm into Lissa's. 'There, I knew as soon as I saw you that you were kind. Clever too, I shouldn't wonder. Not like me, thick as a brush and half blind into the bargain.' She burst into a peal of merry laughter. 'Derry says I should carry a label: "Dangerous. Too vain to wear spectacles." Then everyone would know to keep out of my way. I hate doing the window for that reason, and you did it a real treat today.'

Lissa was laughing quite naturally by this time, and could feel their friendship growing, minute by minute. It was a good feeling, so perhaps things wouldn't be so bad after all.

'Here it is. Colwith Castle. Well, Nab Cottage in point of fact.'

'What's wrong with it? It's lovely,' Lissa said, gazing approvingly at a dapper stone cottage, the end one of a row, with winter jasmine growing up one corner of it. 'Delightful.'

'It's my dad,' Jan blurted out. 'Mam died just three months ago.'

'Oh, I'm so sorry.'

'It was expected. She'd been ill for a long time. But Dad, well, he took it into his head to marry again. Derry thinks it's too soon, too disrespectful, and to the wrong person.' Jan pulled a wry face. 'I dare say he's right.'

'I see. And what do you think of your new stepmother? Do you get on? Is she nice?'

Instead of answering, Jan pushed at a small, green-painted gate and held it open while Lissa squeezed through the resulting gap. They had called at the grocer's on the way home and what with Lissa's suitcase and the shopping they were both heavily loaded. They walked up the short path and straight in through the green front door.

'You can decide that for yourself,' Jan said.

6

The first thing that struck Lissa about the Colwith household was the overpowering heat. The windows and doors were all firmly closed against possible cool spring breezes and a young woman sat huddled close to two bars of an electric fire. It glowed bright orange against the brown tiles of the fireplace – the same colour, in fact, as her lipstick. Her frizzed, bleached hair was held up with combs on top of her head, revealing a pair of purple glass earrings that swayed and bobbed about her rouged cheeks. She wore a pink fluffy sweater and a tight black skirt which she had pulled up to her thighs to warm her bare legs, mottled with scorch marks from the heat.

A blue budgerigar chirped noisily from a cage that hung on a stand in the corner. During the ensuing conversation Lissa watched it, fascinated, as it alternately chattered to itself in a mirror or bashed the life out of a swinging bell. Perhaps the heat was meant for him.

'About time you got here,' the woman grumbled. 'I have to go soon, you know.' She didn't get up, or offer to help, as Jan marched straight through to the kitchen with the shopping. 'Put the kettle on, love. Your dad will be home in a minute and he'll not like being kept waiting for his tea.'

'Why didn't you do something about it yourself then?' said Jan from the kitchen. 'Surprise me for once.'

'I'm off to work soon. And don't I see enough food, waiting on at the hotel, without starting here? Anyroad, it's your house, as you're so fond of reminding me.' She leaned back in her seat with a smile of satisfaction as if she had won some sort of contest.

Embarrassed by the animosity in the atmosphere, Lissa set down her bag and stared at the rings of faded orange flowers on the worn brown carpet, wondering what to say, what best to do. Could this be a sister that Jan hadn't mentioned? Surely not the new Mrs Colwith? She was little older than herself. Twenty at most. And how old would Jan's father be? She glanced at the woman and at Jan who was busily slamming things into kitchen cupboards. Too old.

'So who have we here?'

Lissa started, as if caught out in her thoughts. She stepped forward, one hand outstretched. 'Hello. I'm Lissa – Turner?'

A cackle of laughter. 'Don't ask me, dear. You should know your own name.' Grey-blue eyes, heavily ringed with black mascara, gazed curiously up at her. 'Mind you, I'm having trouble remembering me own at the moment.'

'And you?'

'Old Mother Riley.'

'What?'

'Who the hell do you think I am?'

Jan came to her rescue. Hooking her hair behind her ears in a now familiar nervous gesture, she flickered a smile at Lissa. 'This is Renee. My new stepmother.'

Renee giggled and reached for a pack of cigarettes that were propped on the corner of the mantelpiece. 'Right laugh that, eh? We were in the same class at school, her and me. Now I'm her bloody mother.'

Lissa tried not to let it show that the information jolted her, readjusting the age of the teenage bride from twenty back down to sixteen, seemingly old beyond her years behind the mask of make-up. 'Oh,' she said, ineffectually. 'I see.'

Lissa watched with interest as the match flared and was applied to the cigarette, the bright tip glowing to an orange disc. It seemed to match the unidentifiable swirls on the wallpaper and the worn carpet. Come to think of it, the whole room was filled with strips, blobs and circles of orange and red, some bright and dazzling, others smudged and faded. It made her head spin. No, that must be the heat. Even the linen antimacassars on the brown moquette three-piece suite were embroidered with pretty ladies in orange crinolines and red poke bonnets.

It was a shabby, tired sort of room, rather untidy, with several mugs and cups and saucers scattered on every surface which Jan was now hastily gathering up. A pair of filthy fur-trimmed slippers sat on the tiled hearth looking rather like a dead cat, and an ash tray overflowed with cigarette ends.

'May I sit down?' Lissa considered the settee covered with discarded newspapers and old woollen cardigans and hesitated.

'Suit yourself.' Without moving from her chair Renee called to Jan who had scurried once more into the kitchen, 'What's for tea then?'

Jan appeared at the door, saw Lissa's dilemma and swooped the settee clear, making irritable clicking noises with her tongue. 'I've bought some smoked haddock. I thought I'd poach it with a bit of butter.'

'We haven't got none. Only a scraping of marg left.'

'It's all right. I got paid today so I bought a packet.'

'Is it Friday already? Crikey, how the week does fly when you're having fun.' Renee drew deeply on the cigarette then threw back her head and blew smoke rings up at the yellowed ceiling. Lissa tried not to look impressed.

At that moment the door opened and Renee was out of her seat in a flash, flinging herself into the arms of a man who brought with him a smell of sawdust, the sharp tang of paint or varnish, and damp fresh air. From what Lissa could see of him he was small and stocky, wearing blue jeans and a dark navy sweater. Renee removed his peaked cap and started to run her fingers through his dark hair, instantly twining her pliant body against his so it was hard to tell them apart. Lissa quickly averted her face from the deep, passionate kiss which followed and threatened to continue indefinitely, and her heart went out to her new friend. She could see exactly why Jan had been glad of some company.

Their eyes met for a moment in shared sympathy and understanding.

'Oh my God, you devil you!' gasped Renee, wiping orange lipstick from his lips and cheek. 'Have you brought it then?' And she squealed when Jimmy Colwith grinned.

'It's coming on Monday. A Ferguson. Twelve-inch. How about that? Next-door's is only nine.'

'Oh my giddy aunt! A television of me own.' Renee screamed, flung her arms about Jimmy's neck and started to kiss him all over again.

When the celebrations were finally over, she staggered back to her chair by the fire. 'My God, you do go at it once you start, don't you?

Give a girl a break, will you?' She flopped down, legs sprawling, and again Lissa averted her gaze from the look of almost naked lust in the girl's translucent grey-blue eyes. It made her feel slightly sick.

'Who have we here?' Jimmy Colwith came and propped himself on the arm of his wife's chair, slipping his arm about her shoulders and letting his hand dangle, one finger gently circling her left breast. Lissa could tell by the amusement in his eyes that he guessed she found the gesture offensive. What had she let herself in for, coming here? Meg would be outraged.

Jan was explaining about her taking the job at the shop and needing a room.

'Only for a little while, till I find a place of my own,' Lissa quickly put in, making a silent vow to start looking this very weekend.

'In Carreckwater? You'll be lucky. Rents are sky high these days with all the trippers. It's more profitable to take in summer visitors than shop assistants as lodgers.'

'I suppose it is.'

'We've not that much room here neither. Where did you intend sleeping? Wi' our Jan? Or our Derek?'

Lissa blushed bright scarlet and Jan slammed her hand down so hard on the table, the little cruet set danced.

'Dad, how can you? Lissa is my friend, my guest, and only just walked in the door. She doesn't understand your weird sense of humour.'

'Then we might as well start as we mean to go on, eh?'

'It's all right,' said Lissa, manufacturing a laugh. 'I can take a joke with the rest.'

''Course you can,' said Jimmy, pleased with the small sensation he had created. 'Anyway, she could always bunk in wi' me, when Renee's on nights. I don't mind sharing.'

There was a small, tight silence.

Renee leaned forward suddenly, patting Lissa reassuringly on the knee. 'It's all right, lovey. He won't bother you. He has enough trouble keeping up with me.' And she smiled so warmly that to her surprise Lissa found herself smiling back.

They all sat at the small table, covered with an orange checked cloth, and Jan brought in the smoked haddock which smelled surprisingly tasty. Lissa felt herself start to relax.

Derry caused a slight stir by unexpectedly turning up to share the meal with them. A disagreement at once took place between brother and sister since he had assured her he would not be home this evening.

Lissa cast a covert glance in his direction as he took off the overlong jacket and slackened his tie, leaving it to hang loose over the white shirt. He was really quite attractive close to, she couldn't help but notice. She hadn't paid too much attention in the shop since Miss Stevens had chased him fairly smartly off the premises. Now Lissa caught him returning her scrutiny, grinning mischievously at her, and she bent her head quickly, trying to concentrate on her meal, acutely aware of him as he came to sit beside her.

'You could have warned me that you might change your mind,' Jan was still complaining, cutting her own piece of fish in half, preparatory to shovelling a portion on to a clean plate for him. Lissa felt instantly guilty since she was the extra person at dinner.

'Derry can have mine. I'm not really hungry.' She was starving. She had left home at eight to give herself ample time to conduct her search and had skipped lunch, despite Meg's protests, out of sheer nervousness.

Jan looked doubtful, as if she knew it would be polite to refuse but was sorely tempted all the same.

'Go on,' Lissa urged. 'We can at least share two portions into three, make it better all round.'

So Jan was persuaded, ignoring Derry's grins and winks at Lissa, which made it patently obvious the motivation for his change of plan. Nobody commented upon the fact that neither Jan's father nor Renee volunteered to share their portions. The pair silently got on with their meal, eyes never leaving their plates except to dwell lingeringly upon each other.

'You can come and listen to me practise afterwards, if you like?' Derry offered, as if bestowing a gift.

'Practise is what he needs an' all,' Jimmy said, through a mouthful of fish. 'Spare her ear drums, laddie.'

'Practise what?' asked Lissa, intrigued despite herself.

'My guitar, of course.'

'Fancies himself as Elvis Presley, my son does.'

'No, I don't. We have a skiffle group, not a rock 'n' roll band. Not that you would know the difference for all you pretend to be young and with it.' Derry flung a glowering glance at Renee before returning his glare to his father. 'You're square, you know

69

that? An old has-been. We can't go on listening to Perry Como for ever.'

'At least he sings in tune.'

Jan held up her hands as if conducting an orchestra with her knife and fork. 'That's enough you two. Eat, please. Remember we have a guest.'

There was silence as everyone finished off their meal.

Later, Derry and Lissa dried the dishes which Jan washed, Renee and Jimmy having vanished somewhere upstairs.

'So? How about it?' Derry persisted. 'We practise in the school hall. For the Saturday dance tomorrow. Will you come?'

Lissa glanced at him and in that brief instant longed, more than anything, to say yes, she would love to come. He looked so friendly and smiling, his brown eyes warmly inviting as if he really wanted her to go with him. She longed to live the life of a normal young person, a teenager as they were now called. Somehow Lissa felt she had missed out on so many things. Her clothes were out of date, her hair style flat and uninteresting. She never wore make up or listened to music. She didn't own a single record or record player, so how could she? Why, she hadn't even seen this great film everybody was raving about, 'Rock Around the Clock'. And had never, in all her life, been kissed by a boy.

Sweet sixteen and never been kissed. It was such a cliché it made her cringe. Going to a girls' school had of course given few opportunities but she had not been sorry at the time. She'd seemed to lose all interest in kisses. Those boys she had got to know, brothers of friends, had shown occasional interest but Lissa had always succeeded in freezing them out so that they quickly changed their minds and asked someone else for a date instead.

But then Derry wasn't asking her for a date, was he? He was merely suggesting she come and watch him practise. Probably only wanted to show off. He would have a girl friend already. Someone pretty and very 'with it'.

Best not to get involved.

'No, thanks,' she said airily, lifting her chin so he couldn't guess her real feelings. 'I have to unpack and I'd like a quiet evening if you don't mind. It's been a long day.'

'Give her time to settle in, for heaven's sake,' Jan protested.

70

The expression on his face could have been taken for disappointment had Lissa not known better. 'What about the dance tomorrow then?' he asked. 'Will you come to that?'

She lifted her eyebrows and managed to shrug her shoulders with perfect disdain at the same time. 'I really don't think so.'

But the next day as she watched Jan try on various garments and agonise over what to wear Lissa felt sorely tempted to change her mind. She had felt very strange inside when Derry smiled at her. A warm, tingly sort of feeling that had been most pleasant.

She pictured his face. It was really not at all bad-looking with its long straight nose and curving lopsided smile. Brown eyes, thickly fringed with surprisingly long dark lashes, held an expression of permanent mischief, as if he knew some secret about life that had passed others by. Lissa guessed that he kept his brown hair slicked back with brilliantine in order to achieve that fashionable 'Tony Curtis' hair style he wore. It probably wasn't nearly so dark when just washed, she found herself thinking, and decided on the whole that whatever its colour, the style suited him. Derry Colwith seemed pleasant enough, if a bit full of himself, despite the rather odd clothes he wore.

So why hadn't she said yes?

Because she couldn't be sure he really wanted her to accept? Because he might have touched her in a way she wouldn't like or showed her something she didn't want to see? Because she had to be in control?

'You don't want me hanging on your coat tails,' she said now.

'I hadn't thought of wearing coat tails but it's not a bad idea. Bit different, eh?' Jan joked.

'You know what I mean.'

Jan twirled her circular cotton skirt, checking she showed just the right amount of petticoat and no stocking tops. 'You talk daft, I'll tell you that. The white blouse or the blue, do you think?'

Lissa considered. 'The blue. I'd rather not, if you don't mind.' She had decided long since to have nothing at all to do with sex, or love either for that matter, and she must stick by that decision. She would stay an unmarried virgin, like Queen Elizabeth I. Whenever Lissa thought of sex, which was more than she should, she saw it as unclean, certainly not a pleasure. In her view it was meant only for some strange gratification of the male ego. Going to dances with young men was therefore not a good idea. She did wonder though, if that were the case, why the idea of accepting was so very enticing.

Perhaps she really was wicked, like her mother.

'You should hear our Derry play,' Jan was saying. 'He's really not half bad. Even I, his ever non-loving sister, can tell that much.' She took out some green eye shadow and began applying it thickly to her lids.

Lissa watched with interest, deciding that although Jan wasn't pretty in the accepted sense of the word, there was an attractive, homely quality about her. A friendly girl, she was the sort of person you could rely on, or so Lissa hoped. However, the eye shadow would do little for her eyes while she screwed them up in that squinting way she had. Not for worlds would Lissa say as much, though.

'I'm sure he is,' she said, and watched, intrigued, as Jan outlined her lips with coral pink lipstick. 'Does he have a girl friend?' Now why had she asked that?

'Oh lord, yes, millions. They hang about him like wasps round a jam pot. Sickening it is.'

She should have known.

'But there'll be loads of talent there. Male talent that is. And all our friends. It'll be fun.'

If Lissa had been about to change her mind the mention of all these unknown girl friends at once put paid to the idea. She was an outsider. Jan and Derek were only feeling sorry for her and she had no intention of joining the crowd round Derry Colwith.

'I've nothing to wear, and no money to buy anything,' Lissa said, settling the issue.

'You could borrow something of mine,' Jan offered, not disagreeing with this statement.

Nevertheless Lissa kept to her decision not to go to the dance and sat at home and felt sorry for herself instead.

The following weekend she spent searching the village for a flat or even a room of her own which she could afford, but to no avail. The week after, she met with no greater success. After a month or more of fruitless searching Lissa had almost given up hope of ever finding a place of her own. Everywhere was either too big or too expensive. A winter let would have been easy to find, but with summer coming, the landladies could make more money out of the growing numbers of holiday makers.

She paid the Colwith family a small sum each week in return for her bed and board and she and Jan were getting along famously. Lissa had even grown used to the eccentric behaviour of Jimmy and Renee.

But she avoided any contact with Derry.

Fortunately he was out most of the time, either at work, or with his skiffle group. He enjoyed boasting of their success and of the way the girls were starting to scream whenever he made an appearance. The moment he swaggered in through the door each evening, he would jauntily challenge them with his disarming grin and claim to be worn out by the girls' ardent attentions. Lissa refused to listen and would find some excuse to go upstairs.

Every morning Jan and Lissa walked together to work, enjoying the softness of the air as spring gradually changed into summer and the streets of the small town grew busier. At lunchtime they often took their sandwiches down to the lake, sitting on the benches by the band stand, feeding crusts to the mallards and moorhens that crowded the shore line and laughing at the upturned wagging tails in the water.

Their friendship was now teetering on the confiding stage and one morning as they were happily unpacking a new delivery of lingerie, giggling together over old ladies' pink bloomers and corsets, Lissa felt able to risk a personal question.

'Does it bother you, your father marrying a girl your own age?'

Jan gave her an old fashioned look. 'What do you think? Anyway, she wasn't just any girl, she was Derry's girl friend. Hasn't he told you? He brought her home for tea and she and Dad both clicked, as you might say. Derry never had a look in from the moment they set eyes on each other.'

Lissa said, 'Oh,' and tried not to picture Derry with the voluptuous Renee. It disturbed her somehow. 'Doesn't Renee mind? About the age difference, I mean.'

Jan shook her head in bewilderment. 'She's sixteen, like me. My dad is forty-five. Makes you want to throw up, doesn't it?'

Lissa agreed that it did. 'No wonder Derry won't speak to her.' There had been several unpleasant scenes in the last few weeks when Derry had simply refused to acknowledge Renee's presence, even so far as not setting a place for her at the dinner table. Jimmy often flared up in fury at his son, accusing him of insolence. But Lissa's sympathies were with Derry. She could recognise pain behind the jaunty insolence in his brown eyes. It was how she had felt every birthday when her mother had promised to come and never had.

'What about your family?' Jan casually asked. 'You must miss them. Will you be going to visit them soon?'

'I expect so. Meg will want to know how I'm getting on.'

'Why do you call your mother Meg?'

'Because she isn't really my mother.' Ever sensitive that people might be disapproving of her true status, Lissa had decided to be perfectly blunt about her illegitimacy. She had no intention of pretending to be what she was not. 'I was dumped on her as a baby.'

'Dumped?'

Jan forgot all about unwrapping corsets as she became absorbed in Lissa's swiftly told tale. 'Oh, how dreadful, to be abandoned. So romantic though.' Her brown eyes, so like Derry's, grew round and moist. 'And this Meg person, she's loved you as her own daughter ever since? How wonderful.'

'Yes, I suppose it was. Not that she was given much choice in the matter.'

'Is that your real name then, Turner, or your adopted one?'

'Real? Whatever does that mean?' Lissa shrugged her shoulders with a laugh to show that she didn't care one way or the other and met Jan's sympathetic gaze with belligerence in her own. 'I'm illegitimate. A bastard. So what's in a name?'

Jan blinked, alarmed by the sharpness of the tone, then after a moment said, 'Not your fault though, was it? You didn't ask to be born. Why be so angry about it?'

'I'm not angry.'

'You sound it.'

'I don't need pity or advice, thanks very much.'

Jan flushed and paid excessive attention to opening a new package but couldn't resist asking, 'Have you ever met her then? Your real ma, I mean?'

Lissa shook her head and started to rip up the empty carton, stamping the cardboard flat. It made her feel a lot better. 'No, course not. She's in Canada. I'm sorry I was rude. Didn't mean to be.'

'That's OK.' Jan smiled. 'I wouldn't want sympathy either. Anyway, no one need know if you don't tell them.'

The violet eyes sparkled with the light of battle royal. 'I'm not pretending, not to anyone. I am what I am. This is me. Take me or leave me.'

Jan looked startled for a minute and then grinned. 'I'll take two, thanks very much.' Then they both burst into fits of girlish giggles, the prickly moment past.

'I wish this shop sold something more interesting than old fashioned corsets,' Lissa complained, happily changing the subject and holding up a satinette underskirt with straps two inches wide. 'These slips still have a 1930s look.'

'Some of our stock genuinely *is* that old, very nearly antique,' Jan giggled. 'Miss Stevens wouldn't hear of "going modern". Why, she might get *teenagers* into her shop and heavens, that would never do. The very idea. Anyone would think young people were a new invention, a disease, the way she carries on.'

And they both giggled again as they priced up the unpretentious underwear and stowed it away in the ranks of glass-fronted drawers that lined the walls of the draper's shop.

It was then that the idea popped into Lissa's head, quite out of the blue, and she wondered why she hadn't thought of it before. 'Hey, I know. We could find a place together.'

Jan's eyes opened wider than her myopic vision usually permitted as she gazed in astonished wonder at Lissa.

'Are you serious?'

'Never more so. Why not? It's quite the thing for young career girls to do nowadays, or so I read in Jimmy's newspaper.'

'Is that what we are, career girls?'

'Well, why not? I intend to make something of myself, don't you?' said Lissa. 'Though I haven't quite decided how yet. Having a flat together would be a start in the right direction, wouldn't it? And good fun, don't you think?'

'Oh,' Jan breathed, not able to believe her luck in finding such a friend.

'We could afford more rent between the two of us. Make it much more economic.' Lissa grew enthusiastic as she thought of a place she'd looked at just the other day. She tossed aside a pink corset she had been rolling up to grab her friend excitedly. 'I've seen a converted boathouse. Wooden, close to the lake so admittedly horribly damp, small of course, and with a minuscule kitchen, a spiral staircase and two tiny bedrooms above. But with the most fabulous views. Two pounds ten shillings a week. We could go and take a look this lunchtime if you like?'

'Oh, yes. That would be lovely.' Jan's smile formed a perfect triangle of delight in her small face, and then almost as suddenly faded away. 'We'd have to get permission off our parents. They'd have to sign the lease or something.'

Lissa shrugged. 'So what? Meg trusts me, though no doubt she'd come over and check it all out.' She rolled her eyes in exaggerated style as if saying, Parents, how fussy they are.

But Jan still looked anxious. 'Dad might not care for me going. He likes me at home, expects me to help with the cooking and cleaning since Renee works long hours at the hotel.'

Lissa laughed. 'Huh! Hang that for a life. Let the wonderful Renee look after him for a change. She took him on, didn't she? For better, for worse, for washing and for cooking.' Lissa held up the long pink corset, suspenders dangling. 'She'll be needing one of these if she doesn't get out of that chair soon and start to do a bit more work. That would really please your dad.'

Then they were both giggling so much they didn't hear Miss Stevens come in, eyes slightly glazed from the small comforter she had been enjoying in the stock room. Her stentorian voice, however, had benefitted from the stiff gin and soon put a stop to their hilarity. Suitably chastened, but desperately trying to avoid each other's eyes in case they set off a second attack of giggles, they got back to unpacking corsets.

7

Philip Brandon stared through the glass panel of his office door, peering beneath the gold letters that read BRANDON AND BRANDON, SOLICITORS AND COMMISSIONERS FOR OATHS, and frowned. He could plainly see his young clerk, playing the fool again, dodging about between the desks, no doubt in pursuit of Christine, the new typist, when he had been specifically instructed to sort the morning post and stamp it with the date received. Worse, Miss Henshaw, Philip's personal secretary, sat smiling upon both of them, as if there were nothing untoward in such horse play during office hours.

He got up from behind his wide mahogany desk, tugged at his waistcoat, then took off his spectacles and polished them furiously. The glass in them was quite plain but they were useful in the office as they gave dignity and an air of authority to his somewhat boyish face. He replaced them carefully upon his nose, hooking the wire frames around each ear as he again peered through the gold lettering, bobbing his head up and down to get a better view.

Christine was squealing, dropping papers all over the place as she put up her hands in weak defence, her breasts bouncing beneath her white blouse in delightful unison. Philip contemplated how they would feel pressed up against him. His hand twitched convulsively as if testing the squashiness in his hand, or perhaps as a soft pillow for his head.

For a moment he envied Derry his close proximity to those wondrous orbs and then felt guilt wash over him like a hot tide. Blinking furiously, he straightened, stiffening his spine to a more proper posture. What was he thinking of? He thrust open the door and stepped into the outer office.

'Have you finished with the morning post, Colwith?' he asked in his quiet voice, and the occupants of the room froze, as if captured on camera.

Derry was the first to recover. 'Won't be a jiff.'

Philip winced. 'Can we use the English language within the precincts of the office? Bring them through when you are done. Five minutes, if you please.'

'Yes, sir,' said Derry, adopting a suitably sober expression. Christine had fled to her big black typewriter in the corner and was already pounding heavily upon it, bent on proving how hard she was really working.

Miss Henshaw was looking flustered as if it had been she who had been running about and squealing so outrageously. Philip glowered at her before returning to his desk, to let her know that he did hold her largely responsible. She flushed a dark red and bent her sensible, neatly cropped grey head more arduously to her own typewriter and the conveyance she was laboriously typing. When the telephone shrilled at her elbow she almost snatched it up.

'Brandon Solicitors. Can I help you?' she trilled in her bright telephone voice, pencil poised over her pad. 'Of course. One moment, please.' Miss Henshaw flicked switches and pulled plugs on the ancient switch board. 'Mr McArthur.'

'Thank you,' said Philip, in a tone which indicated she was not forgiven. Miss Henshaw took the point and got back to her typing.

'Behave, you two. You'll get us all the sack,' she complained, trying to sound stern, and failing.

Derry only had to look at her with that butter-wouldn't-melt-in-his-mouth smile and she was putty in his hands. She knew it. It made her day just to watch him strut up and down the office. He certainly gave her a giggle and something to think about in her chill, lonely bed at night. Vera Henshaw rather liked young men. She'd used to dream about Philip at one time, about what might have been between them had things been different and he not a man of affairs and she his simple secretary. Foolish even to have considered it a possibility. Didn't every secretary fall in love with their boss? And Vera knew she wasn't really his type. He preferred smart, attractive young women, not tired ones in floppy cardigans with the first signs of varicose veins.

Vera sighed. It could have been so perfect, she a mere thirty-nine, or thereabouts, and he a mature thirty. But of course he would never marry, not now Felicity, his fiancée, had died. How that poor girl had suffered! But Philip had remained loyal. He'd not so much as glanced at another woman in all the three years since, the dear man. It was as if he was afraid to. As if by doing so, he would in some way blight her sweet memory. Though in Vera's carefully considered opinion he sorely needed some good woman to shake him out of his endless mourning. Unfortunately, she was not that woman.

She mopped up a tear and on finding herself the object of scrutiny from her fellow workers, threw them a sour look, put back her spectacles which hung from a cord about her neck and took out her frustration on the keys, her fingers hammering the words while her mind continued its deliberations.

He looked so sad these days. There was a sort of moody, brooding quality to his dark good looks. The ears flat to the finely shaped head, full lips and dark, unfathomable eyes that gave away none of their secrets. A real charmer he could be when he put his mind to it. No doubt about it, plenty would be glad to be the wife of Mr Philip Brandon.

Miss Henshaw sighed again. Realised she'd got her fingers accidentally on to all the wrong keys and had typed several lines of absolute rubbish. She ripped out the paper with an exasperated click of her tongue. Really, she was becoming as irresponsible as the two youngsters.

'Have you finished that post, Derry?' she barked, venting her wrath on his hapless ears. 'Well, get it along to Mr Brandon or you'll find yourself at the labour exchange next week, mark my words. And poke that fire. My feet are frozen.'

Her poor circulation was not helped by the hours she spent at this desk, she told herself morosely. A martyr to her work she was. Life had been so much easier when she was a junior with old Mr Brandon and they'd had all those clerks with scratchy pens for the laborious paperwork. Miss Henshaw tucked her feet into a small knitted blanket she kept for the purpose and frowned at him so that he could see she meant what she said.

'I shall write a song about you,' Derry was saying. 'Oh, sweet Vera, how a smile from your lips enchants me.' He blew her a kiss, wicked mischief on his grinning face.

'Impudent monkey. Get along with you.' But Miss Henshaw was

smiling too. Derry Colwith brought a bit of much needed sunshine into this gloomy office.

Derry sat most of each day at an old high sloping desk where he could gaze out of the window and dream of fame and riches. And he should have them, she thought fondly. Such a lovely boy. In the meantime, if only she could persuade him to behave more responsibly. Mr Brandon deserved the best.

Derry gathered up the post, winked at her and swaggered to the inner office door, tapping loudly upon the glass with one knuckle.

Had Miss Henshaw been able to hear the conversation that was progressing on the telephone on the other side, she might have adjusted her high opinion of her employer. Though she would have had to pay careful attention. It sounded innocent enough as Derry carried in the stack of letters and laid them on the blotter before his employer.

'Thank you, Mr McArthur. I'm glad we are agreed on that matter. I think you will find it to be the wisest course. Certainly more – shall we say? – beneficial to both of us. One moment, my clerk has entered.' Philip covered the mouthpiece with his hand while he pushed a pile of bank books across the desk to Derry. 'The McArthur probate. Take these books to the bank and inform the manager of Miss Amelia McArthur's death. Her nephew is the main beneficiary.'

'Right,' said Derry, gathering them up and turning at once to the door. This was the part of the job he liked best, wandering about town on some errand or other. If the bank didn't take too long about it he could nip in to see Jan and Lissa, maybe have a quick coffee with them. He brightened at the prospect. He was getting nowhere with Lissa so far, but he still fancied his chances.

'Did you hear me?' Philip barked, with unusual impatience.

'Sir?'

'I said to call at the building society first with the other book, ask them to close the account and have the money transferred into the office account.'

'The office account?'

'Yes, you fool. In preparation for probate.'

'Right you are.'

When Derry had gone, whistling happily and slamming the door too hard so that the ancient glass shook perilously, Philip removed his hand from the mouthpiece, carefully gathered his

80

strained patience and continued with his conversation. He almost purred into the phone.

'Sorry to have kept you, Mr McArthur. Where were we? Ah, yes, death duties. No indeed, no one should be obliged to pay more than is absolutely necessary. Certainly your aunt would not have wished her money to go to the government.'

A pause while the caller on the end of the wire apparently expressed his thanks and Philip Brandon's dark eyes took on a gleam as hard as the polished wood of his own desk.

'Such a gesture would of course be entirely at your own discretion. I shall be in touch.'

He rested the receiver back in its cradle and allowed himself a rare smile. Everything was progressing most satisfactorily, most satisfactorily indeed.

Happiness did not come easily to him. Life had been harder than he had bargained for since leaving Oxford. He'd been lucky, he supposed, missing the worst of the war and young enough to make something of his life afterwards. But he had resented the way he'd had to pinch and scrape, the way austerity had gone on so long. As a member of the professional classes it didn't seem quite fair that he should suffer.

The initial pleasure he had felt at finding himself in sole charge of the practice on the death of his father had soon dissipated when he had learned the true state of it. It had given every appearance of a bustling, one-man practice, dealing with conveyancing, probate and estate work, inventories and valuations. Only a small amount of court work came his way, for which he was thankful. Litigation was rarely profitable and it gave a poor impression for a high-class practice to be too involved with the nefarious goings on of the criminal classes.

He should have been a happy man. He loved his work, spent as many hours in his office as he possibly could, only reluctantly leaving it to return home in the evening to a plain meal served by his housekeeper. But he was not happy. Not at all.

The problem was that people were so lackadaisical about settling their legal accounts. Were everyone to pay him what they owed tomorrow, he would be a rich man, comfortable at least. But they did not. And it had to be said that his father, John Crawshaw Brandon, had been somewhat dilatory on the work front. He'd been far more interested in catching char and pike from the lake than sitting at his desk. Fascinated by points of law he may have been, yet he had shown little head for business, certainly none for turnover. In consequence, matters had suffered interminable delays, clients had grown restless and ultimately taken their business elsewhere. It had all been most unsatisfactory.

It had fallen to him, Philip, to build the practice up again. Not an easy task. Sometimes he was so busy he was fortunate if he had time to prepare any bills at all, let alone reminders. Even when he put Miss Henshaw on the task of ringing people up it brought a poor response. People were happy enough for him to solve their problems, their disputes with neighbours, convey their house or dispose of their dearly departed, but balked at paying the cost.

And so he had taken the matter into his own capable hands. Here and there, not too much and only where there was no risk of it being noted, he managed to keep his pockets fat and his own bank account healthy.

It was while serving in the army that he had learned there were short cuts to everything. One did not have to tread the twisting and thorny path when there might be a smoother, more advantageous route. He smiled again. Great care of course, must always be taken.

The McArthur estate had been unusually easy since the nephew was as flexible in his code of conduct as Philip himself.

McArthur had no more wish than his solicitor to declare the true extent of his aunt's estate. A sum had been agreed upon which would satisfy the Inland Revenue and leave the nephew nicely in pocket. Should the beneficiary of this good fortune choose to show his appreciation by way of a small gratuity, was that any fault of Philip Brandon? No indeed. A small gratuity was no more than common business practice, after all.

But even were this not the case, he usually found a way, without ever stepping too far outside the grey fringes of the law. True, relatives could often be a problem. But thanks to the two wars there was no shortage of widows. Indeed, probate had always proved delightfully lucrative.

Certainly more valuable than divorce, which he disliked as it was so messy and troublesome. He hated disagreement of any kind, so petty and disagreeable, and rarely encouraged it for his clients. Divorce was bad for society. A woman's duty was to her husband after all. Yet there was something about a vulnerable woman that appealed to him, and he was always happy to counsel and advise.

The day passed much the same as any other, sunnier than most which added to his unusually cheerful mood.

This was one of those rare, brilliant Lakeland days when the lake glimmered, the mountains were wreathed in a soft blue mist, and it made you think summer might actually arrive at any moment. It would be a pity, he decided, to waste it.

At lunchtime, instead of eating his sandwiches at his desk as was his wont, Philip decided to take them down to the lake.

On Fridays he usually treated himself to a ham salad at the Marina Hotel where one had a grand view of the goings on on the lake. His budget, as yet, did not stretch to making this a daily ritual. One day he meant that to change.

He was sitting on a bench, quietly enjoying his fish paste sandwiches and trying to avoid the rapacious ducks, when he saw her.

She was not alone but Philip cast the other girl scarcely a glance. His gaze was riveted first upon a mass of black curls. Some attempt had been made to hold the hair back from her face with a scarlet ribbon but tendrils of curls were determinedly springing free, bursting joyously all across her brow and upon the curve of each soft round cheek. His gaze shifted to the smooth golden skin, the dark, violet eyes like great bruises in a perfect, heart-shaped face. And she moved with such grace it was a joy simply to watch her.

He heard her light voice, sensed it like a thrill deep inside him as she laughed at something her friend had said.

They were climbing the wooden steps up to an old boathouse and the wind was pressing her straight black skirt about slender, shapely legs. Philip became acutely aware that he was holding his breath.

He sat for a full half hour or more waiting for them to come out, well past the time he should have returned to the office, but he would have waited twice as long if necessary. An incongruous figure on the bench in his double-breasted, black pinstripe suit, fully buttoned as was right and proper, he tapped one polished toe and then the other.

When he had almost given up hope she burst out of the boathouse like a small explosion of colour. She wore a bright red duffle-coat, swinging open over her skirt and blouse, and he caught a tantalising glance of a slender figure, voluptuously ripe and blossoming. The outfit, obviously new, looked well against her black hair, and he felt a hard knot of excitement low in his stomach.

83

She was laughing as she locked the door, then as she swung round to hug her friend, he saw that she was younger than he had thought by a number of years. The realisation brought a sharp edge of disappointment. How very foolish of him. He should have realised at once. She couldn't be more than seventeen or eighteen. Less perhaps.

Loneliness swamped him and he moved not a muscle as he watched her walk away.

He had to fight hard to pull back his shoulders and get up from the bench, dusting off his immaculate trousers. Carefully folding his empty sandwich paper, he slipped it into his briefcase, ready to use again tomorrow. He told himself he was scarcely into his thirties and not unattractive to women.

He thought of Felicity. Sweet, darling Felicity with her pale blonde beauty, her illness and fragility making him love her all the more. Felicity had been pure as well as beautiful, not like most of the women he came across through his work, who played fast and loose with some poor fool of a husband.

But Felicity had died, leaving him alone in an unfeeling world with a memory that remained a raw wound. What was he thinking of even to be looking at another girl, let alone one so young?

He had his practice, didn't he? His home may be a touch too modest and further from the lake than he would like, but it was bought and paid for and one day he would improve upon it. No mortgages for him. Too disagreeable. And then there was his sailing dinghy. He was thinking of having a new one built, something classy and fast. He'd never yet won in the annual Yacht Club races but he meant to, very soon.

Philip Brandon told himself he was going places. All he needed was a touch more security.

He straightened his shoulders, replaced his trilby hat with care so as not to disturb his carefully combed dark hair, and without a backward glance walked smartly from the lakeside and back to the sanctuary of his office. But he might make eating his lunch on the lakeshore bench a regular feature of his routine. When the weather was pleasant.

'Leave? How can you leave? Why should you? Your dad won't hear of it, I can tell you that for nothing.' Renee's orange mouth drooped at each corner, making her look like a comical clown as she gazed woefully from one girl to the other. The budgie in the corner, reacting to the alarm in her voice, started to squawk.

'I suppose I can please myself what I do,' Jan said, flicking back her hair and raising her voice above the din. 'You didn't ask my permission when you moved in here, did you?'

'I didn't have to. Your dad wanted me to marry him, so that was that.'

'And you wanted an easy life.' Jan stormed over to the cage and flicked the cover over it. Blessed silence fell.

'What if I did?' said Renee, dropping her voice to a belligerent mumble. 'My dad thought it part of his daily routine to batter the walls with my head. So what if I did want to get away from that? It's not a crime, is it? And Jimmy loves me.' She gave a great gulping sob.

Both Renee and Jan were so close to tears that Lissa instinctively put out a hand to each of them, wanting to calm the situation.

'Have you thought, Renee, that it might be for the best? You and Jimmy need more time on your own. We feel a bit in the way with you two so – so obviously in love.' She cleared her throat. 'Anyway, we won't be going for a week or two. There's a heap of work to do on the boathouse before it's habitable. Cleaning it out for one thing, then painting it and finding something to sleep on and cook with. Simple things like that.' She laughed as if she had made a joke. 'So you'll have plenty of time to get used to the idea.'

Renee's eyes filled with a sudden gush of tears, the effect upon her mascara-coated lashes being quite catastrophic. Black rivers ran down her face, adding to the clown-like effect. 'What about me then, after you've gone? I can't cook, you know,' she sobbed. 'I've never so much as boiled an egg in me life. Even me mother didn't do much cooking. Bread and dripping, sausage and HP beans, that's what we were brought up on. He'll kill me, he will. You know how he enjoys his food. He'll kill me.' She opened her mouth into a wide orange oval and began to wail.

Incensed, Jan almost shouted her response. 'He won't do any such thing. My dad would never hurt a flea, let alone a woman. You should have realised you'd be expected to do wifely things. Cooking and cleaning and such like,' she said, astounded by the state her teenage stepmother was getting into, howling like a banshee and shaking her head in despair.

'Oh God,' Renee sobbed. 'He said I didn't have to worry my pretty little head about such things, 'cause you'd never get wed. You're too plain, he said, what with your straight brown hair and squinting at folk all the time.'

There was a small stunned silence though Renee, blithely unaware of the insult she had voiced, continued to howl, working it up to a fine pitch. And her face looked like one of the new zebra crossings.

'Jan is not at all plain. But as for the cooking . . . well, I could teach you,' Lissa said, seeing her friend quite bereft for words.

The wailing stopped instantly and the ensuing silence was such a relief they all sagged visibly with relief. 'Could you?' Renee asked, wonder in her voice.

'Of course. Meg taught me. She's a very good cook is Meg. Steak and game pie, Cumberland sausage, mutton and tatie hot pot. Gingerbread. Oh, and her Rum Nicky Pudding.' Lissa stopped. Both girls were standing gazing at her open-mouthed.

'You a chef or summat? How can anyone have so much food with the war and the rationing and all?'

'I lived on a farm. We produced our own.' Her mouth was watering and her heart beating fast at the memory of the big warm kitchen at Broombank. She could almost feel herself sitting at the huge scrubbed pine table, Meg laughing as she whipped and stirred, Tam tasting and teasing.

What was she doing here? She belonged with them, on her very own fells where the wind blew free.

And ponies ran loose and gypsies waited by grey boulders. Where you could spend a night in a bothy and drive your foster mother into a miscarriage through despair. Lissa shook the picture away. This was her new life and she meant to make it a good one.

Over the following weeks Lissa taught Renee all that she knew. It became clear that no one had ever troubled to teach the girl anything in her life before. And judging from what Lissa learned of her home background, was it any wonder if she had grabbed the first kind man who had come along?

Lissa searched her mind for Meg's recipes and soon Jimmy thought himself the luckiest man in Carreckwater.

'All I want is a quiet life,' he kept saying, tucking into his food with relish. And to be fair, he was most appreciative of Renee's efforts, patting her cheek fondly when she burned something or the meat was tough. 'Better next time, my poppet.' Which increased Renee's confidence and made her more adventurous.

'I'll have to buy meself one of those striped pinnies like Philip Harben,' she said.

In an odd sort of way, seeing their happiness made Lissa feel more insecure than ever. Would anyone ever love her so completely?

Jan was happier, however, as she no longer felt so put upon.

A letter came from Meg, asking Lissa to visit, but she wrote back saying that she was too hard at work renovating the old boathouse and converting it into a flat.

They scrubbed and scoured, painted window frames and doors and sewed rag rugs from scraps of old clothing. The panelled walls needed little more attention than a good sweep down, banishing cobwebs and running spiders by the score.

Furniture was still hard to come by so Lissa scoured house sales and auction rooms and came up with a bed each, a chair or two, and a small table which they covered with green oil cloth. The cooker was the most difficult but they found an old one on a stall in the market, along with a few pots and pans.

It was well into the summer season by the time the boathouse was ready for occupation and they moved in with great anticipation.

'Isn't it lovely?' Jan cried, pink-cheeked with excitement. 'I'm so glad you came to Carreckwater, Lissa. So glad we're friends.'

'Me too,' she said, pleased with their efforts, wondering if at last she had found a place to put down roots. She could scarcely believe their good fortune in finding it. She loved it already. They could sit in their tiny living room and gaze out across the lake to Wetherlam, Tilberthwaite Fell and the Langdales. They could watch the visitors bobbing up and down on the lake in their clinker-built boats, see families picnicking on the small island in the centre. Life was suddenly fun again and Lissa wanted to sing with joy.

'I just know we are going to be happy here,' she sighed.

'Oh, me too,' echoed Jan, giving her impish, triangular smile. 'I feel this is a new beginning, a new life.'

Yes, thought Lissa. A new beginning, as I once gave to the kingfisher.

A second letter came from Meg and this one made Lissa sit up and take notice.

She read it in the stock room while she had her morning coffee break and found herself gaping with shock. She had to read it twice more to be sure that she had it right.

Ashlea belonged to her. Meg said so, plain as day. Jeffrey Ellis, the man she had always referred to as an honorary uncle but was in fact her grandfather, had left her the freehold.

Meg's letter gave the details. 'It has only this moment come to light as the family solicitors, as trustees, have written to ask if you wish the rent to be reviewed. It is a safe tenancy, still in my father's name of course, and he couldn't be got out unless you wished to live there yourself. And I know, darling, that you would never deprive Sally Ann and her family of a home. But it could be purchased for Nick, in Sally Ann's name of course, and she wonders if you would consider selling? Are you planning on coming on a visit soon? I do hope so. It seems so long since we saw you. You could tell us your decision then. Are you enjoying your new job? I must come and see your boathouse. Perhaps you could give it some thought?'

So her grandmother had kept this secret from her? A creeping sickness came over Lissa at the thought. Not that she wanted Ashlea, or any other farm, but the thought that Rosemary Ellis had callously deprived her of her inheritance, and Nick of an opportunity to purchase his home, out of pure spite, was quite beyond imagining. Nor did she feel any more inclined to trust her grandmother's solicitors, who only had Rosemary's interests at heart.

Lissa folded the paper and thrust it into her pocket. She thought about it for several hours then as they walked home that evening, asked Jan.

'Who is that solicitor Derry works for?'

Surprised by the question, Jan gave her an odd look. 'Why do you want to know?'

'I need some advice. Family stuff, you know.'

Jan was at once sympathetic. 'Oh, sorry. He's called Philip Brandon. Has an office near Benthwaite Cross. Bit of a stick-in-the-mud but I doubt he'd overcharge you, being a friend of Derry's. Shall I ask him to fix up an appointment for you?' Her brown eyes were troubled, and filled with curiosity.

Lissa decided the less either of them knew about this, the better. If she started talking about an inheritance, they might get the idea she was rich and nothing could be further from the truth. 'That's OK. I'll call in one lunchtime. See if he's got a minute.'

8

Philip couldn't believe his good fortune. 'Please take a seat, Miss Turner.' His mind whirled through the possible reasons for her visit. Close to, she was even more attractive than his first glimpse of her by the lake. Young and fresh, with her hair in a swinging pony tail, the same wayward tendrils framing her face in a most beguiling manner; her beautiful slender body prettily decked out in a pink shirt waister dress. 'What can I do for you?' he asked, smiling his charming smile. 'May I offer you coffee?'

'No, thank you. I don't have much time as I must get back to work.' She looked uneasy, embarrassed by whatever had brought her here. Philip Brandon's heart sank. Surely she couldn't be married, seeking a divorce from a rake of a husband? No, no, she was far too young. He held out a chair, not taking his eyes from her as she sat. Her legs were sweet perfection, long and smooth-skinned. He slipped his spectacles into his top pocket and realised with a jolt that she had launched into some tale and he had missed it.

'So you see I have no wish to keep it. What would I do with a farm? But Nick is an old friend. There was a time when he might have liked . . . anyway, I want him to have Ashlea.'

Very gently he took her back to the beginning and piece by piece, with the very gentlest questioning, he had her entire life story from her. He guessed that she told more than she'd intended but then he was a sympathetic listener. It was a shock to learn she was only sixteen, though clearly mature for her age. He was astute enough to guess the effect the stigma of illegitimacy would have upon her.

He came round to sit upon the edge of the desk. Pansy eyes looked up into his, brimming with unshed tears and his heart clenched. 'It must have proved such a burden for you. Heartrending for a sensitive child to feel rejected at birth.'

'You *do* understand. Oh, I'm so relieved. Few people do, you know.'

He gave her his wise, compassionate smile, debated whether he might take her hand but decided against it. 'Ah, but I am different. Rather like a father confessor or family doctor. You can tell me anything, anything at all and I would not divulge a word of it.'

She warmed to him instantly. 'I'd really like Nick to have Ashlea. He works the land and lives in the house so he deserves it. Can that be done?'

'Nick is presumably your own age, so too young for a mortgage. No bank would consider him.'

'What about Sally Ann?'

'Of course. You could offer her a private mortgage, though farmers are notoriously irregular payers, preferring as they do to deal strictly in cash.'

'Nick is very reliable.'

'I'm sure he is. I should warn you that property with a sitting tenant has a very poor sale value.'

'I don't care about the money. I don't want anything that belongs to the Ellis family. Nothing at all. Do you see?'

'I do. Absolutely.' He paused, hooked his thumbs in the pockets of his waistcoat then went to sit behind his desk again. 'Pardon my saying so but that is a rather short-sighted view. There may be other property, or funds, to come.'

Lissa thought of Larkrigg and of her hard-hearted grandmother. Where would she leave her money? To a daughter whom she considered wicked and undeserving? To a granddaughter she refused to acknowledge? And what did it matter? Lissa straightened her spine, smoothed her short white gloves and gave a dry smile.

'It's possible, I suppose, but unlikely. My grandmother is more likely to leave her property to some charity or other. Probably the church. I sincerely hope so.'

'Not to your mother?' Eyebrows raised in query as he had become very still.

'Who knows? They haven't seen or spoken in years, which gives you some idea what I'm up against.'

'Indeed,' he said thoughtfully and gave a gentle smile. 'How very sad for you.'

'It's all in trust, of course, until I come of age and I wondered if there was anything we could do about that?'

'Certainly there is. I could write to the trustees and ask them if they could deal with the matter in this way. They may even agree to transfer the trusteeship of Ashlea to my firm, if I persuade them.' He smiled, as if she had favoured him in some way, then became at once brisk and businesslike as he explained to her, most carefully, the ins and outs of the transaction but finished with a smooth word of advice. 'You should perhaps reconsider your view of the future. Sell Ashlea to your friend by all means but income, from any source, is a valuable asset in today's rapidly changing world. Is there no chance of a reconciliation?'

Lissa stood up, face tight. 'No. That is quite out of the question. She would never . . . And neither would I. Please arrange this matter for me and send me your bill. I have a little money to pay the fee.'

He had offended her. Damn!

He led her to the door and risked taking her hand. It felt small and soft in his. The urge to raise it to his lips was almost overpowering. 'I will carry out your wishes to the letter,' he said.

'I don't want anyone to know about this. Not even Derry. I work with his sister and I'd rather keep my affairs private.' She half glanced through the glass panel, thankful she had chosen a time when he was out at lunch.

'You may rely upon my absolute discretion.' She smiled at him then, a brilliant, wide, shining smile that revealed perfect white teeth and the smallest, pinkest, most delightful tongue.

'Thanks,' she said, issuing a deep sigh. 'I do appreciate your help. It's a real joy to be able to do something for Nick.'

He gave a light laugh. 'You must be fond of him.'

'Oh, yes. We've always been close. Like family, you know.'

'I can see that you are a girl to whom family is important.' A shadow flickered across her face and he was at once all contrition. 'Oh dear, I seem bent on offending you this morning. How very clumsy of me.' He lifted the hand now and pressed his lips against it. Her skin tasted delicious but he would need to be very patient. 'Forgive me,' he murmured, smiling into her eyes. And unable to help herself, Lissa found herself smiling back, responding to his charm.

91

As she hurried back to the shop she decided that Philip Brandon was really far more attractive than Derry had led her to believe. And so kind.

It was Derry's idea that they go on a day-long hike the following Sunday, and Lissa and Jan readily agreed. The weather was calm and settled, the sun shining like a big soft round cheese and there were few holidaymakers to disturb the peace so early in the season as they caught the bus out to Skelwith Bridge.

The three of them were dressed sensibly in slacks and warm sweaters, for mountain weather can change even as you are wondering if it might. On their feet the girls wore strong shoes, Derry his favourite boots for he was a keen climber.

Lissa cast him a glance from beneath her lashes. He looked different today in his windcheater and rough cords, woollen socks replacing the hideous lime green. He seemed more approachable somehow, dressed this way.

'Do you really go rock climbing?'

He pushed back his shoulders, preening himself, brown eyes glinting with such a cocky arrogance she almost wished she hadn't asked. What a peacock he was. 'Sure I do. Love it. Would you like to try?' Lissa haughtily assured him that she would not.

They got off the bus and walked along the lanes to the bridge where there were a few people sitting about having picnics. Where only a short while ago there'd been limp dead grasses, the verges were now clotted with yellow primroses thick as cream. Violets, bluebells and meadowsweet filled the clear mountain air with their fragrant scents. In a few weeks the scene would change yet again and foxgloves, wild roses and ox-eye daisies would have their moment of glory.

Lissa felt the excitement of a day free from the dusty confines of the old fashioned draper's shop.

They walked up a dusty lane by the river that led up through the quarry work sheds. A few shirt-sleeved men sat joking and whistling as they worked the stones, splitting it on the grain with their special tools.

'This is where they quarry the blue-green slate that makes Westmorland famous,' Derry told her as if she'd never seen such a thing before.

She almost told him that they quarried stone on her fells too, but it sounded too petty. Besides, she had no wish to think about quarries, or the roads that led to them. Not today.

They stood on the huge flat rocks at Skelwith Force and watched with wonder as the small waterfall rushed down in a cloud of white froth into the river below, swirled around huge boulders which forced it to gush and froth and gather in deep dark pools. It was like a fairy glen, a magic place where a water sprite would be sure to live, reminding Lissa suddenly of that other day in early summer when she and Nick had played their wishing game.

For a moment, homesickness claimed her. It didn't happen so often nowadays and she knew it was foolish for she could visit Broombank at any time, only she rarely did. Transport was a problem and she felt instinctively that she wanted to make a place for herself here first, before she dared risk it. Or she might never have the courage to come back.

After a while they left the force and walked on up the rough footpath. Then they were walking across flat water meadows where the river widened and spread out until it reached Elterwater. Here they stopped to admire the view.

Ahead lay some of the most dramatic scenery in Lakeland. Primitive blue-grey crags jagged against the pale sky, dark rocky grandeur dropping precipitously to a thickly wooded fringe of trees below.

'It's like Switzerland,' she said, breathing deeply her delight. 'Or how I imagine Switzerland might look.'

'It's the Langdales, a special place,' Derry said. 'Almost secret. We'll go there next. Surprisingly not all that well visited, which is a relief. More space for us, eh?'

They reached the village of Chapel Stile and went on past the school and the post office, and up the big hill.

When they grew hot from their walking they pulled off thick sweaters and settled in the lea of a drystone wall to eat their lunch. It felt cool and sheltered, whorls of yellow lichen rough and scratchy on their bare arms. They watched an Orange Tipped butterfly light on a bloom of lady's smock and laughed in delight as a tree pipit descended like a spinning top in a graceful spiral of song.

Lissa said, 'I was ready for a rest,' as she pulled out sandwiches and bit into them with relief.

'Not used to walking then?' Derry teased and Lissa was infuriated with herself for giving him yet another opportunity to show off.

'I grew up on the fells so it is hardly a problem for me,' she said scornfully. Her annoyance was made worse by the fact she could feel her cheeks grow warm under his amused gaze.

She turned quickly to Jan, offering her more sandwiches, a piece of cake, a sip of water.

'No, I'm fine, thanks,' Jan said and Lissa heard Derry make a sound very like soft laughter.

After a while they walked on.

'We'll just walk up the Band today,' Derry said. 'We haven't time to go as far as Bowfell and I don't think Lissa is quite up to it.'

Flushing a deep red Lissa longed to deny it but dare not, for she was indeed tired. It had been a hard week in the shop. Jan settled the matter.

'Thank heaven for that. My legs are like jelly already.' Proving her worth on a high mountain peak must wait for another day.

They set out from Stool End to walk up the broad smooth incline, and after a while Derry made sure Jan was striding ahead, as she so loved to do, so he could talk to Lissa on his own.

'You don't say much, do you? Are you always so touchy?' he asked. 'Or have I done something to offend?' His voice sounded so genuinely concerned for once that she was quite taken by surprise. He thought her standoffish, a bit uppity no doubt, when all the time she was simply – simply what? Nervous of men? Of possible rejection? Something of the sort. She didn't like to think too deeply about it. Lissa only knew that she felt better, safer, when there was a certain distance between herself and others.

'I don't know what you mean.'

'Is it because you think I'm a Ted? It's only a style, you know, not a way of life. I don't beat old ladies over the head with my comb.'

Despite herself, Lissa giggled and he gave her an answering grin, lopsided and so full of impish good humour that she very nearly laughed out loud. Derry Colwith might be a bit too full of himself, but he surely wouldn't hurt or offend anyone.

Then he spoiled it all by starting to tell her about the climbs he'd done and how difficult they were.

'But you, being Mr Wonderful, managed them with no difficulty whatsoever,' she said drily.

He blinked at her. 'How did you guess?'

'Derek Colwith, you're impossible.' She flounced away from him, walking so fast he had to run to catch up with her.

When he did, he launched into yet another long tale of his latest climb and how his prowess with a rope had helped him survive a bad fall.

'Pity you didn't land on your head. Might have knocked some sense into you,' Lissa said.

'Hey. Aren't you interested? Most girls enjoy my stories.' Since she stubbornly chose not to respond to this, Derry decided his exploits were not having the desired effect and tried for a more intellectual approach. 'There used to be a stone axe factory on these mountains once. Quite a thriving industry in neolithic times,' he told her proudly, as if he'd set it up himself. 'Exported stone all around the country they did, the continent too I shouldn't wonder. Not that they called it the continent in those days, you understand.' He frowned. 'At least I don't think they did.' He felt he was getting a bit deep here so closed the subject with a knowledgeable remark he remembered his geography teacher making. 'You can tell where stone comes from, just by looking at it. Did you know that?'

'So what? Meg can tell all her sheep just by looking at them. Most of them anyway. And the sheep know their own fells.'

'How do they do that?'

And for some reason Lissa found herself talking to Derry about Broombank and the sheep, Nick and Daniel and how they had played in the beck as children. She wondered for a moment why she bothered, but made no mention of gypsies or mothers or lost babies. And Derry listened, asking questions from time to time as if he were really interested. Perhaps he wasn't so bad after all.

Once, he took hold of her hand as she stumbled and a series of tiny shocks ran right through her. For a moment she was the old Lissa again as she lifted her face up to his, violet eyes coaxing and teasing. His stunned expression warned that she trod on dangerous ground and quickly she loosed his hand. But she regretted its loss.

'I think we'd better hurry and catch up with Jan,' she said, increasing her pace. 'What a speed she walks at.'

'Jan loves walking, as I do. We spend days out on the mountains in the summer.' He was staring down at his boots, as if something was troubling him.

'Oh, so did I once,' Lissa agreed.

'Once? Why not now?'

She hesitated, feeling she'd blundered. 'I mean when I was at home.'

'You'll soon get to know and love it here too,' he said sympathetically and she felt emotion suddenly block her throat. She couldn't deal with sympathy.

'I'm not really homesick. Well, sometimes I am. It'll pass.'

'But you are going to stay? You won't go home yet, will you?' he asked, sounding suddenly so anxious she glanced up at him in surprise. As their eyes met Lissa felt something warm unfold inside. He seemed to be passing some sort of message to her and her cheeks flooded with heat. Quickly Lissa turned her attention back to setting her feet carefully on the stony path, and for the next several minutes ignored him completely, just to prove to herself that she could.

At the summit they sat on the wiry grass to catch their breath and admire the panorama of mountains. Lingmoor and Wrynose Fell, Tilberthwaite beyond, and Bowfell Links above, achingly green beneath a clear blue sky.

'Isn't it grand?' Jan said, and Lissa, hugging her knees and drinking it all in, had to agree.

'You'll come on another walk some time?' Derry asked, and he sounded so hopeful she simply couldn't find it in her heart to say no. He rewarded her with a wide beaming smile.

'Great.' Derry was thinking, I've done it. I've broken through that cool reserve. He wasn't used to girls who hung back, they were usually all over him. He judged that Lissa had probably only been playing hard to get. 'I knew we'd get on,' he grinned. 'Knew it the first moment I saw you looking in the shop window.'

'Hark at him?' Jan laughed, getting up and dusting down her jeans which were bright green and cropped just below her knee. 'Right, last down pays for tea.'

'Oh, no,' Lissa mourned, all pride gone. 'I can't rush, really. I'm shattered.'

'There're some clouds gathering behind us,' Derry said. 'So come on, let's make tracks.'

Jan won, of course. She looked like a tiny fairy perched on a stone by the lane. But Derry held his pace to match Lissa's, for which she was truly grateful. She never enjoyed going downhill.

'Don't you feel we get on OK?' he asked. 'I can see you're not really stuck up. You're just shy. And I know you like me, so stop pretending you don't.'

Lissa might have thumped him for this patronising remark but he'd taken her hand again, as if to prove the sincerity of his words and she quite liked the feel of it. He held it tenderly, tracing each of her fingertips with his own. 'Such lovely pearly nails you have. I certainly like you, Lissa. I like you very much.'

There was a pain suddenly, in her breast, and Lissa realised that she'd been holding her breath. She expelled it on a tiny sigh and then suddenly his lips were on hers, warm against the cool mountain breeze, tender and deliciously soft. Lissa leaned against him, wanting the kiss to go on and on, startled by the pleasing sensations swirling through her.

Somewhere high above a lark sang and her heart lifted with each climbing note.

When the kiss ended he squeezed her fingers, very gently, and smiled at her with that lovely secret message again passing between them, his brown eyes seeming to dance over her face. She wished, with a piercing sweetness, that he would kiss her again and swayed gently towards him, her head giddy with longing, then quickly pulled back, shocked by her own wantonness.

But when he held on to her hand for the rest of the way down the steep mountain track, Lissa did not pull away.

Afterwards they ate scones and jam and drank tea at the Old Dungeon Ghyll Hotel, which Lissa poured from a silver pot. It was the perfect end to a perfect day.

Summer passed in the blissful pursuit of uncomplicated happiness. It seemed to be filled with raspberries and ice cream, happy laughter and daring pursuits.

They often took one of the many footpaths or trails that traversed the heights around Carreckwater, Ambleside and Rydal. From those windy tops the visitors looked liked ants, riding the toy steamer up and down the lake.

Derry's friends would often come along too, bringing their many and rapidly changing girlfriends to form a happy, relaxed group.

They would spend whatever time they could spare from their work, either on the lake messing about in boats and dinghies, or high on the fells. Loughrigg was a favourite walk. Or they would explore the eastern sides of the lake, even so far as Jenkyn's Crag, from where they had a wonderful view of the whole Windermere valley. Once they climbed right to the summit of Wansfell Pike, relishing the sparkle of clear fresh air after the dusty days confined to shop and office.

But Lissa took care never to walk alone with Derry. She studiously avoided being anywhere near him, preferring to keep a safe distance between them at all times. And he made no move to repeat that magical kiss, which she knew proved how little it had meant to him. She watched the other girls hang on his arm and told herself she was above such nonsense. Derry Colwith was not her sort at all.

And if she saw the puzzled irritation, perhaps something like disappointment, in Derry's eyes she refused to let it trouble her. He was only playing a game, wanting to notch her up on his belt along with his other conquests. She was not so stupid.

In July she paid a fleeting visit home and found she could return quite happily to Carreckwater. She worked hard in the shop during the week and the Sundays when she wasn't out with the gang she spent tidying the boathouse, resting by the lake where she loved to hear the slip-slap of water against the shingle, or cooking a good meal for herself and Jan.

Once Lissa saw Philip Brandon eating his lunch on a bench by the lakeshore and she stopped for a chat. He seemed embarrassed to be caught doing anything so human as eating and she very nearly giggled out loud, only that would have been unkind.

'I have been meaning to call upon you,' he said in a rush and she took him to mean concerning the sale of Ashlea.

She was anxious suddenly. 'No, I should have called on you. I'd rather you didn't come to the shop.'

He looked attentive and sympathetic. 'Of course. Then perhaps you could call at the office one evening next week?'

'No problems I hope? Meg wrote to say that Nick was happy with the price.'

'Oh, everything is splendid. Yes, splendid. I need you only to sign some papers. Though I'm sure you could have got a touch more for it.'

Lissa shook her head. 'I told you. The family have lived there for donkey's years. It wouldn't have been fair.'

Mr Brandon very kindly assured her that she might call upon him at any time, should she feel the need of advice. And Lissa thought how much smarter he looked now summer was here. He'd stopped wearing that old fashioned trilby and given up the dull black suits. Today he was wearing pale grey and looked quite dashing.

'You'll think of me as a friend, I hope,' he said, and Lissa felt grateful and humbled that he could spare her so much time from his busy schedule.

But even as she talked to him, her eyes lifted to scan the path that led out from the church yard through St Margaret's Walk, in case Derry should appear as he sometimes did at lunchtime. 'Must get to work,' she said, backing off. 'I'll settle my account with you next week if you'd like to have it ready.'

Then she whirled about and skipped away on light steps, looking so young and free it made his heart ache to watch her. He wished he'd thought to ask her out. What was the matter with him? missing such an ideal opportunity. He wished she'd look back and give him a bright wave then he could call her back, perhaps offer to take her for a sail.

But she didn't. Lissa was too busy wondering where Derry was and feeling ridiculously disappointed that he hadn't come.

But then why should she care? He was far too interested in himself anyway, in her opinion. If he wasn't talking about his music and his guitar he was planning how he would win the Yacht Club races which were held every year in the first week of September.

'Have you ever won one?' she had asked him.

'No,' he'd said, the light of battle in his eyes. 'But I intend to. This is my year. I can feel it.'

But when September came and the races were held it was Philip Brandon who won, as apparently he usually did. His yacht was so smart and fast, Lissa didn't wonder at it. Derry was disappointed, of course, and vowed to persuade his father to help build him a better boat for next year.

'I'd give anything just to win one race, so he couldn't lord it over me in the office and make me feel so small,' he said. 'If I got a boat like his I could enter in the same class and maybe beat him.' Derry's eyes lit up. 'God, that would be something.'

'He wouldn't like being beaten by his clerk,' warned Jan. 'I should stick with your little dinghy if I were you.'

Lissa kept quiet, not understanding all the fuss. Later, Jan asked her to come to the Yacht Club dance and hear Derry and his group play but she refused.

'I don't think it's really me.'

'Come on,' Jan urged. She moved about their small home, closing windows against the growing chill of the September evening,

99

clicking the latch on the door then shutting it firmly against the world. Lissa had lit the lamp and it was cosy here, by the fire. 'He won't take no for an answer, not this time, he says. The group has never played at the Yacht Club before and they've been asked to fill in at the interval while the main band is taking a break. They're a bit toffee-nosed up there, more into trad jazz, and he says he needs all the support he can get.'

'Do you mean that rock 'n' roll stuff?' Lissa asked, feeling herself weaken. She wished Derry no harm, for all his arrogance.

'They play skiffle mainly, but some rock 'n' roll too, and the dancing is pretty much the same.'

'You go. I'll be quite happy here. I could start to crochet that cover for the old arm chair.'

Jan laughed. 'Or knit socks?'

Lissa's lips curved into a smile. 'Don't mock. People in my dale are good at knitting socks. And sweaters. Meg and I spent hours each evening doing it. Sally Ann too.'

'What a talented family you have.'

Lissa grinned. 'Not really, there's not much else to do up there.'

'Well, we don't knit socks in Carreckwater, we wear them on the hills. But in the evening we jive and rock. So do come, you'll be an old woman in bed socks soon enough.'

'I don't know how.' There was a tremor of longing in Lissa's voice and Jan burst out laughing.

'Is that what all this shyness is about? Right,' she said. 'No time like the present.' She selected 'Hound Dog' from her collection of 78s and put it on the record player. The music rang out with a tinny fervour, echoing wonderfully in the wooden building. What followed was the most hilarious hour and a half of Lissa's life. She twirled and shook, and jived and rocked, till her head was spinning and both girls fell gasping on to the rag rug.

But she agreed to attend her first dance.

9

The dance floor was crowded when they arrived at the Yacht Club and Lissa very nearly changed her mind and went straight home again. She hadn't wanted to come in the first place. Now they had actually arrived, fighting for space against a tide of other girls in a stuffy cloakroom, Jan was urging her to put on some pink lipstick. 'And do try to smile.'

Lissa looked doubtful. 'I've never worn lipstick.' But seeing Jan's expression, obediently took out a small mirror from her bag and complied. She did feel rather good in point of fact, in a lavender linen dress that had a small Peter Pan collar and turned back cuffs on the short capped sleeves. Its skirt was full, the waistline fitting snugly, nipped in with a broad black belt.

Jan nudged her. 'Look at these toffs coming in, all dressed up to the nines in their little bow ties. Lord, they look like penguins.' She started to giggle. 'I can't see them getting up and dancing to our Derry's racket, can you?'

Since Lissa hadn't yet heard any skiffle in her entire life she felt unable to comment but took the point. They did seem somewhat forbidding, very stiff and formal. The two girls put their cloakroom tickets inside their shoes and headed for the dance floor.

It was crowded with people, hot and stuffy with a big silver ball hanging from the ceiling that sent little coloured lights all over the walls as it turned. The band was playing 'Love Is A Many Splendoured Thing', and a host of stout dowagers in stiff taffeta and satin were dancing, elbows at 45 degrees, with even stouter men in evening dress.

101

There were girls in long dresses with elbow-length gloves and matching satin slippers, and others like themselves in bright summer dresses. And such a rainbow of bouncy net petticoats that Lissa wondered how some couples could get near enough to dance together.

When the dance ended everyone stood about gossiping, as there weren't enough chairs for everyone to sit down. Then the band on the dais struck up a cha-cha and there was much chatter and laughter as people found their partners and started following each other to pick up the steps.

Jan went off at once to dance with a young man with a toothy grin while Lissa watched, entranced, snuggled down in a corner and hoping no one would notice her. It was a world far removed from the quite fells of Broombank. Would she ever have the courage to get on to that floor herself? She thought not. The prospect seemed too daunting.

A waltz followed, then a succession of quicksteps. Lissa could see Jan changing partners, clearly enjoying herself, but she declined every offer, though she had several. Privately she wished Derry would come and ask her to dance but knew he was too busy getting his skiffle group organised. She longed for the interval when she would see him up on stage.

A picture of how he had kissed her on that day in the Langdales rose in her mind, making her stomach go all wobbly inside. Yet she knew for a fact he'd been out with several girls since then, so it was just as well she hadn't thought too much of it.

Even so, she wanted tonight to go well for him and didn't envy him facing this lot. Lissa hoped he wasn't dressed too outlandishly. Somehow she knew that she would be embarrassed if he looked too much the Teddy Boy.

'Would you do me the honour of this dance?'

Startled, Lissa was about to refuse when she looked up into a familiar face. 'Oh, Mr Brandon.' He looked different, smartly attired in evening dress with what must be a silk shirt and cummerbund. His best bib and tucker, as Jan would say.

'May I?'

'Well . . .' she temporised.

'It's a slow waltz so not too difficult. I noticed you don't seem too keen on dancing but you look far too lovely to hide away in a corner. Perhaps you would care to try? It's not difficult. I'll be most gentle with you, I promise.' He smiled and his face softened. It made him look younger, somehow. Very debonair.

'I'm not really hiding,' Lissa protested, smiling shyly up at him. She didn't want to appear a complete fool. 'Well, perhaps I was, a bit. Thanks. I'll give it a try if you don't mind my two left feet.' She placed her hand in his and let him lead her out on to the dance floor.

'No legal matters tonight. Agreed?'

'Agreed,' she said, her smile warming.

He guided her with perfect style and expertise right around the floor, not once crashing into any other couples. Nor did he step on her toes or attempt to take liberties by pulling her too close. Lissa began to relax and enjoy herself, squealing with delight and clinging tightly to his shoulders as he whirled her around. And she couldn't help noticing that his dark eyes rested upon her in a most admiring way.

When the music ended he didn't take her back to her seat as she expected but stood smiling down at her, chatting about the weather, saying how good the band were, waiting for the music to start up again.

He talked to her all through the next dance and listened most carefully to her replies, as if he were truly interested. Though what he asked and how she answered Lissa could not afterwards recall.

'You must remember something,' Jan insisted as they exchanged notes over a Coca-Cola in the bar. 'You do realise who you were dancing with, don't you?'

Lissa looked puzzled. 'Yes, of course. Philip Brandon. What of it?'

'He's not normally one for dancing. You must have caught his eye.'

'Don't be silly.' Lissa felt herself flushing.

'He's a very good dancer as a matter of fact. A real gentleman.'

'He never goes out these days, though he used to at one time. Or so Derry says.' Jan pulled Lissa close to whisper in her ear against the loud chatter of voices all about them, and above the music coming from the other room. 'Such a sad tale. He was engaged, just after the war, to a girl called Felicity. Only she had some mysterious illness or other. Very highly strung and delicate she was. He was supposed to be absolutely devoted to her but she died.' Jan's myopic eyes were wide as she nodded at Lissa's expression of horror. 'Found her drowned in the lake, they did, just like the poor mad girl in that fairy story.'

'What fairy story? Oh, you mean Ophelia? That was in Shakespeare, not a fairy story,' Lissa laughed. 'Are you telling me the truth, Jan?'

''Course I am.' Jan looked affronted. 'Just because I'm not informed on books and stuff, like you, doesn't mean I don't know the truth about life and death.'

'Sorry. When did she die?'

'About three years back.'

A wave of compassion for Philip Brandon washed through her. Why was life so filled with pain? 'How terrible for him. No wonder he looks so sad.' As they walked back on to the dance floor Lissa's eyes circled the room and found him gazing across at her. She turned quickly away, blushing in scarlet confusion.

'He's been a lonely bachelor ever since, so watch out. Don't get mixed up with him,' Jan said.

'Why not? He looks harmless enough.'

Jan wrinkled up her tiny nose. 'He's *thirty*.'

'Then he's probably learned a bit of sense,' Lissa smartly replied.

And as luck would have it, Philip Brandon chose that moment to ask for another dance. 'How are you on the tango?'

'My favourite dance for getting in a muddle,' said Lissa, and cocked a cheeky grin at Jan's stiff-faced disapproval as he led her out on to the floor.

'Yes, but have you any sense, lass?' Jan murmured.

The band departed at the end of the square tango and Lissa and Jan held hands, and their breath, as Derry's Skifflers sprinted on to the stage. Would he be successful? Would the Yacht Club members like him?

Lissa's heart suddenly swelled with pride. He was dressed in smart narrow black trousers topped with a red silk shirt shot with silver thread, and a black bow tie. He carried a guitar which he at once started to pluck with something he held in his hand. Jan explained it was a pick, to save his fingers.

'You should have seen them when he first started to learn. Made them bleed it did.' But Lissa wasn't listening. She was swaying to the lilt of the music, a Lonnie Donnegan number, thrilled by the skill with which Derry played, the way his hips swayed to the beat of the music. He looked so good up there, different again from the young man in cords and sweater. It was hard to work out what kind of a person Derek Colwith really was.

Her eyes shone, her smile widened and she nodded her head and tapped her pointed toes in time to the music. It was pulsing and irresistible. Yet the dance floor remained empty.

There were five in the group. One other guitar, played by Tony who strummed the chords while Derry picked out the melody. John who rattled a washboard with dancing fingers tipped with silver thimbles. Another boy was getting a surprisingly rhythmic and pulsing beat from a single string attached to a tea chest and broom handle while the fifth member of the group played his heart out on a set of drums. Even if Lissa had not known the hours they had spent in practice she would have been able to tell. They were good, no doubt about it, they deserved to be appreciated.

'Oh, why didn't I come before?' she shouted to Jan, clapping her hands in time to the beat. 'They're great.'

Jan grinned delightedly. 'Told you. Think of all those dances you've missed, sitting at home, sulking.'

Lissa glanced sharply at her, realising Jan had guessed her unhappiness but had made no comment on it. But she wasn't miserable now. Oh no, this was glorious, this was living. Just to listen to this music made you happy.

She glanced about the room and found that the stuffy, over formal Yacht Club types were not even paying any attention to the skiffle group playing their hearts out. They simply stood about in tight little groups, their backs to the stage as they chatted to each other and laughed too loud. It was as if the group didn't exist.

'Why aren't they dancing?' she hissed at Jan, forgetting that only a short time ago she had been the retiring wallflower, reluctant to join in.

Jan's face was grim. 'They wanted a trad jazz group in the interval and since they didn't get one, they're determined to make their feelings known. They like to imagine themselves above this sort of music. Derry was afraid it might be like this. If no one dances, the MC will get fed up and could sack the group on the spot. Then they mightn't get paid at all and certainly wouldn't be asked again.'

The prospect of Derry failing, of not being liked by this crowd, had not until that moment occured to Lissa.

'Then we must do something.'

105

'What can we do?'

'We must *make* them dance,' Lissa said.

'Oh, yeah? How? Brought your magic wand, princess?'

Lissa spoke without even thinking, aware only of the expression of pain and discomfort that was tightening Derry's face, and of the faltering beat as unease began to affect their confidence and make their hands clumsy. 'If no one else will dance, then we must.'

'What?'

'We'll shame them into it.'

'Go out there alone, d'you mean?' Jan sounded appalled.

'Why not? Come on, don't stand there moaning. Action is called for.' The two girls' eyes met and mischievous excitement bubbled out of Lissa. She could have been that young girl again, daring Nick to swim or catch her a jar of fish.

But still Jan hesitated, glancing anxiously at the empty dance floor, the stiff backs turned resolutely away. 'We'd look a proper pair of clucks dancing out there all on our own. All eyes upon us.'

Lissa tilted her chin. 'We won't be on our own though, will we? Your brother is out there already.'

A slight pause, then a grim smile. 'Too right he is. OK, you're on. Let's see how good my teaching was.'

The two girls stepped out on to the floor and began to rock 'n' roll. And not a moment too soon it seemed. The MC was already looming close, the music having lost its excitement, and everyone was expecting Derry's Skifflers to be evicted at any moment. The whole room seemed breathless with anticipation, liking nothing better that a little fracas to liven up the evening.

Derry, who a moment ago would have welcomed being struck down by a bolt of lightning, missed a beat as the girls came on to the floor. Then, beaming his delight, yelled, 'Come on, lads, let's give it to 'em.' He started singing and thrumming for all he was worth, backed by the renewed enthusiasm of his group.

'We'll give it everything we've got,' Jan gasped, crooking her arm and catching Lissa expertly as she spun her round. They made a colourful, arresting sight in their pretty cotton frocks and can-can petticoats showing just the right amount of shapely leg as they twirled about. Not a male eye in the room missed one moment of the dance.

By the time the two girls had rocked 'n' rolled a second time around the dance floor they came close to the dais where Lissa

106

caught the full force of Derry's lopsided smile. He winked at her and she felt again that lovely warm feeling flow within her, that secret message flash between them as if only they existed.

Now some of the audience were smiling, picking up the beat as they started to clap.

'They think we're a floor show. We ought to get some of them up,' Jan whispered, gasping for breath as they swirled and rocked and skipped about the waxed floor.

'Oh, my.' Lissa hadn't bargained for this. 'D' you think we should?'

'Come on. Don't weaken now. I'm game if you are.'

So they split up, Jan dashing off to choose a rather good-looking young man who had danced with her earlier. For a moment Lissa felt stranded, alone in the centre of the floor with all eyes upon her.

And then she became aware of a particular pair of eyes, of a dark, familiar face, and she crossed the floor in a whirl of floating colour to stand before Philip Brandon.

'Would you do me the honour of this dance?' she asked, very properly, face alight with laughter.

In the normal course of events Philip Brandon would have refused instantly. Not for the world would he ever risk setting himself up as a stooge. For him to rock 'n' roll was unthinkable. But this girl was smiling up at him with such a radiant smile, and such a delightful beckoning in her beautiful eyes that he knew he could not refuse. Besides, he was flattered that she had chosen him and wanted everyone to see how wonderful they looked together.

'You must show me what to do,' he said, taking her hand and following her on to the floor.

'I'll be very gentle with you,' she teased, and they both laughed at her repetition of his own earlier promise. As she turned into his arms he noted the firm roundness of her young breasts, the smiling pink mouth that he had a sudden urge to kiss. His arm felt extremely comfortable around her trim waist. 'Take my hands. I'll show you the basic step,' Lissa said. 'It's very easy. Lean on this foot, then back on the other and do a kind of wiggle. Like this. Do you see?'

'Yes,' he said, eyes on her swaying hips. 'I do.'

Moments later the dance floor was filled with happy, laughing people. Even the fat dowagers in regal satin and swinging pearls were attempting to learn the steps of this new-fangled dance and loving every minute of it.

'Thank you,' he said at the end, dark grey eyes on her flushed face. 'I really enjoyed that. You made me feel young again.'

She looked surprised. 'You are young. At least . . .' She shrugged her shoulders in a captivatingly elegant gesture. 'I never think age is of any importance, do you?'

He held her close for just a shade too long, the pressure of his fingers at her waist strangely compelling, before letting her go with obvious reluctance. 'You don't know how happy it makes me to hear you say that.'

Lissa was thoughtful as she watched him walk away. Were the idea not entirely silly she might have imagined he was making a pass. But then Derry and the group bounded up and she forgot all about Philip Brandon.

'How about that?' Derry cried. Lissa was astonished to find herself gathered into his arms. The scent of his hot skin against her cheek was heady and for a moment she wondered if she dared hug him back but he'd let her go before she'd made up her mind. 'That was great. Thanks.'

He hugged Jan with even greater vigour, face flushed with triumph. 'That was brave of you, Sis.'

'It was Lissa's idea. You can thank her, not me.'

Derry cast Lissa a thoughtful glance then took out his comb and started to adjust his quiff as if the embrace had ruffled it. 'They loved it, didn't they? Did you see the young girls come up to the stage afterwards? Screaming and crying, some of them were.'

'Yes,' Lissa said, an unusual tartness to her tone, eyes upon his laughing face. 'We did notice.'

He winked at her. 'Didn't make you jealous then?'

'Why should it?' Deliberately cool.

The pressure of his strong body against hers had felt delicious, better than she had ever imagined. Did that mean she was getting over that silly phobia about having to keep folk at a distance? In fact, tonight she had been embraced by two men, though once during the course of a dance. It really felt quite good to be wanted. If only for a moment.

She longed for Derry to stay, to ask her to dance and hold her close again, but from the corner of her eye she saw Philip Brandon approaching. He took hold of her hand as if he owned her and she very nearly protested. But remembering what a good sport he had been Lissa bit her lip, smiled, and went meekly with him on to the dance floor, acutely aware of Derry's eyes piercing her back.

She could barely wait for the dance to be over before excusing herself and hurrying to Derry. Only she was too late, he had gone. To get changed, Jan said.

'They're to play again later. The MC has arranged a second interval 'specially. They're going for a quick pint now, Derry says.' She raised disbelieving brows. 'Never had a quick drink in his life.'

Keen disappointment bit into Lissa. 'That means we won't see them until after the dance then?'

Jan raised surprised eyebrows as she glanced at her friend but said nothing, even when Lissa, catching the expression, blushed furiously. Then suddenly he was there, at her elbow, and her heart jolted, shocking her by the astounding affect he had upon her.

'Hiya,' he said. 'How was the dance?'

'Fine, thanks.' She could feel herself shaking. Not that Derry noticed. A group of young girls hovered close and half his attention was upon them, a smile curving one corner of his mouth, self-satisfaction lurking in the deep brown eyes. 'Coming for a drink?' he asked, his gaze suddenly switching to Lissa, then flicking over to include his sister and back to Lissa again.

Heart beating rapidly, she was about to accept when she saw one of the girls, a blonde with forget-me-not blue eyes who couldn't be a day over fifteen, edge closer. Derry turned his head and winked at the girl who gave a tiny squeal of delight and at once came to hang upon his arm. When he turned back to Lissa, he was grinning from ear to ear.

'It has to be a quick one though because Tony's broken a string so we must fix a new one and tune it in with mine before we go on again,' he said.

'Then don't let me keep you,' said Lissa, in a frozen voice, as if she couldn't care less what he did.

His smile faded. 'What's biting you?'

She saw him shake his arm free of the girl but it was too late. Lissa had seen the pleasure it gave him. 'I don't drink beer,' she said, in her loftiest tone.

'Fine. Well, I haven't brought any champagne.' Then he glanced down at the blonde still hovering close. 'Come on then, Karen. I bet you drink beer.'

'Ooh, yes,' she squealed, in a poor imitation of Marilyn Monroe.

Derry glared at Lissa for another half second then took a step back, evidently itching to be gone. 'If you two want walking home you'll have to wait. It'll be late by the time we've changed and cleared away.'

'And you've signed autographs for all your adoring young fans,' said Lissa, while Jan watched the growing tension with interest and immense amusement.

'Yeah, maybe that too. Any objections?'

'You can take as long as you like. It's no concern of mine. And we certainly don't need you to see us home,' Lissa haughtily informed him, determined to let him know she wasn't hanging around waiting for any favours.

His eyes narrowed as he glared at her. 'Maybe you've got an offer already?'

'Maybe I have,' she said, hating him for letting her down, wishing he'd take her in his arms and tell her he wanted to be only with her, not any foolish young blonde. But she was done with wishing, wasn't she? 'I haven't gone short,' she said.

'So I noticed. Suit yourself.' And pushing back his ridiculously wide shoulders, he strolled away, the fifteen-year-old blonde scurrying after him.

'Arrogant young fool,' said Jan, crisply. 'Still, at least we saved him from a dire death, eh? Fun, wasn't it?'

'Yes,' Lissa said, swallowing bitter tears of disappointment. 'At least we did that.'

So when Philip Brandon asked her for the last waltz she accepted, and afterwards she let him walk her home.

He judged the moment of their meeting with a perfection that owed more than a little to careful planning. But then Philip Brandon approved of planning, of order and organisation. He liked perfection.

And Lissa was perfection. From the sweet oval of her face, the curves of her slender body, to the last curl on her beautiful head.

He could see her sitting on a stone wall by the lake, her head bent over a letter she was writing as he willed the fickle breeze not to change direction at just the wrong moment. The yacht had tacked bravely across the lake as if knowing its own destiny, skimming fast and sure across the waves.

Philip swung the jib round and brought the little boat safely to shore with well-judged skill.

'Ahoy there,' he called. 'How about a sail?'

She glanced up from her work, her expression vague and unfocused. Then as they fixed upon him, the smile of recognition that followed was his reward.

'Mr Brandon.'

She seemed lost for words and he longed for the ability to make some witticism, a little quip that would remind her of the fun they had had in their attempts at rock 'n' roll, and of his prowess in the yacht race. But he was not good at quips. They were not his forte.

'It's a lovely evening,' was all he could manage. He was quite close to her by this time, the tiny yacht bobbing gently up and down, the clear water slapping against the boat's sides. 'I did promise you a sail and this is probably the last chance we'll get. I'll be laying her up for winter soon.'

'Did you?' She looked confused, shaking her head, pursing her soft pink lips. Was that what he had talked of at the dance? His yacht? 'I-I don't think I should.' She half indicated the letter in her lap.

'I can see you're busy,' he said, playing on her sense of guilt. 'But a spin across the lake and back wouldn't take more than a few minutes. Bring some colour to your cheeks.' Wonderful cheeks, and a perfect straight nose. If she would only stop dithering. All he needed was an opportunity to give her a sample of his charm.

He could see she was tempted. Her gaze kept straying across the lake, ruffled by just the right amount of breeze for a sail on this lovely September evening. With summer gone and the quiet of autumn approaching, the water was the colour of amber, like a Chinese water colour with sky and lake melding together, reflecting upon her skin till it glowed like molten gold.

Then she was climbing into the boat, laughing with delight as it rocked beneath her feet, and Lissa couldn't have said quite when the decision had been made. Or why. Perhaps she still grieved for the old Lissa who would not have hesitated to accept such an adventure. Or simply wished to show Derry Colwith, and herself, that she was her own woman.

Whatever the reason she longed suddenly to feel the spray in her face, the keen wind in her hair, to trail her fingers in the rippling chill of the water. Lissa wanted to experience the hard thump of the waves skudding beneath the hull of the boat and banish the blues from her mind.

She laughed when a swan took off, beating its wings in temper, flurried by the winter geese newly arrived from the north.

'I can finish the letter at any time,' she told him. 'So why not?' It was to Meg and could wait.

'Good.'

Their eyes met. She had such wonderful eyes, he thought. Exciting, mysterious, sensual. If he saw any hint of rebellion or stubborn independence in them he chose to pay it no heed. If a wildness came into her expression he interpreted it as fear. She was young, and therefore impressionable, but malleable, he was sure. And he knew that soon, very soon, his patience would be rewarded. The thought excited him almost beyond endurance.

Lissa found the sail exhilarating, and terrifying. She was afraid that at any moment she might slip from this crazy 45-degree angle right into the foaming water that crested the hull. Yet oddly enough, having complete faith in Philip's skill with rope and tiller, she loved the fear, revelled in it, as if living on the edge made her feel more alive.

She couldn't think of him as old. He seemed friendly and charming. And no one could deny he was good-looking with his dark hair, charcoal eyes and lean, bronzed body.

'Are you all right?' he asked her and she smiled and nodded, lifting her hair from her neck to let the breeze run through it. And so much more considerate than Derry Colwith. No screaming fan club in tow here.

Philip sailed the yacht close to the far shore, white sails cracking in the wind, wondering if he dare land it. Should he take her now? Should he risk mooring the boat and make love to her with a passion that would have her begging for more? He could feel his arousal and hastily busied himself with the jib and the sheets.

'Ready about,' he called. What was he thinking of? He mustn't blow it, not now he was so close.

By the time he had returned her safely to shore he had asked her for a date in the form of a gentle invitation to dinner that evening.

Lissa climbed out of the boat, cheeks aglow, curls bursting loose from the restraints of the bobbing pony tail. 'That was wonderful, so exciting. Thanks a lot, I loved it. And thanks for the offer of a meal but . . .'

'You're pretty busy?'

She smiled, flushing pinkly. 'Yes.'

His dark eyes looked sad as she walked away and Lissa almost regretted her refusal. But Philip Brandon was reminding himself of the need for patience. She was young still. He could afford to wait.

1957

10

Carreckwater, like many another of its kind in Lakeland, was a town with a split personality. For most of the year it was a quiet, sleepy place where people walking up and down its slate cobbled streets felt obliged to smile or say good morning to everyone they met. In the summer they thought themselves lucky if there was room to walk on the pavement let alone see a familiar face.

Lissa loved the hustle and bustle. She enjoyed the clatter of walking boots even if bulging haversacks did constantly bump her off the narrow pavements. The visitors came in droves down the mountain paths which descended like the spokes of a wheel into the little town. Lunchtime and late-afternoon were popular times, when they came to partake of a substantial lunch or a high tea in the many cafes and hotels along Carndale Road. They tramped their mud in and out of every establishment, bought one postcard to send to Aunty May back home, oohed and ahed at the many little shops and picture galleries, replaced a broken pair of boot laces and went away thinking they had done the town a favour by bestowing their meagre business upon it.

At Stevens Drapery they were rushed off their feet. Lissa soon discovered there wasn't time in the summer to do anything but deal with customers and their endless enquiries. Often these were not at all concerned with the goods in the window, which grew increasingly dusty since there was no time to change it. More often than not the visitors asked the most unlikely things, like where to buy fishing nets or what time the next steamer left. They wanted to know where Beatrix Potter had lived and if they sold postcards.

115

'The fish shop.'

'Half-past two.'

'Far Sawry.'

'Sorry, no, we don't. Try the post office,' answered Jan to each in turn, smiling all the while. Lissa, impressed by her friend's efficiency and unfailing good spirits, felt herself flagging. June had been hot but July was proving to be breathless, the air heavy and sultry with heat. It made her almost long for a cold snap.

But perhaps all this rush and her long working hours was the reason she hadn't seen Derry lately. The streets were so crowded she had missed him. Not that she'd seen much of him throughout the winter either. He always appeared to be busy, what with his work as clerk during the day, his evenings devoted to skiffle practice and his weekends given over to playing at dances. The group travelled half across the county in their little van at weekends.

She had only herself to blame in a way, she supposed. Frozen him out, as she always did. She'd given up going to dances, certainly those at which Derry played. Not that there were many dances in Carreckwater itself but she couldn't bear to watch the crowds of screaming females all clamouring around him. Derry seemed to revel in their silly attention. Even Jan had told him off for letting it all go to his head.

'You're turning into a prig,' she'd said, with her usual lack of sisterly affection, but he merely grinned and told her he couldn't help it if he was popular, puffing out his chest all the more. Lissa knew she should be glad that she hardly saw him and would have been, were it not for that other, secret part of Derry Colwith she'd been given a glimpse of, and the memory of which still haunted her.

But she really shouldn't let it bother her. By and large she was glad she was busy. That way she could maintain her determination to keep him at a distance.

Lissa brought her wandering attention back to the reality of a long, hot and tiring day, pushing back damp tendrils of undisciplined curls as she bid good day to yet one more grumbling customer who had taken thirty-five minutes to choose two yards of lace trimming.

'Why doesn't Miss Stevens spend more time in the shop?' Lissa groaned, propping herself on a stool so she could massage her aching calves. 'We've been run off our feet from the moment we opened. One minute she's in the middle of serving that rather plump lady with some lyle stockings and the next she's vanished.

116

Where? Why? I was left with two not very happy customers to attend to.'

Jan raised her eyebrows, giving the decided impression that she knew the answer to that one but it wasn't for her to say. 'Best not to ask too closely when it comes to our Stella,' she advised, wrapping braid back on a reel with alarming dexterity. 'It don't do to upset her.'

As if on cue, Miss Stevens stuck her head around the stock room door, hair awry, looking faintly flustered, with flags of colour lighting each prominent cheek bone.

'Ah, there you are Jan,' she said, as if it were a surprise to find her two shop assistants still behind the counter. 'Will you kindly take a selection of brassières along to Mrs Elvira Fraser. She has sent a request for same in this morning's post.'

'But she lives right up on the Parade,' groaned Jan, thinking of the long hot trek staggering under a weighty parcel. 'Why can't she come here?'

'Because she is quite old and rich enough to do as she pleases,' snapped Stella Stevens. 'Two states of affairs which will never prove to be a problem for you, my dear gel, if you don't jump to it, as you will be unemployed and expire of starvation before you reach twenty.'

Jan hung her head. 'Yes, Miss Stevens.' And gathering a selection of corsetry of suitably ample dimensions, and studiously ignoring Lissa's giggles, she set out.

Stella Stevens' temperament was indeed quixotic. She could storm through the shop finding fault with everything but then return later all syrup and smiles as if they were the dearest girls on earth. Which was what she called them, her 'dear gels'. The tone was not always complimentary. Customers she referred to as 'Modom'. And that wasn't necessarily complimentary either.

She sat now in her office, staring at the wad of unpaid accounts in her hand and reaching for her bottle of Milk of Magnesia. Her nervous stomach was really giving trouble this morning, a little sip or two might help.

Stella Stevens was a large lady with a healthy appetite, a low-slung bosom and hips that were a walking advertisement for her corset department. Her 'nerves' were aided and abetted not by the worthy Milk of Magnesia but by whatever liquid the innocent blue bottle actually happened to contain. Today it was brandy.

'Something must be done,' she informed the Kangol beret poster stuck on the wall above her desk. 'Clients no longer seem to have the good taste of former years. Turn their noses up at true quality, they do. "But is it in fashion, my dear Miss Stevens?" they say.' Stella mimicked the warbling tone of one of her customers and took another sip from the Milk of Magnesia bottle, found it empty and threw it in the waste paper basket. Then realising what she had done, took it out again and went to her washroom to rinse it. She would buy another small bottle of something, perhaps of gin, at lunchtime. She was not herself this morning and could do with a bit of comfort. Surprising really how bad her stomach got after the monthly bank statement arrived.

'My shop is as good as ever it was,' she declared to Jan and Lissa as she faced them later that day with the unpalatable truth that despite the high volume of customers who had walked through the door, the takings in the till were pitifully small.

'Yes, of course it is, Miss Stevens,' Jan hastily agreed and Lissa privately thought that that was the problem. Stevens Drapery had not moved with the times. It fell very much between two stools. The clothes were neither stylish nor classic, merely old fashioned. Admittedly they did well with a jumble of useful bits and pieces of haberdashery, but not enough to sustain a thriving business.

'What I wouldn't like to do to this place!' Lissa said, as Miss Stevens retreated to her office like a crab scurrying sideways to bury itself in sand, safe from the harshness of the world.

'Oh, me too,' Jan agreed. 'Burn it down?' And they both burst into fits of giggles.

The girls were always thankful when five-thirty came round and they could lock the door, hand over the takings and return home to the little boathouse where they took it in turns to make the evening meal. Then they would sit outside by the lake in the evening sun and talk about how blissful it was to be seventeen and free.

Occasionally Derry came over, declaring himself tired of practising and in need of some fresh air, though he always managed to make a point of rubbing Lissa up the wrong way. Tonight was no exception.

'Not going out, are you?' he asked, staring almost accusingly at her and she wondered why.

'Nope,' Jan answered for her, eyes closed as she sat sprawled in a deck chair, her neat figure clad in a blue and white swimsuit that sported a dashing skirt about the hips.

Derry was dressed in a blue check shirt, open at the neck to show off his tan, and tight blue jeans that no doubt sent the young girls crazy, Lissa thought, averting her eyes from his neatly shaped rump. 'You two stay in too much,' he informed them loftily. 'Wouldn't get me leading such a dull life. It isn't cool to stay in, y'know?' He started skimming stones across the lake, yelling with delight when he got a high number of bounces. 'Out every night, I am.'

'Good for you,' said Lissa drily. 'Anyway, how would you know what we do, since you're never around?' She lifted violet eyes to his, a challenge blatantly written in them, and felt a curl of delight to see the swaggering arrogance slip slightly into doubt as he frowned at her.

Lissa's swimsuit was a two-piece, of a modest cut but revealing enough to give Derry pause for thought.

'You could come with us on our gigs.'

'Perhaps we have better things to do.'

'What? Who do you go out with?' he asked, finding to his surprise that he preferred to imagine her sitting serenely here, by the lake, waiting. For him? He wasn't quite sure. He'd thought at one time that she quite fancied him, now he'd given up hope. Almost.

'None of your business,' she said.

Violet eyes met brown, and held.

'Maybe. Maybe not.'

For the first time Derry looked troubled and uncertain, almost as if he wished he hadn't asked. He skimmed a stone with such fierce vigour it bounced half across the lake before sinking.

'Did you see that? Thirteen.'

'Unlucky,' said Lissa and sank back in her deck chair, closing her eyes as if she weren't interested.

He took out his comb and flicked at his quiff with quick, agitated gestures. ''Course, this town is boring. You won't find me hanging around here much longer. I'll be away. Starting to make real good money with the group now.'

Despite herself, Lissa's eyes flew open again and saw the triumph register as he recognised her interest. 'Going where?' The thought of never seeing Derry again sent her heart plummeting. Could he be serious?

'Haven't decided yet. Manchester. London. Who knows?'

'You were born and brought up in the Lake District. How could you ever be happy anywhere else when you love it so much? There are no mountains to climb in London.'

He looked thoughtful for a moment then shrugged his shoulders.

'Life goes on. I'm going up in the world. Or I might get a place of my own here. I could if I wanted. Good as this, or better. Renee's a bit of a pain, though her cooking has improved out of this world and Dad isn't too bad. He's building a boat for me, you know. So I can win the races this year.'

'You're staying on at Nab Cottage because you get well fed and Jimmy is building you a boat? You selfish, arrogant . . .'

Jan lifted her hands in her favourite conducting gesture. 'Now children, no more squabbling. Why don't we go for a row on the lake? A little gentle exercise will do us all good, don't you think? Cool us all down?'

But Lissa was still stinging from his accusations of dullness as they dragged the wooden row boat over the shingle. 'Where's your fan club tonight? Deserted you already then?'

Derry stopped tugging at the boat to grin at her, his face so close to hers that to Lissa's immense fury her heart gave a little flip. Drat him, she thought. Why won't he stay out of my life completely then I could forget him?

'They do tend to wear a bloke out, it's true. But I'm between dates, as you might say.'

A wave of sickness hit her and Lissa would have liked to knock the supercilious expression off his beautiful face.

With strenuous efforts on Jan's part, good humour was restored as they puffed up and down the lake and were soon squealing with delight every time they 'caught a crab' and were splashed with the ice cold water.

'This is lovely, we should do it more often,' Lissa gasped, on a sudden burst of enthusiasm.

Derry glanced at her in surprise. 'My, my. We are coming out. Take care. Dangerous to unstuff your shirt and mingle with the peasants.'

'*Derry*!' Jan said, horrified. 'What a thing to say.'

'Sorry,' he said, but didn't look it and Lissa decided she'd been right about Derry Colwith all along. He was perfectly horrid.

With the fickleness of Lakeland weather the skies had turned iron

120

grey, promising rain, held off only by the wind which tore through the valley, turning the leaves upside down on the trees, churning the waters and scurrying the ducks into flustered huddles.

It was a day to be indoors. Renee was spending it defrosting her fridge.

'Drat the thing,' she screamed, jabbing her knife into the huge lumps of ice stuck fast to its shining surface.

'There's more water on your kitchen floor than in the mere,' said Jimmy, watching her wring out cloths and shift bowls about. 'Our Derry'll have to swim in for his tea tonight.'

'And all the food's going off.' Renee almost sobbed her frustration. 'Why didn't that salesman tell me it'd take half a day and a night to defrost the damn' thing?'

'He told you to do it every week. You do it once every two months, and the ice builds up.'

'Looks like the bloody north pole in there. I wish I had one of those huge American fridges, like on "I Love Lucy".'

Jimmy groaned and got up from the kitchen table where he'd been enjoying a bacon and egg breakfast. 'Aw, don't start, Renee. Not summat else. Enough's enough.'

'I only want what I deserve, pet. What I've never had.'

'I know, sweetheart, but there's only so many working hours in a day.'

'We could get it on the Never-Never.'

'And never never bloody pay for it? I thought you wanted a gramophone that way?'

'I do.'

'I'm not a walking bank, Renee.'

Tears were streaming down her face now and Jimmy watched her with a sad expression. It was the nearest they'd come to a quarrel. 'I'd give you the earth, love, you know I would, but it'd cost too much.'

The knife jerked in her hand and flew off into some distant hidden recess of the kitchen. Renee doubted she would ever see it again, and didn't rightly care.

'To hell with it. Oh, Jimboy, I'm sorry. And I wanted things to be real nice this evening when they all came.'

'They will be nice. Don't you always make things nice?' Then she was in his arms and in seconds the quarrel was forgotten. He was lifting up her skirt, grabbing like a teenager with eager hands. He

121

took her there and then, slipping and sliding in the pools of ice on the kitchen floor.

'I'll get you a telephone installed, so you won't feel so alone,' Jimmy gasped, when he could breathe again. 'How about that?'

Renee screamed her delight and hugged his tousled head close to her soft round breast. 'Oh, I do love you, you soft old fool. Now get off to work, and take care.'

He smacked a kiss on one damp nipple. 'When do I not?'

When he was gone Renee sat for a minute longer on the damp floor, eyes glazed with soft love.

'Mind you,' she said to the budgie as she went off to change, 'it's all very well being a modern woman and Jimmy working hard to buy the latest gadgets, but there's so much to learn to operate the damn' things you need to be a trained mechanic.'

The little gate had been given a fresh lick of green paint and the tiny garden was crowded with blue delphiniums, hollyhocks, pink rambling roses and pale crinkly honesty as the two girls walked up the path to Nab Cottage.

Renee loved to invite them for a meal and they were always glad to accept. It gave her a chance to show off her latest culinary efforts.

The electric fire was out since the rain had stopped and a fitful sun was warming the August day but the little blue budgie was still squabbling noisily with its alter ego in the mirror.

'You are really getting very good,' Lissa told Renee as they all tucked in to delicious lake trout, baked to perfection with smoked crispy bacon. There were plump ripe strawberries to follow, piled high on a meringue nest.

'I've you to thank for that,' Renee told her. 'No one else has ever bothered to teach me anything.'

'You'll have to teach her to knit socks next,' Jan said.

Renee looked puzzled, as well she might. 'Why socks?'

'Lissa's family are experts but haven't the first idea how to dance.' And nobody else quite understood their hilarity.

But that's the way they were. Silly and careless. Joking all the time. Life was fun and Lissa wanted to keep it that way.

Jimmy Colwith let his eyes rest on his young wife with pride. Dressed in her usual black pencil skirt which flattered her shapely figure, she wore a pink top with raglan sleeves and a wide vee neck that kept slipping off one lovely bare shoulder. Ripe as one of those luscious strawberries she was. It had been a lucky day for him when she'd walked through the door. He'd quite forgotten she'd ever had any connection with his son.

Lissa hadn't. She was letting her own gaze stray to Derry's face and found his warm brown eyes riveted upon his young stepmother. Her heart plummeted. So that was why he was reluctant to leave home? He still wanted Renee. The thought filled her with a sick dread. What a foolish innocent she was.

'She'll be running the Marina Hotel before she's done,' Derry was saying. The expression in his eyes was filled with laughter and admiration and Lissa almost hated him for being happy. But when they turned to her, instinctively sensing her gaze upon him, the eyes narrowed and noticeably cooled. 'She could hold dances for the Yacht Club set. I'm sure Lissa would love to attend. She likes men in penguin suits.'

'They certainly wouldn't let you in wearing that jacket,' she tartly replied. 'Not to mention the purple shirt. Where did you find it? At a fancy dress party?'

She lifted her chin with haughty disdain, turning her attention to the dessert as it was placed before her, then found the lump in her throat would not allow her to eat it. She really shouldn't waste time on him. But Lissa knew, even as she chastised herself, that it wouldn't have made any difference. Despite all her efforts to keep him at a distance she was falling in love with Derek Colwith and there wasn't a damn' thing she could do about it.

There was a balmy warmth to the evening air as Derry walked the girls home later that evening.

The black mountains huddled about the shoreline seemed to protect them in a secret world all of their own. Soon summer would be over, the visitors would leave and the quiet riches of autumn would be theirs to enjoy, unfettered by overwork.

Contentment warmed Lissa. What did it matter if Jan had a good-looking, infuriating brother? On the whole, taking everything into account, she was happy here in Carreckwater, for all she still missed Broomdale, and Meg.

'What more could we ask for?' she sighed. 'But a job that puts money in our pockets and friends to enjoy life with?' She really mustn't let him guess how she felt. She must fight her emotions, every inch of the way. If Derry still had a thing going for Renee, that was his problem. And Jimmy's. He was the one she should feel sorry for.

'Well,' Derry said, smiling mysteriously, 'I could think of one or two other things I might ask for.'

'I can guess,' teased his sister. 'A Vespa scooter maybe, or a recording contract with Decca?'

He cast a glance at Lissa across Jan's head as if trying to judge her reaction. 'We're buying a bigger van next week, then we can travel further, to play at other hops. Maybe go as far as Manchester.'

Lissa stared at the ground, not wanting to show that it mattered whether Derry stayed in Carreckwater or not. But the rapid beat of her heart told its own tale.

'What about your job?' Jan asked. 'You can't take too much time off from that.'

'He's too grand to be a clerk,' Lissa said, hating the way her voice sounded peevish. But Derry only told her that she was absolutely right, he was. 'I'd give it all up tomorrow for one chance at the big time.'

'Fool,' Jan laughed. 'Fat chance.'

The boathouse was bathed in a pool of pale moonlight as Jan turned her key in the lock, still chuckling over her brother's foolish dreams.

The soft lapping sound of water slipping over stones echoed magically in their ears. Pewter grey, its polished surface reflected a half moon and the need to be alone with Derry was suddenly so compelling that the blood hummed in Lissa's veins.

She wished Jan would go to bed so she could walk with him along the shore, hand in hand, gazing at that moon, talking softly together, perhaps feeling his lips on hers. Lissa shook the dream away, knowing it to be false and dangerous, and then as if her thoughts had been spoken out loud, Jan declared she was tired and would go at once to her bed.

'If you two don't mind? G'night.' She flashed them a cheery wave then went up the spiral staircase to her tiny bedroom in the eaves.

And now the very opposite emotions ruled. Cold fear gripped Lissa's heart. She was alone for the first time with Derry. He stood in the tiny living room smiling at her, hands in pockets, and to her complete shock and dismay she felt her limbs start to tremble. Foolish as it might seem the sensation persisted, filling her with a cloying panic. How ridiculous. He wouldn't hurt her, she told herself. Yet all she wanted was for him to go. To leave her alone with her pain.

'I'm tired too,' she blurted out, more harshly than she intended.

He considered her for a long moment before answering and Lissa saw his shoulders tense. 'I'd best be on my way too, I suppose,' he said at last, not making a move.

'Yes,' Lissa agreed through stiff lips, and after a moment found the strength to walk to the door.

Derry took his hands out of his pockets, wiped the palms on his trousers and slowly followed her. She held open the door, stiff-backed, as she waited for him to leave. Then the panic dissolved into a wave of shyness as he brushed past her and Lissa lowered her chin, unable to meet his shrewd gaze. She was aware that he had paused in the doorway, that he was looking down at her, waiting for her to say something. But she dare not move, dare not return his gaze. Couldn't think what to say.

'Good night then,' he said.

'Good night,' Lissa said, falsely bright, and moved as if to close the door. Derry stopped it with his foot, then catching her chin between finger and thumb, tilted her face up to his.

'I don't understand you,' he said, and there was a grating quality to his voice that she'd never heard before.

'I-I don't know what you mean.'

'Yes, you do. Think about it. Sometimes you give me the real come-on. Slanting those delicious smiles when there are other people around and I can't do a damn' thing about it. The next minute you're as cold as ice, don't want to know. You've avoided me for months. What is it with you? I hadn't thought you a tease but it's looking that way.'

'I-I really . . .'

'I'm only human, Lissa. Its not fair to lead a bloke on, you know, then freeze him out.'

She was appalled. 'I never led you on.'

'You let me kiss you on that walk. You said you'd come with me again but never did. You danced for me and saved the group from certain death. Then you went off with Philip Brandon. Now you've hardly a good word to say to me.'

Lissa remained silent, hanging her head as if with shame. She had never considered the situation from Derry's point of view before, never imagined that he might have feelings of his own and could be injured by her blow hot, blow cold attitude.

He was saying it was all her fault. That she was a tease. It must be true since this was not the first time she'd been told so. This was exactly what Kenyon Parker had said to her. *'It's all your fault,'* the gypsy had said, and he was right. She had encouraged him, she had.

'You'll end up wicked like your mother,' her grandmother had told her.

She didn't want to be wicked. She didn't mean to be a tease. Oh, what was wrong with her? Why did she behave in this way? Everything that had ever happened to her was all her fault. The gypsy's obscene act, Meg losing her baby, perhaps even something she had done or neglected to do as a child which had driven her mother away. Now even Derry hated her. Lissa suddenly felt so unsure of herself, so certain nobody really liked her she wanted to lay her head on his shoulder and burst into tears.

'I'm sorry,' she got out at last, her voice barely above a whisper. 'I didn't mean to . . . I-I suppose I was protecting myself.'

'From what? From me?' His voice had softened and the anger in his face eased a little. 'Do I look such a villain? OK, so I wear cool clothes. That doesn't mean I carry a flick-knife and knuckle-dusters, does it? Bit of a swank but Honest Jack, that's me.'

She met his frank, open gaze and was troubled.

'Yet you love to encourage all those females to hang about you. I mean it when I say I've no wish to be numbered among your fan club, Derry Colwith. A notch on your gun.'

'Is that what you think you'd be?' His hands grasped her shoulders, the weight of them burning through her thin dress, and he gave her a little shake. 'You really believe those girls matter to me?'

'I don't know what to believe.' She didn't want his hands on her, they confused and frightened her. They made her want things she shouldn't want.

'Miss Henshaw told me you'd been up to the office once or twice. Were you looking for me, or developing a schoolgirl crush for my boss?'

Lissa tossed back her hair on a spurt of temper. 'Don't you dare call me a schoolgirl. Why on earth would I look for you? That was family business.'

He glowered at her, disbelief in his brown eyes. 'And was it family business when she saw you walking by the lake, talking with him?'

Lissa felt herself grow pale. Miss Henshaw must have seen her on that day Philip Brandon had taken her for a sail. Office gossip? Drat Derry Colwith.

'I really don't see that it is any concern of yours who I talk to,' she said, in her haughtiest tone.

He was so close she could taste his breath on her tongue, smell the aftershave he wore, mingling with the maleness of him.

'No wonder you're so cold with me. My wallet not big enough for you?'

'Perhaps I don't trust any man.'

'Known a lot, have you?'

Without stopping to think, Lissa lifted her hand to slap him across the face but he caught and held it fast with his own, a white line of anger showing above his full top lip. Lips she longed to kiss, even now.

'Don't class me with the likes of Philip Brandon,' he said, voice no more than a low hiss. 'Not ever. There's more to him than he lets on.'

'I reckon you're jealous,' she taunted. 'Serve you right.' And Lissa laughed, delighted to have the upper hand again, but he was pulling her closer, holding her tightly in his arms and his mouth came down upon hers, hard and demanding, bruising her by its intensity.

A great giddiness swept over her, a desire and panic so overwhelming it was like claustrophobia, as if she were a prisoner in a confined space and must fight to get out. Lifting her hands Lissa thrust him from her with all her strength. 'No!' she screamed, and fell back, gasping for breath.

There was shock on his face and a curl of contempt at his mouth. 'What the hell . . .?'

'I-I don't like to be used,' she said.

Then he held up his hands, palm outwards as if offering surrender. 'There's no danger of that.' And turning abruptly from her, slammed the door so hard it rocked on its hinges. Even so she could hear his last words. 'Don't worry. Your virginity is quite safe with me.'

11

.

There were times when Philip Brandon thought he would have liked to escape this tight valley community, were his fortunes not so firmly tied to it. Crowds irritated him, the happy bustle of the visitors seeming to intensify his own intrinsic loneliness. Particularly today when a summer storm seemed to be brewing and the air grew heavy with promised thunder. Huge purple and grey clouds gathered above the lake which lay like an amethyst in the fading afternoon light. Neither poet nor artist, yet he was aware of its beauty from his vantage point in the bay window of one of the more flamboyant Victorian villas on the Parade.

He allowed the voice of Elvira Fraser, his esteemed client, to flow over rather than into his consciousness. She would run out of steam soon, or her maid would turn up with the long promised tea, then he might bring her to the point.

Philip adjusted his gaze to the fine mouldings and carved cornices slightly above her head, giving every appearance of attending whilst thinking how much he appreciated a house of style. This one would suit him very nicely, though it had about it the stale, close to death smell, of a house occupied by the old.

He'd made good progress over the last year and his bank accounts were looking modestly healthy, but he felt sure he was running out of time. His patience was wearing thin.

'So you see, *dear* Mr Brandon, I do depend upon you absolutely. My father made his fortune in the cotton mills but times are not what they were.' Elvira emitted a heavy sigh. 'Too many imports, don't you know? If only my family would recognise my need, yet they

129

would rob me of my last farthing given half a chance, I am quite sure of it.'

Philip offered his most reassuring smile, not unsympathetically. Yet he was so accustomed to hearing the woes of distressed gentlefolk whose ample funds had first brought them to the Lake District and were not now quite so abundant, that his concern was limited. Poverty was relative.

Reaching across the small table set between the two chairs he patted the old lady's hand. The flesh was soft and papery and made him cringe.

'You may rest assured that I have your best interests at heart, Mrs Fraser.'

'I know, I know, dear boy,' she said, dabbing at a tear with a lavender-scented handkerchief. 'It is so rare these days. Everyone has become so greedy since the war. Do you not think so?'

The door opened and a tiny maid staggered in carrying a loaded tray. Silver teapot, silver milk jug and sugar basin, and of course a tea strainer. Cups and saucers of the very finest porcelain, he noticed. Even one of those old fashioned cake stands dangling from her arm to set by her mistress's right hand. Philip considered the peaked ridge of cucumber sandwiches and wondered how quickly he could conclude the small ceremony and be out of here in the fresh air, bank books in hand.

It took less time than even he had anticipated. Mrs Elvira Fraser, having been vilified once too often by an indiscreet son-in-law, was only too pleased to hand over her financial affairs to *dear* Mr Brandon without any fuss at all. It took no more than two triangles of cucumber sandwich and one slice of seed cake and the deal was done.

'I shall be only too happy to invest your funds for you, Elvira.' This concession had been granted with the second sandwich. 'A sum of interest will be paid each month into your bank account, more than sufficient for your needs. The balance will grow and add to your securities.'

'Oh, what a relief.'

He leaned forward and rested his hand on a stout, tweed-clad knee, allowing it to linger until a slight stain of colour touched the sagging cheeks. He could feel the elastic garter just above her knee that held up the thick lyle stockings.

Elvira Fraser was perfectly enchanted. No one had paid her this much attention since her own darling Charles who had departed this life believing her to be well provided for, though that had been a full twenty years ago, before this last war. It was a different world today and one's children never turned out quite as one hoped.

Philip Brandon was smiling at her. His dark good looks set her old heart racing so much, for a moment Elvira feared for her health. 'So charming,' she said, showing her yellowed teeth as she simpered at him. 'And *so* dependable.'

'Certainly you may depend upon my services,' he beamed, leaning back in his chair, glancing at his watch as he did so. The air in here was growing stifling. 'I have enjoyed our little chat but unfortunately, Elvira, I have other clients demanding of my time.' He stood up. Hastily, she set down her cup and saucer with a clatter and did the same.

'You will call again? I must see you *regularly*, mustn't I? Now that we are doing business together.'

'But of course. And what a pleasure it will be,' he murmured solicitously. At the door he turned and regarded her with all due seriousness. 'Now if you have any worries, any little thing bothering you, you have only to call.'

'Oh, yes, I do know that, Mr Brandon,' she sighed.

'Philip, please, if we are to be friends as well as business colleagues. You may rest assured that all your affairs will be in safe hands. You need never worry again.' Taking her wrinkled hand, he kissed it. It was the final accolade. Sometimes he made himself sick with such sycophancy.

'Oh,' Elvira breathed. 'Oh, dear me.'

'Good day to you.' And he bowed himself out of the room while she shooed away the little maid, declaring that she would show dear Mr Brandon to the door herself.

'You must call at twelve o'clock next Thursday,' she informed him. 'We will enjoy a small sherry and partake of a light luncheon.' It was a summons not to be ignored.

Somewhere across the lake there was a faint rumble and the waters shivered. 'I would be delighted.' Better than sandwiches on a bench, he thought, but then a picture of black curling hair and a scarlet duffel coat lit like a beacon in his head and he wondered. The memory prompted a question.

'Are you, by any chance, acquainted with a family by the name of Ellis?'

'Ellis? Dear me, now let me think.' Elvira Fraser and her family had lived in the Lake District for almost a century. If the Ellis family held any status locally, then she would know of it.

'Of Keswick?' she brooded, struggling to bring her recalcitrant memory to heel. It was not so biddable these days.

'The south eastern part of the county. High on the fells?'

'Ah, that would be the medical chap, Jeffrey Ellis. Charming man, charming. Played golf sometimes with my darling Charles. Married some jumped up daughter of a quarry owner. Pretty little piece, but opinionated I seem to remember.'

'The family owns a fine house, I believe,' Philip prompted her.

'Yes, of course. Larkrigg Hall, over Broomdale way. Had some wonderful parties in that house as a girl I do recall.' Elvira's eyes glazed, her mind slipping back to pleasanter times and then as quickly sharpened. 'Why do you ask?'

'Met someone who claims to be related. I was curious.'

Elvira Fraser's own curiosity was well and truly aroused. 'No family to speak of, so far as I can recall. No, wait a moment. They had one daughter. Left home over some scandal or other.'

'What kind of scandal?'

'Affair, I shouldn't wonder. Always having affairs, young girls, eh? Particularly during the war.' She cackled with laughter and offered him a leer that in younger days might have been alluring. Philip shuddered.

'This person claims to be the grandchild.'

'Indeed? Well, it might be so. We never saw the Ellis girl again, but then we wouldn't, would we, if she'd gone off to have this child? What is it?' she asked, as if speaking of a puppy.

'A girl. A lovely young girl.'

'How sad. Jeffrey would have enjoyed a granddaughter. A darling man. So kind. Handsome too. Wasted on that creature he married. Dead now, or so I'm told.'

'Mrs Ellis is still alive.'

'She would be. Hard-faced madam.' There was nothing Elvira enjoyed more than a good gossip and today was proving to be most fruitful, in so many ways. 'This granddaughter will come into a tidy sum one day. Violet, no . . . Rosemary, that's the woman's name. I remember it was something silly and flowery. She's the one with the real funds of course. Family made a fortune in copper mining and slate quarrying.'

Philip's mind was racing. The only grandchild of a wealthy

woman. Better and better. Pity about the illegitimacy, and disturbing that Mrs Ellis still refused to acknowledge her, but they could be persuaded into a reconciliation yet. He smiled at Elvira Fraser. 'Now if there is any little thing, don't hesitate to give me a call.' He had such a delicate touch with old ladies.

The storm finally broke just as they'd got the fire blazing and the sausages were only half cooked.

A whole group of them had been enjoying a barbecue by the boathouse. It would probably be the last of the season so they were determined to make it a good one.

The reflection of the fire's flames dancing in the waves was suddenly shattered by a warning shoreward breeze, and broken into a million sparkling remnants of light. Lightning tore open the sky, thunder rolled and the lake seemed to heave like a live thing. The roar of it rumbled endlessly along the valley followed by sheeting rain that put out the fire and drenched everyone in seconds. There were squeals and screams and shouts of laughter as pans and bread rolls were grabbed and people ran for cover into the boathouse.

The girls found towels and dried hair then got on with frying the sausages in the little kitchen while Derry picked up his guitar and started to strum and sing, trying to outdo the noise of the thunder. 'Singing the Blues', 'Love Letters in the Sand' and Tab Hunter's hit, 'Young Love'. These were his current favourites.

His singing sounded so good, making her heart do funny acrobatics, that despite her determination to have nothing more to do with him, Lissa was tempted to abandon the sausages. She sat by his feet, looking up into his face as he sang. She would have liked to stay there for ever.

They drank several bottles of Coca-Cola with supper and there was much speculation about the coming yacht race, a major event at the end of the season.

'This is going to be my year,' Derry boasted and they all laughed.

'To justify your poor old dad spending all his free time building you a fancy boat?'

'Cool it, will you? This boat is a winner. I'll come zooming in first, you'll see. Or die in the attempt.' Lissa jumped, but saw everyone else hide their smiles behind their hands and offer to help him spend the winnings. She guessed this must be an annual resolution.

After supper, since it was still raining, Tony suggested they play some party games, winking at a little brown-haired girl called Helen he'd had his eye on all evening. And so an empty Coca-Cola bottle was found and spun.

Lissa was amazed how often it pointed to Derry whenever it was one of the prettier girls who had spun it. She found herself counting the minutes he was out in the kitchen with them, thinking it grew longer every time.

Once it stopped at her and it took all her courage to walk out of the room with Dave and let him put his cold lips against hers. But only for a minute. She was back so quickly, complaining about the draughty kitchen, that everyone laughed.

Derry didn't look so amused. He was frowning, probably disappointed in her for not being a good sport. So what? She hated these silly parlour games anyway. Who wanted to be kissed by this lot?

Then it was Derry's turn to spin the bottle. At that moment Sam offered her another Coke and almost spilled it as he popped off the metal cap. Laughing, Lissa turned back to find the bottle pointing at her. She could feel her cheeks start to burn as she got up and followed a silent Derry out to the kitchen.

They stood face to face in the darkness, saying nothing, not even looking at each other. She could feel her lips tingling with the expectation of his kiss which confused her somewhat since she'd taken fright the last time he tried. But there was no denying that her heart was hammering so fiercely it cannoned against her rib cage and she was sure he must hear it. Was he never going to speak? Never to kiss her?

It occurred to Lissa with sickening disappointment that perhaps he didn't want to. He was letting this time go by so that everyone would think he was kissing her, imagine he was playing the game, when really he was seeking a way out. The very idea of kissing her obviously repulsed him.

'You don't have to,' she said, her voice sounding weak and unconvincing even to her own ears.

'I know,' he replied. It was not at all what she had wanted to hear. 'I don't suppose you want to either?'

'I didn't say that.' Did she sound too forward? she worried.

Lissa stared at the floor and decided, inconsequentially, that they really should have varnished these floorboards which were all scratched and splintered. Maybe if they put down lino . . .

After a further long moment she could bear the suspense no longer and of its own volition a tiny agonised cry came from her throat. Lissa half turned to the door, desperate suddenly to escape. 'Let's go back,' she mumbled, wanting to die on the spot, wishing this old wooden floor would open up and swallow her.

'No, wait.' Then his hands were on her arms. He was pulling her towards him and the next instant he was kissing her. His mouth was soft and compelling, warm and coaxing, not cruel and hurtful; every bit as exciting as that first time. Except this time was different. This time she was kissing him back. They wrapped their arms about each other and clung as if neither would ever let go. The kissing went on far too long of course, and they returned to the living room looking flushed and rumpled, anxious to avoid each other's eyes and the knowing grins of their friends.

It was a long time before Lissa slept that night. She went over and over the kiss in her mind till a thousand pains of sweet agony pierced her, all mingled with uncertainty, confusion and regret. It had shocked her how much, in that moment, she had wanted him.

Why had she allowed it?

Why couldn't she make up her mind about him?

He could leave any day.

Well, she could leave too.

It was reported that two thousand people a week were emigrating to the Commonwealth; to Australia, New Zealand and Canada. Maybe if she'd gone out with them, gone to look for her mother, she wouldn't have this problem over Derry.

Maybe she should still go.

What a fool she was. Lissa thumped her pillow and squeezed her eyes tight, trying to shut out the picture of his tender smile, the memory of his touch searing her skin, the excitement of his mouth against hers.

She enjoyed her work, had found in Jan the friend she'd always wanted. She was sweet and funny and kind. Practical and sensible and easy to get along with.

They both loved the boathouse, had money in their pockets to spend on fun things, such as a new lipstick or a hooped petticoat which were all the rage. And each week they considered most seriously which singer's latest record to bestow their hard earned shillings upon. This week it might be Guy Mitchell, the next Johnnie

135

Ray or Elvis. Then they would carry the prize home with pride and play it till they knew every word by heart. Life was good.

Now she was risking all of this for a few kisses. Derry only took his music seriously, nothing else. He had every intention of leaving Carreckwater to follow his crazy dream to be famous, and he certainly had no intention of taking her with him when the music world was full of silly screaming girls. She was simply an amusement, to pass the time.

But how could she avoid him? He was Jan's brother, for goodness' sake. And when he left, she would feel abandoned all over again, no doubt end up an old maid sitting on some shelf or other.

Lissa gave up trying to sleep, and throwing off her sheets lay on her back to stare miserably up at the ceiling. The storm rumbled in the distance, moving away, leaving the air still warm but slightly fresher in its wake.

Did she never learn? Gypsies, Teddy Boys, what idiots she chose. But then you couldn't even trust mothers so what hope was there? Hadn't that fact sunk in yet? Hadn't she packed her heart away, where no one could damage it ever again? Not well enough, obviously.

There had been no word from Kath in years, no suggestion that her mother would ever wish to see her. The rejection still rankled, deep down, so all things considered Lissa felt she'd made the right decision in staying in Lakeland. This was her home, where she belonged. Yet she'd wasted years longing for something she couldn't have. Her mother hadn't wanted her, Meg hadn't really wanted her either, being more concerned with loyalty and duty and with a baby of her own. Even a passing gypsy had scorned her friendship. And here she was, risking rejection all over again by falling for a swollen-headed young clerk with his heart set on fame and his eyes on any girl who happened his way.

Lissa closed her eyes again, turned over her hot pillow and curled up, willing sleep to rescue her tortured mind. She told herself firmly that his kisses were part of a game, a giggle at a party. Nothing more.

Perhaps the fault lay in her own naivety. She'd never been kissed by anyone but Derry, after all. She was an innocent, with no experience at all.

Why, for two pins she'd accept a date with someone else. That would show him. Yes, she thought, that might be the answer. And on this comforting thought, Lissa fell asleep.

*　　　*　　　*

136

For some reason Lissa couldn't quite explain, the day of the races brought a flutter of nervous tension to her stomach.

It was a perfect day for a sail, warm and sunny. Puffy white clouds danced across an azure summer sky while the prevailing wind seemed almost eager to fill the white sails and power the little boats along by the unseen miracle of aerodynamics. The lake had never looked more inviting with lacy tips to a blue-grey ruffle of waves.

Competition at the Yacht Club races was always fierce. There were several classes taking part from small dinghies to huge, spanking yachts. Great kudos was attached to winning.

She and Jan had walked down to the little jetty early to watch events, though not as early as Derry who had been trimming sails, checking his mast and rigging, and oiling, scrubbing and greasing since dawn.

'It's tricky, sailing these lakes,' Jan told her. 'The mountains affect the wind currents which are constantly changing. It's important to know how to play it, how to use the wind, whether to put the spinnaker up or not to get the most speed from the boat. One mistake can slow you down and lose the race.'

'Do you think Derry will win?' Wanting him to, very badly.

'He's a good sailor, decisive, which is what you need to be.' Jan considered a moment. 'Perhaps a touch impulsive at times.'

It all sounded most complicated and Derry seemed so young and inexperienced against the rest of the entrants, Philip Brandon being one of them. Lissa could see his yacht with its showy blue sails standing serenly at anchor some way off shore. Derry will never beat that, she thought, and wished it didn't matter.

They found a space on a low wall where they could get a good view of proceedings.

'Wish me luck,' Derry said, appearing at her elbow with a wide grin on his face. He looked so young and eager, handsome in his white T-shirt and navy shorts, hair slick with brilliantine, skin so smooth and bronzed that Lissa felt a surge of longing to put her arms about his neck and kiss him, just as they had done at the party. Her cheeks pinked, almost as if he could read her thoughts.

'Good luck then,' she said, clasping her hands firmly in her lap.

He said, 'Now if I were a knight in shining armour going into

137

combat you might offer me a favour,' and for all he was smiling his brown eyes were serious, almost intense.

'Depends what kind of favour you want.'

He reached out a hand and before she could guess what he was about, slid the ribbon from her hair, releasing her pony tail. The wind at once caught her black curls and whipped them about her face but she only laughed, her face instinctively lifting to his. And as her gaze slid to his mouth she watched it move slowly towards hers.

'That won't help. No pretty ribbon will win you this race.' The deep voice cut in and they both broke away, pretending innocence, as if they had not been irresistibly drawn to taste each other's lips.

'Mr Brandon. What a surprise.' Lissa covered her confusion by desperately trying to gather her hair together and bring it under control. 'How's the jiving these days?'

'I've given it up. Sailing is much easier.'

'You have a fine yacht. I've been admiring it.'

'You must come out on it later,' he said. 'I'll let you take the tiller.'

Derry said, 'There's no need for that, Mr Brandon, thank you. As you can see I have one exactly the same, *The Fair Maid*. My father built her for me. If Lissa wants a sail she can come out on mine.'

Philip Brandon smiled, though it lingered only upon his lips. 'Perhaps she may be permitted to choose for herself. She certainly enjoyed it the last time, did you not, Lissa?'

Lissa's cheeks fired with confusion as she felt Derry's stare upon her.

'The last time?' he asked, very quietly.

'Oh,' she said at last, disturbed by the gleam of admiration in Philip Brandon's eyes and by the undercurrents she could feel flowing between these two who were to be adversaries in this race. 'Really, I'm not sure. I mean, dry land is my favourite place. I know nothing about boats.'

Philip chuckled. 'Nor does my clerk, for all he might think differently.'

Derry was glowering like a sulky child. He longed to say that he didn't care if Lissa had sailed in Brandon's yacht, that he'd grown up with boats, that his father had taught him to sail almost as soon as he could walk, but aware of the sensitive nature of his relationship with this man, and the fact that he had no wish to lose his job, he managed to hold his tongue. Lissa, sensing his problem, spoke up on his behalf.

'You don't need to feel sorry for Derry. He'll manage well enough. I'm not sure you're right about the ribbon though. An emblem of good luck never did any harm, particularly if you believe in it. My own family puts great store by a simple Luckpenny.'

'And Dad is crewing for him,' put in Jan, eyes hot with pride at Lissa's stout defence.

Now it was Philip Brandon's turn to look displeased which he tried to disguise by taking off his peaked cap and running his fingers through his dark hair. 'It isn't luck which wins a race but skill, evaluation of all the relevant factors such as wind, competition and current, and of course perfect planning. Something I am adept at.'

There was a small, awkward silence.

Lissa tried to smile at them both. 'Well, a bit of luck won't go amiss for either of you. That's fair, isn't it? Let the best man win, as they say.'

A gleam came into Philip Brandon's eyes, which she didn't see as she was too busy looking at Derry.

Dark eyes met brown and for a moment the air crackled with tension. Then Brandon relaxed, his smile at its most urbane. 'It should be an interesting contest.' He bowed slightly to Lissa, giving her his most charming smile. 'That dinner invitation still stands, by the way,' and he walked away, leaving Lissa bright red and Derry furious.

The start of a race, Derry knew, was of vital importance. Get this wrong and precious time would be lost, time not easily made up. He had his own stop watch so he could keep an eye on those first vital minutes. He knew when the first shot sounded, the distance he must tack away, and at what moment he must turn so that he was crossing the starting line exactly on the sound of the starting pistol. He knew how and when he should trim his sails, and had worked out his plan for tacking to the first marker buoy to the very last detail.

And it seemed, at first, that everything was working well. Derry got off to a flying start and *The Fair Maid* hummed along, pointing well into the wind.

What he hadn't properly taken into account when he devised his plan was Philip Brandon.

It was Jimmy who noticed him first.

Brandon had taken the opposite approach, going first to port as Derry tacked to starboard, so when Derry went about on to the port tack, he came about too on a starboard one and was heading straight for the *Maid*.

'He's coming a bit fast,' Jimmy called to his son, indicating the approaching yacht, sailing at a killing angle in the wind.

Derry scarcely glanced at it, he was too busy judging how closely he could risk running behind the buoy. 'Don't worry. We'll be well past by the time he reaches us.' He lifted his voice above the slapping waves. 'The rules allow him to come pretty close and try to unsettle us. Only he won't unsettle me.'

'So long as he doesn't risk a collision,' Jimmy muttered, not entirely mollified by his son's confidence. Could he be getting a bit old for this caper? Was that why he was so jumpy? Derry seemed calm enough.

'Ready about,' Derry shouted, as he saw they were approaching the buoy.

Jimmy slipped the sheets from the cleat and held the rope ready, waiting for the next call when Derry had swung over the tiller, then he would let the jib sheet go so that the boom and mainsail could follow it. But before that could happen his attention was caught once more by Brandon's boat.

'Bloody hell, he's cutting it a bit fine. What the . . .? He's letting his sail out. Watch it, Derry, he's swinging this way.'

Derry's face was as white as the sails as he watched Philip Brandon deliberately alter his course so that instead of crossing safely some fair distance behind Derry's yacht, he cut right across the bows, narrowly risking collision. The spray hit Derry in the face, running down him like a cold shower and the boat lurched, very nearly overturning in the wash.

'You damn' fool,' he shouted.

'Scared of a bit of competition?' Brandon called back, and neatly turned about ready for the next tack. 'I told you that bit of ribbon wouldn't help.' His laugh rang out and Jack Callan, who was crewing for him, likewise grinned while the scrap of scarlet, tied to one of *The Fair Maid's* main ropes, waved bravely in the wind.

The next few minutes needed Derry's entire concentration if he was to stay on course and not lose the advantage of his flying start. But anger curdled within. Had he not been an experienced sailor he could very easily have been overturned.

When they were on an even keel again, Jimmy was the first to speak. 'You should bloody well report him for that. Plain bad sailing, that's what it was.' But Derry only shook his head.

'Who would believe me? A mere clerk complaining about his boss. And that boss a real big-wig in the Yacht Club. What do you think I am, Dad, suicidal?'

'It was deliberate.'

'Concentrate. We can still win, which is all that matters.'

The teamwork of father and son was superb, working as one, anticipating the other's thoughts and actions, horn hard hands on sheet and tiller, keeping the weight right, the sails at the proper tension and swinging over at exactly the right moment. At one point Philip Brandon tried a bit of serious blanketing, to rob *The Fair Maid* of vital wind for her sails, but it did no good, she flew over the line several feet ahead, with both Derry and Jimmy yelling for joy.

'We've won.'

Derry was jubilant, barely able to wait to see the girls' faces and wallow in Lissa's admiration for once. He'd won the race for her, hadn't he?

It was much later, after everyone had moored and anchored, that he was called to the committee room. Philip Brandon and several other members were already there, and a very sad-looking official.

'I'm sorry, son, but I have to disqualify you.'

'What?' The blood seemed to seep from Derry's veins. For years he'd dreamed of winning this race. 'I don't understand. I won it easily.'

The official looked even more uncomfortable, clearing his throat, smoothing a hand over his bald head. 'These matters are always difficult, and as you know it's not possible for the committee boat to be everywhere at the same time, to see what's going on, particularly at the start of a race when everyone is so spread out. Mr Brandon here has reluctantly put in a complaint.'

Derry stared blankly at his employer. 'Reluctantly? What kind of complaint?'

'He says you cut too close. If he hadn't taken evasive action you and he would have certainly collided.'

'But he . . .'

'I was on the starboard tack, Derry,' Philip gently pointed out, his face sad, as if he hated to be the cause of these ill tidings. 'And thus had right of way.'

Jimmy opened his mouth to protest, anxious to point out the finer points of the ruling. Right of way or not, Philip Brandon had been the one on the attack. Hell-bent on collision, if he was any judge, which dammit he was after years of racing. But his son kicked his ankle so he closed his mouth again, remembering in time the particular relationship of these two antagonists. Losing a yacht race was preferable to losing a job. He cast a hasty glance at Derry's face, pale but inscrutable you might say, and surprisingly calm. You had to admire the lad for holding his temper.

'And nobody saw what happened?' Derry asked, quiet as you please.

The official cleared his throat again and rubbed his hands together. They made a harsh rasping sound in the quiet of the office. 'As I said, Derry, it's very difficult . . .'

'Yes. Thanks. I understand.' Derry nodded to them both and, turning on his heel, walked out of the room. Once outside he found he was trembling. He thrust his hands deep in his pockets and drew in several harsh breaths to regain control. After a moment he became aware of Jimmy standing quietly beside him.

The two men exchanged a long speaking glance, each telling the other that they understood perfectly what had happened. Philip Brandon had failed to overturn Derry so had put in a fallacious complaint, to get the result squashed. And there wasn't a damn' thing they could do about it.

'Come on, son, I'll stand you a pint.'

'You're on,' Derry said.

Later, the girls wanted to know what had gone wrong. Derry looked at them both, considered telling them the truth then changed his mind. It would only sound like the gripes of a poor loser. 'I lost. That's what went wrong.' What else was there to say?

12

First thing the next morning, astounded by her own daring, Lissa telephoned Philip Brandon at his office.

'Is that offer of a meal still open?'

'Of course,' he said, sounding slightly breathless.

'I'd like to accept then, thanks very much.'

He picked her up on the dot of seven and took her to a very smart little restaurant in Fisher's Gate. What a relief, she thought, that she'd worn a smart little navy and white polka dot dress that just skimmed her knees.

Even so, she felt ridiculously nervous. Lissa told him she'd never been in such a place before, its clientele being the kind of businessmen and visitors who had been least affected by war and the years of austerity since, perhaps even profited from them.

'We've moved into more prosperous times,' he agreed as Lissa looked about her at the plush atmosphere and the candlelit tables, quite outside her experience. 'Never had it so good, isn't that what Mr Macmillan tells us?'

The waiter came and Philip ordered for them both without even consulting her, which surprised her. She felt relieved and strangely irritated all at the same time.

'I could never imagine coming to a place like this with my friends,' she laughed, feeling slightly self-conscious.

'With Derek Colwith? You count him a friend?'

Lissa smiled across the small table at him, quenching the curious disquiet she felt in talking about her feelings for Derry. 'Derry's sister is my best friend.' She saw by his expression that he was not convinced it was quite so simple.

'I would have thought a girl like yourself could do better than my clerk,' Philip said, his handsome face taking on a scathing expression which did not suit him. 'He's a young tearaway who thinks only of himself. Take the yacht race, for example.'

Perversely, though Lissa had said the very same thing about Derry, she now wished to defend him. 'What about the yacht race? Derry had set his heart on winning. I felt rather sorry for him actually, coming so close. But you were the better sailor, evidently.' She smiled, to show how sporting she was.

'I may well be the better sailor, but I can also win without cheating. The trouble with young Derek Colwith is that he is so determined to be the best he is perfectly unscrupulous.'

For a moment Lissa was stunned into silence. 'Why? What did he do?'

'He cheated.'

'Derry? I don't believe it.'

But by the time Philip had finished explaining his version of events she had no choice but to believe it.

'I would never have thought it of him.' Lissa was horrified. She'd come out on this date to prove something, to herself certainly, and to make Derry jealous perhaps. To make him want her so much he'd give up everything for her. Now she felt sickened by this new aspect of his character. 'You say he deliberately tried to create a collision? There could have been a terrible accident. One of you injured.'

'Undoubtedly, save for my own skill, though I have no wish to sound immodest.'

'I'm sure it's the truth.' Lissa's eyes were bleak, her mind so distracted she did not notice when the waiter placed a dish of prawns and salad before her until Philip Brandon gently reminded her.

'May I pour you a glass of wine?' And the conversation moved smoothly on to safer topics but Lissa's appetite had quite gone. She couldn't stop thinking about it.

'You sound as if you weren't surprised that he cheated.'

'I wasn't.'

She considered this reply as she toyed with her prawns and supposed Brandon must know him well enough, since Derry was his clerk. She pushed back a curl that had escaped from her carefully executed chignon which she'd thought made her look especially grown up and sophisticated. 'Then why employ a man you know to be a cheat in your own office?'

The question, asked point blank, seemed to surprise him, as if he were unsure how to answer. Then Philip slid a hand over hers.

'You mustn't fret over Derry Colwith. Leave him to me. He's a young fool with his head in the clouds. You are far too beautiful to waste time over him.' The hand gently squeezed hers and she lifted her eyes to his, reading a message she could not deny. 'You deserve better,' he murmured. 'Someone to care for you as you should be cared for. Someone to give you only the best of everything.'

He liked her. With a tiny shock she saw that he really liked her. Perhaps this was why he objected to her friendship with Derry, Lissa thought, astonished and excited by his flattering words. He thought her beautiful. He thought she deserved the best. Surely this charming, good-looking man couldn't be jealous, could he?

As they ate a delicious meal he got her talking of Broombank and Ashlea, laughing over tales of her childhood with Nick and Daniel. Lissa found she felt quite at ease with him and was almost sorry when the evening ended.

A perfect gentleman to the last, he took her to the door of the boathouse, unlocked it with her key and bade her a polite good night.

'I have so enjoyed our evening. Perhaps we may repeat it some time?'

'I'd like that,' she said, and was surprised to realise that she meant it.

'Hello, Peter. Who's a pretty boy then?' Renee poked a finger between the bars of the budgie's cage but her attempts at friend-ship were met with a loud squawk and a vicious nip from the sharp beak.

'Bloody hell.'

She pulled the finger away and ran to the kitchen tap. No blood appeared but tears stood out in her childlike blue eyes. 'What a day this is,' she mourned, switching on the electric fire, kettle, radiogram and the television set all at once in a fit of pique and unmindful of the huge electricity bill they had recently received.

Music blared out from the one while the television set blinked blankly at her, too early for its programmes to have begun. Peeved, she switched it off again.

'Waste of money, that was,' she said and went to glare out of the window instead. It was, in Renee's view, a typical Lakes day, grey

145

and miserable with rain coming down in stair rods. Poor old Jimboy. He'd hoped to get a bit of fishing in later.

'Anyone would think it was bloody November instead of September,' she mourned. 'And nobody to talk to half the time, what with Jimmy working long hours and Derry never in.'

She'd been glad at first when Jan and Lissa had taken the boathouse. Give Jimmy and me more time on our own, she'd thought. But in the twelve months since then she'd found it hadn't worked out that way. Jimmy worked all hours and she'd found herself more and more alone. Derry was still hanging around, making a nuisance of himself, always argufying with his dad.

'Not that he isn't still fanciable,' she admitted, mouth lifting into a knowing smile. 'That's part of the problem though, isn't it, Peter? Don't do to have two gorgeous men in one house. Particularly when you wouldn't mind sleeping with either of 'em. Not that I would, you understand,' she said, soberly shaking her head at the budgie. 'But thinking about it can have a funny effect on a girl, eh?'

She sat with her hands cradling a mug of tea, her skirt pulled up over bare thighs so she could warm her legs by the glowing bars of the electric fire, and began to plan.

They were having a nice pair of lamb cutlets tonight, baked with a sprinkle of rosemary on top and accompanied by mash potatoes and some nice Batchelor's peas out of a tin. Amazing really that she had taken so well to cooking. There'd never been the opportunity before, not at home where you were lucky if you got a bag of chips. Nor at the Marina Hotel where she worked, skivvied more like, as a waitress, general dogsbody and bottle washer.

Renee hated working at the hotel. Jimmy hated it too. He felt threatened by all the young men she met there.

'Just because I like to dress with a bit of flair,' she constantly assured him, 'men think they can take liberties, cheeky buggers. Forever pinching my bottom they are, and I don't like it. Not while I'm serving 'em, I don't. No respect for women, that's what it is. Not like you, pet.' Then she would kiss him and in no time at all he would feel better. He was a good man, her Jimmy.

'Deserves the very best, don't he, Peter darling?' She reached for her packet of cigarettes and lit one.

Having beaten out its ill temper on its companion in the swinging mirror, the budgie chirruped back, quite equably.

Renee pulled out her own small spotted mirror from her crocodile plastic handbag and, holding it in one hand, started to titivate her hair with the other, cigarette stuck between orange lips, eyes creased against the ensuing curl of blue smoke.

'I'd hand in me notice only I enjoy a bit of money of me own, d'you see? Point of fact, we could do wi' a bit more.'

The budgie attacked its millet spray, quite unconcerned.

'Jimmy works hard all day at the boat yard, comes home knackered sometimes he does. And a tired man ain't no good to woman nor beast.' She laughed. 'You know what I mean, Peter boy?'

He blinked at her through the bars then bashed his bell, just to assure her that he understood perfectly.

'I fancy one of them new Hotpoint washing machines. A Hoover vac and a new electric cooker. So clean they are, you wouldn't credit. And 'oo knows? We might even save up enough for a motor. An 'illman Minx would be nice.' She blew smoke rings up to the yellowed ceiling. 'Ooh, that would be lovely, don't you think?'

A plan had been forming in her mind for weeks now. Sometimes she could hardly sleep, the idea took such a hold on her. She stubbed out the half-smoked cigarette and set off up the stairs to investigate the bedrooms.

There was hers and Jimmy's, the biggest in the house of course. Next to that was Jan's which she had shared with Lissa for a time. At the end of the landing, next to the bathroom, was Derry's. That was only a single but it was a good-sized one all the same. You might fit a three-quarter bed in it if you got a smaller chest of drawers.

Her mind busy with plans she took a tape measure out of her skirt pocket and started to measure.

With these three bedrooms in operation she could take in two, four, five, maybe six guests at ten shillings and sixpence a night bed and breakfast. She started doing sums in her head, got lost and went searching for a bit of paper on the kitchen mantleshelf.

Back upstairs again, satisfied with her arithmetic, she faced her major problem. Jimmy.

First off she'd have to persuade him to convert the loft into a bedroom for them. It had a proper staircase to it, that was one good thing, narrow but solid. But the room itself was a junk heap with cracked floorboards that didn't quite reach the plastered walls, and no electricity. She stood rather gingerly on the floorboards and stared out of the small attic window.

The rain had stopped and though the mountains beyond were still wreathed in mist a faint sun was attempting to break through the grey cloud, sending shafts of sunlight down on to the grey water. Needing no further indication of a brighter day ahead, she could see two elderly couples taking to the water with gusto, pulling up masts and sails, swinging jibs about, wheeling dinghies down the slipway.

'You get a good view of the lake from up here, that's one consolation that might appeal,' she announced to the empty room, so used to talking to the budgie she hardly noticed when it was absent.

But she'd have her work cut out to persuade him though. It wasn't so much the joinery in the loft that would be the problem, if she were honest. Best craftsman in Carreckwater, Jimmy was. Had built their kitchen cupboards easily and with the same spit and polish as the clinker-built boats he worked on for his boss at the yard.

Oh, no. It was the idea of having strangers in his house. Now that might not go down too well at all. She'd have to prove her figures, show him how much money they could make with bed and breakfast. How it was the coming thing, with all the tourists about.

Renee upturned an old box and sat on it, licked the tip of her pencil and started totting up the figures again, just to make sure she'd got them right.

Yes. She could make more money out of letting three bedrooms than she could working four nights a week skivvying at the hotel. They could spend the winter getting ready for next season.

But were there any rules and regulations she ought to know about? she worried. Jimmy would be sure to ask. Stickler for doing things right, he was. Wouldn't want his precious house messed up for nothing.

And then she was back to the most difficult problem of all, which, if she didn't solve it would cause all these plans to go up in blue smoke. Getting rid of Derry. Renee thought about this for some time, chewing on the pencil till it was a frayed soggy mess, as she had used to do with the pencils the teacher gave her at school. Got a right telling off for that she had.

But she was a married woman now, not a schoolgirl, for all she was only seventeen. She could make her own decisions about life. If she wanted to chew pencils, she would chew pencils. If she wanted Derry out, then out he would go. And she could handle Jimmy. When had she ever not been able to handle Jimmy? B and B. That was her future.

And then the solution came to her. Mr Brandon. He was the man to see. He could tell her all about the possible problems and regulations the council might throw at her. And he might also be able to help with Derry.

The rain had stopped and the sun was glinting on pale pebbles and chips of greeny-grey slate, lapped by the waves on the shore. A breeze shuffled across the water and the reflections of cloud and boats and sunbeams broke into a brilliance of disorganised fragments then pieced themselves together again, like a jig-saw. It made Derry feel quite lighthearted as he hurried to the boathouse. The two girls would have finished early since it was half day closing in Carreckwater and he'd made it his habit to take lunch with them every week at this time. Whether there'd be a welcome for him today was another matter.

He wished they hadn't quarrelled. He couldn't really imagine Lissa fancying Philip Brandon. Jan had told him she had family problems that needed dealing with. He'd no idea why he'd bitten her head off in that way. Could he put it right? that was the point.

He almost broke into a run as he passed the bandstand, his heart fluttering in anticipation. He wanted, just once, to see her face light up into a smile when she opened the door to him. Why did she always think the worst of him?

Derek Colwith might like to give the impression of the tough, swaggering man-about-town, but in truth he was as shy and very nearly as inexperienced as Lissa herself. He knew she was jealous of the attention he got when he was singing, and that excited as much as it irritated him.

How could he not enjoy it when all the girls screamed at his music, or hung around waiting for him afterwards? Gave him a good feeling. Made him look real cool to his mates, that did. But he couldn't quite see himself as a lothario. Was that the word? Though he'd given it a try, it hadn't proved quite so successful as he'd expected. Up close, they unnerved him a bit with their long nails and bright pink lipstick. Girls liked you to spend money on 'em and that was his main problem, he decided. Money.

Money was something he would never have if he stayed at Brandon's, a small, rather down-at-heel solicitors.

In any case he was no fool. He had no wish to get stuck with the wrong girl. Derry believed he could afford to be choosy. He was going to be famous, wasn't he? Some days he thought that girl might be Lissa Turner. Other days, when they quarrelled, he thought not. He couldn't quite make her out. She'd thawed a bit recently but still kept him very much at arm's length. And they never had a minute to themselves. He was sure she positively encouraged Jan to hang around. Maybe she only tolerated him because he was Jan's brother.

Once he got a recording contract, then the money would really start rolling in. Derry had no doubt that given the opportunity he could make it big. The fact that half the teenage boys in the country had the same dream did not occur to him. He was special because he was Derry Colwith.

She'd take more notice of him then, wouldn't she?

He clucked to the ducks as he swung along, whistling happily, his natural optimism restored, keeping well back so the ducks didn't follow him. He took no notice of the people sitting upon the green benches as he sprinted up the steps to the boathouse. His heart was racing, much to his own astonishment, and he bounced from one foot to the other with impatience as he waited for Lissa to open the door.

It took no more than five seconds and there she was, exactly as he had imagined she would be.

'Hello.'

'Hello.'

He itched to leap across the doorstep and take her in his arms but knew his nosy sister might appear at any moment with a bowl of chicken soup and her weekly lecture.

For several magical moments he had the joy of simply looking at her. 'Sorry I'm late.'

'Don't be silly. You're early.' He was always early. Could hardly wait to get to the boathouse. He could scent the sweetness of her skin, and the longing to run his hands over the slim curves of her back and up into those silky black curls was almost overwhelming. She still hadn't let him cross the threshold, nor had he noticed.

'It's turning colder.'

'Yes.'

'Winter coming on, I suppose.'

'Hm.'

They talked like strangers and looked at each other like lovers.

'I'm sorry about the other night. You've every right to go out with whom you please.'

150

'It was a legal matter. Family business, that's all,' she said, wondering why she felt the need to explain. 'I over-reacted.'

'No, no. Like you said, none of my business. I shouldn't have rushed you. Right blockhead I am. Won't do it again.'

'It's OK.'

'Will you go out with me?' he blurted out, at once breaking his promise. Oh God, he thought, I've messed it up again. What is the matter with me? No wonder she simply stared at him. Probably thought him raving mad, wondering how to let him down easy and get rid of him without giving offence.

Lissa was in fact too stunned to speak. Blushing hotly she felt oddly trapped as he set one hand at each side of her head on the door frame. Yet she could easily walk away into the living room if she wanted to. Not that she did want to. She couldn't move a muscle in fact. Her legs had quite turned to jelly. 'I-I don't know,' she said at last, looking up at him through lowered lashes. Waiting. When the kiss came, with only their lips touching, she felt a shudder of desire run right through her like an electric current. It was as if her mouth had found sanctuary and yet opened the rest of her body to an excitement she had never believed possible.

'Lunch is ready,' called Jan's voice from the kitchen and they broke hastily apart, giving a half laugh, embarrassed, as if she had actually come and caught them.

But if Jan had missed the kiss, more than half the people on the lakeshore benches certainly hadn't. They had thoroughly enjoyed the moment, sighing as they remembered sweet young love.

Except for one gentleman in a pinstripe suit, who not only sat frowning his deep displeasure into his uneaten sandwiches but was coming swiftly to the conclusion that more drastic action was called for, if this situation were not to escalate quite out of control.

Renee Colwith stood before Miss Henshaw wearing what could only be described as her mulish expression.

'I'll wait,' she said.

'Mr Brandon has appointments well into the afternoon,' replied Miss Henshaw through pursed lips. It wasn't true but she didn't believe it gave a good impression for the General Public to imagine they could simply walk into a solicitor's office and be seen right away. Oh dear me, no. Particularly a madam such as this one who was clearly no better than she should be.

151

'He will see me,' Renee insisted, bending her knees slightly so she could peer under the gold lettering on the glass panel of the inner office door to see if anyone was inside.

Miss Henshaw was incensed by such impertinence and stood up at once, ready to bar the way with her own frail body if need be.

'You should have rung for an appointment,' she chided.

Renee laughed. 'The only bells that get rung in our house are in the budgie's cage.' She resented the secretary's hard gaze, judging, making assumptions. And after she had put on her best pink fluffy wool coat and black gloves too.

The stand-off might have continued indefinitely had not Philip Brandon chosen to return early from his lunch that day. Disturbed by the sight of the girl he desired being man-handled by his own clerk, his appetite had been quite ruined. He'd waited too long it seemed and fear was thick in him.

'Yes?' he barked, as he saw a young girl with an orange smiling mouth, bright pink coat, and the most ridiculous bleached blonde hair, hopping about on heels that were drumming holes into his office lino.

Trapped into making the introduction, Vera Henshaw made plain her disapproval of such an unexpected visitation by introducing Renee as 'this lady'.

'This lady is desirous of speaking with you,' she began. 'I told her you were engaged, and have offered to make her an appointment later in the week.'

'It'll only take five minutes,' Renee assured him, batting her spiky eyelashes furiously, which usually did the trick where men were concerned. This one, however, wasn't even looking at her.

Had Philip paused long enough for an introduction it is doubtful whether Renee, with her close relationship to one particular young man, not in favour at that precise moment, would have got past the door. But in his current mood he had no more patience for his secretary than his client. He stormed past both of them, burst into his office and flung off his coat in a single movement of fluid rage.

'Right,' he said. 'I can spare you two.'

It was enough.

Renee's voluptuous body wriggled with delight as she cast Miss Henshaw a sweetly venomous smile and sashayed into the inner sanctum, shutting the door with a cheery wiggle of her fingers through the window.

When she had finished telling Philip Brandon what it was she wanted, he reached past her and drew the green blind down over the glass.

'Sit down please, Mrs Colwith. I think you and I should talk.'

Derry had been given the task of calling upon Elvira Fraser to ask her to sign a document for the bank. The old lady was disappointed that it wasn't Philip himself, naturally, but warmed instantly to the fresh-faced young man who was shown into her parlour.

'Do please sit down,' she encouraged. 'Would you care for some tea? Indian or Earl Grey?'

Not understanding what she was talking about, Derry politely declined. If he got this over with quickly he would have time to call in and chat with the girls, assuming the old dragon wasn't anywhere about. He explained his need to hurry to Mrs Fraser in more diplomatic terms.

'Mustn't be seen to be wasting time,' he joked, bringing a smile to the old lady's drooping mouth.

'Admirable, admirable. Not all young men would see it in that light. But Mr Brandon would inspire loyalty in his staff. He is such a caring man.'

Derry made a non-committal grunt. 'I've brought you a form to sign, something to do with releasing funds.'

She reached for her glasses and hooked them on her long nose as he handed her the papers. 'Ah, yes, this will be concerning the investments I referred to. Now, should I read it, do you think?'

Derry inwardly groaned. If the old dear read every word on these two close-packed pages she might well ask all manner of questions to which he did not know the answers and a proper cluck-head he would look. It might as well be Greek for all the sense it made to him.

'I shouldn't worry,' he said, anxious to be off.

'Will I have enough income to keep on my dear housekeeper, do you think? And then there is the man who does my garden. I really couldn't manage it on my own.'

She fiddled anxiously with the rings on her plump fingers and Derry felt suddenly sorry for her. Old and vulnerable, Elvira Fraser reminded him of his own gran who used to test him on his homework as a boy. 'Never get anywhere if you don't ask questions,' she'd been fond of telling him. Never missed a trick, his old gran. But his gran had been poor, Elvira Fraser was rich. House by the lake, servants, what was he worrying about? She was loaded.

And if there was something Mrs Fraser didn't understand about the document and he explained it all wrong, then he'd be the one to get it in the neck. Best to leave it.

'I'm sure Mr Brandon will explain it all to you when he calls next time.' Derry stood up and held out the pen he'd brought with him for the purpose.

Elvira smiled at the young man, charming of course but clearly not up to the task set him today. Yet what did it matter? It would give her a lovely excuse to invite Philip to luncheon, and he could explain it all then. They could have salmon mousse. Oh, how she loved salmon. And finish with a nice glass of port.

'Very well, dear boy. Now, where do I sign?'

It was the Monday following Renee's discussion with Philip Brandon that Derry burst into Stevens Drapery, his face crimson with outrage. 'What do you think she's done? She's put me in the garden shed.'

Jan and Lissa stared at him for a moment, nonplussed. 'Who has done what?'

'Renee. She says she wants my room and she's put my bed in the shed. I'm to sleep in there or get out. She says I can please myself.'

Both girls exchanged a long glance, then burst into merry peals of laughter.

'It isn't funny.' Derry sounded deeply hurt. 'It'll be damn' cold out there this winter.'

'You could buy a paraffin lamp. Weren't you a boy scout?' his unsympathetic sister suggested.

Derry took out his comb and began to smooth back his quiff as he always did when he was agitated. 'I wondered if I might kip down on the floor at your place?'

'Well, you can think again,' Jan told him as Lissa's heartbeat quickened, though whether from fear or excitement she couldn't rightly have said.

'Why is she throwing you out?' Lissa asked.

'Would you believe she's going to do bed and breakfast? It's all your fault, Lissa. You started her on this cooking lark.'

Lissa couldn't help but giggle at the look of astonished outrage on his face. 'Why shouldn't she do bed and breakfast? Sounds like a good idea to me. But that isn't till next season surely?'

154

'Claims she needs to redecorate and refurbish. She's got Dad doing over the loft to use as a bedroom for them.'

'Fumigate your room, more like,' Jan said, hurrying behind the counter safe from any retaliation. 'You'd best get out of here before our Stella catches you. Like a bear with a sore head she is this morning. The last thing I need is my notice because of your troubles.'

'But where am I to sleep? I might catch pneumonia in a shed,' Derry mourned. 'I'd rather stay at your place.' He'd taken quite a fancy to the idea of staying at the boathouse. He could get all his meals made without any effort on his part, and see Lissa every day. A nagging landlady clocking him in and out was not his idea of a peaceful life.

Jan rolled her eyes heavenward. 'Why should we help you?'

Because if he couldn't find a room, he might leave, Lissa thought. But later that evening Jan made it perfectly plain that this idea did not even reach the starting post.

'You'll have to ask around town,' she said, and Lissa had to agree it was for the best. And so the matter was settled.

13

Autumn was coming to Carreckwater. The numbers of visitors had declined. Families had gone home, children had returned to school, students to their universities and colleges. A different breed of tourist occupied the narrow streets.

Elderly couples not tied to school holidays came to enjoy a little gentle walking. Gentlemen in good sound windcheaters, ladies in sensible twin sets and tweed skirts, woollen socks and walking shoes. And both sexes sporting cherry wood walking sticks and little trilby hats.

The locals seemed to heave a deep sigh of relief and returned to their favourite haunts in the pubs and on the lakeside benches, reclaimed the pathways and streets for their own use, pulled down the shutters on their guesthouses, left their summer occupations and started their winter activities in the numerous societies that proliferated in the town: bellringing, flower arranging, photography and amateur dramatics.

Along the lakeshore the water seemed to lap more loudly and across in the woods could be heard the sound of chattering red squirrels and the bark of deer.

Now was the time to pick up real life again with the promise of a restful, quiet autumn and winter ahead. Now was the time, Lissa decided, to pay a visit home.

Meg had written asking her to go home in the summer but she'd been too busy with the tourists. Now she could ask Derry for a lift in his new van, knowing it was only an excuse, for she was itching to show him off. She was almost sure that Meg would like him. How could she not when Lissa adored him?

The sun came out to match her buoyant mood. Puffs of cloud bounced perversely across an azure sky that the summer visitors would not have believed possible in the last drenched weeks of August. The mountains preened themselves in their new cloak of gold and there was that special scent in the air, of moist earth and crisp leaves, bonfires and woodsmoke.

'This van of yours. I don't suppose you'd give us a run in it?' Lissa asked the very next time she saw him, and explained how she longed to go home to Broombank and see Meg and Tam. 'I was hoping Miss Stevens would allow me an extra day off but she won't hear of it. So it will have to be a day trip. I thought perhaps Sunday. It's ages since I saw them and it's difficult to get home without transport.'

His heart leapt. A whole day out with Lissa alone. 'Rightio. You're on,' he said, brown eyes gleaming.

'Great.' Lissa turned to Jan. 'You'll come too, Jan? I'd like you to meet Meg.'

Jan looked pleased to be asked but suggested, catching the frown on her brother's face, that she might be in the way.

'Don't be silly. We're friends, aren't we?' And Lissa hugged her, just to prove it.

''Course we are,' Jan agreed, and beamed over Lissa's shoulder into Derry's scowling face.

It was almost seven months since she had last been home and though Lissa felt a little unsure of her reception she couldn't wait to see them all. She strained her head for the first glimpse of the familiar white-walled farmhouse crouching in the lee of Dundale Knot. She wanted it to look exactly the same, hoping nothing at all had changed.

Ruff, Rust's grandson, was waiting at the farm gate as they drew up, tail wagging, tongue lolling, ready to bounce all over her long before she had climbed out of the van.

'Hallo, old boy,' Lissa said, kneeling down beside him in the grass while he leapt about her in such a frenzy of delight he was quite beside himself. 'I've missed you too,' she laughed. 'I've missed you all.' Then he rolled over, grinning, and permitted her to rub his tummy.

Meg and Tam came running down the fells where they'd been checking the sheep, Meg happy and smiling, looking almost girlish.

There were tearful hugs and kisses which set Ruff off all over again.

'It's lovely to see you all,' Lissa declared on a happy sigh. 'And to see the fells again.' She gazed upon them with affection and thought the crisp fronds of bracken had never looked more like a matted bronze beard, left behind by some ancient Viking. Familiar sounds rushed in, of hens clucking about the yard, sparrows squabbling in the hedge, the moan of the wind through the ash trees. And the dearly loved scents of green grass and woodsmoke.

When she returned her gaze to Meg, it was to find her glancing across at the two smiling visitors, a query in her grey eyes.

'Oh, sorry. This is Jan Colwith, my best friend.' Lissa felt proud to be able to introduce her as such.

Jan stepped forward, hand outstretched. 'I'm so pleased to meet you at last, though I feel I know you already.'

Meg smiled an acknowledgement of Jan's words but her eyes slid across to Derry.

Lissa had grown so used to Derry's outlandish style, knowing it didn't give a full picture of his complex personality she had come to ignore it. It didn't affect the way she felt about him, particularly when he kissed her, which she wanted him to do at every opportunity. It was the most delicious experience in her life and she wondered now why she had ever felt so alarmed about it.

But looking at him through Meg's eyes, her heart shrivelled a little inside. He cut an odd-looking figure in a leather jacket, narrow black trousers, huge crêpe-soled shoes and string tie. A skiffle king with a fancy to be a cowboy?

Is this the best my darling girl can do? the grey eyes said. Is this why I brought her up with such care, to have her throw herself away on the first dandy that crosses her path? All this was evident, and more, in the set of Meg's mouth, the tightness of the skin around her shrewd eyes, the whole stance of her body.

And Lissa could see that Derry too had noted some hint of disapproval for he'd adopted his defensive, insolent look.

Lissa drew in a deep breath. 'And – this is Derek, Jan's brother.' She could have kicked herself for the slight hesitation in her voice, and the way she had avoided linking him with herself. 'He prefers to be called Derry.'

There was a long awkward pause as Meg made no move towards him.

Then Derry, responding to Lissa's fierce stare, took a step forward and held out his hand.

159

'Howdy,' he said, as if he really were a US Marshal, and Lissa inwardly cringed.

'Good afternoon,' Meg coolly responded, not taking her hands from the pockets of her jeans. For a moment the awkwardness deepened before Tam slapped Derry on the shoulder and ushered them all inside.

'So good it is to see you, we're forgetting our manners, are we not? I'll put the kettle on. Meg, you fetch out that fruit cake you made the other day, since we haven't got a fatted calf.'

Everybody laughed and the moment of tension passed.

An hour drifted by pleasantly enough with Lissa learning all the latest news and gossip, though the conversation grew stilted at times. Derry did not say a word and nobody spoke to him. He sat and gazed upon them all with impudent arrogance on his face and Lissa chewed on her fingernails and worried.

Tam finally excused himself, saying he'd catch them a rabbit for tea. 'Would you be wanting to come with me, lad?' he asked Derry, who blenched and shook his head.

'N-no thanks. I'm OK here.'

Tam chuckled and went off whistling.

Lissa recognised a flicker of annoyance in Meg's eyes, as if she'd been hoping that Derry would disappear in a puff of smoke and leave them alone. So she hurriedly started to talk about the draper's shop, anything to lighten the atmosphere.

'You wouldn't believe how old fashioned it is and what little help we get from Miss Stevens. She spends all her time in the office though what she does there I can't imagine. I'd love to be let loose on the place,' Lissa declared, suddenly realising that she meant it.

Meg, scraping potatoes for lunch at the kitchen sink, looked up in surprise. 'Why, what would you do with it?'

'I could make it beautiful. And profitable.' Lissa's sudden flush of excitement increased as she considered the idea, seeking confirmation from her two friends. 'I'd get rid of all that old stock for a start, and bring in something quite new.'

'Paint the front,' Jan suggested, coming to sit at the pine table with her. 'Get rid of that awful pea green.'

'Oh, yes. And turn that draughty old stock room into a second display area. There's plenty more space upstairs after all, for the extra stock.'

160

'Oh, my, will you listen to her? Why not open two floors while you're at it,' Jan quipped.

'Why not?' Lissa laughed, blushing bright pink.

Meg rinsed the potatoes, put them in a pan and set it on the stove with a clatter. Then she checked the progress of the meal. A casserole of pork in cider with whole onions was bubbling nicely in the oven. For afters she had made a lovely apple pie, spiced with a pinch of cloves. It would go down well with a hunk of home-produced, crumbly cheese. She wiped her hands on a cloth and took off her apron.

'You seem happy anyway,' she said, forcing her voice to sound pleased and wondering why she wasn't.

'Oh, we are. Life's great.'

Meg wanted Lissa to be happy, she really did. If only Carreckwater were nearer, and they saw a bit more of her. And if only she wouldn't pick up every bit of rubbish she felt sorry for. First gypsies, now Teddy Boys. Meg felt the familiar fear in the pit of her stomach. Didn't Lissa realise how unreliable men were?

'Tell me about this boathouse you live in,' she said, wanting to get away from the subject of a shop, which in Meg's opinion was not good enough for Lissa.

So the girls told how they had come upon their lovely boathouse, how they had cleaned it up and attended auctions and sales to find furniture for it.

'Now we are helping Derry look for a place,' Lissa finished with a grin.

'Really?' said Meg vaguely, glancing across at Derry who was strolling around the living room, peering into corners, opening cupboard doors. She got up from the table and followed him. 'Are you looking for something?'

'Your record player. Wondered what kind of music you cats play. Are you cool or square?' His eyes challenged her, the insolence almost mocking now. Derry hated to be ignored.

'We have no electricity here, as yet. But I think we have an old wind-up gramophone and some ancient records upstairs if you like?'

'No electricity?'

'No.'

'No television set?'

Meg shook her head, grey eyes growing annoyed at the inquisition.

'I'd settle for a washing machine myself, or a vacuum cleaner. Five years they've promised us, then we'll be on the national grid and can start catching up with the rest of the world. I'll believe it when I see it.'

Derry gazed at her in awe, a life without the gadgets of the twentieth century being quite beyond his comprehension. 'How do you survive?'

'We get by.'

'Renee couldn't.'

'Renee?'

'My – stepmother.' He hurried on, not wanting to be questioned further on that particular relationship, 'Doesn't it get a bit, well – quiet?'

Meg allowed herself a wry smile. 'Believe it or not, Derry, we quite like it that way.' Except that sometimes, without Lissa, it had been a bit too quiet recently, she thought, but refrained from saying so. You had to learn to let your children go, she scolded herself for the umpteenth time, however hard it might be. But not to this creature, for God's sake. Spinning on her heel Meg left Derry to puzzle it all out and returned to the kitchen. She'd do everything she could to put a stop to that young man's arrogant ambitions, certainly as far as Lissa was concerned.

After lunch Lissa offered to show Jan and Derry around her home. They were halfway out the door when Meg stopped them.

'We're a farm, remember, and the lanes are muddy,' she reminded Lissa, eyeing the pretty blue shoes with the kitten heels. 'Had you forgotten?' Meg tried to make a joke of it but she felt awkward, out of touch with Lissa, as if her own daughter were a stranger to her. 'Not really suitably dressed, are you? You look so different.'

She hadn't meant to say anything of the sort. She hadn't wanted it to show that she felt faded and tired and uncomfortable with this newly minted, coolly sophisticated young miss who had replaced her own laughing, lively country girl. But then that girl had vanished long since, in a muddle of adolescent emotion. It was sad really that daughters had to grow up at all, Meg decided.

Lissa was bridling at the implied criticism. 'Sorry. I wanted to look smart for you, that's all.'

'So I see.' Now all the wrong words came tumbling out. 'Fancy

162

shoes, lipstick, eye shadow. Is that mascara on your lashes? And what makes your skirt stick out like that?'

'A paper nylon petticoat. Do you like it? I starch it with sugar.' Lissa spun about to show it off then flushed slightly as she saw Derry's smile out of the corner of her eye.

'Paper nylon? Whatever next?' Meg said, wiping the table top with unnecessary vigour. 'You must be earning plenty of money then?' She bit her lip, realising she sounded silly and mean.

'I earn enough.'

Tam laughed in his cheery way, as if it were all great fun and the air was not crackling with an undercurrent of tension. 'I think I'm a bit out of touch with your young world,' he said.

'You and me both,' Meg agreed sharply.

Wellingtons had to be found for them all since Jan's shoes were even sillier and Derry's were quite beyond the pale for farm lanes. But there was no shortage of sensible footwear in the Broombank kitchen. Yet the fact that she had forgotten to come properly shod seemed to be a black mark in some way. Lissa felt hurt by this unspoken criticism, seeing it again as a form of rejection.

Lissa walked her friends down to Allenbeck, telling them how she used to dam up the stream and catch minnows. 'We even found a baby kingfisher here once,' she said. 'I raised it myself, then let it fly free.'

'Did you ever fall in?' Derry teased.

'Oh, yes, I expect so,' Lissa agreed. The memory of the disappointment she had felt that day rose with bitter clarity into her mind. 'There was the odd occasion, I'll admit. But not too often.'

'Don't believe a word of it. She fell in all the time,' said a voice from above. 'When she wasn't throwing others in, that is.' Then Lissa was scrambling up the bank and both Derry and Jan watched in amazement as she flung herself into the arms of a tall, broad-shouldered, fair-haired young man with a round, laughing face.

'Oh, Nick. I am *so* glad to see you,' Lissa said. 'Let me look at you.'

'Let *me* look at you.' He held her away from him so he could let his gaze wander over her. At the smart bell-skirted dress and matching jacket, the bow at the neat waistline at odds with the cumbersome wellies.

It was the fashion to look rather grand and snooty and Lissa carried the style off to perfection with her long neck and easy grace. She'd pinned her hair up in a French pleat, letting tendrils curl free on her forehead, and her skin still had that golden quality, as if she had been kissed by the sun. Her eyes were as darkly mysterious as ever, made more so by a whisper of blue eye shadow. He let out a low whistle. 'My word, Meg's right. What a picture. Quite the young woman about town, eh?'

Lissa, flushed with happiness and pleasure, pulled a wry face. 'I wore the wrong clothes. Meg disapproves. Should have put my jeans on only . . .'

'You wanted to show off, as usual?'

'Horrible boy.' And Lissa laughed, feeling happy and light-hearted at last, then hugged him again. 'How well you do know me. You look just the same, Nick,' she said, feeling pleased that he did.

'Still a country bumpkin, you mean?'

She aimed a playful slap at him. 'No, I don't.'

Nick's gaze strayed over Lissa's head and came to rest upon the other two. 'And these are your friends?'

His amused, half questioning glance told plainly what he thought of Derry and Lissa felt her cheeks grow hot with embarrassment, though she hated herself for it. She wished she'd asked Derry to wear something a bit less − provoking, to tone down his stylish image a bit. But it was too late now. The damage, if that's what you could call it, was done.

Nick, however, had released her and was making his way over to Jan. There was no amusement in his eyes now as he stretched out one broad rough hand to her, carefully wiping it on his working trousers first.

'Hello,' he said. 'You must be Jan.'

She nodded, and Lissa waited for some pithy response, her friend rarely one to be stuck for words. None came. Jan simply stood there, her hand swallowed up in his, smiling up at Nick for so long it almost became embarrassing.

Lissa met Derry's questioning glance with a smile and gave a polite cough. 'How are Sally Ann and Daniel?'

Nick dropped Jan's hand only with reluctance and on the walk back up to the house told his family news.

'Grandad is back at Grange-Over-Sands, still trying to get the hang of retirement. At least that's how he sees it.' Nick chuckled. 'He'll no doubt think of some excuse to abandon Connie for Ashlea before too long. Meanwhile we're enjoying the rest.'

They all laughed and Lissa had to explain that Joe really wasn't as bad as everyone said. 'He has his own rather narrow view of life, that's all.'

'Very like you in fact,' Nick agreed, then realised his blunder by the stiffness that came to her mouth, for she and Joe were in no way related so how could she be like him? He hurried on to talk about his brother. 'Daniel's taken himself off to college to be a vet, would you believe?'

'Oh, good for Daniel. And Sally Ann?'

'Mum's the same as ever. Always busy. Nothing ever gets her down. She'll want to see you.' He cast a half glance in Jan's direction. 'All of you.'

'Of course.'

Nick's grey eyes, so like Meg's own, rarely left Jan's small, pixie face. He stayed by her side as they walked back to the house for tea, asking her about the shop and how she spent her free time. Jan, seemingly overcome with unaccustomed shyness, answered in monosyllables.

To Lissa's delight she saw that Sally Ann had arrived and further kisses and introductions were exchanged before everyone settled before a table laden with salad, fresh fruit and yet more cake. A delicious feast over which Meg had plainly taken considerable trouble. But when she placed a slice of rabbit pie before Derry he went as pale as the tablecloth.

'I-is this one of the r-rabbits I saw Tam bring in earlier?' He could clearly recall the sight of their dangling, bloodied heads. And when Meg agreed that it was, he fled through the kitchen to the lean-to and threw up what remained of his dinner.

Everybody thought it highly amusing. Only Meg and Lissa didn't laugh.

After the meal had been cleared away the men went out to check the sheep. And while Lissa helped Meg with the washing up, Sally Ann settled in the ingle-nook with her knitting. Plumper than ever as she approached middle age, yet she had the same open friendly smile which gave a sweet, girlish quality to the round cheeks. She had never been known to raise her voice or lose her temper with anyone, not even with Joe.

But she was far more shrewd than her benevolent smile might reveal. She'd seen the way her elder son paid special attention to this pleasant-faced young woman with the straight brown hair. Had sat next to her, passing plates, talking more than she'd heard from him in a long while. But the girl seemed sensible enough, apart from those daft shoes. Taken them off now and was sitting curled up on the floor at her feet, watching Sally Ann's needles fly, eyes creased in amazement as if she didn't want to miss a stitch.

'Lissa told me how you all knitted the whole time but I didn't really believe her,' Jan said, and Sally Ann chuckled.

'Dalesfolk always have their knitting by them,' she said. 'In the old days it was men and women alike, shepherd or farmer's wife, at work or play. Though admittedly not so much now. Too many other demands upon our time. Must have been grand before the war with lots of hired men working on the land and servant girls in the kitchen to do all the rough work. Those were the days, eh, as Joe is so fond of telling us.' She wanted to ask the girl what she thought of her lovely son but couldn't quite frame the words.

'What is that stick coming from your belt?'

'This is the sheath, or knitting stick, which holds one needle. Very special these are, often lovingly carved and passed on through the generations, as is the skill of knitting from mother to daughter. Stockings were the favourite in the Kendal area. When I first started, I knit me first pair so tight they could stand on their own.' She burst out laughing and Jan joined in. 'Over Dentdale way they go in more for jerseys. Have you never tried knitting then?'

Jan gave a shamefaced smile. 'I did some corkwork once, at school. You know, knitting with a safety pin on four nails hammered into a bobbin? Ended up with yards and yards of rainbow-coloured coils that I hadn't the first idea what to do with.'

Sally Ann liked the easy way the girl chatted and smiled. No side to her, that was for sure, nor dressed quite so daft as her brother. Happen Nick could do worse. It was hard for a man on these fells. Neither sight nor sound of a woman for weeks on end. 'Would you like to have a go?'

'Oh, do you think I could?'

And so a chair was brought, a set of needles and ball of Herdwick wool found. 'We put the ball in our apron pocket or in a yarn bowl on the floor. In the old days the women would hang it from their belt so they could knit wherever they went, even walking to the market at Kendal. Important source of income it was.'

Sally Ann's work worn hands guided Jan's fumbling fingers, urging her to keep short needles and work as close to the tips as she could for a better speed. 'Let your body weave with the rhythm and once you've got going you should strike each loop faster than the eye can see.'

Jan's efforts were very far from this ideal and several dropped stitches had to be found and retrieved before she got the hang of it. But by the time Nick and the other menfolk returned the first lesson was well under way with a narrow inch of grey knitting to show for her efforts. Nick took the seat opposite so he could watch, an odd smile of pride and pleasure upon his homely face. And for some reason, Jan found that she had entirely lost all of that carefully acquired rhythm.

Lissa stood on the knoll gazing up at Dundale Knot and breathing deeply of the clear air, letting it bubble inside her like champagne.

'I love this place. Carreckwater is pretty, and great fun but I do miss all this majesty, all this freedom of space.'

'You can come back any time,' Meg said at her elbow.

Lissa turned to gaze at her foster mother. She thought Meg seemed quieter these days, a rather sad and lonely figure. No more babies had come and she would be forty next year. Lissa wanted to wrap her arms about her and say how sorry she was to have caused the loss of that precious burden, but Meg was moving away from her, saying something that brought Lissa's wandering attention to heel quite sharply.

'What did you say?'

Meg turned to her. 'I said where on earth did you find him? He's not at all the sort of boy I would've expected you to bring home.'

'Derry?'

'Yes, Derry. Even the name is rather silly.'

'Why? What's wrong with it, or with him?' Lissa was instantly on the defensive.

Meg gave a self-conscious little laugh. She'd spoken her thoughts out loud when really she shouldn't have but it was far too late to call them back. She ploughed on, hoping to make Lissa understand how anxious she felt. 'I should have thought that was obvious.'

'Not to me.'

'Look at his clothes. We may live high on the remote fells but we read the newspapers, we listen to the radio for all we haven't yet got the wonders of television and – what was it? Oh, yes, record players. We are nevertheless aware of the trouble such people have been causing.'

'Such people?' Lissa could feel a cold sensation creep into her stomach. Why could they never now be friends as they used to be, a long, long time ago? 'He isn't a separate breed. Anyway, what sort of trouble?'

'Teddy Boys. Ripping up cinema seats, that sort of thing. We've read all about it.'

'Derry never ripped up a cinema seat in his life. He wouldn't know how to start.'

Spots of colour marked each high cheek bone but Meg's lips remained tight and thin, determined to stick to her point. 'Nevertheless, he seems a bit common, don't you think? Unreliable. Not at all the sort of boy we would have chosen for you.'

'Then it's a good thing I can choose for myself,' said Lissa tartly, feeling the sinking of misery in her stomach as the gulf between them widened. And she had hoped to bridge it today, to bring them close again.

'You're too young to make choices,' Meg unwisely said. 'It's too easy to make mistakes when you are young.'

Lissa struck back in the only way she knew. 'Like you objected to my choosing to write to my own mother?'

Meg's face was the colour of cold ash. 'I was afraid for you. I wanted to keep you, yes, I'll admit. But I was afraid it might not work out with Kath, that she'd make you feel even more rejected.'

If the words made sense Lissa was no longer receptive to it. Meg had disapproved of her own and Jan's silly high heels, and of her new dress. She'd commented upon the hair so carefully pleated on top of her head with pin curls curling on each cheek. And worst of all, she had criticised Derry. 'I needed to understand *why*. Why my mother didn't simply drop everything when she realised she was having me. Why I wasn't the most important thing in the world to her.'

Meg did not reply. She could not. It all seemed so long ago. How could she explain the hurt, the passion, the lost hopes and fears of that time to this young woman who saw everything in black and white, and only as it related to herself. Lissa was young and selfish as all girls were, as Kath had been. But Meg couldn't say that. It would be too unkind. She had often thought how unfair it was that the major decisions of one's life had to be made when one was often too young to make the right ones.

'There was a war on,' was all she could say. 'It changed things.'

'I don't believe that.' Lissa spat out the words, stepping back from Meg, as if wanting to distance herself from the simple truth. 'Anyway, the war has been over for years. Everyone is entitled to know who they are, where they came from, what makes them behave in a certain way. You never gave me that chance.'

'I told you about Kath, about both of us and – and Jack. I told you what happened. I did my best.'

'Eventually you did, but much too late. The damage had been done.'

Meg looked Lissa squarely in the face but she did not beg for understanding now. She showed annoyance, that she was fighting an unjustified attack. 'What damage? I told you what I thought you were old enough to understand. I loved you. I wanted to protect you.'

Lissa gave a grunt of disbelief, hot tears standing proud in her eyes, wanting to extricate herself from the terrible hurtful words pouring into her head and out her mouth but unable to do so. 'If that were true you wouldn't have needed a baby. But you did, so you couldn't possibly have loved me.'

Meg jerked with shock and at last she did raise her voice, the anger in it sharp and acrid. 'That's a terrible thing to say.'

14

The two women faced each other, hot with dismay and frustrated emotion. 'I have this memory,' Lissa said, with stilted calm, 'I think it's a memory, of me crying in a cot. I'm holding on to the sides and you look as if you are about to pick me up, then you turn your back and walk away from me, a baby, leaving me screaming. Was that true? Did that really happen?'

Meg was gaping at her. 'No one can remember so far back. Someone has told you.' It was the worst possible thing she could have said, for it proved Lissa's point. Lissa stared at her for a long, silent moment, shaking her head in bewilderment.

'So it did happen. You really didn't want to pick me up.' It was a statement, cold and bleak.

'I was young. Hurt and betrayed by my best friend and the man I had meant to marry. I was afraid . . .'

'For yourself,' Lissa cut in bitterly, not wanting to hear any more. She turned and started to walk away. Meg hurried after her and grasped her arm.

'Don't go, Lissa. Not like this, angry with each other. I do love you, and I've been the best mother I could be, not perfect maybe, but the best I could manage. I knew from the start that I loved you as if you were my own child. But I also knew that I might lose you, that Kath might come back at any time and take you from me. Can't you imagine how that felt?'

There was a desperation in her voice, one that suddenly Lissa longed to respond to. But too much had been said, too much hurt inflicted. 'Kath made promises over the years that she never kept

171

and you refused to understand this terrible need I have. You stopped me going with her when I was seven. You stopped me writing to her. Now you want to stop me from seeing Derry.' Lissa shook off Meg's restraining hand. 'You criticise me, tell me which friends I should choose, decide my life for me, but you really have no rights over me at all, have you? You never even adopted me, not offically. You are not my mother.'

It was the final cruelty and Lissa's heart clenched as she saw the spasm of pain that came into Meg's face at these words. What had she said? What had she done? She hadn't meant to go this far. But all the disappointments she had suffered over the years had boiled up and spilled out of her like a hot tide of evil lava, destroying everything in its path.

'Oh, Lissa,' Meg said, tears running over her fingers as she held her hands to her face in a helpless gesture of despair. 'I didn't realise. I never thought it was so important to you. You should have said.'

'I *did* say, but you weren't listening, were you? You only heard what you wanted to hear.' Lissa's voice grew thick with unshed tears and not a little self-pity while Meg, knowing there was too much truth in the accusation to deny, bit on her lip and said nothing.

Then Lissa tossed back her head, eyes blazing, and in that moment she had never looked more like Kath, with the same wild, devil-may-care beauty about her. 'And as for Derry, he's good and kind for all his odd notion of fashion. And more importantly, he's my friend.'

She very nearly said that she loved him but decided against it at the last moment, her instinct for self-protection being too strong. 'I choose my own friends even if I couldn't choose my own mother. I'm free to make my own decisions now, and one day I'll marry whom I damned well please. Not that you'll be interested, since neither you nor Kath wanted me at all really, did you?'

And she walked away, not waiting for Meg's reply.

Lissa wept as they drove along the lane out of the dale. She had hurt Meg very badly and wanted it not to matter. Knowing that it mattered very much.

The rain had started by the time they reached the fork in the lane. A fine mist gathered momentum into a dampening shower, swirling about the dale, rolling down from the rounded knobs like a bolt of gossamer silk. To Lissa, the weather seemed to echo the

172

awfulness of the day. It also served to harden her need for self inflicted agony.

Let's see how much I bleed, she thought, and instructed Derry to turn left and take the van up towards Larkrigg Fell instead of right, towards the main road.

He exchanged a surprised glance with his sister in the driving mirror but held his own counsel. Jan was too wrapped up in her own thoughts to care where they drove and Derry privately hoped that wherever it was Lissa was taking them would cheer her up and make her smile again. The visit home seemed to have done her no good at all.

He cleared his throat, thinking he'd best make his own position clear.

'Didn't go too well, did it? Sorry about everything, particularly the rabbit.' A stain of pink embarrassment threatened to rise up his throat. Lissa saw it and thought it such a fine throat, so strong and smooth she longed to lean over and put her lips against it where she could see the flutter of a pulse beating.

'You aren't used to country ways, that's all.'

'I didn't make a very good impression.'

'It isn't important.'

'Tam was OK. He just laughed. Said I looked like a spiv, then talked about horses all the time.'

'Yes.'

'Suppose I shouldn't have worn this pink shirt. Bit much, was it?'

Lissa came out of her reverie to look into his warm brown eyes and felt herself melt inside. 'Wear whatever you like, Derry. People should accept you for yourself, not what or who they think you are. Stop here. Stop the car.'

He slammed on the brakes at the urgency of her request and stared at the rain now streaming down the windscreen. 'You're not getting out in this?' But she was.

Lissa was out of the car in a trice, gazing out across the rainswept fells.

'What's she doing?' Derry asked Jan, disbelief in his voice.

'Haven't the faintest.' Jan tried calling through the window but Lissa didn't even turn her head. Then she darted an agonised glance at her brother and on a mutual decision they both sighed and climbed out of the car, stepping gingerly through the puddles to go and stand

173

beside her. Derry turned up his collar as the rain flattened his hair and ran down his face and neck, soaking the front of his best pink shirt. They'd be quite ruined, he thought.

Lissa was lifting her face up to the rain as if she loved it.

'What is it?' he asked, following her gaze into the sweep of mist that cloaked the fell.

'There. Do you see it? High on that ridge? This track winds around to it eventually, by those two huge boulders like standing stones over there.'

Derry squinted through the rain, trying not to think that he could be somewhere warm and dry, enjoying a pint in the King's Arms with his mates maybe. 'There's a house,' he said in surprise. 'Surrounded by tall trees.'

'Larkrigg Hall. Yews and oaks all about it.' Lissa smiled. 'Or yows and yaks as Grandfather Joe would say. That's where I might have lived, if my mother had kept me. It's where my grandmother still lives.'

'Saints alive!' Derry said, forgetting all about the rain as his mouth dropped open. 'That's some pad.' No wonder she'd appeared so stuck up at first, with a place like that behind her.

'I suppose it is. But I hate it. And I hate my grandmother. She doesn't want me and I don't want her. Any more than my mother wanted me. Any more than Meg wants me now.'

They were both staring at her, not daring to challenge her words because of the venom and desperation in her voice.

'Even when I wanted to leave the dale after . . . well, after I'd had some trouble as a child, my witch of a grandmother still refused to help. Meg went up especially to ask, swallowed her pride to do it.' Lissa tilted her chin, letting the rain wash away her tears. 'I don't care any more. I *won't* care. I don't need anyone. Not Rosemary Ellis, not Meg, not my mother. No one.'

'Everyone needs someone,' put in Jan quietly.

But Lissa only shook her head, flicking back the wet curls from her face with a defiant gesture. 'I'm a woman now, not a child, and can cope on my own.'

'Hear hear,' murmured Derry, but not with any great conviction. Her mood bothered him, as it clearly bothered Jan.

Lissa turned away suddenly and if either of them noticed her dash a hand across her eyes, they put it down to the rain. Best not to question her any more today, Derry decided. He put his arm about her. 'Come on, you're wet through. We all are. Let's go home and put the kettle on.'

She smiled up at him, slipping her arm into his. 'Yes, let's go home. I've looked my fill for today, perhaps for a lifetime. There's nothing for me here.'

So there we are, she thought, as they ran back to the van and drove off down the bumpy road. I didn't bleed at all. Not too much anyway.

There was a note pinned to the garden shed door when Derry got back that Sunday evening. It was from Renee.

'Mr Brandon called. He wants to see you in his office, first thing.' There followed several exclamation marks.

It's Mrs Fraser, Derry thought, spirits slumping. She'd complained because he failed to explain the papers to her. Oh, crikey!

The thought of the interview kept him awake half the night, worrying himself into more discomfort than usual in the narrow bed that just about filled the small wooden shed. A cold wind blew fiercely through the gap under the door, lifting the newspaper he'd used to block it and giving Derry cause to wonder what he was doing here. Why he didn't find somewhere better to live?

The cold light of Monday morning found him tapping politely on the glass panel of the inner office door, his heart in his boots as he prepared for the worst.

He wore his usual grey office suit, a pristine white shirt and his blue tie with silver diamonds down the middle, since it was the most subdued he could find. He wished he'd found the courage to wear his new blue silk waistcoat. It wasn't strictly businesslike but it might've given his confidence a boost. Derry was shocked to find his hand actually shaking as he turned the knob in answer to the command to enter. He thrust back his shoulders and swung into the room. It was a pale imitation of his usual swagger.

'Morning, Mr Brandon. Renee said you wanted to speak with me.' Whatever he had to face he'd do so with courage. Even so he was shocked by the cold anger in every line of Brandon's face.

'You've gone too far this time. There's no excuse for such loutish behaviour.'

Derry hastened to his own defence. 'I thought you'd want me to

175

leave it to you. OK, I didn't read the papers, I didn't do my homework properly. But it's not really my job, is it?'

'What the hell are you talking about?'

'I gave it a quick once over but couldn't make it out. She did sign though, and said she'd ask you about it.'

Brandon was glaring at Derry in perplexed and silent fury. 'I haven't the first idea what you are jabbering about.'

Derry said, 'Mrs Fraser, of course, who else? She didn't understand all those long words and to be honest,' he flushed beetroot red, 'neither did I.'

'I'm not talking about a foolish old woman, nor any dratted document. I'm talking about my *boat*.'

Now it was Derry's turn to gape. 'Your boat?'

Brandon punched his knuckles on the polished mahogany surface of his desk and leaned across it to glare at Derry. 'Why did you do it? In revenge for the yacht race, I suppose.'

'D-do what?'

Philip jerked his body so violently that instinctively Derry drew back, never having seen his boss so angry, not in all the years he'd worked here from the age of fifteen. Smooth, cultured, patient, that was Philip Brandon.

'Don't play games with me, I'm not in the mood. You never forgave me for getting you disqualified, did you? Though you certainly deserved it.' He seemed to be waiting for Derry to speak but he couldn't have spoken if his life had depended upon it. Philip Brandon continued, a soft menace in his voice, 'You holed my boat in revenge.'

'Holed your . . .?' An awful realisation dawned. 'Good God, are you saying someone has damaged your yacht?'

Brandon rolled his eyes up to the ceiling as if for assistance. 'Stop pretending, Derry. I've no time for lies.'

'I'm not lying.' Every vestige of colour had drained from his cheeks, leaving them almost as white as his shirt. 'Why would anyone make a hole in your yacht?'

'That is exactly what I'd like to know. You had the motive and no doubt the opportunity, knowing as you do where I moor it. Who else could it be?' He let the words hang in the air and in the long moment that followed Derry desperately searched for an answer.

'One of your clients, someone with a grudge?'

Philip put back his head and almost laughed. 'I don't take that kind of client on, as you well know. This isn't a criminal practice. You don't suppose Mrs Fraser goes in for vandalism, do you? Or perhaps Mr McArthur? Come, Derry, admit to it. Your air of innocence doesn't convince me and it certainly won't convince the police.' Philip reached for the phone and Derry's face filled at once with alarm.

'*No*, don't ring the police. I didn't do it, I swear. I didn't touch your damn' boat. It hasn't sunk, has it?'

Philip's fingers drummed on top of the telephone. 'Fortunately not. I found it in time. But you've made a savage mess of the hull. It'll cost a small fortune to repair.'

'Oh, God. I didn't do it, I swear I didn't.' Derry stood transfixed with horror, appalled by the accusation. 'I wouldn't do such a thing. Why would I?'

'Save your winsome charm for your lady friends, it cuts no ice with me. We both know why you did it. Because I beat you in that damn' race.'

Derry was desperately trying to pull himself together, to think, but his mind refused to operate beyond the horror of his predicament. 'I did win, you know I did. It was you trying to ram me, not the other way round.'

'Can you prove it? I was on the starboard tack, remember. Therefore I had right of way.'

'In theory. I'm innocent and that's the truth.'

Philip's voice almost purred. 'The truth? What is that? In law the truth is only what you can make people believe. You should have taken evasive action sooner in that race, instead of being so determined to win.'

'Not at the cost of safety.'

'If you're so certain of being able to prove your innocence, you've nothing to fear from police questioning, have you?' Philip lifted the receiver. 'Assuming they take your word against mine.' Charcoal eyes seared into brown.

'They'll believe what you tell them,' Derry said, hopelessness in his voice. 'Look at me. I wouldn't stand a chance. They'll call me a Ted, a rabble-rouser, a trouble-maker.'

Philip almost smiled and slid the telephone receiver back into its cradle. Then he picked up a paper clip instead and started carefully to unbend it. 'Very well, I will agree not to call in the police. But I feel bound to terminate your employment.'

Derry gasped. *'Why?* My dad could repair the boat.' His offer was treated with silent contempt. Philip Brandon continued as if he'd never spoken.

'On numerous occasions you've been given warnings for insubordination. You cavort all over town when you should be working. Pester Miss Henshaw and Christine, and play foolish games in the office. Now you have gone too far. You're beneath contempt, Derek Colwith. I'm perfectly justified in having you sacked. My patience is exhausted.'

'But I . . .'

'I strongly advise you to leave town,' Philip continued, the paper clip no more than a crumpled piece of wire in his fingers. 'Go and seek this fame and fortune you've talked so much about. If you are capable of achieving it.' With a faint raising of sceptical dark brows.

Derry was appalled. 'You've declared me guilty without a trial. That's not fair.'

Philip said, 'Take a week's notice like a man, or we can let the local constabulary decide the matter. The choice is yours.'

Derry spent hours during the ensuing week in deep discussion with the rest of the group, when he wasn't running down to the post office with carefully hoarded coins to make telephone calls. Perhaps it would all turn out for the best, he decided. Philip Brandon's unfair accusation may well have given him exactly the kickstart he needed.

'What are you up to?' Renee wanted to know, changing a sixpence into pennies for the fourth time.

'Getting out of your hair for good maybe,' he said.

'Oh, well, in that case.' Perking up, she dug deeper into her crocodile plastic handbag and handed him more coins. 'I've four more pennies here, that'll make another call.'

Derry took the coins with a dry smile. 'Thanks for your support.'

By the following Friday he had the whole thing sorted. He'd rung every name and contact he could think of, who in turn had passed him on to others. In the end he'd finally found a bloke in Manchester willing to give them an audition. If he liked their music, he said, he'd get them work. Derry's hopes were high.

Miss Henshaw was upset to hear that he was leaving, and wept damply into his collar before wishing him luck for the future and giving him a pair of hand knitted gloves she'd meant to give him at Christmas to remember her by.

'You must look after those precious hands if you are to be famous,' she sobbed.

Philip Brandon handed Derry his last pay packet, telling him how lucky he was to have a generous-hearted employer.

Jimmy offered him no advice at all, as was his wont.

All Derry had to do now was to tell Lissa.

Lissa felt oddly nervous as they stepped off the bus. There'd been no problem with Jan as she'd claimed to have plans of her own, so here they were. Just the two of them. She could feel her heart beating fast at the prospect of a whole day alone with Derry on the fells. Clothed in their tawny brilliance, they looked so achingly inviting Lissa could hardly wait to get up there. With a pale, shining sun and clouds too high for rain, it seemed a perfect autumn day, and a perfect opportunity to prove she wasn't as frozen and stuck up as Derry imagined.

The bus dropped them close to Troutbeck and they did not speak as they started to walk up through the village. Lissa shyly kept several feet of track between them as they made their way past farmsteads, seventeen-century statesman houses with their quaint spinning galleries, along narrow walled lanes and beside the bubbling Trout beck that gave the village its name.

As they laboured uphill the distance between them had shrunk to a matter of inches.

'I need to talk to you,' Derry told her, and she was surprised to hear a nervousness in his voice even greater than her own. Then a farmer stopped and offered them a lift.

'It's a bonny day.'

'Aye,' Derry agreed.

'Ganin oop the fell?'

Derry agreed they meant to walk up to High Street by way of the Tongue.

'Joomp in then. Ah can save thee the boring bit oop this road. Then you'll know where you're at.'

And so he did. Lissa sat with Derry on the bumpy leather seat and thought how lucky she was to have him for a boy friend. It was all very exciting.

The farmer dropped them above Troutbeck Park Farm, thus saving

179

two or three miles on their journey. They thanked him and he waved them off, warning them to take care.

'Watch the weather. It'll coom in from the west.'

'Thanks.' And they set off at once, through the gate and down into Hird wood. It was hard going at first. They had to cut across country, over rocks and through thick clinging bracken, climb stiles, bridge the beck and negotiate boggy ground which sucked at their boots whilst stretching before them falsely green and beguiling.

Yellow loosestrife bloomed and the sedge grass and rushes were thick beneath their feet. A family of meadow pipits 'pheeped' crossly at them, in a frenzy of flight at being so rudely disturbed. When they finally reached firmer ground with Ill Bell rising above them, they stopped by mutual consent for a rest and a sip from their water bottle.

'Eat your mint cake now,' Derry suggested. 'To give you energy for the ascent.'

Lissa gazed up at the steep climb which faced them, Thornthwaite Crag to the left, Ill Bell to the right, and grinned. 'I reckon I'll need it.'

'It's a tough, steep haul of two and a half thousand feet,' he told her.

'I can do it.'

'We'll take it slow.'

They sat companionably together, crunching on the sweet brown candy.

'What was it you wanted to talk to me about?' Lissa asked, casting him a shy sideways glance. His answer surprised her.

'Philip Brandon.'

Violet eyes sparkled. 'Fancy you being jealous of your boss,' she teased. 'But you've made your apology, no need to go on about it.'

'But I . . .'

'No, no,' Lissa insisted. 'Every time we talk about Philip Brandon, we quarrel. Not today. I want nothing to spoil this wonderful day. I'm looking forward to our walk. I've shown you my favourite places, now you can show me yours.'

'Maybe you won't enjoy my company as much as you do his.'

'Oh, for goodness' sake. Didn't I say we'd quarrel?' Lissa stood up. 'Come on. I won't hear another word about Philip Brandon.' And she strutted ahead in high dudgeon, forcing him to hurry to catch her up.

How could he explain about him being forced to leave if she refused to let him mention Philip Brandon and explain what he'd done? Derry worried as they started up the steep fellside. Not that Lissa would necessarily believe him. She hadn't believed him about the yacht race, had she? Accused him of making it up and of being a bad loser. So why should she believe him innocent now? He sighed heavily. Girls! You couldn't understand them.

And he had no more wish to spoil this day than she had. He straightened his spine, eased the rucksack on his back and closed his mind to the future. He'd tell her later. Plenty of time. It'd taken him over a year to get her alone like this, he wasn't about to mess it up now.

'You might be able to see some of your own home fells when we reach the summit.' He grinned at her, sheepish and conciliatory, and she responded with a shy smile. He edged closer.

'That would be lovely,' Lissa agreed.

Derry pushed back his shoulders, drawing in a breath of deep contentment. He was never happier than when out on the hills. 'It's getting steeper now, can you manage?'

'Watch me.' Whatever you can do, I can do better, her expression said. But seconds later she was regretting her confidence, gasping for breath while she plonked her bottom on a flat stone, knees shaking with her efforts.

'I think I'm out of condition,' she groaned. 'Too much shop work.'

Derry waited for her, grinning. 'Twenty steps then a breather, eh?'

And that's how they climbed, fingers catching from time to time then breaking shyly apart again. Lissa had been brought up on the high fells but she never underestimated their challenge and Derry took care to match his pace to hers. The first peak she'd been aiming for proved not to be the summit at all but merely a hump with the mountain continuing its relentless ascent beyond.

They stopped for a much needed rest and to admire the view. 'Isn't it utterly breathtaking?' Lissa said, rubbing the cramp in her calves, though it was getting easier as she found her second wind.

'This is the same path the Roman soldiers would have taken from the Windermere valley to reach High Street, where they marched right across the tops in their quest to get as close to Scotland as they dare. They fought a battle here with the Britons, on Scot's

Rake. Can't you just see it?' His brown eyes shone and Lissa had to laugh.

'I wouldn't like to do this climb in full armour, with breastplate and sword.' They both gasped at the thought then Lissa continued, 'I'm sorry if I've been a bit – well, blow hot and cold, as you put it, Derry. I've had a few things on my mind lately.'

'I'd like to think we've called an end to our own battles,' he agreed.

Lissa smiled at him, feeling the warmth of his response flow through her, setting her blood surging. He did like her, he really did.

It came to him then, with a jolt, just how much he would miss her when he left. But he had his career to think about, didn't he? Which was more important? He wished he could decide.

'I've thought about that question you asked me,' she was saying, 'and I've decided. I will be your girl, if you still want me to be.' She was blushing furiously and Derry was puffing out his chest as if she'd told him he was the handsomest man in the universe while inside, his heart was jumping and sinking, all at the same time, knowing this made it worse. But what could he do if he stayed in Carreckwater? Be a waiter at the Marina Hotel? Build boats that fewer and fewer people wanted to buy because they preferred the new moulded plastic and fibreglass. What could he do? How could he give up his music?

'That's great,' he said, meaning it.

When they reached the beacon on Thornthwaite Crag, a solid chimney of stones fourteen feet high, they were breathless and stopped to eat the sandwiches they had brought with them.

'Isn't it beautiful?' Lissa breathed, the freedom of the fells seeping into and soothing her soul, as it always did, the undulating surface of the summit stretching out invitingly all around them, just waiting to be explored.

'Makes you feel so insignificant, doesn't it? As if your own troubles are so slight in comparison with those nature has to contend with.'

Spread out below them, beyond the fans of scree and craggy boulders, lay all of the Troutbeck valley. The silver thread of the beck could be traced right down until it disappeared around the hump of the Tongue, dwarfed now by the sweep of greater mountains all around. And beyond that, from their vantage point could be seen the blue ribbon of Lake Windermere and the smaller Carreckwater.

'Yes,' Derry agreed, wondering if he could tell her his troubles now, then bit hungrily into a thick cheese sandwich. Lissa did the same.

'And over there, to the east, are my own fells. When I was at home I always wanted to see what was beyond this line of mountains,' she mumbled through a mouthful of crumbs.

'That's easy,' scoffed Derry, offering her another sandwich before she had finished the first. 'It's another mountain. Bit like life really, if you think about it.'

'I suppose it is.'

They ate in companionable silence. When they had finished, Derry rolled over and cupped his chin in his hands to stare up at her. 'OK, so tell me what you intend to do with your life? Where are you heading?'

She stared at him in surprise. 'I don't know. I've never really thought about it.'

'You should. Everyone should have a life plan.' He'd tell her now. He'd say, quite casually, 'I'll be away for the next few weeks, trying to get a recording contract.'

'Plans don't always work out,' she said, with such sadness in her voice that he bit back the unspoken words. 'Long ago, when I was very young, I vowed to have no more plans, no more wishes. It's too disappointing when they don't work out.'

'I suppose so.'

'What about you? Do you have a life plan?'

He sat up and stared at her. She looked so beautiful, so trusting, gazing at him out of those soft, entrancing eyes. 'Oh, you know me,' he joked. 'I intend to be rich and famous. Make a million records and have my skiffle group play on television. The usual stuff.'

Lissa tried to laugh, though she found it surprisingly difficult. 'You'd have to leave Carreckwater in order to do all of that. Is that your aim? To go off to London to seek your fame and fortune?' She smiled up at him, waiting for him to deny it.

'Would you blame me if I did?' He was watching her and she answered equally carefully.

'Everyone has the right to pursue a dream. And it's no business of mine what you do, is it?' she said, trying to give the impression that she wasn't concerned one way or the other. And though she meant what she said, in her heart she longed for Derry to assure her that he would never leave, that his only dream was to stay with her. But he was chewing on a piece of grass, saying nothing.

15

The black knuckle-bone rocks, the cry of a lone curlew in the silence which clung like a presence Lissa almost felt she could touch . . . all these ingredients, familiar as they were, seemed to intensify her sudden and intense sensation of loneliness. As if Derry had slipped from her in some way when really he was still beside her, reaching for her hand, urging her to move on.

Why hadn't he denied it? Oh, she didn't want to think about him going away. The very idea opened up a deep void that frightened her. He wouldn't go, not really. Head in the clouds. A dreamer, that's all he was.

As they walked on, hand in hand, perhaps because of their talk, or because of the silent sweep of the empty panorama of mountains all around which made her feel as if they were the only two people in existence with the world at their feet, Lissa told him of her illegitimacy, brandishing it like a weapon as she usually did, so he could stab her with it if he wanted to. 'That's why I hate my grandmother.'

'I know,' he said, as if it were of no consequence. 'Jan told me. So what? It's not your fault, is it?'

Violet eyes opened wide and she pushed back the wayward curls of her tumbling hair with an impatient hand. 'Don't you understand? I was dumped. Can't you see how rejected that makes me feel? It's not as if Meg decided she wanted a child and went along to an orphanage and chose me. Kath, my own mother, didn't want me at all, and got rid of me at the first opportunity. She left Meg literally holding the baby. *Me.*'

Derry considered this for a moment as he helped her negotiate a pile of fallen rocks, the peat cracked and brown underfoot. 'And so because you hate Kath for dumping you, you blame Meg? That's not very fair, is it?'

Hot fury rose in her breast. 'Fair? For all I know, Meg might've driven Kath away, as punishment for stealing her fiancé. How do I know what happened?'

'Exactly. And it's so long ago, does it really matter?'

'Of course it matters. Don't blame me for not being fair. I'm the victim here.'

'What sort of victim?' He gazed at her, genuinely puzzled that she was so close to losing her temper, simply because he did not see her point of view.

'Nobody wanted me. None of them. Don't you see?' Lissa longed for him to tell her that he wanted her, would want her for as long as he lived.

Derry had been watching her face, reading the expressions that flitted across it in the space of a few seconds. Hope, pain, disappointment and disillusionment. 'You know your trouble, don't you?' He grinned at her, crooked and teasing, but she refused to respond, only tilting her chin and pursing her lips, determined not to be affected by it. Nevertheless she had to ask.

'What? What is my trouble?'

'You don't know where you're going because you're too busy looking where you came from.'

'What?'

'In climbing we're taught never to look back. Onward and upward, that's the thing. Come over here. I'll show you something.'

Lissa very nearly refused but then let him take her hand and lead her to where a drystone wall lay tumbled right across their path. She stood at the wall and looked over, gasping at what she saw. It was the most amazing sight.

A whole new vista had opened up before her eyes. She looked out on to a complete new set of dales and mountains, lit by the sun in brilliant green and gold patches like a magical stage set with a backdrop of blue mountains and the glimmer of yet another silver lake.

'This is known as Threshwaite Mouth, probably because the mountains yawn wide open, giving you a grand view of the Northern Lakes. If we carried on walking we would reach Patterdale and

186

Ullswater. There's Ullswater, a shining water every bit as beautiful as Carreckwater and the Windermere valley we've just left.'

'Oh, it's magnificent,' she sighed. 'It takes my breath away.'

'We could stay in the softer valleys for ever of course, in the lush intake land, taking no risks whatsoever. We don't have to come up these mountains. We could venture on through the rigours of Skiddaw forest. We could choose to climb Helvellyn or Scafell, or go right over the border and up into the highlands of Scotland if we wanted to go that far. Or we could take a bus and play it safe. It's up to you.

'But if you want to know what lies beyond the next mountain and the one after that, and find out your own worth at the same time, then don't look back, look forward. You might surprise yourself.'

He turned to her and found she had tears in her eyes. 'Oh, crikey, listen to me playing the philosopher. Still, I mean what I say, Lissa. Life isn't about what other people make for you but what you make for yourself. It doesn't matter where you came from, only where you're going.'

'I don't believe all that. I believe that who you are and where you start out determines where you are going.'

'Maybe, to a certain extent. But a lot of it's up to you. When my mum was dying,' he said, fixing his eyes on the middle distance, 'she told me not to remember her as sick and unhappy. "If you must look back," she said, "think of the happy times when I was healthy and full of life. But better still, look forward. Live your life to the full. Live for tomorrow," she said. "You only get one shot." And much as it hurt at times, I've tried to do just that.' He gave a half laugh, embarrassed by his own words. 'Listen to me, prattling on. It must be the air up here, it gets to me. Always fills me with this great sense of achievement that I managed it, under my own steam.' His eyes were shining now as brilliantly as the lake waters themselves while Lissa regarded him with a strange expression, admiration and something like awe in her own.

Could he be right? Had she spent too much of her life looking back, worrying about other people? Maybe she should push herself forward a bit more. It seemed wonderfully possible with Derry beside her.

He was looking at her with the kind of intent gaze that made her shiver with longing. 'I wish I could be brave like you. Dream, make plans, go anywhere, do anything I wanted.' She slanted a glance up at him. 'Perhaps I even wish I dared to let myself love you.' She

187

wanted instantly to take back the words but they were spoken now, bursting out of her, answering the need she felt inside.

His response was everything she might have hoped for. He leaned forward and kissed her softly upon her lips. The thrill of it ran through her like a forest fire. 'Why can you not, if you want to? And I know that you want to. So why fight it?'

'Because I'm afraid.'

'Of me?'

'Of rejection, I suppose. I expect people not to want me or care for me, except out of duty or selfishness. I've always thought that people are really only concerned about their own needs, not mine.'

He looked shocked, pulling her close into his arms. 'Because your mother didn't want you, you imagine everyone else is the same? Even me? That's a bit strong, isn't it?'

'Other people have used me.'

'Who?'

She hung her head, avoiding his searching gaze. 'I can't say.'

'Yes, you can.' He brought her round to face him. 'You can tell me anything.'

'I've never told anyone.'

He stroked her cheek. 'I'm not anyone.'

It surprised her how easy it was to tell Derry about the gypsy. The words slipped out as if she needed to purge herself of their pain. Derry listened, at first with sympathy and then with growing horror, a look of disgust on his wholesome young face.

'My poor little love,' he said, his arms tightening on a convulsion of fierce anger. 'He didn't . . .'

'No, no. I think he did it just to punish me, because Meg had sent the gypsies away. She didn't care that they were my friends.'

'She probably only wanted to protect you. But not all men are so horrible and cruel, Lissa.'

'I know,' she murmured against his lips. 'I know that now.'

He was cradling her in his arms, smoothing back hot tendrils of hair from her brow, kissing the tears from her cheeks, telling her that he loved her and would do so for as long as he lived. Inside Lissa an unexpected excitement mounted as his words soothed her, making her grow weak with the need to surrender to the compulsion of wanting.

He put her firmly from him and she felt the loss like a waft of cold air. 'Hell, we'd best stop now or you'll think I'm as bad as him.'

188

Her eyes were warm and loving as she shook her head. 'No, I won't. I do understand the difference. And I'm no longer a foolish adolescent, you know.'

He grinned, that lovely lopsided grin. 'I had noticed.'

She reached for him then, kissing him of her own volition, full upon his mouth, and heard his groan, heard her own soft sigh of pleasure as his arms came about her. They both sank quite naturally upon the sweet grass.

'I won't hurt you,' he murmured against the fevered warmth of her skin. 'I won't do anything you don't want me to.'

'I'm not cheap,' she said, aware in that moment that there was little she didn't want him to do. 'I want you to respect me.'

'I do respect you, silly.'

Her heart exulted when she felt the muscles in his arms tighten about her. Lissa had never felt more alive, more wanted in her life before. They rolled and clung together like young puppies, teasing, touching and kissing as they explored and discovered the joys of love. She stuffed bracken down his neck and he tickled her mercilessly, stopping her squeals with increasingly demanding kisses.

It was meant to be no more than harmless fun, of course. They'd neither of them intended to take it too far but he couldn't disguise his hunger for her, nor she her need for him. And though he was a young and inexperienced lover, a little clumsy in his eagerness, they came together quite naturally and made love without restraint, pulling off clothes which got in the way, ignoring others till a tide of passion took them over and the laughter faded. Their loving seemed right, the most natural thing in the world. Lissa gave herself to him freely and with love, cleansing herself of all unpleasant memories. And yet there remained a tender sweetness and sensitivity in their loving that moved her to tears and brought Derry to a shuddering climax.

Afterwards they both lay upon the yielding bracken staring into the blue sky, stunned by their emotions and shaken by the result.

'I shouldn't have let you do that,' Lissa said, filled suddenly by the enormity of what had happened. What had she been thinking of? She hadn't been thinking at all, that was the trouble. Now that the passion had faded she began at once to worry. 'I don't know what came over me.'

'Me neither.'

A dreadful thought struck her and she sat up, all hot and bothered. 'Oh lord, what if I get pregnant?'

189

Derry took her hand and squeezed it consolingly. 'You won't get pregnant. I'm not daft. I was careful.'

Violet eyes gazed pleadingly into his. 'But what *if* ?' It didn't bear thinking about. 'I'd die,' she said. 'I'd just *die*.'

He pulled her into his arms and kissed her brow with great tenderness. 'I promise you, Lissa, you are quite safe. I'll look after you.'

'I love you,' she said.

'And I you.'

'For ever?'

'And ever.'

They were sitting on Kidsty Pike. Not too far, had they but known it, from where Jack Lawson proposed to Meg nearly twenty years before. Where he'd given her his mother's engagement ring and she had kept by her promise to marry him, throughout the long years of war that followed, through all the pain and suffering, the realisation of his betrayal and her love for another man.

Lissa and Derry were children of a different world. A world which promised peace. There was no fear of their young lives being torn apart by Hitler's ruthless ambitions. They believed it would be an easy world to live in because of that simple fact.

'Over there, in the next dale,' she told him, lifting his hand and lovingly pointing with his fingers to the gleaming curve of Haweswater beyond, 'is Mardale. Grandfather Joe told us all about that doomed valley. So sad. How a great dam was built and it was flooded and turned into the Haweswater reservoir.' When she told him about the old corpse road, a shiver rippled through her body and for an instant she was back in the old bothy by the tarn, darkness falling, quite alone. Except somewhere, out on the empty fell, a gypsy might be waiting for her still.

Derry laughed at her expression and squeezed her tight in his arms. 'Don't tell me you're superstitious? You surely don't believe it's still trodden by the ghosts of corpses? That legend is told about every corpse road in Lakeland.' He was kissing her neck, smoothing his fingers over her bare throat and down to the swell of her breast beneath her blouse. He could feel her excitement vibrating against his rib cage, hear her small gasps of pleasure. Something most strange and wonderful had happened to him today and he wanted it to go on and on.

190

'Of course not.' Lissa tried to speak with her usual hauteur but her limbs felt like liquid fire and she could find no strength to give emphasis to her words. 'You mustn't go any further,' she said, pulling her blouse close and struggling for breath as his tongue circled the hollow beneath her ear and a pain started up somewhere it shouldn't. It had all become far more intense than she'd intended. She'd committed the unforgiveable sin without a thought. Yet she loved him, and Derry loved her, so didn't that make it right?

'I won't, I promise.'

'Well, see you don't then.' She tucked her head into the curve of his shoulder, loving the warm hardness of his chest against her cheek, pushing aside her anxieties for she didn't want to regret this beautiful afternoon with him, not ever.

'And a few miles further on is my own dale,' she resolutely continued. 'We must visit Meg again and I shall try to be a better daughter.'

'Stop worrying over it,' he murmured, but she could not. Any more than she could keep from twisting round to kiss his smiling mouth. For did she not need constant affirmation of his love?

His earlier kisses, on their walk with Jan to the Langdales, and at the Spin-the-bottle party had surprised her. But could not compare with the positive storm of kisses he'd bathed her face in today, nor with the love they had readily given and received. Lissa knew she should feel sorry about losing her virginity in this way, but how could she when she loved him so much? And hadn't he promised he would stand by her, no matter what? They were one person now. Hadn't he told her so?

'When did you realise?' Lissa asked, wanting to examine his emotions, swathe herself in the assurance of this glorious new discovery.

'When did you?' he parried, not quite knowing the answer.

'Oh, for ever and ever, I think.' She laughed. 'We only had to find it.'

'And now we have.' His arms tightened about her and she sighed her contentment.

'Yes, now we have.' A pause for more kisses, warm and increasingly demanding, and then Lissa pushed him away to study his face more seriously, her own cheeks warm with embarrassment. 'That was my first time, you know.'

'I guessed it was.'

191

'Was it yours?'

'Does it matter?'

She considered this for a moment then decided that at least one of them needed to know how to go about things. She guessed she was a bit naive in these matters but a worrying image came into her head. 'Will you tell me about Renee?'

'What about her?'

'Don't play games, Derry Colwith. Jan told me how you were seeing Renee before she married your dad. What went wrong?'

'She went wrong. She married the wrong man, that's all.'

Lissa went cold. 'Wrong man? Do you mean that you still love her?'

'Now who's jealous?' Derry chuckled and tried to kiss her sulks away but she was having none of it.

'Tell me the truth. I need to know.'

'OK.' He sighed with exaggerated patience but his brown eyes were twinkling. 'I fancied her for a while, that's all.'

'Oh?' Hope was growing inside her.

'Then she got serious. Desperate to leave home she was. Started looking at engagement rings in shop windows and talking about settling down. Worried me to death, that did. She's fun is Renee, but not the girl for me to marry. Then when she finally realised I'd no intention of ever falling in with her plans, she tried to make me jealous by going out with my dad.'

'And did it?' Lissa asked quietly, watching his jaw tighten ominously. 'Did it make you jealous?'

'Not in the way you mean. I get on well with my dad, as a matter of fact. We've always been good mates despite him being a bit, well, you know, old fashioned and liking to rib me about the way I dress and everything. But then fathers are supposed to be like that, aren't they?'

'I suppose so,' Lissa said, thinking of Tam, who was all she had ever known for a father, and whom she loved dearly. He too had teased Derry for his fashionable, almost Teddy Boy look. 'Go on.'

'It annoyed me because I thought she would make a fool out of him. He's more than twice her age. What could she see in him?'

'Comfort? Security? Her home life doesn't sound as if it was too good.'

'Exactly.' Derry was gritting his teeth, biting on his anger. 'So she used him, didn't she? Got her feet under our table and now she's for chucking me out because I cramp her style.'

There was a slight, awkward pause. 'Jimmy seems to adore her. And she him. They're happy together.'

'But it can't be right, can it? She manipulates him. Money, that's all she ever thinks of. What she can buy next. He works his socks off at the boatyard every day to buy her things . . . television set, fridges, telephones. But there's always something else she has her eye on. Greedy little tyke, that's what she is.'

Lissa buttoned up her blouse then snuggled close in his arms, wanting to calm his agitation. 'Thoughtless perhaps. She's never had anything of her own so now she wants it all. But I wouldn't have thought there was any malice in her.'

'Huh, I'm not so sure. On at him all the time she is, with her want, want, want.' He snapped the words out in a cold, hard fury and Lissa wished she'd never broached the subject, yet somehow had to pursue her final questions, as if probing a sore tooth.

'And does she still fancy you?' She asked the question carefully, quietly, resting her head in the crook of his shoulder so as not to look at him while she waited, what seemed an age, for a reply.

'She tried it on once,' he said quietly. 'But I soon put her right.'

Lissa's heart was hammering. 'Because you wouldn't want to hurt your dad, I suppose?' A part of her started to cry inside. She couldn't lose him, not now, not after this. 'Are you saying that but for the love and respect you have for your father, you'd have no hesitation in continuing to enjoy Renee's charms?' She wanted him quickly to deny it, to say that he loved only herself. Instead he burst out laughing, told her she was making a mountain out of a molehill and changed the attack on to herself.

'What about you, little Miss Innocent? I take it you won't be going out with old Brandon ever again?'

Lissa's strong sense of independence made her want to toss her head and say she would do as she pleased. But the last thing she wanted was to quarrel with Derry so instead she reached up and very gently nipped the lobe of his ear with her tiny, pearl white teeth. 'Whatever you say, oh, master.'

Then he was reaching for her and all their quarrelling was forgotten as he began kissing whatever part of her sweet body he could find, unfastening buttons to find more. Lissa fastened them up as quickly again, gently protesting as the golden sun slipped closer to the

193

horizon, bathing the landscape and the two entwined figures with a glorious glow. 'I'm not letting it happen again, you know. I must need my head examining.'

To Lissa it felt glorious to feel so loved, so free, so *safe*. Derry would never ask her for anything distasteful or unpleasant, never let her down.

'We should go,' he murmured, kissing every contour of her delightful, beautiful face. 'How smooth and silky your skin is.'

She felt warm and languorous, heady with the joys of the tenderness that flowed between them, pushing aside her niggling worries. She wouldn't get pregnant, she wouldn't. Not from just one mistake. Neither could bear to break the spell, and when they were quite exhausted with kissing, they both fell asleep.

Lissa woke to find the clouds had gathered and darkened, clotting the skies like thick cream. She looked beyond his beloved face and stared into a blank, soft white nothingness. Then she was pushing him away, trying desperately to wake him and examine the seriousness of their situation.

'Oh, do wake up, please, Derry. The mist has come down. We're smothered in cloud.'

He sat up and rubbed his eyes, gazing about him as worried as she. The last thing anyone needed on a mountain walk was to be engulfed in mist. He cursed quietly under his breath though the face he turned to Lissa was reassuring, fixed with a careful smile.

'It'll be all right. We'll simply have to sit it out until it's gone.'

'Sit it out? Here?' She was pulling her sweater over her blouse, reaching for her coat. The golden fantasy had faded, leaving cold reality in its wake. 'We must go home. At once.'

'We can't see where we're walking. One wrong step and we'd be tripping down the cliff into Riggingdale. That's a fair drop and I'd prefer not to make it, if you don't mind,' he said, making a joke of his anxiety.

She hesitated, understanding the sense of what he said but unwilling to accept it. 'We know where Riggingdale is, we can avoid it.'

'It's easy to lose our sense of direction in thick mist like this. No, much better we stay put.'

The argument continued for some time, but in the end Derry won. They put on every item of clothing they had brought with them and waited.

'It's lifting.'

'I don't think so.' A soft rain had started, sweeping in, as the old farmer had warned, from the west. 'Stop fretting, Lissa, I'll keep you safe, I promise. All night if need be.'

'All night?' The last time she had stayed out all night, Meg had lost her baby. She felt the familiar cold panic close in. 'You wanted this to happen. You shouldn't have fallen asleep. It's all your fault,' she accused, with no sense of reason as fear took root.

'Oh, sure. I ordered it by mail order and told it not to be late. Calm down, Lissa. You're getting hysterical. Come here, love. Let's cuddle up and keep warm. You can have my coat as well if you're cold.'

She was too overwrought to trust anyone, even Derry. She hated to be told to calm down. She'd been a fool yet again, she told herself. He'd coerced her here, persuaded her to believe in him, *seduced* her and planned the whole thing to humiliate and use her as others before him had done. Oh, what had she done? What had she been thinking of to let things go so far? 'If we stay here all night everyone will know. It'll be all around town that we've slept together.'

'Well, it's true. We have.' He laughed and she felt suddenly exasperated with him, almost crying with frustration.

'That's not the point. I don't want anyone to know.'

'Why? Are you ashamed of me?'

'Don't be silly. It should be our secret. Just between us. What will people think? They'll say I'm no good.'

'To hell with what people think. That's their problem.'

Now that the sun had gone and the beautiful green grandeur of the fells been swallowed up by ghostly mist, Lissa felt cold and vulnerable and alone. All her growing worries exploded in her head, numbing her with their implications. 'Oh dear God, what if I do get pregnant?' She was as bad as her mother. Wicked. She'd proved everyone right.

'You won't get pregnant. I promise, Lissa.' He was stroking her hair, smoothing her cheeks, trying to reassure her. 'It's all right, love. You're quite safe.'

But she wasn't listening. 'What will Meg say? She must have guessed I was really bad inside. Wicked, like my mother.'

'It's not wicked to love.'

The mist seemed to be thickening, pressing against her like soft padding hands. Lissa was slapping his hands away and the next

195

instant she was on her feet and running, stumbling and falling over her own feet in her desperation to find the beck.

She was good at falling into becks, she told herself. If only she could fall into this one now. Dear God, how far down was it? Please let her feel the glory of its wetness on her legs. Then she'd follow it, walk in it if necessary safely through the long miles back down to the village. But she ran the wrong way. Disorientated, his voice ringing in her ears, telling her to take care, Lissa ran blindly along Racecourse Hill where in the past farmers had tested their horses and won or lost their bets. To one side of her, smothered by the thick cloud, was a long perilous drop to Blea Water, two hundred feet or more below. Then her foot caught on something, there was a loud crack and blackness closed in.

'Lissa. Wake up, Lissa. Are you all right? Lissa, please open your eyes.'

Derry's voice came as if from a great distance and then his face swam into view before her eyes. At least the glimmer of his eyes shone, reflecting her own image in them like twin pale ghosts.

'Thank God,' he said when he saw her blink. 'You tripped and hit your head against a rock. Are you all right?'

He helped her to her feet and they huddled together, wrapped in each other's arms in a small hollow they found beside a rock until she felt recovered enough to go on.

'I'm sorry I panicked,' she murmured, snug against his hard chest. 'Only shows my foolish insecurity. I will learn to trust in you, really I will.' Her teeth were starting to chatter with cold. 'You're very special to me, Derry Colwith, d-do you know that?'

'We'll have to risk going on now,' he said, trying not to show his concern. 'You're cold and it's starting to rain. Come on, love, hold on to me. If we can find the cairn that marks Nan Bield pass, there's a shelter there and we can rest up for a while, until the weather improves.'

But search as they might they missed the cairn, smothered as it was in the mist. With visibility so bad and the rain running down their necks it soon became plain they had gone too far and were almost on the Longsleddale ridge which went ever higher and miles out of their way.

'I should have brought my compass,' Derry mourned. 'There's nothing for it but to go back and try again.' And Lissa almost sobbed with tiredness and frustration. What was she doing on this mountain with Derry Colwith who didn't seem to have the first idea where he. was? Could she really trust him with her life? For that was what this could amount to. Worries about lost virginity seemed small by comparison.

'Do you think you can find it this time, Derry?'

'Sure.'

Turning back and retracing their steps was the worst thing Lissa had ever done. The rain was in their faces now and the grass grew slippy underfoot. After half an hour Derry admitted they must have missed it again.

'We'll have to go down the scree into Kentmere valley,' he said, and Lissa's heart jolted. Scree walking was dangerous at the best of times. In mist, late in the afternoon, it was very nearly foolhardy. She said as much, protesting vigorously.

'This bit isn't too steep, I promise. We can't go west over Kirkstone in this weather and Longsleddale would be a long, hard walk in the opposite direction. Much too far. Kentmere is the best bet. There are farms down there, houses and people. Trust me.'

What choice did she have? Lissa slid her hand in his and gave it a little squeeze. 'I do.'

It took them two hours to get down off the fells. It was the worst two hours of Lissa's life. Sometimes the mist lifted, giving them tantalising glimpses of the way ahead. At other times it blanketed down, sweeping them with rain so that they were soon soaked to the skin despite thick woollen sweaters and waterproofs. It ran down their necks and into their socks, making puddles between their toes. It soaked right through their clothing and plastered their shirts to their backs.

Underfoot it was treacherous, slipping and sliding over rain-slicked grass, patches of scree, and jagged stones where a cricked ankle seemed inevitable and would have been a life-threatening catastrophe.

Lissa felt certain they would never reach the soft meadows of the valley below, but at last they did, almost stumbling with relief on to the long flat road. Drenched and shivering, Derry knocked at the first door where a light showed.

'Eeh now then,' said a warm friendly voice as the door opened, letting light spill out into the gloaming, 'what hev we 'ere?'

197

'I wondered if perhaps you could provide us with a cup of tea?' Derry held fast to Lissa's hand, shaking violently in his.

The farmer's wife stood on her slate doorstep, her mouth agape, and gazed at the two miserable young figures before her. 'Well, I niver. George, see what we hev here. Come in, the pair of you, afore you turn into a couple of puddles.'

Mrs Bowker wouldn't hear of them settling for anything less than a substantial spread. Fresh bread was brought and stinging hot soup, followed by thick slices of ham, pickle, spiced sausage, and enough tea to float a battleship.

Their clothes steamed on the rack above the big farmhouse fire while Derry and Lissa snuggled sleepily into huge blue-checked dressing gowns that smelled of pipe smoke and cold cream respectively.

'I've made up two beds,' she told them, whisking away empty plates and gathering up the tablecloth to flick the crumbs out the back door for the hens.

'Beds?' Lissa managed weakly.

'Thee doesn't think I'd send you bairns off out on a night like this, do you?' She grinned at her husband. Happily ensconced in the chimney corner he had said not a word, happy to leave these domestic matters to her judgement. 'It'll be reet by morning, George, won't it?'

'Aye,' he said, and returned to his pipe.

'I'll tek the young lady oop fust then,' Mrs Bowker said, in a voice which said she would have no nonsense, not in her house, thank you very much.

'We're truly grateful,' Lissa said as she followed her up the broad oak staircase.

Lissa was sure she wouldn't be able to sleep a wink. She wanted to go over in her mind everything that had happened that day, and its possible implications. But the moment her head touched the pillow, she was asleep.

Derry, however, lay wakeful for some time. He couldn't help wondering what he had got himself into. He did love her, at least he felt almost sure that he did. But he was young, with all his life and his ambitions before him. He wasn't ready to be responsible. Not for himself even, let alone another person.

How can I tell her that I've lost my job? How can I say I'm leaving, after all of this? he worried. She'll think it sure proof that I didn't

198

mean what I said, that I don't care for her. His eyelids began to droop. Perhaps next week, he thought, when I've finalised everything with this chap in Manchester. It'll be time enough to tell her then.

And so they each slept, with reasonable contentment, in their chaste beds.

16

Lissa woke to a crisp autumn day, the fells glowing like molten honey as if to prove how benignly innocent they were.

Mrs Bowker wouldn't hear of their leaving until their stomachs were well filled with bacon and eggs and fried black pudding. Neither of them made much of a protest and tucked in as if they hadn't eaten for a week. When it was time for them to leave she looked offended when Derry tried to pay for their stay.

'If you can't do someone a good turn, don't do 'em a bad one, that's what I say,' she said. 'What's a bit of bacon anyroad?' Then in dry clothes, feeling full and warm, they walked to the little fellside church and caught the bus back to Windermere, and from there to Carreckwater.

'How did it go?' Jan wanted to know as they polished the windows and swept out the shop but Lissa made no reply, smiling as she worked.

'Ah, like that, eh? Good. About time you two got together,' Jan said, as if she had arranged it all. 'And you only got home this morning? Well, well, well.' There was a question in her voice and Lissa flushed, unable to prevent herself from looking guilty.

'There was a mist and we got a bit lost. Derry thought it safer to go down into Kentmere where we were offered accommodation by a very proper farmer's wife, so there.'

Jan's eyes danced. 'I'm sure. Very sensible on the hills, our Derry.'

'Weren't you worried when we didn't come home? We thought you might call out the mountain rescue.'

'Er, I stayed over at a friend's house myself,' Jan said. 'So, come on. Tell me all.'

'Stop it, Jan. It was very, very . . .'

'Innocent? Sweet? Passionate?'

'Oh, do stop asking questions,' Lissa complained, rubbing vigorously at the glass, already sparkling with her efforts.

Jan tucked her hair behind her ears and grinned. 'So nothing happened? How very disappointing.' And Lissa marched away, chin high, to beat her duster on the door post, setting both girls off in a fit of coughing, well mingled with laughter.

'To more mundane matters, did you see dear Stella on your way here this morning?'

Lissa shook her head, not really concentrating on what Jan was saying, her head too full of the delights of her Sunday walk and the way Derry had lingered over his goodbye kisses this morning at the bus stop.

'She isn't usually this late. And she has the stock room key. Until she comes we can't get in there, not even to make our morning cuppa.'

Lissa frowned. 'How did you get in the shop then?'

'Oh, she trusts me to keep a key for that, then we can get in and start cleaning. But we can't serve anybody until we get the change from the safe.' Jan was looking worried. 'I think I'll nip to the post office and telephone her home. She might be ill or something.'

Moments later she was back, looking more anxious than ever. 'No reply. What do you think can have happened? This isn't like her at all.'

'She's probably on her way right now.' Lissa started to polish the glass counters. She felt so good this morning, as if a new life had begun, which in a way it had. She and Derry had made arrangements to meet again this evening and her stomach was churning already with the agony of anticipation. How could she wait a whole day before seeing him?

It was when she carried some old stands out to the narrow dark corridor which ran behind the main shop that Lissa heard the sound. No more than an echo, it made her spine prickle and she wondered for a moment if she had imagined it. She froze, one hand caught in

202

mid-air. When it came again she knew it was real.

It was a groan. Miss Stevens was locked in the stock room. Dropping the stands with a clatter, Lissa ran for Jan.

'I should have realised,' she mourned. 'I knew something like this might happen one day. She's probably drunk as a lord.'

'Drunk?'

'Likes her little G and Ts, does our Stella. And her brandy. In fact she has no discrimination whatsoever. She's discreet, I'll give her that, but she can't count. *And* she has a bad stomach. Oh my, what if she's been there all weekend?'

They banged on the door, tried to force the lock but it wouldn't budge and there was only silence now from within. The two girls gazed at each other in horror.

'What ought we to do? How can we get her out without a key? Is there a back door?'

Jan shook her head. 'Nope.'

'Who will have a spare one?'

Jan thought about this for a minute then her face brightened. 'Her solicitor. He has a complete set as a precaution, since she is a maiden lady with no relatives. I remember her telling me soon after I came to work here.'

'Which solicitor?'

'Derry's boss, of course. How many do you think we have in a small town like Carreckwater? Philip Brandon. Well, there we are then, since you know him so well and have been given the privilege of a sail in his spanking yacht, you can have the pleasure of informing him that his esteemed client is three sheets to the wind.'

Lissa giggled but then quickly sobered. 'This isn't funny. Miss Stevens could be in dire difficulties. Perhaps we should call the police or an ambulance?'

Jan looked alarmed. 'Then they'd break down the door and she'd be furious. No, fetch Philip Brandon. He'll have a key and know exactly what to do.'

'OK.' Lissa was putting on her coat.

'Anyway, gives you the chance to see our Derry again, doesn't it?' Jan said, grinning wickedly, and Lissa's cheeks flamed.

'Really, Jan, there's a time and a place.' And she dashed off, trying hard to ignore the fast beating of her heart which had very little to do with Miss Stevens' predicament.

*   *   *

When Lissa reached the offices of Brandon and Brandon, there was no sign of Derry. It didn't surprise her. Probably out on one of his many errands.

Miss Henshaw showed her straight in for once, and when Philip had heard her tale he put on his coat right away.

And so it was that as Derry turned the corner of Benthwaite Cross on his return from the post office where he'd been making yet another of his long-distance calls, he saw Lissa climbing into Philip Brandon's car. She was smiling up at his ex-boss, apparently thanking him most profusely and Brandon was preening himself, as he usually did. Probably talking about him, Derry decided, and why he'd been sacked.

He hid in a doorway as the car drove slowly past, his own face tight with misery as he watched the two of them chatting with great animation within the upholstered interior.

No wonder she'd asked him so many questions about Renee. She was about to play the same trick. Go for the older man with money and status. That was all women thought about these days. Money. Fridges. Telephones. And to think he'd actually felt sorry for her and been nervous about admitting he was going away. She wouldn't miss him for more than a minute.

Miss Stevens was found in a crumpled heap in the corner of the stock room, an empty bottle of Milk of Magnesia clutched tightly in her hand and vomit all down the front of her best fair isle jumper. She was still alive, though how she had survived all weekend was considered a miracle. After the ambulance had carried her away both girls gave way to weeping.

Philip held them gently in his arms, patting, soothing, paying special attention to Lissa.

'If I hadn't heard her,' she mourned, 'how long might she have stayed there? Oh, I do wish we'd found her earlier. We were so busy talking all morning we never . . .' And she was off again, borrowing his great white handkerchief and sobbing her guilt into it while Jan recovered sufficiently to pull down the blinds and lock the door.

'We'd best close for today, out of respect,' she decided. 'Though how we'll manage now, I don't know. What will she want us to do? Will she be in hospital long, d'you think?' Philip took it upon himself to supply the answers.

'Who can say? You must carry on as before. I shall leave you with a complete set of keys, and you can bring the takings to me each evening when you lock up. I'll keep a watch on matters for Miss Stevens, never fear,' he reassured, delighted with this turn of events that would give him the opportunity to see more of Lissa. 'I can call in every day if need be.'

I'll bet you will, Jan thought, but only smiled, and agreed to do as he asked.

The letter was waiting for her when she got home to the boathouse. It lay on the mat, and Lissa picked it up with a soft smile on her face.

'It's from Derry,' she said, and hurried off to her room to read it in private.

'Lissa, Lost my job. Can't explain everything now but am on my way to Manchester. We've a chance of a recording contract. Who knows where it might lead? Can't believe our luck. Will write later and let you know when I'll be back. Derry.'

She read the letter again, read it several times before the full meaning of the words finally soaked in.

As a love letter it left much to be desired. He hadn't even signed it 'with love'. Only his precious recording contract seemed to matter. Yet he said that he would be back. Lissa, grasping at straws, read the letter over again. Yes, it definitely stated, *Will write later and let you know when I'll be back*. So it wasn't over. She simply had to trust him, and wait.

During the following weeks the note almost fell to pieces, so often did she open and read it. Jan kept on reminding Lissa how he'd promised to write and explain and tell her when he'd be home. Lissa would smile and nod and wonder why a letter never came. But then she knew all about promises in letters.

'Don't give up on him. He's not the best letter writer in the world but he's honest. Believe in him.'

'I do. Oh, I do,' Lissa said, making herself mean it for didn't he deserve to be trusted? Hadn't he guided her safely down the mountain?

Not that Jan was around as much as Lissa would have liked. Most weekends she went off to visit this new friend she had acquired, and since she volunteered no further information, Lissa did not like to

205

ask. But she felt the loss and a slight coolness sprang up between them for the first time.

Miss Stevens made good progress following an operation for a stomach ulcer, but would be away from business for some months, recovering. Philip Brandon informed them that she was happy for the current system to continue until she had decided what best to do about the shop.

'You mean she might close it?' Lissa asked, stunned.

'She may well decide to retire. She is well past fifty and not as healthy as she might be. But there is no immediate cause for concern,' he assured them. 'I trust you will not desert her for some other employment in her hour of need?'

Lissa was shocked. 'Of course not.' If she lost her job, she could go with Derry. Manchester, London, anywhere, what did it matter so long as they were together, and he wanted her?

But still there was no word.

Then one day Mrs Courtney came into the shop and told them that Tony had written to say that the recording deal had been a flop and they were all coming home. 'He and Helen have got engaged, you know, so we have a wedding to look forward to in the spring.'

'Oh, how lovely!' Lissa gazed enviously at the woman, so obviously pleased with herself. 'They're coming home, you say?'

'Yes, my dear. Next Wednesday, on the midday bus.'

'Derry too?'

'Of course Derry too. He said for you to meet him at the bus station. Since it's your half day.'

When Mrs Courtney had gone, making them promise that they would be sure to come to the wedding, which was certain to be the most spectacular event Carreckwater had ever seen, Jan gave a loud cheer and Lissa lifted shining eyes to hers. 'He's coming home.'

So thrilled was she, that she even told Philip Brandon the moment he walked into the shop that evening.

He'd taken to calling for the takings and helping them to lock up, often walking the girls home afterwards. Jan's presence irritated him but he hadn't quite worked out a way to avoid her yet. Though today she'd left early for once, and gone off somewhere. Nor had Lissa yet agreed to go out with him again, though he'd asked her a couple of times. Now he saw the excitement in her face at the prospect of his ex-clerk's return.

Philip thought how patient he had been, waiting for Lissa to grow up. Then when he'd seen her fix her attention on his clerk he'd set out to beat him, fair and square, so far as Lissa was concerned, in the yacht race and for her heart. In the end he'd been forced to give Derry the sack. Lissa didn't seem to know about that. Perhaps it was time that she did. Hadn't he been patient long enough?

Taking her elbow, Philip steered her across Carndale Road. 'I hope he has achieved whatever he set out to achieve.' So that he can stay in Manchester indefinitely.

Lissa pulled a wry face as she shook her head. 'Apparently not. Maybe this will bring him down to earth. No more chasing rainbows.'

'You think he'll settle down to a steady job?' There was the very slightest hint of irony in his tone which caused Lissa to bridle slightly.

'Yes, I believe he will.'

'He must, of course, find a job first.'

'Oh, but . . .'

'I'm afraid I have taken on a replacement clerk since he left. I was, in any case, dissatisfied with Derek. Rather too light-minded for the job. He told you, I dare say, that I had been given cause to sack him?'

'*What*?'

Lissa couldn't take in what he was telling her. That Derry, her Derry, would carry out such a criminal act was unthinkable. 'He would never do such a thing!'

Philip looked sad. 'I'm afraid Derek Colwith is not quite the innocent you seem to imagine. Those clothes he wears, for instance, speak volumes. Can't you see? You mustn't let yourself be fooled by his boyish charm.'

'I don't believe it. I won't believe it. He wouldn't touch your yacht.' But her voice trembled, momentarily uncertain. Derry had always disliked Philip Brandon, swearing he'd do anything to beat him and win that race. But he hadn't won the race, he'd been disqualified, by Brandon. And now he was jealous of Philip's attentions to her.

Tears filled her eyes and Philip handed her a large white handkerchief. 'I'm so sorry. I didn't mean to upset you. Let me buy you a drink.' And before she had time to protest, he was leading her into the Marina Hotel, settling her into a comfortable chair and handing her a brandy.

207

It shot like fire through her veins, making her head spin.

'Oh dear, alcohol on an empty stomach,' she said.

And so a meal was ordered and brought, and Philip was all attention, smiling, handsome, charming, nothing too much trouble.

He was really very kind, she thought, if a bit serious for her taste. He talked a good deal about how Carreckwater was developing as a town, due in part to tourism, and partly to the old money that existed here and how those people must never be forgotten. She tried to sound interested but her mind was elsewhere. She must keep her faith in Derry. She must. What else did she have? Even Jan had deserted her these days.

'I think I'd like to go home now,' she said.

'Of course.'

He walked her home, held her hand for a brief moment as he unlocked the door of the boathouse then smiled into her eyes. 'I've enjoyed this evening. Perhaps we may repeat it some time?'

Lissa smiled vaguely, not quite seeing him. 'That would be lovely.' What would Derry's explanation be? she wondered. He must surely have one. She wouldn't think the worst until she'd heard his version.

Lissa could hardly wait for Wednesday to come, her excitement making her tension grow as the week progressed.

Something new must be purchased of course. She could hardly meet Derry at the bus station in any old rag. She bought a smart little suit with a straight skirt and box jacket in a soft powder blue, and small hat to match, with white gloves and handbag. She brushed her hair till it shone and bought a new lipstick in bright coral. It was the most daring colour she'd ever tried.

When Wednesday arrived she would have set off down the road a good two hours early had Jan not prevented her.

'I'll make you a cup of tea.'

'No, it'll spoil my lipstick.'

'Well, sit still for half an hour at least.'

But she couldn't sit still for a minute. 'What time is it?'

'Too soon.'

'If only he'd written himself.'

'He hates writing letters. Tony's mother passed on his message. You know what time to meet him.'

'But what if he no longer cares for me?'

'Of course he still cares. Stop worrying.'

'Do I look all right?'

'Yes,' said Jan on a sigh. 'You look beautiful, as ever. I'm sure Derry will think so.'

Jan settled herself in the big saggy arm chair and picked up the knitting that was rarely out of her hand these days while Lissa went to the window to look out along the shore just in case he might arrive early, though how he could manage that until the bus came at noon she wasn't sure. 'You aren't going out today, are you?' Lissa asked. 'He'll want to see you too.'

Jan smiled and shook her head. 'No, I told – my friend – that I couldn't come today.'

At the sight of Jan's face, Lissa forgot for a moment her own affairs and, sitting beside her, gathered Jan's hands in her own. 'Won't you tell me who he is? It is a man, isn't it?'

Jan set down her knitting and gazed at the floor, eyes half closed in her familiar squint, as if perplexed. 'Well, yes, of course it is. It's just that we – we decided it best not to tell you at first. It was me, I didn't want to hurt you. And I wanted to be sure.'

'What are you trying to say? He isn't married, is he?' Lissa waited with trepidation as Jan raised brown eyes, so like Derry's, and met her questioning gaze.

'Heavens, no. It's Nick. We love each other and he wants to marry me.'

'*Nick*? *My* Nick?' Lissa could hardly believe her ears.

'Not your Nick any more.'

'Oh, lord, that's wonderful.'

'You don't mind?'

'Why should I mind? I'm delighted. You're really going to marry Nick?'

Jan nodded, a wide happy smile lighting her plain face and giving it a new radiance, a sweet blossoming beauty. 'Yes, I am. He wants to marry me as soon as possible so I can go and live at Ashlea.'

Lissa squealed and hugged her in delight. 'I can't believe it. It's wonderful. But why keep it a secret? Why didn't you tell me?'

Jan gave a shamefaced little shrug. 'I know he had a thing going for you, for years. Nick said as how you might not care to have your nose pushed out. He said he'd always meant to marry you himself.'

Lissa laughed. 'That was only schoolboy stuff.'

'Well, he never stopped talking about you the first few times we

209

went out. I had to be sure he really liked me and wasn't just using me to reach you.' Her eyes were bright and Lissa's heart clenched.

'Oh, Jan. I'm sure Nick would never do such a thing.'

She blinked. 'I know that now. He says he does love you, as an honorary cousin, always will. But his feelings for me are . . .' She blushed bright red. 'Quite different.' They were laughing again, squealing with delight and the warmth of friends who might one day be sisters. If Lissa had her way.

'Heavens, Derry! What time is it?'

'Go on. Don't be late. He'll be as impatient as you. Make sure I'm chief bridesmaid, and you can do the same for me.'

They hugged one last time then Lissa set off, heels clicking on the slate pavements, a spring in her step, face shining with happiness. Soon she would see him. Oh, she was so thrilled about Nick and Jan, her two dearest friends. How good life was.

Jan stood and watched her go, not quite so confident. She hadn't mentioned it, but the other families had not heard from their boys at all recently. One letter when they'd arrived in Manchester, but nothing since. It was puzzling. But she was sure it would all turn out right in the end.

Bus station was rather a grand term for two shelters and a newsagent's that doubled as a small booking office. These simple structures linked Carreckwater to the outside world. The railway had never got beyond Windermere, despite valiant efforts by eminent Victorians, so without a car, the bus was the only means of getting in and out of the village. It ran several times a day in the summer. But in the winter, as now, it came twice. If you were lucky. The driver had been known not to bother if he couldn't rustle up enough passengers. Lissa worried that this might happen today. The bus wouldn't drive all the way along the valley simply to bring Derry home. What if he were left stranded in Windermere? What if he had to sleep on the station all night?

She walked restlessly up and down, wishing she'd put on a coat over her new suit for it was bitterly cold. The wind swept down from the hills, through both open shelters, swirling up toffee wrappings, discarded bus tickets and dried leaves and depositing them in untidy heaps in the open road, before blowing them all away again.

Would the bus never come?

And then she saw it. Small, red, and dearly familiar, it rumbled

210

along as if it had all the time in the world. As if she were not waiting for her life to begin, her heart beating twenty to the dozen.

Helen came running up, at the last minute as usual.

'Is it here?' she gasped, flushed and excited, and Lissa tried not to glance at the sparkle of diamonds on the third finger of her left hand.

The bus drew up and then Tony was leaping out, Helen was squealing and flinging herself ecstatically into his arms.

Lissa stepped forward, looking for Derry's dearly loved face, eager for her own turn.

A touch on her elbow brought her spinning around, face alight with love. But it was Tony, pink with embarrassment. He was holding out an envelope and Lissa was staring at it as if it were poison.

A letter? Why had he sent a letter? She looked into Tony's eyes and knew that her own were pleading. Tell me he's here, they said, but Tony only shuffled his feet, thrust the letter into her reluctant fingers and gathering Helen close, walked quickly away into the wind.

She held it unopened in her hand for a long time. The conductor rang the bell, the gears of the bus grated loud in the empty street and slowly the vehicle moved off. Lissa stood alone, staring at the square of paper in her hand.

With trembling fingers she slit open the envelope and quickly scanned the few words on the single page, her heart filled with a fearful anticipation at what she might find.

He wasn't coming. There it was in black and white. He was very sorry but there was no work for him in Carreckwater. Since he'd failed to realise his dreams in Manchester, he thought he might as well try London.

She felt her heart shrivel and her hopes crumble to dust. The pain in her breast was so bad she thought she must be dying.

'I'll be in touch,' the letter said.

In touch? How? With a card each Christmas as if they were strangers?

He'd signed it in his usual way, with not a word of love. She must have imagined that he loved her. She must have dreamt those hours out on the fells when he'd made love to her with a passion that said he didn't want to let her go, even for a moment. Imagined that he'd promised to love her for ever.

For he'd clearly meant not one tender word, not one of those

211

glorious kisses. Derry Colwith had broken his promise and rejected her, just like everyone else.

A wildness came over Lissa following the receipt of that letter. Had her old friend Nick been there he might have recognised a glimpse of the girl she had once been. Her eyes sparkled and her ebony hair crackled. But it was not happiness that wrought this change in her but despair, fury, even hatred. The subdued, withdrawn Lissa had quite gone and in her place was a counterfeit of that early promise.

She wanted to be on the go all the time. She redecorated the boathouse, went dancing every Saturday night, worked far longer than was necessary in the shop, cleaning out corners of the stock room that had never seen the light of day. But she could not eradicate the pain and misery in her own heart.

Christmas came and both she and Jan visited Broombank.

Meg and Tam were delighted to have the family about them again. Lissa played the old harmonium and even Joe joined in with the happy carolling. His wife Connie came, as she always did for Christmas, however much she might avoid farm life for the rest of the year. Sally Ann and Meg put on a huge spread and everyone ate too much and laughed too loud and took turns with the endless washing up. Almost as if life were normal, Lissa thought.

She did her best not to feel envious of the lingering looks, the secret whispers and stolen kisses of the two lovers. Their happiness shone from them like a radiance. Sometimes Sally Ann would whisk her daughter-in-law-to-be off into a corner to talk about weddings and dresses and flowers, when they weren't studying new stitches for their endless knitting.

Meg found she had a new audience who had not heard her sheep stories. Given chance she would talk endlessly about her beloved land, and the different qualities of staple in the wool she produced. And Grandfather Joe told how he had won the war without leaving his own fireside.

The result was that Lissa felt more than ever an outsider in her own home. She didn't seem to belong anywhere, or to anyone.

Jan might tell her not to worry, that Derry's crazy ambitions might take him off chasing rainbows but that he still cared, deep down – Lissa didn't believe a word of it.

'Why promise to come home and then go as far as he could in the opposite direction?'

Jan had no answer.

And there were no more letters. A Christmas card, as expected, to keep in touch. It carried no address and said little beyond the fact that he still had several agents to see.

Lissa didn't know where she would have been during these miserable weeks without the kindness of Philip Brandon. On his daily calls when he checked the shop and reported on Miss Stevens' slow return to health, he also found time in his busy schedule to stop and chat with her, and try to cheer her up. He showed concern over her health and the fact that she wasn't sleeping.

Lissa appreciated his concern. He sent her flowers and once a box of chocolates. He often bought her a coffee in The Cobweb, a new coffee bar that had opened by the shore, when she seemed at a loose end at lunchtimes. He was so attentive that on occasions she found herself very nearly flirting with him, deciding he was really quite attractive, for all he was older than she.

But when he asked her for a date, she refused.

'You must eat.'

'I don't ever seem to be hungry.'

'He isn't worth it, Lissa.'

'No,' she said. 'He isn't.'

'Try me,' he said. 'I promise I'd never let you down.'

'Ah,' she said, a sad smile on her lips. 'Promises.'

When he asked her out to dine with him again, she thought, To hell with it, why not? Recklessly she spent far more money than she could afford on a new dress in a daring off-the-shoulder style. She tucked up her hair into a stylish french pleat, wanting to look elegant. She'd been out with Philip Brandon before. This was hardly a new experience.

It proved to be a wonderful evening. He was charming and flattering, if not quite so amusing as Derry. He treated her as if she were made of Dresden, which right then was how she felt, so fragile she might break. He soothed her jangled nerves and told her not to blame herself for Derry's defection. But she did. If she'd been worth loving he would still be here. As would her mother.

'I don't intend to trust you either,' she told Philip, slanting her violet eyes up at him in a most bewitching manner.

'What have I done?' he asked, his handsome face so bleak she couldn't help but laugh. 'I only want you to be happy, Lissa.'

If she couldn't trust Derry, who could she trust? But then she had loved Derry, and that was why it hurt so much. She had loved Meg and presumably her mother. She didn't love Philip Brandon so how could he ever let her down?

17

Derry sat gloomily shivering in a small bare room at his lodgings. He would have put on the single bar electric fire since little sun peeped through the filthy windows, but he had no shillings to spare for the meter.

He'd been had. He knew that now. The whole thing had been a disaster from start to finish. He'd left Carreckwater on a wish and a prayer, dreaming of his name on a record label, his voice playing on Radio Luxembourg and money pouring in. Instead there'd been a seedy-looking character, a bunch of recording equipment that must have seen better days, and an empty, filthy warehouse. Why the man had invited them to come in the first place was a puzzle because he'd showed little interest in their music.

They'd gone once through the songs they'd chosen and that was it. 'I'll give you a call,' he'd said. But never had. They'd hawked themselves all around Manchester to no avail, then headed for London, which was even worse. No streets paved with gold here either. Only dozens, if not hundreds, of other young look-alike Tommy Steeles and Elvis Presleys.

Derry was alone now because the others had gone home to their caring families, their warm loving homes.

'More sense than me.' Anyway, what home did he have to go to? Renee and her garden shed? Dad looking disappointed in him?

So he'd stuck it out, hoping to find some interest in his playing. He'd practically worn his crêpe soles to shreds trekking up and down the streets, in and out of dozens of agencies, sitting for hour upon hour only to be told there was nothing today, thank you very much.

He hadn't two beans to rub together and make a stew with. He'd spent all his spare cash on bus fares, not to mention a seemingly endless supply of new guitar strings. He had just over a pound in loose change in his pocket and not a scrap of food in the cupboard. He couldn't get a job because if he was working he couldn't be selling himself in the agencies.

He'd tried busking, that way he could eat. But he'd come to London looking for his name in lights not pennies in a cap on the pavement. Derry forced himself to ignore the gnawing fear that however hard he practised he might never be good enough to make it.

He owed a week's rent and hope was dead in him, dry as ash in his mouth. His belly ached with hunger and his knees knocked with cold. And all he could think of was Lissa. Her bright, smiling face, her silken hair, her long limbed loveliness haunted him day and night. What a complete idiot he was.

Had he lost her?

Whenever he thought of her the ache in his gut felt worse. He'd been so wrapped up in his dreams, he hadn't given proper thought to how he really felt about her. He'd wanted to impress her. The last time he'd seen her she was fawning at the feet of his oh-so-charming boss. He couldn't compete with Philip Brandon's cheque book. He couldn't afford to take her to fancy restaurants, couldn't promise her any sort of future. And she deserved a good future. Lissa needed stability and security, which were the very things he couldn't even provide for himself, let alone a mixed up kid with a great chip on her shoulder.

The only things he'd had in his favour were his looks and his ability to play the guitar. He'd wanted to come back with a recording contract, the promise of riches. How could he face her as a failure?

He sat in abject misery, rubbing his hands to get the circulation going, shivering with cold.

On the other hand, Derry reasoned, desperately searching for a shred of hope, she might wait for him. If he asked her nicely. Perhaps he'd given in too quickly? Maybe there was a good reason for her being in that car? He couldn't stand meekly by and let Philip Brandon set him up for a crime he didn't commit, then pinch his girl.

He looked at the piece of scarlet ribbon tied to a peg at the end of his guitar. At least he still had that. It served to remind him of happier days. Was there still a chance? He was filled suddenly with

216

a rush of hot determination. He'd give himself a few more weeks to try to make it, then he'd go back and find out. Hitch a lift, busk till he had enough money to settle his debts and pay the fare. Anything. He wouldn't give up hope. Not yet.

The winter months passed and the first green shoots of spring appeared. The lilac-veined white blossoms of wood sorrel crowded the woodlands, wild daffodils lined the fringes of the blue-grey lakes. Wheatears and chiffchaffs were, as usual, the first birds to arrive for the summer months, followed by the willow warblers. Lissa sat at her window in the boathouse and wondered if Derry would fly home too. She ached for him so much the pain of her longing made her feel quite ill at times. But he did not come. Nor was there any news of him beyond one scribbled note.

'Not the greatest letter writer in the world, is he?' Jan complained as she re-read a scrap of paper that might once have formed part of a brown paper bag. 'What a young fool he is. Says he's getting some auditions and will you write back? Shall I tell him his stationery leaves much to be desired?' But Jan's eyes were accusing, for all her casual wit as she waited for Lissa's reply.

Lissa only kept her own gaze on the untroubled calm of the lake, for it never failed to soothe her.

'He chose to leave, not me. He knows where I am.'

Jan sighed with exasperation. 'He wants to prove himself.'

'He doesn't have to prove anything to me.' Except that he loves me. Lissa firmed her lips, outlining them with a bright, red lipstick, remembering the time not so long ago when she had watched Jan get ready to go out while she played Cinderella and stayed in all the time. Now the reverse was true. Jan complained she had changed and was never home. Lissa intended to change. Staying in was bad for her. It gave her time to think.

Nor did she care how much make-up she wore. It helped somehow, to see a different face in the mirror than the one Derry had loved. She felt reckless enough to try anything, even going so far as to paint each of her nails a different colour. It was quite the rage, as were her pale blue nylon stockings, snapped seductively in place with a mere scrap of lace.

'Oh, Lissa. How hard you've grown.'

Lissa blinked away the prick of tears that stung the backs of her eyes. 'Not hard, self-protective maybe. Necessary if one is to survive in this world. Or so I've learned. I've no intention of feeling guilty for not writing when he was the one who failed to keep his promises. Tony came back, so did the others one by one. But not Derry. Oh no, he must pursue his dream at all costs. I'm not very high on his list of priorities am I?'

He'd made a fool of her, letting her think that he loved her when really he was simply using her for his own pleasure, as everyone else had done. Lissa thought, If I don't stop, I'll cry, and ruin all my careful composure. Snapping shut her mascara case she flung it into her bag.

Then she calmly smoothed the kingfisher blue satin of her short evening dress with its hip hugging skirt, picked up the beaded black bag and smiled serenely at Jan in the mirror. 'Do you think this colour suits me?'

How could anyone deny that Lissa Turner was beautiful? 'I think you're playing with fire.' And driving me mad, Jan inwardly steamed, but managed to content herself with a nod of approval as she banged the kettle about and set it on the stove. 'You're a cruel, unforgiving woman with a heart of ice. Derry has lost everything and now he's about to lose you.'

Lissa started as if Jan had struck her. It took several seconds to get herself under control.

'Ice keeps things safe and in pristine condition.' She licked a finger tip and dabbed the curls into place, one on each cheek bone, with a sigh that was meant to indicate satisfaction but only sounded discontented.

'He's doing this for you.'

Lissa's violet eyes blazed with sudden fire and she swung about to face her friend, more furious than Jan had ever seen her. 'Don't give me that! He's doing this for himself. Your brother isn't to be trusted, Jan. He led me up the proverbial garden path, letting me believe he loved me. I certainly fell for his line of chat and gave him everything a girl can give to a guy. So there, now you know. He's no good, and I don't ever want to see . . .' Her voice choked on a tiny strangled cry.

'Oh, love, I didn't know.' Then Jan was holding her in her arms and Lissa was biting hard on her lower lip to stop the tears which would surely come if she relaxed her discipline for only a second.

From outside came the sound of a car's horn.

Jan clicked her tongue with impatience and pulled aside the curtain

218

to peer out into the darkness while Lissa searched frantically in her bag for a powder puff. 'Why doesn't he come to the door in a civilised manner?'

'Perhaps he senses your disapproval.' Lissa slipped stockinged feet into high stiletto heels, collecting the cashmere stole Philip had bought her. 'Don't wait up, I might be late. He's taking me to the theatre at Keswick and dinner afterwards.'

She'd partnered him for the New Year Ball at the Yacht Club, causing quite a stir amongst his friends. But why worry? He was good-looking, enjoyed her company and made her feel confident about herself. And he never seemed short of money. If he wished to spend it on her, take her to the very best restaurants and order the finest wines, why shouldn't she accept? It gave him enormous pleasure, he said. With Philip Brandon she could have fun. She was beginning to pull herself together, wasn't she, and enjoy life again without worrying about love and heartache and all of that dangerous nonsense.

And he made no demands upon her. Once, in his car, he had kissed her, and with too much champagne singing in her head she'd very nearly encouraged him to go further. Derry had taught her that loving could be delicious, hadn't he? Would it matter if she did surrender? Lissa had thought. She'd already proved how wicked she was. But Philip had folded her caressing hands into her lap and apologised for his affrontery.

'Oh, Lissa,' Jan groaned, grasping at her arm as she made for the door. 'Don't do it. Please stop seeing Philip Brandon. He isn't right for you, really he isn't. He's too old for one thing.'

Lissa stared at her friend with cold, unseeing eyes. She didn't care to be told what to do any more now than she had as a rebellious adolescent. She certainly felt old enough to make up her own mind.

'Unlike your foolish brother, I'm not a child with my head in the clouds, playing childish games in childish clothes. I gave up such nonsense years ago. I'm a woman and I enjoy the attention of an attractive male, particularly one who is reliable and courteous, gracious and charming and with impeccable manners. Philip is all of those things and I like him. Is that so wrong? And he enjoys my company which is more than your brother obviously did.' She felt her legs start to tremble and knew if she didn't get out of the room fast, she would burst into tears. 'In any case, Jan,' she said, as she flung open the door, 'I really don't think it's any of your business. Do you?'

'Well, look who the wind's blown in,' Renee said.

He stood on her doorstep trying not to look shamefaced. Then Renee blew on her bubble gum and cracked it. 'You'd best come in, I suppose.'

'Thanks.' She hadn't changed, he thought.

Over a cup of very welcome tea and several ginger biscuits which went some way towards abating his hunger, Derry briefly told his tale, trying to make a joke of it and failing miserably.

'Poor love,' she said, as if she were years older and wiser than him. 'All that effort with nowt to show for it.' She watched him pick up two more biscuits. 'Have you eaten lately?'

'N-not today.'

'This week, for instance?'

He smiled. 'Not that I noticed.'

Less than fifteen minutes later Derry was sitting down to a plate loaded with lamb chops, baked beans and chips.

'By heck, Renee, you're a treasure,' he said, tucking in with gusto. He couldn't remember when a meal tasted so good.

'Generous to a fault, that's me,' she said. 'Eat up. I'll make a fresh pot of tea.'

Later, as he sat replete on the opposite side of the brown-tiled fireplace, Derry thanked her.

'You're all right, Renee. I'll forgive you for nabbing my dad. Though he's too good for you.'

'Thanks a bunch. I'd still've been waiting to this day if I'd hung on for you.' She grinned happily at him, content with her lot. 'Instead, you thought you'd got young Lissa in the pudding club, did you? Then ran away, to avoid trouble?'

Derry's cheeks flamed bright scarlet and he was on his feet in a second. 'No, dammit, I didn't.' He stopped, appalled. 'She isn't, is she?'

'Ooh, not far wrong, was I? Well, well. She wouldn't be the first it's happened to.' Renee smiled, orange lips clashing horribly with the shocking pink of her sweater. 'Happen I'm only teasing.'

'What?' Colour rushed back into his ashen cheeks. 'You rotten . . . You mean she isn't?'

220

'Not unless she's carrying it in her handbag. Thin as a rail she is these days. Mebbe Philip Brandon likes her that way though.'

'Philip Brandon?'

'Aye. Your ex-boss, no less.' Renee took an age to light up a cigarette before she continued. 'Escorts her everywhere, or so I'm told. Not that I see much of her these days. Quite the gad-about-town. Wouldn't recognise her, you wouldn't. Come out of her shell good and proper. Ain't that right, my pretty Peter?' she finished, directing her last words to the budgie, busy bashing its mirror, as usual.

Derry stood in the middle of the tiny, overheated parlour and looked so stricken that a wave of maternal sympathy washed over Renee. 'Oh, my poor cherub,' she gushed, going to wrap her arms about him and pull his head down to her rounded breasts. 'She's cheated on you, hasn't she, the rotten madam?' Renee thought how good he felt against her. But then he'd always had a good body, had Derry. She wriggled closer. 'And you're such a wonderful lover, she must be mad.'

He tried to pull away from Renee's clinging embrace but the scent of her was so familiar, of strawberries and lipstick and summer days, and he felt so wretched that when she put her lips against his, he didn't protest but kissed her back. She reminded him of a time long past when he hadn't a care in the world. She placed his hand on the soft cushion of her breast and it felt so comforting the joy of coming home swamped him. He forgot for a moment that it was Lissa he wanted, not Renee.

The front door banged open and the scent changed to wood shavings, rain and the acrid taste of varnish.

'Oh, bugger me,' Renee calmly said, pulling away from his arms. 'Now the cat's among the pigeons, ain't it, Peter my pretty boy?'

Derry found himself staring into the furious eyes of his father. It was some moments of scarlet-faced embarrassment before he managed to speak.

'Christ! This isn't how it looks.' He wished he'd died of starvation in those awful lodgings. Fallen in the Thames or under a Manchester bus.

Renee was the only one who still seemed in possession of a voice. 'Just giving the poor little love a step-motherly cuddle,' she said, going over to Jimmy and smacking a kiss on his cheek. 'Had a bit of a disappointment, our Derry. Come home to lick his wounds, he has. Are you ready for your tea, love?' Jimmy neither moved

221

nor answered. 'A stiffener, mebbe? I think we've got some sherry somewhere. Celebrate the return of the prodigal, eh?'

She went to the new sideboard and poured out three glasses, placing them on a small, tile-topped coffee table. Two stood untouched while she took her own back to her chair by the fire and beamed at her husband and stepson.

'Well now, isn't this cosy?'

Jimmy glared at his son. 'Out.'

'What?'

'Out. This is my home, my wife, and I'll not have that sort of behaviour here.'

'But I never meant . . .'

Jimmy pulled open the front door, every taut line of his wiry body declaring he would stand no argument. He emphasised his words by ominously pushing up his sleeves. 'Don't make me any madder than I already am, Derry. I'm not a man given to violence but I have my limits. You've never shown any respect for Renee. Now you've gone too far. *Out.*'

'OK, OK, I was going anyway. I only came back to see how you all were.' Derry swaggered to the door.

'Go and see her,' Renee called as he sauntered nonchalantly down the front path. Derry did not reply, nor look back. But he winced when he heard the door slam and wished he could turn back the clock and make it all come out different. Now he was at odds with his father, on top of everything else. Dear God, what was happening to him?

Could he still put things right with Lissa if he tried? He'd go and see her, right now. He'd tell her how he hadn't realised just how much he loved her. How he missed and needed her. He'd take a job here in Carreckwater, as a kitchen porter if necessary. Or he'd beg her to wait for him. He could make it big in something for Lissa, just see if he couldn't. He'd work hard to build a good future for them. 'Give me the chance, Lissa, that's all I ask.'

He stepped out with fresh vigour, a breeze from the lake ruffling his quiff but he didn't even notice.

It was one of those beautiful clear nights that often come in early spring. The sky seemed studded with stars while a pale moon floated in the black waters of the lake. Lissa stared at it through the windows of Philip's car and wished she could float with it, deep into a magic world where everything was beautiful and there were no more bitter disppointments.

'You're not cold?' he asked, ever considerate, and she turned to him with a smile.

'No, I'm fine. Thank you for a wonderful evening. Would you like a cup of coffee?'

He glanced across at the boathouse, in complete darkness. 'What about Jan?'

'She'll be in bed by this time.'

He smiled. 'Fine.'

He stood and watched her as she moved about the small kitchen, enjoying the sway of her slender hips, the rise and fall of her breasts. How patient he'd been. He was really quite proud of himself. But not for much longer. He could feel he was winning.

'It was a good meal, wasn't it? I love trout. And the play was superb. Time we enjoyed some culture. Next time we'll try a concert in Lancaster.'

He was growing ever more proprietorial, making decisions for her. Lissa never protested, it saved her the trouble of making them for herself. What did it matter where they went? She smiled her agreement. 'That would be lovely,' she said. Philip knew so much and she so little. She appreciated his efforts to educate and entertain her. And he made her feel so safe.

Miss Stevens had decided to sell the shop and take early retirement so she mightn't have a job for much longer. The prospect of starting again, seeking new friends, new job, perhaps a new home, chilled her.

Nor did she wish to return home to Broombank. Jan was happily planning her wedding and Lissa couldn't bear the prospect of watching her glowing happiness. It would be too much. It would make her feel even more of an outsider and unwanted.

'You don't know what these evenings have meant to me,' Philip was saying. 'You've made me the happiest man on earth.'

Lissa glanced at him in surprise. 'Have I?'

He reached for her, pulling her into his arms, smoothing his hands lingeringly down her spine and over her hips, the sensuality of the gesture catching her unawares. 'You must guess how I feel about you, Lissa. You've filled my rather dull life with joy. You can't imagine how much I needed someone like you, only I never thought I'd be so lucky. Since Felicity died . . .' He stopped and seemed to take a minute to collect himself. Lissa's heart filled with sympathy. She knew about pain.

'It's all right. There's no need for you to talk about it. I understand how you must have felt when she . . . when she died in that tragic way.'

His dark eyes swam with gratitude. 'Of course you do. Because you have known pain too. Darling Lissa, what can I say? You humble me by your beauty. I want you never to suffer pain again. We both of us deserve so much more, a new beginning. To have you here, beside me, makes me the richest man in the world. We are so well suited. All I ask is to spend the rest of my life making you happy. I believe you feel exactly the same way.' He was taking her hand, slipping something into it.

She glanced down, surprised. 'Philip?'

'I've decided it's time we made it official.'

She opened the box in a daze and stared at the ring, no more than a glittering blur in her hand.

'If it isn't the right size I can get it altered. You do like diamonds, don't you, darling? I thought them the most suitable. Let me put it on for you. There, perfectly lovely. Flawless, like you, darling.'

'I am far from perfect.' Diamonds. Ice cold. Many-faceted. Diamonds are right for me in that respect, she thought.

'To me you are entirely perfect.' He kissed her cheek. Chaste and undemanding, it reassured her. 'I thought June for the wedding. Far the best month for weather. A reception at the Marina Hotel, followed perhaps by a smaller one at your own home of course, with your family about you. You have no objection to June?'

She gazed up into his face, his eyes filled with a quiet eagerness to please, anxiety to make her happy. And offering the stability and security she craved.

'I need you, Lissa.'

It was all she wanted to hear. No more broken promises, no more rejection. A simple and uncomplicated relationship, dependable and caring, untroubled by too much emotion.

'June would be perfect,' she said.

Lissa was upstairs showing Jan her ring as Philip had suggested when the knock came. Philip crossed the room and opened the door.

Derry stood on the step, mouth dropping open in shock.

'Mr Brandon.'

Philip half glanced back over his shoulder, then stepping out on to the step, pulled the door to behind him. He spoke to Derry in a low voice, rich with unspent anger. 'What the hell are you doing here? What do you want?'

Derry's brain was spinning so fast he could hardly find the words. 'I-I want to see Lissa.'

Philip made a sound rather like an angry bear and jabbed one finger in Derry's chest, pushing him backwards down the steps and on to the shingle. 'The last thing Lissa wants is you hanging around, creating trouble.'

'I'm not here to make trouble. I need to talk to her, that's all.'

'She has no wish to talk to you.'

'How would you know?' Derry wanted to ask what Philip Brandon was doing in the boathouse at past eleven o'clock at night but couldn't seem to get his tongue around the words. Maybe because he was too afraid of the answer. 'Isn't that something she should decide for herself?'

'You promised to stay away. You know what'll happen if you don't.'

Derry stiffened. 'Is that a threat?'

'My boat is still undergoing repairs.' Quietly spoken, with undertones of menace. Derry gulped.

'I never touched your bloody boat. Maybe I'll face the police and tell them that.'

Philip's dark eyes raked over Derry from the top of his tousled head to his dusty shoes. 'You could try it, but think of the risk. I see you haven't made your fortune yet. Quite the reverse in fact. Scruffier than ever, if you ask me, in that old leather jacket and Teddy Boy jeans. The world is moving on, Derry. It really is time you started to grow up.'

Derry wanted to yell that his jacket cost fifteen quid and wasn't scruffy at all but he'd worn it every day for months, so he ground his teeth together and held his temper with difficulty. Brandon was only trying to rile him. And he really had no wish to get involved with the police. Not the way his luck was running at the moment. 'Where is she?'

'I've told you.' Having reasserted control Brandon was gracious. 'You are history so far as Lissa is concerned. I'll tell her you called.'

'What will you tell me?' A familiar voice from the door. A beloved figure silhouetted against the light that spilled out on to the shingle. And as she moved involuntarily towards him so that the moonlight captured her in its radiance, he gazed up at her, speechless, awed by her ethereal beauty.

'Hello,' he said. Renee was right, he thought. She was too thin. Her eyes were like dark bruises in her face. Oh, but so lovely and fresh, and surely that light which suddenly sparkled on her face was happiness at seeing him?

'Derry?'

Philip walked over to her and put his arm about her waist. 'I was telling Derek that it was rather late for social calls, but he's leaving on the first train from Windermere in the morning, so he's in a hurry. Aren't you?'

'Er, well I . . .'

Lissa cleared her throat, her brain surging with so many questions she could hardly think. What was he doing here? What did this mean? And then reality sank in. 'Train? Are you leaving again, Derry? So soon? Why didn't you tell us you were coming?'

'He has his fortune to make, my dear. Have you not, young sir?' Philip said in a jokey voice. 'Shall we tell him our good news, darling?' He pulled her closer to his side and smiled triumphantly upon Derry. 'Lissa has done me the honour, as they say, of agreeing to become my wife.'

A short stunned silence during which there was no sound but that of the waves noisily slapping the shore.

'Your wife?' Derry's voice had sunk to a whisper, as if he was afraid of disturbing that silence. But there was fury in it. And cold shock. 'Did you say *wife*?'

'Show him the ring, darling.' It was Philip who held out Lissa's hand, since she seemed reluctant to display quite the right degree of pride in it herself. 'Rather lovely, don't you think? A well-cut stone. Only the best, of course, for my own love. We thought June for the happy day. Let us have your address when you get settled, then we'll maybe send you an invitation.'

Derry stared at Lissa, bemused, a question in his brown eyes, but she was looking up at Philip and the expression upon her pale face was quite unreadable.

'I doubt I'd be able to manage it,' he said stiffly, fighting the tremor

226

in his voice. 'Congratulations. You must be very happy,' he said to
Lissa. Only then did she look at him and her eyes seemed distant,
unforgiving, empty.

'Yes,' she said. 'I must, mustn't I?'

1961

18

A coating of rust lay upon the mountains. Mist hung in the valley, trailing ethereally over the glass-calm water. There were fairy rings in the woodlands that clustered along the shoreline, and heaps of leaves in gold and amber and bronze. The mallards hustled together on the lake in restless groups, sometimes springing up into the air with a great whirring of wings, instinct telling them that soon their feathers would be ready for flight to the winter nesting grounds further south. One pair came waddling across the road, as if returning from a shopping expedition in the quiet streets of the town.

'Raarb!' called the showy drake, bossing his dull brown wife, but she refused to hurry, holding up traffic, making people curse or smile as their mood took them.

Lissa tried to smile too but the sight was almost painful. She felt at one with the plain little wife, following on in the wake of her mate, his brilliance outshining hers.

It was three years since she had married Philip Brandon. It had taken less than three months to realise her mistake. A sobering thought.

It served her right of course. No one else had been in favour of the match. Certainly not Jan.

And when Lissa had asked Meg and Tam for permission to marry since she was still under age, Meg's reply had been to urge her not even to think of it until she was at least twenty-one.

'You're too young, sweetheart,' she'd said. 'Do you truly love him?'

Love? What was love? Lissa didn't trust love. Love let you down.

It had no substance. It lasted only for a moment and was all tied up with duty and selfish need. Why should she expect anyone to love her when her own mother and grandmother hadn't even bothered to try? Meg had tried, she supposed, until she'd started wanting her own babies. Derry hadn't. Derry had let her down like all the rest. No, best to steer clear of love. It was unreliable.

So Lissa had married Philip Brandon one sunny day in June, 1958, and twelve months later almost to the day the twins had been born.

Only in that moment, when her babies were put into her arms, did Lissa learn about love. Sarah and Elizabeth were two precious scraps of humanity with soft downy hair, curling fingers tipped with pearl, and bewitching blue eyes. Even at birth Sarah seemed especially alert and enquiring, while Beth, as she at once came to be known, contentedly smiled. They were a part of her and Lissa knew that their birth had changed her life for all time. She could pour all of that damned up love upon them without fear of rebuff.

Not that it was quite fair to blame Philip for whatever it was she felt their marriage lacked. He adored her and told her so all the time. The failure must be in herself. She should be the happiest woman on earth. As well as her beautiful children she had a lovely home on the Parade with a fine view of the lake and the mountains beyond. Beautiful clothes to wear, an interesting social life with a good-looking husband, and money in her purse at all times. Philip gave her everything a woman could possibly desire. So what was the matter with her? She could surely expect no more?

'Come along, darlings, throw the crust to the ducks. We must go home soon.'

The two year olds squealed and giggled as the ducks clustered about, gobbling up the pieces of bread they had thrown with such verve but which had landed only inches from their feet.

Sarah suddenly took it into her head to set off after one unfortunate duck, running on unsteady legs down the shingle to the water. Laughing, Lissa snatched up Beth, who protested vigorously, and ran after her.

The duck took evasive action while Sarah plonked down on to her bottom, missing the water by inches.

'Duck, duck!' she shouted.

'Take care, darling. Mummy doesn't want you to fall in.' She gathered her children to her, one at each side, while she knelt on the shingle and gazed at her own reflection in the still waters. It surprised her sometimes to see how young she still was. No more than twenty-one, for all she felt like a mature married woman.

'Can you see your faces, darlings? Look, there's Sarah with her snub nose, and little Beth with her sweet smile and new tooth. Can you see?'

The twins hunkered down beside her in their matching cotton frocks and gazed very seriously at their reflections, so similar and yet so different. They were not identical. The hair was changing colour now, even the eyes had lost their baby blueness.

'When I was a girl we used to wish by the water every spring for whatever our hearts most desired.' Lissa laughed at the memory, pushing back the errant jet curls that still tumbled upon her brow for all the care she took to pin her hair in a tidy fashion as Philip liked. She never wore it in a girlish pony tail any more and he did not like to see it flying free.

'Me want to wish,' Sarah announced, sticking out her jaw in determined fashion, making Lissa laugh.

'You want everything, darling, even when you have no idea what a wish is. And what do you want, Beth?'

Beth slid her arms about her mother's neck and kissed her damply. 'Sweetie,' she said, at her most alluring, and Lissa laughed all the more, letting them tumble her backwards on to the shingle and search her pockets until the hoarded treasure of two jelly babies had been found. Then she dusted the children down and took their hands in hers, her spirits sinking in the familiar way as they turned towards home.

Sometimes she did wonder why Philip had chosen her. Just as one might wonder why the showy mallard was happy with its dull brown mate. Perhaps it was simply because it had no choice.

Was that how Philip saw her? As the best choice he could find at the time? He was certainly always striving to improve her. And she was grateful for his assistance, oh, she was. How else could she know the correct knife to use at a grand dinner, or which dress was quite appropriate? No, no, she depended upon his care absolutely. If she felt inadequate sometimes, the fault must be entirely hers.

Where was it they were going tonight? The Yacht Club was it, or something to do with the Town Council? She couldn't quite recall but there was plenty of time. It was lovely to saunter by the lake in the September sunshine. And what was there to rush home for? The house shone like a new pin, and was entirely empty.

231

They passed the benches and as she glanced at the boathouse, tears sprang unexpectedly to her eyes. What was the matter with her today? She could remember those happy times as if they were yesterday and not a million years ago.

'When I was a teenager,' she told the twins, her voice brightening for their benefit, 'we used to have parties and barbecues on the shore here, Coca-Cola and burnt sausages. What fun we had!' She remembered the night of the storm and the Spin-the-Bottle party when Derry had kissed her in the kitchen.

She allowed herself to watch an image of him in her mind as he pulled out a comb from an inside pocket and flicked the already tidy quiff into place. Did he still dress in those ridiculous long jackets, tight jeans and brightly coloured shirts? Had he ever got his recording contract? she wondered. His dream?

And she remembered the night he had stood on this very spot and Philip had told him of their coming marriage. She would remember the expression in his brown eyes till her dying day.

A ripple of emotion coursed through her body, shocking her by its intensity. It did no good to remember. She was a mature, married woman. Those glorious youthful summers were over. Strangers lived in the boathouse now. Jan was at Ashlea with Nick, busily knitting for the expected arrival of their first child. Tony and Helen had two. Where the others had gone, she had no idea.

Lissa had no dream, only a confusing jumble of unsatisfied needs. She'd never felt Derry's driving ambition to succeed, would have been happy with more modest achievements. Someone to love her and never let her go.

Yet more often of late she had felt dissatisfied, had started to ask herself questions. Am I happy? Am I fulfilled? The Russians had more control over their rockets flying through space than she had over her own life. And the days seemed so long. She had the twins, of course, and they were such darlings she could eat them. But Philip had insisted on employing a nanny. A plain, stolid woman of uncertain years who dressed predictably in starched overalls and had all the right qualifications. Which meant Lissa was left with too many empty hours to fill, too much time to think.

They had reached the bandstand when Sarah squealed in delighted fear. 'Duck chasing me, Mummy.'

Lissa laughed. 'No, darling, they're greedy, that's all.'

A hopeful troop of ducks had come waddling behind, perhaps in search of a forgotten crust so the twins must be permitted to bend down and talk to them, explain how they would be back tomorrow with more. Suddenly a car came, too fast, along the narrow shore road. The birds whirled up into the air, wings beating madly, crazy with fear before skimming into the water in a flurry of injured pride and flustered panic, scattering all the other ducks in a squawking mass of feathers. In an equal panic Lissa grabbed the twins, her heart beating wildly, and leapt to one side, shouting at the retreating car: 'How dare you? You road hog! Have you no consideration?'

The ducks flapped their wings, shook their stubby tail feathers to restore lost dignity and at once began to preen and groom themselves in order to settle their nerves.

Sarah was screaming. She had fallen down and grazed her knee. Beth was sucking her thumb and crying, wide-mouthed, around it in sympathy.

'Oh, dear Lord.' Lissa held them both in her arms, soothing, kissing, mopping up blood and tears. What would Philip say?

The sun was dropping behind blue-misted mountains by the time she reached home.

'Where have you been?'

He met her at the foot of the stairs in his dressing gown, face tight with anger. 'What have you done with the children? Nanny?' He yelled up the stairs and a starched white overall came instantly into view. Nanny Sue came running, clucking her tongue in disapproval, and bore the children away for hot chocolate and baths and the joy of an Elastoplast. Lissa's heart sank. She so hated to displease him.

'It's all right. It's only a graze.'

'They shouldn't have been out so late. What were you thinking of? I came home to find the house empty. You weren't here, Nanny on her afternoon off, the twins not in bed and my bath not even run.'

Reaching up she kissed his cheek, hoping to placate him. 'We were feeding the ducks.' And smiling, she brushed past him and walked up the stairs to the blue and white bedroom they shared at the front of the house. Ten minutes in the bathroom, she dare waste no more time, and she was standing before her dressing table in her slip, dabbing her face with cream when he entered.

'Is it the Yacht Club dinner tonight?' she asked, in her interested voice.

'No, that's next week. Don't you ever listen? We are due at the Cheyneys' on the dot of seven-thirty.'

'The Cheyneys. Of course.' Nothing to do with either the Town Council or the Yacht Club. Don Cheyney was a magistrate of some standing, so the talk this evening would be of legal matters. 'How delightful. It won't take me long to get ready.' It would be boring in the extreme. His wife would be no help at all since she was at least fifteen years older than Lissa and constantly trying to persuade her to join some worthy ladies' group or other. Lissa stifled a sigh and started to pull the pins from her hair.

'I'll do that.' She looked up, catching sight of his expression through the mirror, and felt her stomach clench.

Lissa stood unresisting as he released her hair, spread it upon her shoulders and combed his fingers through the tumbling curls from scalp to tip. Then he lifted it with one hand so he could kiss a bare shoulder. Lissa suppressed a violent urge to slap his hand away.

'You said we were in a hurry.'

He half glanced at the clock but his eyes were already glazed, the pupils darkly dilated. It was an expression she had come to dread.

'Not that much of a hurry,' he said thickly, letting his lips linger over the silky skin. His hands slid to her buttocks. 'Damn, you're not wearing suspenders. Did you go out in those ankle socks again? Haven't I told you always to be properly dressed?'

Lissa said nothing. She had learned the art of silence.

But he made her put them on now, and as she did so, she was aware of his growing eagerness. She watched him taunt himself by making her remove the silk slip and walk around the bed to him. He could barely wait for her to come to him before he was running his hands over her firm body and pushing her back on to the bed. He dropped his own robe to the floor, spread her legs and the next instant he was on top and inside of her. The pain of it was unbearable and she tried to lift her knees in order to ease it, putting her arms about him. His impatience was always at its worst when she had displeased him.

'Wait for me, Philip. Give me time.'

'Keep still, for God's sake. You're so clumsy.' He shook her arms away, took hold of her wrists and held them back while he pounded into her, pouring out his frustrations till moments later it was all over, for which she was deeply thankful.

'Oh God, that was good,' he said, slumping against her on a great gasping groan. Lissa eased herself from beneath him. He never asked if she had enjoyed it, which, oddly enough, she found a relief. At least it spared her any pretence of pleasure. He didn't seem to require it.

'I'll have to shower again now,' he said, sounding irritable as if it had been her intention to distract him with unplanned sex.

He pulled on his robe and went into the bathroom while Lissa rolled over on the bed and curled into a tight ball, her hands between her legs, testing the sore tenderness there. But she did not cry. She never cried.

When they were first married his love making, if that was the right name for it, had perhaps pleased her. He'd certainly behaved with more consideration, being gentle and kind, calling her his darling virgin bride, and she'd taken care not to disillusion him on that score. It did her no good to remember it either. But she'd been young then and was so grateful to Philip for choosing her as a wife that she'd been eager and anxious for love, not minding if they didn't quite reach the heady heights of ecstasy she'd found with Derry.

It was all her own fault of course. Somehow she'd failed in that as in everything. And as time went by Philip became surprisingly more ardent and demanding than she'd expected. Lissa found she simply could not bring herself to comply with those demands. No matter how hard she tried, she could not do as he wished. Her inadequacies had at first distressed and then annoyed him. She was either too slow or too clumsy or too tired. She never quite seemed to please him.

In the end he'd lost patience, accusing her of being frigid and abandoning all consideration for her.

'Some women find no pleasure in sex,' he told her on countless occasions, and were it not for the dreams which haunted her at night of reckless young love on empty golden fells, she might well have believed it to be true. 'But I must have it, Lissa. You do understand that, don't you, my dear? It is a physical necessity.'

'Of course, Philip,' she would assure him. 'I want so much to please you.'

And he would smile and pat her cheek as if she were a child not able to understand such adult mysteries. 'Of course you please me, my darling.'

In their everyday life together he remained everything she could wish for in a husband, she told herself now. Exquisitely caring, in his own way, helping her to cope with the complexities of her new life. But in the bedroom his charm too often vanished, replaced by a driving need. He took what he required as and when he required it and her own needs were forgotten or ignored. Sometimes, as today, she made an effort to respond, to kiss or caress him. But it rarely worked.

More often than not her efforts distracted or annoyed him and she had learned it was better to damp down her emotions when he was in this mood, and not think of what he did to her. But sometimes it took all her courage simply to stay ice cool in his arms, waiting for him to be done, glad when he was.

And really he was not unkind, Lissa thought as she struggled to pull the hair brush through her tangled locks. Sometimes he could be Prince Charming himself, sweet talking and caressing her, making her feel like a young bride again, precious and beloved. He would often let her massage his shoulders and bring him breakfast or supper in bed and would read snippets of his newspaper to amuse and educate her. She loved to make him happy for that made her happy too, and they had grown used to each other, developed a sort of contentment. So if she found little pleasure in their love making, how could she blame him? The fault was entirely hers. She was the one with hang ups about love, and belonging, and sex, as he very reasonably pointed out, not him. And where would she be without his love?

'Wear the burgundy suit with the navy trim,' he told her later as she reached for her favourite silk dress in lupin blue, which so suited her eyes.

'It makes me look old,' she demurred, but he took the blue silk from her hand and hung it firmly back in her wardrobe.

'Let me be the judge,' he said, kissing her hand. She put on the suit with its pleated skirt of a demure length, and short, fitted jacket, and he told her how beautiful she looked.

'Perfect, my darling. The very thing for a magistrate's dinner.'

She couldn't help but smile. 'How fussy you are, Philip. But I'm glad you like it.'

He had thrown away all her pretty cotton dresses and rainbow net petticoats, declaring them too young and frivolous. It was a new decade and a new era in her life, so she had made no protest.

Lissa called in to kiss goodnight to the children and Philip did the same. 'We should have a nurseryful,' he said, gazing on their sleeping faces. 'Girls are very pretty and appealing but a man needs a son.' As if in some way this would prove his virility or perhaps his status. Lissa made no reply. It had been a difficult pregnancy carrying two babies, a prolonged labour and worse delivery. It had taken her months to recover from the exhaustion and she had no intention of

236

repeating the experience. Not until she had sorted out the problems in her marriage anyway.

He led her out to the car as if she were a princess. 'You will be the most beautiful woman there and you know how much that means to me. I need you beside me,' he told her. 'I'd be lost without you.'

'I know,' she said, smiling radiantly up at him, loving this evidence of his adoration.

'I may decide to join the Golf Club and Don Cheyney is the Vice Captain this year.'

As he pulled the front door closed he happened to glance at the coloured patterns in the pane of glass in the top of the door and ran his finger along the strip of black lead that divided each portion. He stared at the tip of his finger, grey with dust. 'Have you cleaned this door recently, my sweet?'

Lissa's heart sank. 'I'll do it tomorrow.'

'Tomorrow never comes though, does it, darling? We've discovered that before, haven't we?' He glanced at his watch. The fingers stood at twenty past seven.

'You'll have to hurry. We mustn't be late.'

Lissa was appalled. 'You can't mean that I clean it now?'

Dark grey eyes opened wide. 'Why not? Now is when it is dirty. What have you been doing all day? Wasting time feeding the ducks with crusts they do not need. And keeping the children out far too late.'

'I did not waste . . .' What was the use? 'I'll do it first thing in the morning, Philip, I promise. I can hardly start cleaning windows in my best suit.'

He was unlocking the door. 'You should have thought of that before, my pet. It won't take a moment to get a damp cloth. Wear an apron and rubber gloves. We don't want you to spoil those lovely nails.'

He stood on the doorstep, tapping his foot impatiently while Lissa hurried into her pristine kitchen, smartly decked out with every modern appliance, and collected the necessary items. She was flushed and flustered by the time the task was done to Philip's satisfaction, and tendrils of carefully lacquered hair were already escaping to lie with clammy heat on her brow.

By the time she'd hurried back to the kitchen with the bowl, wrung out the cloth and hung the gloves on the taps to dry he was calling for her, a note of hard impatience in his voice. 'It's twenty-five to eight.'

237

'The fault is all Lissa's,' he informed their hosts as they arrived twenty minutes late with everyone else well into the soup course. 'You know how women are. Such perfectionists.'

And all she could do was bite on her lip and try to smile so that the tears that blocked her throat would stay there and not betray her.

She cleaned the house from top to bottom the next day. Not that it needed it. Every surface gleamed, the mahogany table in the hall reflected a carefully arranged copper bowl of gold chrysanthemums as if it were made of glass. The pristine white paintwork glistened in the sun. Even the tastefully plain blue carpet looked untrodden. Indeed she kept out of the drawing room for fear of marking the pile with her footprints.

But she knew that once Philip had spotted an imperfection he was likely to go on the hunt for more. And it made her feel so very dreadful when he found her wanting in some way, that it simply wasn't worth the risk.

When she had vaccuumed every square inch of carpet and dusted and polished the furniture till it glowed, she switched on the electric kettle and settled herself with a thankful sigh on one of the lemon yellow kitchen chairs, a magazine and a plate of biscuits to hand. She felt more comfortable in the kitchen. Lissa pulled the pins from her hair, fluffing it free with her fingers, the way she preferred it.

When Susan brought back the twins from their shopping expedition she would play with them in the nursery until it was time for their afternoon nap. That was her escape. The twins made her life worthwhile.

Even so the day stretched endlessly before her. There were times when she longed for the heady freedom of the drapery shop, with Miss Stevens chivvying them and calling them 'my dear gels' in that frosty manner she had. You knew where you were with old Stevens, dragon though she undoubtedly was. Lissa was never quite sure with Philip.

But Stella Stevens had long since retired. The old drapery was now a not very successful Gifte Shoppe, providing the increasing numbers of visitors who crowded the streets of Carreckwater with rather tacky souvenirs. And even if it had still been there, Philip would never have countenanced her working. She was a wife and mother, that must be enough. Lissa wondered why it wasn't.

He had been quite shocked once when she'd suggested she might take a part-time job, almost as outraged as if she'd suggested taking a lover.

'I hope I can keep my wife without her needing to demean herself by clocking in every morning.'

'But the house doesn't fill my day and it would only be in the mornings. Nanny Susan is with them in any case.'

'I won't have you worn out when I come home from the office.' Since then he had perversely made sure that her day was filled to capacity. If she could not find sufficient tasks he found them for her, or complained she could not have done them properly in the first place and made her do them all over again.

It was a large house. Six bedrooms, attics, cellars, and three reception rooms all on different levels. Spacious lofty rooms filled with old fashioned furniture, cornices, picture rails and stained glass windows that were all difficult to clean. The fact that most of the rooms were never used did not prevent the necessity of their having to be turned out regularly. Certainly not in Philip's view. He was punctilious in keeping her up to the mark, as he put it.

'They still get dusty,' he told her. 'What if someone should call or come to stay?'

'Who?'

'I've no idea. Does it matter? We must be prepared for all contingencies.'

'I could use dust sheets to cover the furniture in the rooms we don't use.'

'I will not live in a museum.'

'I'm sorry, Philip. I didn't think.'

He shook his head with a sigh of exasperation as he kissed her. 'You never do. Leave the thinking to me, darling.'

It was easier to acquiesce than argue. Lissa hated conflict and Philip could cap every point she made with another, and never lose his cool. While she would end up hot with frustrated temper.

The house had apparently once belonged to an old lady. Farquar? No, Fraser, that was it. She had kept a maid and a gardener in happier days, and probably a cook, Lissa thought, with some displeasure. She had now retired to a home for the elderly and Lissa was expected to attain the same standards with the assistance only of her modern appliances which seemed to break down every time she looked at them. Renee might worship at the feet of vacuum cleaners, they left Lissa perfectly cold.

As she sipped her tea, Darjeeling from the very finest porcelain, she experienced a deep aching need to be back in a corner of the stock room with a mug curled in her hand and Jan's ceaseless chatter in her ears.

She went to the phone and dialled a number. Meg's voice rang out, as clearly as if she were in the next room.

'Broombank.'

'Hello, it's me.'

'Sweetheart! When are you coming to see us? We haven't seen the terrible twosome for weeks.'

Lissa laughed. She and Meg had become a little closer since the birth of the twins and Lissa was anxious to build on this progress. 'They nearly fell in the lake yesterday, got chased by the ducks and almost run over by a car. Status quo really.'

Meg chuckled, not taking this dire list too seriously. 'Jan is so small she hardly looks pregnant, but not long to go now. She misses you,' Meg said, the tone of her voice changing slightly.

Lissa propped herself against the telephone table and agreed that she'd been thinking the very same thing. 'I miss her, but she'll soon have her hands full.'

'Like you, sweetheart.'

'Yes,' said Lissa. 'Like me.'

The front door opened and two tiny figures in neat canary yellow coats and bonnets burst in. 'Ah, here they are. Must go.' And she hurriedly rang off, repeating her promise to visit.

'Hello, my darlings.' Lissa knelt on the hall carpet as she swept them both into her arms, nuzzling against their soft cheeks, breathing in the sweet baby scent of their skin. Her heart soared with happiness. How lucky she was. Nothing to complain about at all. 'What shall we do now? Play soap bubbles? Or paint pictures to take to Granny Meg?'

Nanny's hand came down upon each small head. 'The children must have their lunch and go down for their nap.'

'Of course. How silly of me. I'd forgotten. Run along then, darlings. Nanny's waiting.'

She remained kneeling on the carpet for several moments after they had gone.

It was late-afternoon when they woke and Lissa spent a riotous hour or more in the nursery right at the top of the house, playing Ride-a-Cock-Horse, daubing glorious pictures in red, yellow and purple on pieces of old wallpaper, and building huge brick towers which the twins knocked down with screams of delight.

She was telling them a story while Nanny Sue clicked her tongue over the mess they had made when Lissa heard the sound of a clock chiming in the hall.

'Oh lord, it's five o'clock. And I still haven't decided what we're eating this evening.' She hurriedly finished the story, attempting to placate the protests and prevent tears. Then after raiding the kitchen larder and flinging together some scraps of pork and vegetables into a casserole, she flew back upstairs to bathe and change, paint her nails and attend to her hair.

At six-thirty precisely Lissa was waiting in the drawing room for the sound of his key in the lock, his gin and tonic already poured and standing on a silver tray on the walnut sideboard. She might have been Grace Kelly waiting for her prince to come, were it not for the deep and abiding unhappiness that was eating away at her soul.

19

The Yacht Club had opted for a formal dinner this year, to be held in the Marina Hotel at the end of September as usual. Afterwards there would be dancing for those so inclined. The band would be a classic trio and there would be no skiffle in the interval. The craze had long since died. Lissa was glad about that.

She sat at the long, white-clothed table in her little black dress, shorter than she was used to wearing but slim-fitting, expensive and flattering, with a red silk rose bud pinned to one shoulder. Philip had wanted her to wear a long one in heavy white satin, as if she were a debutante, but for once she'd refused. Lissa could sense waves of disapproval emanating from him as he took the chair next to hers and slipped his hand proprietorially over a black-stockinged knee.

'Please, Philip,' she whispered, anxious someone might see. 'Not here.'

'In a dress so short you are clearly inviting such attention, and I am your husband,' he remarked, sliding his fingers under the dress right up to her stocking tops and then back to the knee, much to the amusement of the man on Lissa's right who, catching her angry glare, hastily addressed his attention to the woman on his left.

Lissa gently removed the hand and attempted to appear unconcerned, smiling into the mild gaze of Doctor Robson, seated opposite.

'Good evening, Lissa,' the doctor said. 'Looking as lovely as ever, I see.'

'You're looking rather spry yourself.' Lissa liked Charles Robson. A patient, rotund man, rather old fashioned but unshockable, like the rest of his profession. Yet he managed to maintain an affable quality

243

that made him entirely approachable. Lissa had visited him on several occasions, and he of course had delivered the twins.

They chatted for a while about the health and beauty of her two offspring, a subject Lissa never tired of.

'Ah, Robson old chap.' Becoming aware that someone was addressing his wife, Philip smiled expansively. He had already enjoyed several whiskies, though not of the best quality. He was not normally one to indulge in alcohol but felt he needed to relax this evening. It had been a tedious day. Now he poured himself a second glass of a rather fine claret, hoping to soothe his irritation which had increased with Lissa's obdurate stubborness. It occurred to him that this might be the very opportunity he'd been seeking to discuss a matter of some importance with the good doctor. Man to man. Fellow professionals and all that. 'When are you going to help my wife, you old duffer?' he asked. 'Came to you months ago and you've achieved nothing.'

The doctor looked startled, though not half so startled as Lissa. She attempted to laugh it off, then flinched as once more Philip's hand came down upon her knee. 'Please, Philip. Doctor Robson is enjoying an evening out. He has no wish to discuss medical matters.'

But Philip rarely relinquished an argument once begun, certainly not when his inhibitions were at their lowest. 'He knows well enough what I mean. What sort of a quack are you? Damned inadequate in my view.'

'I'm sorry you're dissatisfied, Brandon,' the doctor said, quite equably, lifting his soup spoon. 'Whatever it is I've done, I hope you're not about to sue me for it.' And several people tittered, partly from amusement, partly embarrassment.

Lissa could hardly contain her shame at the scene. She could feel her cheeks firing up, acutely aware of the growing interest about her. Voices deliberately lowered as people waited to hear what it was the doctor had done or failed to do. Waitresses pretending not to listen to what sounded very like the start of a matrimonial dispute, which they would be sure to relate with relish in the kitchen the moment they returned from handing out the dishes of asparagus soup and bread rolls.

'How long is it now that you've been treating her? The twins are two and a half years old and still no sign of another child. You're incompetent, you old fool.'

Lissa's cheeks flared to bright red. '*Philip*, please! Not now.'

'Hush, woman, I'm talking to this nincompoop.' The hand on her knee gripped tighter and Lissa let out a tiny whimper.

Doctor Robson had turned to her, a frown on his round face. 'Come and see me in the morning, Lissa. We'll talk about it then. There's certainly nothing we can do tonight. Perhaps not even tomorrow. We shall see.' He again applied himself to his soup.

Philip leaned forward across the table, pushing his flushed face as close to the doctor's as he could get and speaking in a loud whisper that not a soul in the room could miss: 'Are you saying the case is hopeless? That my wife has turned barren?'

In the loud and dreadful silence which followed, all movement ceased. Not a hand moved, not a soup spoon lifted.

Except for one red-headed waitress who chose that precise moment to place a bowl of soup before him. Perhaps Philip moved or jolted her elbow, no one could be entirely sure, but the bowl missed the edge of the table and hot soup poured all down the front of his black evening trousers.

Pandemonium broke out and low-pitched, stifled laughter. Philip leapt to his feet, shouting his rage and agony, demanding the waitress be dismissed on the spot. Bringing the manager scurrying.

'I'll go,' she said. But not before she had placed one hand on Lissa's shoulder and given it an affectionate squeeze. And Lissa had looked up into Renee's bright and smiling face.

'Common as muck, that's me, but I don't let nobody push me around. Certainly not a jumped up, full of himself, no good tyke like Philip Brandon.' Renee's hands stilled in their kneading of bread dough and she stared, appalled, at Lissa. 'Crikey, what've I said? I didn't mean it like it sounded. He's your husband, for God's sake.'

In bright tartan trews and an emerald green T-shirt, the whole covered by a huge white apron, and her once bleached hair now a bright orangey red to match her lips and backcombed to within an inch of its life, Renee looked the very picture of a fulfilled and happy woman. Apart from the fact that her voluptuous figure filled the clothes a touch more tightly, gone was the lethargic, whining creature who had never moved from her fireside. Lissa felt a pang of envy at her obvious contentment.

'It's all right. I do understand what you're saying and in a way I agree with you, it's just that . . .' Lissa searched her mind for a way to explain the complications of her marriage. 'Philip needs me, and I want to make him happy, d'you see?'

'Except in this. You don't want another kid?'

'No.'

'But they're gorgeous.' They both gazed at the two girls, happily swathed in tea towels and rolling out grey pieces of dough on the end of the table.

'I know. And all my maternal instincts are quite satisfied, thank you. I don't need to go through it all again.

'So tell him.'

'I can't. He's keen to try for a boy but I . . .'

Renee glanced sharply at her. 'You've been using summat. Right?'

Lissa, hunched on a tall stool, nodded her agreement. 'A diaphragm. Doctor Robson didn't know Philip wanted another child. Until last night.'

'And now the fat's right in the fire.'

'Yes.'

Renee sucked in her breath, then picking up the lump of dough flung it back on to the floured board and began pummelling and rolling it with vigour. Clouds of flour flew up and settled in drifts on her red hair. In her mind the dough might well have been Philip Brandon's head. She wished it was, for the contempt with which he'd treated Lissa at the dinner last night. Humiliated her, rotten toad, fondling her before everyone and then revealing her private business. 'So what did the good doctor say when you saw him this morning?'

Lissa, an incongruous picture of elegance in the untidy kitchen in a sleeveless dress of ice blue linen, hair hanging in a single plait down her back, gave Renee a woebegone look. 'He was a bit surprised.'

Both girls' eyes met and held and once again the dough was neglected. 'I'll bet he was. Let me get this straight. Your husband thinks you've been going to the doc for help to get pregnant again, only the doc has actually been helping you stop babies from coming? Is that the way of it?'

There was a glint of merriment now in Renee's eyes and for the first time that morning Lissa began to see the funny side of her predicament and twisted her lips into a smile. 'It does sound a bit odd, I suppose, put like that.' She glanced at the twins, stopped Sarah from putting some of the disgusting mixture into her mouth while she helped Beth stick currants into hers. 'No, darling. We must cook it first.'

'I'd say it was pretty confusing for any chap to understand, even someone as clever as a doctor. A woman now, would get the drift right away.'

'Oh, Renee.' And then the laughter was bubbling up in her throat. Where it came from, Lissa couldn't imagine. She certainly hadn't felt like laughing earlier when she'd faced Doctor Robson's glowering disapproval and listened to his lecture on filial obedience and a wife's duty. It had taken all her courage and skill to persuade him not to divulge this information to Philip, which he'd threatened to do for all it would mean breaking a patient's confidence. Now she was holding her sides as if it was the funniest thing that had ever happened to her.

Renee was screaming with laughter, flour going everywhere as she circled the kitchen gasping for breath. The twins, entranced by the sight, started to shout with laughter too though they had no idea why. 'Oh Gawd, what a laugh. Crikey, I'd love to see his face when you tell him the truth!'

Lissa tumbled from the stool and grabbed hold of Renee, shaking her slightly to make her stop laughing and take the matter seriously. 'He must *never* know. That's the whole point. I don't *ever* want him to find out. Do you understand, Renee?'

Renee stopped laughing long enough to look carefully into the violet eyes, darkly shadowed in an unusually pale face. She could feel the very slightest tremor in the hands that held hers, the wrists seeming so frail and thin they might snap in two at any moment. 'I'll put the dough to rise then I think we might have a drop of sherry. For medicinal purposes.'

'Maybe I should be getting back. Nanny Sue will wonder where I am.'

'Let her. Old po face. Come on, you two whipper-snappers. You can go and sleep on my big bed while I bake your dough men. OK?' She swept Sarah into her arms while Lissa followed on with Beth.

Ten minutes later they were more comfortably seated in Renee's living room, still untidy with newspapers and discarded clothing everywhere. Exactly as Lissa remembered, except that the chirping budgie seemed to have departed, for the cage stood empty. Renee did not remark upon this, so neither did Lissa.

She was suddenly glad to be here, in Renee's uncomplicated

company, and for the first time in months began to relax. She wondered why she'd kept away so long.

Renee took a sip of the sherry, sighed with pleasure then set her glass on the mantleshelf.

'Why did you marry him then?' The bluntness of the question took Lissa by surprise.

'I-I'm not sure. I liked him, I suppose, he was charming and kind and good-looking. He seemed a safe bet.'

'So what's gone wrong? Come on, lovey, let's be having it. Has he been knocking you about? Because if he has . . .'

'Oh, no, nothing like that.'

'What then? You and me have a lot in common, y'know, both being married to older men like. Mind you, Jimmy could give your Philip a few years and he's a long way behind in the looks department. Is it the age thing that bothers you?'

Lissa shook her head, finding herself quite unable to speak. How could she explain the depths of the terrible mistake she'd made by marrying Philip? She'd made her bed, as they said, and must lie in it. With him. But she couldn't talk about all that, not with Renee, not with anyone. It was too intimate, too obscene.

'I never did understand why our Derry left the way he did,' Renee was saying. 'Mind you, what a mess when he came back that time! Took me days to calm Jimmy down.' She hurried on, not explaining how he'd found his son in his wife's arms. 'You two seemed made for each other.'

Lissa pressed her lips together and stared out of the window on to the back garden. She could see the shed at the bottom of it, the one where Derry had presumably slept for several months at Renee's instigation. But he hadn't left Carreckwater simply because Renee had asked him to move out. He could have found other digs in town. Even after all this time Lissa had come up with no answer except the obvious.

'His head was full of his own ambitions. I couldn't compete with a guitar or the promise of a recording contract,' she said.

'He never got it, you know.' Renee looked mournful as she reached for her sherry again. 'Poor mite. Played his socks off all over Manchester and London to no avail.'

Lissa told herself not to ask. Where Derry was, or what he was up to, was no longer any concern of hers. 'What is he doing these days?' The words came of their own accord.

'He's gone abroad, hasn't he?' Renee nodded.

'Has he? Where?' She didn't care where he was. She only hoped he was miserable as hell, as miserable as she was.

'America, would you believe? Do you think he might meet Acker Bilk? Ooh, I love that record don't you, 'Stranger On the Shore'?' And she began to hum the tune.

'I'd believe anything of Derry Colwith.'

'Aye, well, that's men for you. Never there when you want 'em.' Renee took several sips of her sherry. 'Broke Jimmy up it did, his only son and heir going off like that at a moment's notice. Mind you, we've talked it over and decided against kids of us own,' she continued. 'Too much responsibility. I fancy this new pill, don't you? I'll give it a try when they get it sorted out.' She half glanced at the cage. 'And I might get a parrot.'

Lissa felt a sudden spurt of laughter hit her throat but managed to restrain it. It would be too cruel. Renee might be brash, greedy, oversexed, possibly verging on the amoral judging by the gossip there was about her guest house, but no one could doubt that her heart was in the right place. Renee Colwith meant well for all her clumsiness on occasions, and was the only person Lissa had found in an age who was prepared to be on her side now that Jan had gone.

'I'll never forget the look of shock and outrage on his face when the soup poured down his legs,' Renee said, spluttering over her sherry.

'Oh, golly.' And they were both off laughing again. It made Lissa feel so good to be young and careless again. When they had mopped up their tears and more sherry had been poured she said, 'I shall continue to lie, about wanting more children. If it saves an argument.'

Renee looked doubtful. 'You can't keep it up for ever.'

'I know.' Lissa turned her face away, not wanting to meet the inquiring gaze.

'So what is it? What's really wrong? I'm not daft. I can see there must be summat else.'

'Perhaps I'm bored.' Lissa felt her heart jump as the words popped out and realised for the first time how true they were and how much that bothered her. She took a deep breath and began, at last, to talk.

'Philip expects me to be the perfect little wife. Beautiful, charming, hosting his dinner parties, entertaining him each evening with a gin and tonic and my adoring attention.' The sherry had loosened her tongue and she warmed to her theme.

'I don't even get to spend much time with my own children, except for an hour or two each afternoon. He expects his house to look like something out of the Ideal Home Exhibition with me devoting my entire life to achieving such a miracle. He's so very particular and has such high standards yet treats me like Dresden china, or a weak fool incapable of intelligent conversation let alone holding down a job.' She lifted clenched fists in helpless appeal to Renee. 'He goes out to meetings most nights and sometimes I think I'll go mad, with no one in the house to talk to but two babies, a starchy nanny and the vaccuum cleaner. Can you understand?'

'Oh, yes,' said Renee, nodding sagely. 'I understand perfectly. That's why I miss my Peter since he passed over. Jimmy's never away from that boat yard. Mind you, I have my guests, in the summer at any rate. The long winters can be a bit of a drag. That's why I help out at the Marina Hotel now and again. Bit of company like, as well as a few bob in the pocket. You should try it.'

Lissa shook her head in despair, an expression raw with lost hope on her drawn face. 'There's nothing I can do. He wouldn't allow it. I'm a possession, like a sofa or a fine picture. And, if I'm not careful, the bearer of an increasing brood of children which will keep me very securely within doors.'

The familiar sensation of crawling fear beat slowly in her stomach, the sickness sweeping right up into her gullet. She felt like a prisoner. Yet how could she ever escape without a job, without money of her own? And did she really want to? 'He needs me at home. He's said so a million times.' And she wanted him to need her, didn't she? What else did she have? She couldn't risk losing him.

'I wouldn't let that stop me,' Renee was saying.

Lissa drew in a trembling breath, aware she must remain composed. 'Philip won't hear of it. Simply not on the cards, he says.'

'Bugger his cards,' said Renee, reaching for the sherry bottle and refilling the glasses. 'If you can lie about the baby thing, why can't you lie about this too?'

Lissa blinked. 'What are you saying?'

'How will he know if you're working, if you don't tell him? So long as you're home by the time he is and the house is done and dusted, he'd never notice. Men never see what's right in front of them, everyone knows that. Anyway, you could employ a cleaner. Surely you can afford one?'

'He expects me to look after our home myself. Anyway, Nanny would tell. She's very proper. Likes to do everything by the book.'

'Not if you bribed her not to.'

'Bribed?'

Renee smiled. 'Threatened her with the sack if she split on you.'

Lissa looked shocked. 'I couldn't do that.'

'Yes, you could. Ask her nicely then.'

'I'd never get away with it. Would I?' Why was she even talking about it? The idea was utter madness.

Renee propped her feet on the mantleshelf while she considered. 'Pretend to take up charity work. Most ladies of your class, if you'll pardon the expression, are out and about all day and nobody has a blind idea what they're up to. Take up good works. The Lissa Turner – sorry – Brandon, Save-Her-Sanity Committee.'

And they were both hooting with laughter again. Before the sherry bottle was halfway down they had begun to devise a plan.

Following the evening's débâcle, which he blamed entirely on the clumsiness of the stupid waitress, Philip insisted that the hotel at least pay for his dinner jacket and trousers to be dry cleaned. He returned three days later to collect them, repeating his annoyance at the incident and his hope that the waitress, whoever she was, would pay out of her wages. When he had vented his wrath to his satisfaction he agreed to be mollified by a glass of malt whisky in the bar, courtesy of the management.

'Got to keep 'em on their toes,' said a voice at his side. Philip swivelled round to find himself addressed by a young man with fair, floppy hair and tortoiseshell spectacles that kept slipping down his nose. His dark grey suit was clearly brand new and the white collar he wore looked odd against the pale grey of his shirt, giving him an almost clerical appearance. A clipboard and measuring tape reposed on the bar counter beside a half empty glass of beer.

Philip said, 'Very true,' and returned to his whisky.

After the usual discussion about the weather and the failings of hotels in general, a subject close to the man's heart apparently, he informed Philip that he was a consultant. 'Andrew Spencer.' He held out a hand which Philip reluctantly shook. 'For Manchester Water Board. They're the bogeyman round here, in case you didn't realise.'

251

Philip gave a dry smile. 'I believe so.'

'Aye, well, they've learnt a bit since Thirlmere were built. That's what started it all off.'

'Indeed?'

The Manchester man warmed to his theme. 'The mistake they made then was to concrete the shoreline. Too hard and unnatural, d'you see? And then they stopped folk from using the lake, which again didn't endear them to the natives, as you might say. They don't make those sort of mistakes these days.'

'I see.' Philip tried to look interested though his mind was on Lissa and how she had actually refused his essential needs these last three days and nights. He blamed it all on that doctor. If he didn't set her right soon, Philip meant to go and tackle Robson himself, women's complaints or no. A man was entitled to a son if he wanted one, to carry his name forward to the next generation. And he never loved Lissa more than when she was soft and vulnerable with pregnancy, smelling of babies with breasts swollen with milk. He felt an ache start up in his loins even now at the thought and hastily took a large sip of whisky.

'Eighty million gallons are pumped from the Lakes area each day,' the man was saying. 'But we could do with another fifty at least. Maybe more in time. Industry must have its water, eh?'

'Quite.' God, what a bore he was. Philip drained his glass, preparatory to making a hasty departure, but the man clung.

'The demand goes on. Industry versus tourism, I suppose. I've to speak at a meeting tonight. You'll have read about it in the local paper, I dare say. All these stories about Manchester Water Board being on the lookout for another site? Most of it is wild scaremongering of course. Rumours abound.' He rolled his eyes and laughed. 'People panic and come up with all sorts of daft notions. They'd have everyone believe we're ploughing up half the Lake District to hear some talk.' He continued with his tale without pausing to draw breath.

''Course, you can understand how they feel. But if we don't find a suitable valley for a holding reservoir soon, we'll have to extract from the main lakes, and they won't like that any better now, will they? Think they're holy, these waters, some folks do. And it's my unenviable task to help find the right spot. Do preliminary survey work before calling in the geologists and the rest of the engineers. I don't mind telling you this is my first big job, so

252

it'd be a feather in my cap if I came up with the goods, so to speak.'

'I see,' Philip said, his face thoughtful.

Andrew Spencer puffed out his chest with self-importance then took a swallow of beer, wiping the froth from his upper lip with the back of his hand. 'No doubt I'll be questioned by the local big-wigs and the press *ad nauseam*. I've given two interviews this morning already.' The man sighed at the trials of unwanted fame. 'Not my favourite task, I can tell you.'

Philip was back on the bar stool by this time, dark eyes alert. He glanced at the empty beer glass. 'You must be worn out. Can I get you the other half?'

'Aye,' said the Manchester man. 'I wouldn't say no.'

Lissa stood in front of the shop windows which someone had painted white on the inside and felt an unusual stir of excitement. Renee had been right. The Gifte Shoppe people had packed up and gone. Miss Stevens' old drapery looked sadly neglected. The paintwork was chipped and there were posters and sale tickets peeling off the filthy windows.

Of course the idea was preposterous. How could she take on the lease? Who would arrange it for her? Where would she find the money? Nor could she hope to keep it a secret from Philip. That had soon become apparent, even to Renee.

'Don't you think someone might notice me behind the counter?' Lissa had said, giggling over her third glass of sherry.

'Wear a disguise. Buy a wig and a pair of dark glasses.' And Renee had been off again, opening wide her orange mouth and letting the laughter ring out. Lissa hadn't had such a good time in ages. In the end, however, common sense had prevailed and new strategies been devised.

'Sex. That generally gets you what you want,' Renee had bluntly suggested. But on seeing Lissa's face muscles tighten and a shudder ripple down her spine, she did not pursue the subject further. Not that Renee didn't puzzle over her reluctance. He was good-looking, Philip Brandon, in his way, for all he was a bit lean and a stuck-up cold fish. He needed warming, that was all. Mebbe Lissa wasn't the one to do it. 'Sweet talk then. That can work. Worked with my Jimmy when I first thought of doing B and B.' Her face had softened. 'But then he's a pet, bless him. Wouldn't refuse me a thing.'

'Philip isn't like Jimmy.'

'No, and even Jimmy has his limits. I'd like us to sell this place and move to somewhere bigger.' Her expression grew dreamy. 'We could do with the money and we can only take five guests here, six at a pinch, so it'd be grand to have a couple more bedrooms, and a separate dining room. Feeding 'em is a problem. At the moment we have to put up tables every morning in the front parlour. Bit of a fag that is, I can tell you. We did try 'em in here, but Jimmy didn't like it. He enjoys his privacy, you see.'

Lissa, remembering how the pair had seemed to be permanently glued together at lips and hands, didn't wonder at it. 'I can see his point of view.'

'Well, the poor lamb deserves his little pleasures. He works hard enough. And he is a creature of impulse. We both are.' She winked outrageously, the spiky eyelashes wriggling like spider's legs. 'But you can't go having it off on the rug if some old dear could walk in at any minute for her cornflakes, now can you?'

Lissa flushed, then giggled. 'Do you never take life seriously?'

Renee grinned. 'Not if I can avoid it. Jimmy does. Off to a meeting tonight in point of fact. To protest against the threat of water extraction from the lake. Says it would ruin the boating business. I've said I'll go with him, to hold his hand like.' She laughed. 'Want to come? We could go on to the Marina Hotel for a bite of supper afterwards. What d'you say? It'll be a laugh.'

'It's silly, I know, but Philip doesn't like me going out in the evenings, except with him.'

'Bloody hell.'

'It's all right, I'm used to it.'

'Then you shouldn't be. Does you good to get out. Anyroad, we should have a say in what they do to the lake. I reckon so, don't you?'

Lissa was about to refuse again when she thought, Renee's right. It is important. I should go. Why not? And an evening out would be good. She couldn't remember the last time she'd been anywhere that Philip hadn't arranged for her. 'Right,' she said. 'You're on.' For a few mad moments, high on alcohol, her future looked suddenly bright.

'That's the ticket. I'll teach you to stand up and fight, lass. Get that cleaner organised for one thing. Plan your campaign carefully. Be canny. And determined. If you want summat in this world, you

254

have to go out and get it. Nobody's going to hand it to you on a plate. Not without charging you for the service, they aren't.'

Lissa had smiled, feeling filled with optimism. Funny how she and Renee got on so well when they were as different as chalk and cheese. Renee so robust and unashamedly sexy, and herself having forgotten what it was really to love a man. Well, almost. And now was not the moment to recall it.

Then Renee had switched on the electric fire and drawn the curtains. The gesture had reminded Lissa of the time.

'I must go.' And she'd hurried to find her coat which matched the pale blue dress exactly. Renee had smoothed her hand admiringly over the fabric as she helped her on with it.

'You're so good with style. Not like me. I buy summat 'cause I like the colour, then throw things together and hope for the best. I like bright colours, d'y'see?'

Lissa thought about this now as she stared at the peeling paintwork. Was it possible? Could she run a shop, build a career for herself? Would Philip agree? Dare she ask him?

20

'I've been thinking that I might try a business of my own.'

Philip stared at her, then laughed. She could have suffered it better had he shouted at her. But he simply put back his head and roared with laughter, as if she'd said the funniest thing. 'What do you know about running a business?'

'I could learn.' But he only laughed again. Then he lifted his head, smiling and handsome, and sniffed the air. 'Is that the dinner I can smell burning?'

'Oh, *no*.' Lissa dropped the knives and forks she was carefully laying on her best white lace tablecloth and flew to the kitchen to rescue the steak and mushroom pie which she had baked especially to please him this evening.

'The Cheyneys will be here at any minute,' he warned, getting in her way as she flustered about with oven gloves. 'You are utterly incompetent, Lissa. Why can't you be more organised?'

Because I've been run off my feet all day cleaning this place from stem to stern, she thought furiously, but said nothing. Perhaps he was right. Mortified by failure as the kitchen filled with acrid smoke Lissa decided that she probably was incompetent. She did make a dreadful mess of everything: their marriage, their sex life, even apparently her own children. What made her think she wouldn't make a mess of a shop as well?

He came to stand beside her at the kitchen sink, watching as she tried to salvage the pie by scraping off the worst of the blackened pastry. It always made her feel worse when he watched. 'How silly of me to forget it,' she apologised. 'I've some cold

257

duck left in the fridge. We could have that and I'll do a salad instead.'

'I would prefer the pie. This only proves you must keep your mind on your true purpose in life, being a good wife to me. What can be more important than that? Business indeed.' And his handsome face filled with derision.

'But I would so like to be a success at something,' Lissa said, turning pleading eyes to his, the oven cloth still in her hands. There was no sign of compassion in his face, not a trace of understanding. In that moment she truly hated him. 'Can't you see, Philip? I need a life of my own.'

'You have a life, looking after me and the children.'

'And I need some independence. More than that, I need to feel proud of myself, have my own self-esteem. I want to be a real person, not a shadow of what you have made me.'

'How terribly pompous and melodramatic you sound.'

'Only because it's true.'

Now all she had to say was, I've got a business in mind already as a matter of fact. The old drapery shop. Somehow the words wouldn't come. Lissa flushed at the very thought. Quite impossible.

'Have you done?' he asked. 'Is this supper ever going to be ready? You do care enough about me to give my friends a decent meal, I suppose?'

'Of course, Philip. Don't be silly.' She gazed at the pie in despair. And Hilary Cheyney was such a wonderful cook. She went and stared into the fridge, seeking salvation.

'Oh, it's me being silly, is it? It's you who wants to abandon your children, and your loving husband, to go and play at being a businesswoman and no doubt lose all my money in the bargain, but I'm the one who's being selfish and uncaring. Typical. And you can't even manage one simple dinner.'

'If you'll just let me get on with it, I can manage very well. And I'm not asking you for any money,' Lissa said, very quietly. 'What if I grill this pair of trout, add a bit of a bacon and a nice sauce?' She started to chop lettuce.

He pushed his face close to hers and spoke to her in staccato fashion as if explaining something to an idiot. 'You need capital to start a business. Did you not realise, my sweet innocent child? It isn't a new toy to play with and throw away when you get bored.'

He took the trout from her and put it back in the fridge beside the cold cuts of duck.

Anger rose so hot and sour in her throat she could even taste it in her mouth. Lissa wanted to shout at him that she knew all of that, that she did have money. Money which was all her own and that she could manage very well without him. But some part of her made her hold this information back, as if she needed to keep the knowledge secret, for protection.

In any case, how could she defy him? Philip loved her. He said he needed her and she believed him. Wasn't it her duty to make him happy?

'You're probably right,' she said, shutting the fridge door. The anger had faded, swamped by depression. There could be no escape. Philip would have his own way in everything, never understand her desire for an independent life of her own.

She reached for the cloth again but he took it from her with finger and thumb, grimacing with distaste as he dropped it to the floor and gathered her in his arms. 'You are so young, so vulnerable, that I want only to protect you and keep you safe from harm. I need you here, Lissa, my darling. What is so wrong with that? For my pleasure alone, free from all outside troubles and influences. Forget the pie,' he murmured against her ear. 'I'll ring the Cheyneys and tell them you're not well. I find I'm not hungry this evening after all, not for food anyway. Perhaps it was meant that you burn it. A lucky omen to make us take an early night.'

He was leading her from the kitchen and a tide of panic flooded her. She couldn't face it, not now, not tonight.

Unbidden, the image of Derry came into her head. She saw his smile, heard his laughter and his cheerful chatter, felt the smoothness of his skin, his loving arms about her as they had been on that day at Kidsty Pike. The truth was that she still wanted him, as much now as ever.

'No,' she said, very quietly and rather firmly, removing herself from Philip's grasp. 'I said, not tonight.' And picking up the oven gloves Lissa calmly proceeded to carry the pie dish into the dining room. Philip blocked her way, face dark with annoyance.

'I said I'd ring and cancel. Go upstairs.'

'Cancel the Cheyneys by all means, if you wish, but I said no, not tonight.'

'Are you disobeying me?'

She laughed as she adroitly side-stepped him, and though she quailed inside at her daring she revelled in the expression of shock that came over his face at her temerity. 'I suppose I am,' she said, feeling the exhilaration of her defiance soar through her veins.

Lissa marched into the dining room and placed the dish with care on the cork mat.

Philip's voice was cold and forceful. 'Didn't you hear me? I said, forget the pie.'

'And didn't you hear me? I'm hungry and rather tired. I've had a busy day.' She drew in a deep breath and sat down, arranging her skirts, more composed than she had felt in a long while.

What had come over her?

Where was she finding this courage? From fear? Or an echo of that old Lissa, not quite dead after all?

Philip towered above, angry, menacing, and Lissa lifted her chin to smile up at him. 'Do stop huffing and puffing, darling. Are you going to ring them or not? The pie will go cold.'

He lifted one arm and swept it from the table. The dish broke as it hit the floor and rich gravy and pieces of blackened crust spilled out on to the blue carpet.

'There now,' said Lissa, not the faintest tremor in her voice. 'Now we can't possibly have the Cheyneys to dinner. Not until we buy a new carpet.'

It was an insubstantial victory. Philip rang and put off the Cheyneys till the following Friday. Lissa spent an hour on her knees cleaning the carpet, and knew that she dared never mention the subject of taking a business ever again.

A cold winter changed into an indifferent spring and then into a summer of sweet scents which lightened her heart. She loved to see the boats bobbing on the lake, their masts bristling with importance, white sails flapping, children squealing with delight. It made her think of that long ago joyous summer when she too had felt her blood sing with the promise of youth, all her future before her. Lissa had constantly to remind herself that she was still young, though she dare not imagine her future now. The thought of growing old with Philip somehow made her shudder.

She felt as if time was slipping through her fingers and she had no control over it. But then she had no control over anything. And every time she passed the old drapery she felt that it symbolised in some way the loss of her freedom.

She devoted more time to her children, to Nanny Sue's increasing annoyance. Any change in routine was strictly frowned upon but Lissa took to impromptu picnics, even longer walks by the shore, bus rides to neighbouring towns. Anything to keep her occupied and out of the house. Not that she could stay away too long. Philip rang the house regularly and though he smiled in fond amusement when she told him of little incidents which had occurred on her walks, he expected her to be home at an appropriate hour to be ready for him.

'My own sweet darling. You mustn't do too much,' he would say, kissing her brow. 'Is my drink ready?'

The twins, of course, loved these little 'ventures, as they called them. But however much she might fill her days, there was no escaping the nights. Each evening Lissa found herself filled with an increasing dread, though whether from the fear of his unremittingly polite interrogation about her state of health, or the sense of ruthlessness that was edging into his lovemaking, she couldn't quite decide.

Clad in her silk robe, hair brushed and face cleansed of make up, she looked like an innocent young girl and Lissa often found herself trembling as she walked into the bedroom. Today the humidity had developed into a summer storm, wrecking her plans and keeping her within doors, making her edgy.

'I'm so tired,' she said, the moment she saw Philip's face. 'It's been a long day. The twins were fractious because the rain spoiled their walk.' It was still beating now on the window panes, emphasising her claustrophobia.

'You do look a little pale,' he agreed, his voice warm with consideration. 'Are you well? Is there no sign yet?'

'I'm afraid not,' trying to disguise the tremor in her voice.

'You must see Doctor Robson again.'

'Yes.'

'And take more care. We don't want you overdoing things.' There were times when he wanted her to appear sensual and sophisticated, when he liked to invite men to dinner and watch them drool over her beauty and their wives grow cold with envy. He loved to sense their need, bask in their jealousy. But in the bedroom he preferred a more virginal appeal. 'You must rest more. I shall insist upon it.'

261

She saw at once her mistake. If she became too tired to please him he would confine her to the house even more.

'No, no, I'm ready for a good sleep, that's all,' she said, sounding bright and cheerful as she went to draw the curtains. 'What a dreadful night.'

He moved up behind her and slid his hands over her hips and down between her legs, making her jump, loving it when she gasped. 'I need a contented wife. Willing and loving.'

Lissa eased herself gently from his grasp to attend to the other window.

'I thought I might take the children for a drive tomorrow. I promised Meg. I haven't seen her in ages.'

'A drive? Alone?'

'Why not? May I use the new car?'

He looked doubtful. 'I would feel happier if I were to drive you.'

'I can drive. I took lessons and passed my test, remember?' It had been one of her minor successes.

She had finished attending to the curtains and moved back to the dressing table. Philip watched every nuance of the way the silk gown clung to her slender body, the peak of her nipples thrusting against the flimsy fabric. The need in him was growing and he revelled in anticipation, only half aware of her words, laughing softly. 'You are such an innocent, my darling. Driving a car is quite a serious business.'

'I'm perfectly capable.'

'We'll discuss it later, shall we?' He smoothed his hands about her throat, kissing the nape of her neck.

Her chin came up, neatly evading his hand. 'No, Philip, we'll discuss it now. I want to go. I'm perfectly capable of driving myself.' Rebellion was crisp in her voice and he felt a flush of irritation that she should spoil this sensuous moment for him.

'Dear me. You sound like a sulky child.'

'I mean to go.'

'Perhaps your little 'ventures have gone to your head?' He kissed her bare shoulder and she shrugged it away. A look of irritation came to his face. 'You'll do as I say. I'll take you on Sunday if you wish and we can fit in a visit to Larkrigg at the same time. More effort on that score wouldn't come amiss.'

Lissa bit down on a sigh of vexation but said no more, taking her frustration out on her hair as she dragged her brush furiously through tangled curls.

Philip smoothed them with his fingers, noting how she shivered at his touch, how she really wanted and loved him to touch her.

'I can understand how you might have a problem with families, having been rejected by your mother. I know Meg claims to have loved you once, but you've failed to keep her love, haven't you? My own mother, now, was a wonderful woman, absolutely devoted to me. But you must put it all behind you. You have me to take care of you now. I will never let you down, my darling. Some effort to visit Rosemary more often wouldn't come amiss, as I have told you many times. You could try to build a good relationship.'

'Perhaps,' Lissa said, tired of the old arguments, wishing he didn't make her feel so inadequate, and knowing the subject would be brought up time and time again until in the end she would be forced to agree for the sake of peace. 'I dare say you're right, Philip.'

'Of course I am right.'

Lissa closed her eyes in despair. How could she fight him? It was like hitting a marshmallow that bounced and clung to you, resolutely sticky and sweet. What was happening to her? she wondered. Once she had longed to be loved devotedly, to feel she belonged to someone. And there was no doubt that Philip loved her. He couldn't bear her out of his sight. Yet now she longed only for freedom.

'We should give Rosemary a great-grandson. That would do the trick.' And win me Larkrigg the easy way, he thought.

'I very much doubt she would care. Even if it were possible.'

His tone sharpened. 'Most women find no difficulty at all in conceiving. Yet you're dealing with this matter with your usual degree of incompetence. You don't try.'

'That's not fair,' Lissa cried, spinning about to face him, feeling the pain of his accusation as if it were really true, as if she didn't spend hours each day dealing with revolting jelly from long white tubes. 'I have tried. I never resist you, do I?'

He looked surprised at the very idea. 'You make it sound as if you're doing me a service.'

'Sometimes I feel that I am.' Reckless words, bravely spoken. Philip was not pleased by them. Dark eyes sparked with a quiet fury and the expression she most feared, as if he enjoyed these little spats, as if they added to rather than detracted from his arousal.

'I need no favours, Lissa. I need a son.'

She fought for breath, for courage. 'And I need a little more love and care.'

'Enough of this foolishness. I devote my entire life to loving and caring for you.' He took the brush from her hand and tossed it impatiently away, then gripping her wrist he led her to the bed, urgent now, stripping his clothes off as he went.

'Take off your nightdress. No, don't bother. I'll do it. I'll teach you how to please a husband as a good wife should, then there'll be babies. Just do as I say for once. No protests.' As Felicity had done so very nicely, meekly obeying his every whim as a woman should. Dear, sweet Felicity.

'Philip, please, you're hurting me. Give me time.'

He had hold of both her wrists now and was pushing her backwards on to the green silk cover. Then he took one of her hands and thrust it down between his legs, closing her fingers about his member. He felt her stiffen and flinch, and her resistance filled him with annoyance, firing the anger in him. He tried to push her head in the same direction but she wriggled free, pretending she didn't understand what he asked of her.

Hot temper showed itself as a white line above his tight upper lip. 'What's the matter with you? I'm your husband, dammit. You should be happy to love me, to do as I say. Try to be obliging for once, can't you? Instead of chasing after independence and stubbornly resisting me at every turn.'

She knew he was right. She should want to love him. But she didn't. Lissa could hardly bear to be near him any more, let alone touch him. 'P-please. Not tonight, Philip. Not like this. I'm very tired.'

'Damn you, woman!' If she didn't become more amenable to his needs, he might have to consider chastisement, a touch more discipline. And if he did ever resort to such actions, she could blame no one but herself. He pushed open her legs, brushed aside her reluctant hand and drove himself into her, enjoying the sound of her cries. It gave him the proof he needed that he could control her body if not her obstinate mind.

Philip cried in her arms the next morning, begging her forgiveness for his rough treatment of her last night.

'Did I hurt you, my darling?' he asked and Lissa assured him that he had not. Not much anyway. 'I'm impatient for you sometimes, and my black moods get the better of me. You won't leave me, will you? I couldn't bear it if you left me.'

'No, Philip,' she had told him. 'I won't leave you.'

Two days later Lissa went to call upon Miss Stevens.

She lived in a cottage clinging half-way up Benthwaite Crag, its precipitous garden held in place by a border of clipped laurel, surrounded in turn by a thicket of hazel and beech that stretched across the hillside and hid other, similar properties. A glass conservatory fronted the little house, offering a magnificent view of the lake and it was here that Lissa found her former employer, busily watering her plants. She smelled of damp earth and dahlias and welcomed Lissa as if she were an old friend. 'How lovely to see you. How is Jan?'

'In rude health, as they say. Produced a beautiful baby boy.'

'Oh, how wonderful. I must send her a card.'

Once Lissa had enquired about Miss Stevens' own health, admired the geraniums, commiserated over the loss of a favourite rose due to the notorious black spot and exchanged other family news she came swiftly to the point.

'I'm interested in taking on the lease of your old shop.'

'Oh, goodness me. Really?' Miss Stevens looked slightly startled. 'But I thought you were married, to Mr Brandon?'

'I am.'

'With lovely twin daughters?'

'Yes, but . . .'

'Then surely a lady in your station in life has no need to work.'

Lissa cleared her throat. 'I need to feel fulfilled.'

'My dear, isn't marriage to a wonderful man fulfilment enough?' Miss Stevens would have given anything for such a joy.

Lissa clearly did not share this view for taking a deep breath, she continued, 'May I speak in complete confidence?'

Miss Stevens looked suddenly panic stricken, having little knowledge of matrimony. 'Oh, well, I – of course, only . . . He is my solicitor and . . .'

'I need to do this, Miss Stevens.' Lissa nervously tapped the hanging bell petals of a pink fuchsia. 'I need something of my own, and for my girls. I think my marriage may be in trouble.'

'Oh, my dear.' Shock registered in the other woman's eyes. 'Has he left you? Oh, my goodness.'

'No, no, nothing like that. I simply . . . We are not particularly compatible, I suppose.' How to explain her feelings of being held in a trap? That although her husband plainly adored her, he must control every part of her life, even in bed, and she couldn't bear it, she really couldn't. But Lissa couldn't explain all of this to Miss Stevens. 'He is so possessive he is driving me quite mad,' she said, on a falsely bright laugh.

Stella Stevens set down her watering can and considered her ex-employee more seriously. She had suffered enough romantic disappointments in her own life to recognise the distress Lissa was suffering. She could see it in the haunted expression in the girl's eyes, the pinched quality of the skin about the mouth, the darting glances and quick gasps for breath.

'I think a cup of tea might be the thing. Would you care for one?' Stella politely enquired and flushing bright red, Lissa accepted.

'That would be lovely.'

The tea was made and brought, along with triangles of cucumber sandwiches with the crusts neatly cut off. Lissa struggled to eat one. This meeting was even worse than she'd expected.

'Not that it is any concern of mine, my dear, but have you seen a doctor, for your nerves at least? And you'll do that fuchsia no good at all if you don't leave it alone.'

Lissa guiltily relinquished the flower petals and pleated her fingers tightly together in her lap instead, trying to keep them still. 'Could we discuss the shop, do you think? I don't have much time.'

'Of course. I hadn't really done anything more about letting it. It's very rundown, you know.'

'It doesn't matter.'

Stella Stevens liked Lissa, who was a lovely girl, sensible and intelligent, though at this moment her beauty had taken on a brittle quality quite at odds with the liquid, golden grace of the young girl who had first come to work at her drapery. She looked in dire need of help today. She warned herself not to get involved, that it was no business of hers if Philip Brandon was proving to be a possessive husband. For all she knew he may well have cause. And he was not a man to cross, for all his outward charm. He was a professional, a man of affairs. And a gentleman. A thought struck her.

'Goodness me, you weren't considering . . .' she paused, breathless with horror. '*Divorce*?'

The word jolted Lissa. She had not dared to go so far in her thoughts. 'I-I hadn't quite – decided,' Lissa admitted, and Stella grasped her hand in a gesture of relief.

'Oh, thank goodness.' And lowering her voice to a confidential whisper, 'Divorce is not at all the done thing, you know. Not quite proper. You would lose your reputation, my dear. Only the lower classes and women who are no better than they should be, get involved in divorce. If you understand me?'

Lissa stared at Miss Stevens in obvious distress. Would this be how everyone would view her if she did leave Philip? Vulgar. Wayward. Wicked. *Just like her mother*. She could almost hear Rosemary's purr of satisfaction at being proved right. 'Perhaps it won't come to that,' she said. 'I have my children to consider.'

'Of course you have. I appreciate your confidence in telling me of your troubles, and not a word of it shall pass my lips, but I really think you should consider the matter most carefully before you make any rash decisions. There is great stigma attached to – to the subject. Why, every week my magazine implores women to be good wives and mothers, make their husbands happy and be satisfied with their lot. It is up to the woman to make a marriage successful, they say.'

Lissa set down her uneaten sandwich with a small sound of exasperation. 'Then they are living in the past. You'd have thought that the war would've changed all of that, wouldn't you? And here we are at the start of a new decade, as tied as ever. Duty. Obedience. Responsibilities. Making our husband's happy. What about *our* happiness? Are we not entitled to some of that ourselves?'

Miss Stevens looked flustered. 'I know nothing of marriage, you understand. As a maiden lady.'

'You are a woman, Miss Stevens.'

'Quite so, quite so.' She got up hastily from the small table and picking up a small pointed trowel, dug it into a pot of begonias, the soil as rich as fruit cake. 'I don't necessarily agree with these opinions but they are generally held. There might even be sensational reporting in the local paper.'

Lissa swallowed and hung her head, feeling shame and guilt, as if she were already in such a dreadful situation. She had few illusions about what she faced, were she to try and seek her freedom. She could lose everything. She'd need to find a home for herself and the children and some means of earning enough money to keep them all. And who would take care of the twins while she worked? The problems were enormous. But that was a matter to be considered in the future. In the meantime her life remained intolerable and must be improved. She squared her shoulders and met Miss Stevens' probing gaze with a brave smile. 'I'm only asking to rent the shop, that's all. I can't go on like this, I really can't.

267

If I could only make my life a little more – livable – gain some independence or . . .'

Or the girl would break. Any fool could see that. Miss Stevens nodded her head, looking thoughtful. 'Perhaps then your marriage would improve. Have you thought that it might make it worse?'

'I must take the risk.'

'Well, I shall give your request my careful consideration but I make no promises. And you must think deeply about all of this,' Stella warned, wagging the trowel at her as a schoolmistress might. 'I really think you should take advice before coming to any decisions. See your doctor, or the vicar. And certainly a lawyer.'

'But Philip is a lawyer.'

'I know, my dear,' said Miss Stevens in her sharpest tones. 'So he will know everything and you nothing. And the law is a terrible thing to face for a woman alone, shunned by society.' The dragon could still roar. And speak utter sense.

'Yes,' said Lissa, suddenly deeply depressed. 'I hadn't thought of that.'

1963

21

The months dragged by and Lissa heard nothing more from Miss Stevens. Gradually she lost hope, nor ever found the strength to ask Philip again. The idea died, stillborn.

'Don't give up,' Renee told her. 'Tell him you want to be a typhoon like Mr Woolworth.'

'Tycoon. And I'm not sure that I do.' And Lissa would laugh and change the subject. She enjoyed her visits to Nab Cottage. Renee always managed to make her smile. And Lissa did decide to take up one of her suggestions. Surely there must be something useful she could do. It wasn't exactly the kind of freedom she'd had in mind but it was a start.

'I thought I might take up some voluntary work,' she said one evening as she handed Philip his drink. 'Just an hour or two a week.'

'Good idea,' he said, his attention on his newspaper.

'I thought perhaps I'd ask Hilary, she might know of something I can do. Would you mind?'

She kissed him on his forehead and he glanced up, surprised. It was rare for her to be demonstrative and the gesture touched him. 'No, of course not, darling. The woman always seems to be dealing with some good cause or other.' And it would do him no harm with Don Cheyney.

Lissa smiled her delight, as if he had offered her a gift. He loved her best when she was weak and gentle, showing her dependence upon him. She had turned out to be surprisingly stubborn, not at all like dear, sweet Felicity. Far less malleable than he'd expected or hoped for. There was the matter of her grandmother, for instance. He always had great difficulty in persuading her to visit Larkrigg Hall, and there was still no sign of a reconciliation between them. Not that he had given up hope of winning that one. But then he always did win, in the end.

'Did you see Doc Robson again today like I asked?'

Lissa turned away, busying herself with arranging flowers that were already immaculate.

'Yes.'

He wanted to know what treatment had been offered and if she must go into hospital for it. This necessitated so many lies that Lissa's head was spinning with the complexity of the web of deceit she was weaving. The prospect of yet more lies were she to acquire the shop, was daunting. Perhaps it was just as well nothing had come of it.

Doctor Robson had been totally unsympathetic when she tried to explain her problems. One of the old school, he very much believed it was the woman who made or broke a marriage.

'Philip wants a son,' he'd reminded her in his usual blunt manner. 'And you are depriving him of one.'

'As he tries to deprive me of my freedom, of any say in my own life, even in whether or not I want to make . . .'

'Make what?'

Lissa, blushing with embarrassment, had stared at the worn carpet in the doctor's surgery and pretended she'd forgotten what she was about to say. She couldn't talk about sex, not with the doctor. 'He seems obsessed by me,' she tried. 'He must have me near him at all times. Constantly checking on where I am and what I'm doing. It's unhealthy.'

'It sounds as if you are a very lucky young woman. Few men care so much for their wives. It's a woman's responsibility to create a happy home,' he reminded her. 'Your duty to keep your husband content.'

She'd looked at him then with pleading eyes, begging for him to understand. 'I was too young when I married Philip, too inexperienced. I don't know what I expected from marriage, but not this. I didn't realise what I was taking on.'

At this point Doc Robson had looked very sternly at her over his spectacles. 'It is time to grow up, Lissa. You have made your bed and you must lie in it. Marriage is for life. You must fit your expectations to suit your husband's requirements. That is your responsibility as a wife.'

She'd argued no more. There had seemed little point. More worryingly he'd refused to refurbish her contraceptive supplies.

'I think I'd like to discuss the matter with you both together,' he'd said, and Lissa had felt herself go quite white and shivery.

'No, no, anything but that. It would be too awful, too embarrassing.'

'Don't be silly, Lissa, he is your husband.'

Taking her courage in both hands she'd tilted her chin and outfaced the doctor with a courage she did not quite feel.

'I'm not ready to have any more babies yet. I had thought about trying this new pill which a friend told me about.'

He'd been so shocked, Lissa thought he might have a heart attack there and then. Then he'd proceeded to give her a long lecture on sinful promiscuity, as if it automatically went with the pill, but she had won her case. He gave her the prescription she needed.

Victory was sweet. How long it would last was another matter. She did her best now to set the subject aside.

'He said not to worry. There's nothing wrong with me,' she insisted. 'We must simply be patient.' She went to Philip and put her arms about his neck, wanting to distract him. 'If we're meant to have another child, one will be given to us. The twins are young yet. Doctor Robson says I'm a perfectly healthy young woman.' That, at least, was true.

By February, not on the pill either, Jan announced that she was pregnant again. And around the time of Lissa's birthday in late March, Philip insisted they visit Larkrigg Hall. She always protested vehemently but it was hard to deny Philip anything when he had set his mind to it. And she wanted to see her family, so what excuse could she give?

They sat now in the shrouded sitting room, Lissa's heart filled with dread as usual, Philip at his most charming. It was like a scene from her childhood bringing back all her old feelings of rejection.

Rosemary Ellis poured tea brought by Mrs Stanton, the housekeeper, more ancient and crabby than ever, and responded to small talk with such a frosty politeness they might well have been strangers, quite unknown to her, instead of a part of her own unacknowledged family.

Lissa made no attempt to enter the conversation, having learned long ago that any remark from her was not even granted the courtesy of a polite reply, receiving no more than a chilling silence. She wondered why the woman even received them. Lissa fixed her gaze on the panorama of mountains through the trefoiled windows, which brought their usual comfort and tried to detach herself from the scene being played in the stuffy drawing room.

She sipped her tea, not tasting it, longing for the agony to be over so she could return to the warm cocoon of Broombank kitchen and gather her children on her lap.

'I'm glad to see you looking so well after your difficult winter,' Philip was saying, his warm smile lighting his face. He really could appear a most charming, handsome man when he wished, she thought.

'I'm old,' said Rosemary starkly. 'And prone to colds and chills. Which no doubt pleases you.'

'My dear lady, you have no idea how it distresses me.' Philip set down his cup and saucer on the polished table and edged closer. 'Forgive me for saying so, but you should not live alone in this big house, now that you are reaching your most vulnerable years.' His voice seemed filled with genuine concern so that even Rosemary seemed to pause before barking out her reply.

'What a way to put it. Vulnerable years indeed. And I do not live alone. I have Mrs Stanton. We do very well.'

'I'm sure you do. But for how long? And there is really no necessity when you have a family only too ready to care for you. You could come and live with us, or we could move in here if you prefer?'

'I do not prefer,' she snapped, over Lissa's gasp.

Thank God, thought Lissa, horrified by Philip's unexpected suggestion. She certainly had no wish to live with Rosemary Ellis.

'You would love the twins. Perhaps we could bring them to see you one day?' No response. 'Did we tell you that Melissa and I are trying for another child? A boy this time, hopefully.'

'There's no hurry,' Lissa interjected, then flushed as Philip frowned at her.

She had said the wrong thing. Yet again. But sensible thought seemed to desert her when she had the eyes of these two people resting so critically upon her.

For the first time that Lissa could recall, Rosemary turned interested eyes upon her. For a full half-minute grandmother and granddaughter's gaze locked and she saw a terrible bleakness in the faded eyes. She's unhappy, Lissa thought, and lonely.

A part of her ached to reach out and put her arms about the woman, beg Rosemary to forgive her for whatever it was that had turned her so firmly against her in the past. She wanted to ask for her love, her acceptance at least, but then the face seemed to close and turn away and Lissa felt the familiar rebuff, like a slap.

Her grandmother had never wanted her, not when she was small, not now. She would never accept her. Even as a child when Lissa used to clamber on to Jeffrey's knee and he would give her sweets and presents, laugh and play with her, Rosemary had never unbent a fraction from her rigid disapproval.

Now Lissa stiffened in the straight-backed chair, staring into the empty grate as she remembered doing as a child. Could that be the same cobweb? The very same spider? She would not allow the woman to see that she cared, that her words could still hurt.

'There seems to be a problem, but we'll solve it,' Philip said.

'At least you are respectably married,' Rosemary commented, glaring accusingly at Lissa. 'I suppose we should be grateful for that small mercy, in view of her hoydenish youth.'

Philip laughed. 'Hoyden? Hardly a word I would use to describe my wife.'

Rosemary stared at him without expression. 'Then you do not know her very well. Or she has disguised her true character from you, as Katherine did from me. You have my sympathy.' She did not look at all sympathetic and Lissa felt a tremor come into her limbs. He would interrogate her later, ask what Rosemary meant. And she would feel guilty even though there was nothing to feel guilty about. She felt a prick of annoyance that they should judge her so harshly, and talk about her as if she were not there. Lifting her chin, she outfaced them both.

'I was no more a hoyden than any other child. Nick and I fell in the beck a few times it's true, as children will. No other terrible misdemeanours that I can recall.'

Rosemary fixed her with the same cold unblinking stare and continued to address her remarks to Philip. 'I used to see her riding the fells on a pony, reckless and alone. Or wandering about on foot. Meg exercised no control over her. None that I could see. She ran

273

wild and free, to do as she would, and meet all manner of unseemly people.'

'Unseemly people? Who can you mean?' Philip laughed, amused and intrigued, turning questioning eyes to his wife.

Lissa could feel the blood draining from her cheeks. What mischief was the woman up to? Was she implying that she had seen her with the travelling people, with the gypsy? Oh, please no.

'How should I know? Odd folk do come into the dale from time to time. You must ask her yourself. Ran wild she did.'

'She doesn't now,' Philip said, with a grin.

'No. It is a relief to see you exercising some discipline over her. She has long been in need of it. More tea, Mr Brandon?' Rosemary twisted her face into what might pass for a smile, as if Lissa's burning discomfiture pleased her.

Red hot fury was pouring through her veins. How *dare* Rosemary Ellis talk about her in that cruel way, as if she were a child needing correction, or a dog who needed to be trained? She found herself on her feet, limbs trembling, and two pairs of eyes swivelled to hers, surprised that she had dared move without their permission.

'I think it's time we returned to Broombank, Philip,' Lissa said in her stiffest manner. 'I must see to the twins.' If she relaxed her control for a second she would burst into tears and shame herself before them both. 'And Meg will be wondering where we are.'

'Sit down,' he said, in his quiet voice. 'Finish your tea and treat your grandmother with more respect.'

'But . . .'

'*Sit* down.'

And now Rosemary Ellis smiled widely, if only with her cold narrow lips.

Lissa was shaking, the cup and saucer clattering in her hand as she searched blindly for the table. The cup wobbled, fell over and rolled to the floor where it snapped into two pieces. The sound was like gunfire in the still room.

Lissa stared appalled at the broken flowered porcelain, then at the two coldly furious faces. 'I-I'm sorry,' she whispered, her throat constricting with fear and shame. But the anger was still there, deep inside, burning right to the heart of her. And then she started to speak, the words spilling out without control. 'I won't have you treat me like this, as if I'm some sort of problem to you both. I'm a living, breathing person who needs to be loved. *Can't either of you*

274

see that?' She looked wildly from one stiffly blank face to the other, then she was running from the room and the sobs were coming from her in great tearing gulps.

Philip did not speak to her for days of course. And when he did it was to demand an apology which she absolutely refused to give. 'I've done nothing wrong. I'm not a wilful child in need of discipline.'

'That is exactly how you were behaving.'

'I won't do it.'

'I say you will. Old ladies sometimes say foolish, hurtful things but she is your grandmother, the only one you have.'

'She doesn't think so.'

'All the more reason for you to try harder to be pleasant to her and then she will.'

'I won't do it.'

Philip's dark eyes glittered with anger though his tone remained as cool as ever. 'If you wish us to remain friends, you will do it.'

He brought pen and paper and stood over her, instructing her what to write, blotting the angry marks of blue ink, folding the paper, slipping it into the envelope with resolute fingers and taking it to the post box himself.

When he had gone, Lissa hammered the desk with her fists in a moment of rare fury then sobbed out her despair. But what else could she have done? His control was absolute and she couldn't bear him to be angry with her.

Whenever she could, Lissa escaped to Nab Cottage. She and Renee would drink sherry or Coca-Cola, and gossip. Those times were a blessed relief, an oasis of warmth in a life stultified by frozen emotion and a growing fear that it would never be any better.

Hilary Cheyney was delighted to acquire a new volunteer with her charity work but though Lissa might fill an afternoon with a rummage sale, or spend a morning serving coffee, it did not make her feel any more fulfilled. She even felt an outcast from her own children.

The twins seemed to grow with each passing day and Lissa found herself competing for every moment with them, asking Nanny Susan if she might take them to the park or to feed the ducks, if Beth might be spared egg for tea since she did not care for it. It was as if she had no say over her own children's welfare. Philip saw little of them but laid down a strict routine which he was adamant must be kept.

275

Nanny must answer to him, of course, if it was not, so what hope did Lissa have of changing anything? She grew increasingly frustrated.

Yet any resolve to defy him was demolished by his continual criticism of her. He was like a tightly coiled spring, barely restraining his anger. Each month he would scowl accusingly, bark out his disappointment at the regularity of her periods which seemed to mock his manhood. His increasing complaints and demands left her brain too numb to argue, made her question her own self-worth and wonder if she had anything of value to offer anyone, let alone her own children.

Nevertheless Lissa continued to take precautions against conceiving. She refused to contemplate bringing another child into this less than perfect marriage.

And every time she walked past the old drapery shop her heart clenched, as if it represented the depth of her captivity. Dare she contact Miss Stevens again?

'You shouldn't let him dictate your life to you,' Renee told her, not for the first time. 'Make a stand for women's rights. The sixties are here, for goodness' sake.'

Lissa was sitting on the rug in front of the electric fire, playing with the twins who were happily engrossed emptying Renee's capacious beige plastic handbag and filling it up again, trying out comb, powder puff and hair pins as they did so. Sarah had daubed lipstick on Beth's mouth and was pretending to be a hairdresser and put rollers and pincurls in her baby soft hair. Lissa, for once, was laughing and happy, Nab Cottage seeming to be the only place where she could relax and enjoy her children.

'I know, Renee. And one day I mean to make a stand.'

'Huh. One day.' Renee was washing out the budgie cage in preparation for a new resident. A hot pot was bubbling in the oven and Jimmy would be home in an hour or two but for now she was concerned about Lissa. Renee had grown quite fond of her over recent months, and the terrible twosome who were delicious and not terrible at all.

'Look, love. If I thought he was making you happy I'd say bugger the shop, have another kid and be done with it. Except that nobody but a one-eyed catfish would call you happy.'

Lissa looked mortified. 'Is it as obvious as all that?'

'I can see that there's more to this than you're telling. No, it's all right. None of my business. It's your life. Only don't let things drag on too long. Make up your mind to put it right, one way or t'other. Everyone deserves a happy life. This is the only shot you get at it.'

'Derry used to say that.' The unexpected admission brought a blush to Lissa's cheeks, and a wry smile to Renee's bright lips.

'Don't fret, lass. I know you've never got him out of your system but I won't tell on you.' The doorbell rang and she swore silently under her breath, annoyed by the interruption. 'Who the hell can that be? It's too early in the season for paying guests.' She peered through the lace curtains. 'Oh my God, it's your beloved himself. In person. What the hell is he doing here?'

Lissa leapt to her feet, reaching for the twins. 'He must be looking for me. Oh, Renee, he mustn't find me here. He'll stop me coming again.'

Renee didn't pause to question why, or feel offended by the implied criticism. She was too busy finding the twins' coats and bonnets, and bundling the three of them out the back door. The doorbell rang again.

'Won't be a minute,' she shouted. 'Down the garden, out the back gate,' she hissed. 'Takes you directly to the lake path.'

Renee closed the kitchen door and hurried back to the parlour with the sound of continuous ringing in her ears. Drat the man. Had he no manners?

Moments before she opened the door, her eyes alighted on the spilled contents of her handbag, all over the rug.

'Mrs Colwith?'

'What is it?' she snapped. 'Am I on fire or summat?'

Philip Brandon looked startled by the question, as well he might. 'I don't quite understand?'

'All that damned ringing. Thought it must surely be the fire brigade.'

He gave a half laugh. 'Very droll.'

'Didn't you hear me call? I was out the back.'

His face tightened and the smile vanished. 'I don't have all day. My friend here is looking for a room,' indicating a bespectacled young man who might have been a vicar, fidgeting beside him. 'I seem to recall you are in that line of business.'

Philip Brandon looked unusually tall in the late-afternoon shadows and Renee suppressed an unexpected shudder. Daft, when you came to think of it. She'd always thought him quite a pleasant gent. A real charmer he'd been once. He was smiling friendly enough at her now.

277

She said, 'I do bed and breakfast for summer visitors. I don't take lodgers.'

'He'd be no trouble. A professional man who must visit the area from time to time for the purpose of his work, which may take two or three weeks or more on each occasion. The Marina Hotel is somewhat expensive for a long-term stay.'

Ah, so that was the way of it. She'd had those sort of folk before. Travelling salesmen who pretended they were staying in an expensive hotel, wanting her to bill them as if they were, so they could claim extra on expenses while paying her cheaper rates.

'I don't think so,' she said, giving the man a scant glance of disapproval. 'I never take folk this early in the season. My husband doesn't like it. Sorry.' And thinking of her hot pot and the half clean cage, she started to close the door.

'Let's see if I can change your mind.' Philip brushed past her, as if she were of no account, and marched into the front parlour. As she told Jimmy later, it was as if he owned the damned place. And the young man followed like a spaniel at his heels.

Turning a smiling face to hers, Philip took in her appearance for the first time, starting with the hair. 'Well, well, well. You're the red-headed waitress who tipped soup down my trousers. I didn't recognise you at the time, Mrs Colwith, being otherwise occupied.'

Renee didn't feel too happy about this identification even now, but carelessly shrugged her shoulders, trying to show that it didn't trouble her one bit. 'These things happen. I nearly lost my job over it.'

'Nearly?'

'They're very fair at the Marina Hotel,' she said, meeting his stare with her own. And if you humiliate Lissa in public again, I'd do the same again, her eyes said. Job or no job.

'You do seem rather accident prone.' He was staring at the jumble of items on the hearthrug. Purse, bus tickets, spare stockings, safety pins, an open lipstick, powder everywhere, all spilled from her bag. And then his gaze took in the rest of the untidy room. 'Housekeeping not your forte?'

Renee shrugged, not troubling to reply. She wouldn't be bullied by him. He wasn't her husband. Though despite herself a feeling of intimidation was creeping over her and she felt vaguely uneasy with these two men in her parlour. 'Jimmy'll be home in a minute.' She didn't know why she needed to say that. Something about the expression in his eyes. 'There's naught I can do for your friend. I've told you. My guest house is closed.' That would show him she wasn't scared of his high-handed tactics. She half glanced at the young man, pale and freckle-faced, skinny, glasses sliding down his nose, probably single and lived with his mother, she decided.

But Philip Brandon didn't seem to be listening. He circled the small room as if he owned it, filling it with his tall, lean, pinstripe presence. He poked a finger at the budgie cage and laughed, picked up newspapers and tossed them down again. Even walked into the kitchen and inspected her cupboards.

'Here, where d'you think you're going?' Cheeky bugger.

He turned to her with a dry smile on his lips. 'I was told you were a good cook. Is that so?'

Renee drew in a deep breath and puffed out her chest. 'There in't lighter pastry in Lakeland.'

Philip was rubbing the bridge of his narrow nose with the tip of one finger, his dark eyes measuring her. The woman was proving obstinate but he had little patience to waste on persuasion. Time was of the essence. Money went nowhere these days, what with nannies and children, the new car he had bought, enormous fees for the Yacht Club and the Golf Club next year. Not to mention all the entertaining that was expected of a man in his position. He needed a fresh injection of capital and thought he'd found the way to do it. No blowsy female too big for her stocking tops was going to get in his way. 'I once recall doing you a favour,' he said.

'Eh?' Renee was startled, wondering for a moment what he meant.

'I remember you coming to me for advice on how to rid yourself of Derry Colwith. Isn't he your brother-in-law?'

'Stepson, as a matter of fact.' Uncertainty crept into Renee's voice. 'I wanted him to move out, that's all. And I asked your advice on doing bed and breakfast.'

'That's right. And I suggested you put him in the garden shed and leave the rest to me. Now it's time to repay the favour.'

'What?' Renee stared at him, appalled. 'I only asked you to pay Derry more money so he could afford his own place.' She remembered wanting more privacy for herself and Jimmy but somehow the conversation had got out of hand. Philip Brandon had promised to help persuade Derry to leave town though how he'd intended to achieve that, she hadn't asked. She wished fervently now that she'd never interfered at all. If Lissa, or worse, Jimmy, found out that she'd been to see Derry's boss who'd then sacked him, they'd blame her for everything. 'Oh, hecky thump,' she said.

Philip smiled. 'Your husband wouldn't be too pleased to learn how you conspired to drive his son out of town, now would he?'

'Conspired?' Renee wasn't good on long words, but she understood this one. And when she was beaten.

'Look, it doesn't matter,' the young man said, speaking for the first time. 'If there's a problem I can go elsewhere.' They both stared at him, as if they'd forgotten his presence.

'There's no problem,' Philip said, suave and confident. 'Mrs Colwith will be only too pleased to take you. Mr Spencer here is a consultant, for Manchester Water Board. A respectable man,' Philip continued. 'He requires a clean, comfortable bed, a substantial breakfast and an evening meal. You can manage that, I suppose?'

'I don't do evening meals.'

'You do now. You can provide him with a monthly account to send to his employers but the exact sum will be settled in cash, privately. Is that clear?'

As crystal. 'Jimmy might object,' Renee mumbled. 'He likes his privacy.'

'I'm sure you can persuade him, if you put your mind to it. Well, that's splendid,' taking her agreement for granted. 'It is so much easier when people are obliging. Don't you think?'

He's nuts, Renee thought, finding herself suddenly feeling sorry for the young man who looked as bemused as she felt. But she agreed to take him, evening meals and all. She knew when she was cornered, and when there wasn't a damned thing she could do about it.

22

Lissa stayed away from Nab Cottage for a while, just to be on the safe side. She had gone home in trepidation that day, expecting the usual lectures, but rather to her surprise Philip had said nothing. Nevertheless, his visit had made her jumpy. How often did he follow her? Did he watch everything she did? Surely not, he was far too busy to concern himself with her mundane routine.

For two pins she would leave him, start a new life of her own. Then almost before the thought had formed she would quash it with a sigh of despair. Look at the scandal there would be if she did. She would be looked upon as a loose woman. No, wishing to be liberated was one thing, carrying it out was quite another matter. Lissa did not think she could face the shame of the whispers, the sly looks and comments which Miss Stevens had rightly warned her of. Her case was hopeless.

She concentrated on keeping busy and not thinking at all, filling her life with good works as if that would solve everything. So when Hilary Cheyney rang and asked her to fill in for her with a visit to an old folks' home, Lissa was happy to oblige.

The Birches seemed better than most, being a spacious, rather sedate, ivy-clad building, set in its own grounds. It looked like a grand country house hotel and the residents appeared lively and busily occupied. She talked with several, listening to their stories, admiring photographs of grandchildren and beloved, long dead husbands looking impossibly fresh and young in smart WWI uniforms.

Lissa approached one frail old lady who sat apart from the rest, in a corner all alone. Her head flopped oddly to one side, the mouth twisted, and Lissa's heart flooded with pity. How dreadful to be overset by old age and abandoned by one's family. It made her own problems seem insignificant by comparison.

'Hello, how are you today?' she asked, taking the old woman's hand gently in her own.

'Charles will be home soon,' the woman snapped. 'He's in the war, you know.'

'Really? So was my husband. The Second, of course. Perhaps you know him? He's a solicitor. Philip Brandon?'

Lissa did not at first associate this rather sad woman with the one-time owner of her own gracious home. It was Elvira Fraser, locked in her own confused world but still clinging to a fragment of that indomitable spirit, who struggled to make the connection.

'Brandon? Do I know you?' The faded grey eyes focused a moment as if they struggled to capture a wayward memory, but as quickly became blank again, the effort too much. And then Elvira spoke in a loud sharp voice that made Lissa jump. 'I *won't* stay here a moment longer than necessary. I just can't find my bank book at the moment.'

She leaned forward to speak in a loud conspiratorial whisper. 'The people here steal my things, don't you know? Taken my bank book and savings certificates, every one. But I'll find them.'

Lissa was so troubled by this outburst that she called over a nurse.

'Don't worry, Mrs Brandon. She's easily upset. Tomorrow it might be her slippers or her liberty bodice that she'll claim has been stolen.' A lowering of the voice. 'The poor lady gets very confused.' And smiling cheerfully, the nurse went happily on her way. 'Now then, Mr Marshall, what about your bit of exercise?'

Lissa flickered an uncertain smile at Elvira and prepared to do her best. 'I'm sure you will find your bank book soon. Philip likes to have things tidy too,' she said.

'You know him?'

'Who?'

'Philip.'

'He's my husband. Didn't I say?'

Irritation flashed. 'No, Charles. My husband is called Charles. When he arrives he'll sort this muddle out. Never stands any nonsense, doesn't my darling Charles. He'll take me home. I'm not staying here.'

'Of course he will.' This was the craziest conversation Lissa had ever experienced. Yet she'd taken a liking to the old lady, the way she kept her shoulders square with a certain regal air and dignity in her bearing for all the obvious disability of a recent stroke. Here was a woman who must once have been a beauty, with a position in the world and proud of it.

'I have a lovely house, don't you know?' Elvira said, in a rare moment of clarity. 'On the Parade.'

'Fraser, of course. I hadn't made the connection.' Lissa was delighted. 'I believe we bought it off you.'

The old lady glared fiercely. 'Bought it? Nonsense. I'm going home soon. How can they sell my house? It's mine.'

Lissa stroked the old lady's hand, filled with compassion. 'You must have been sorry to leave it.'

'I haven't left it, have I? Call that silly maid to bring us lunch. We'll have salmon. I love salmon, and sherry trifle to follow.'

'Did you live there for a long time?' Lissa interrupted, trying to keep her in the present.

'Live where?'

'In your house, on the Parade?'

'I'm here now, aren't I? Silly child. Lived here all my life. Born here. Father would never hear of my leaving it. And certainly not now that I've married my darling Charles.' She smiled, as if she were an excited young bride.

How terribly sad, Lissa thought, moved almost to tears by the blank confusion in the old lady's eyes.

Elvira suddenly grasped Lissa's hand in a fierce grip. 'Wait for Charles. He'll sort this muddle out. No money indeed! They come in the night and take my things. Won't stand any nonsense, my darling Charles. He's in the war, you know. He'll be home soon, when it's over.' And she was off again, round and round the same senseless conversation. Lissa exchanged sad glances with the nurse who hurried back, offering lunch and Mrs Fraser's favourite bread pudding.

Lissa said her goodbyes and left, wondering if she'd been at all successful in her visit and thinking that perhaps voluntary work was not her thing, after all.

* * *

283

It was when she was coming out of the The Birches that she ran into Stella Stevens.

'My goodness I was only just thinking about you. How fortuitous,' Miss Stevens said. 'What on earth are you doing here?'

Lissa told her and Stella shook her head sadly. 'I remember Elvira Fraser. We were in the WVS together during the war. I call in to see her myself every now and then, to try to cheer her. Poor old soul. Had a terrible stroke, you know.' Then, brightening, she took Lissa's arm. 'Come along, let me buy you lunch.'

'Oh, there's no need . . .'

'There's every need, I wish to talk to you.'

How could Lissa resist? Besides, Philip wouldn't be home for an hour or more yet. She had plenty of time. 'Lunch sounds good.'

'Splendid.' Miss Stevens took her to a charming little café on Carndale Road which still had lace tablecloths on polished mahogany tables, instead of the newly popular formica. They ordered ham salad and a pot of tea.

Stella at once adopted a businesslike pose. 'Now, are you still interested in the shop? I rather expected you to come back to me.'

Lissa flushed slightly. 'I rather thought it was a waste of time.'

'Good heavens, girl, you'll need more stamina than that if you are to be a successful businesswoman. As you can see, it remains empty, but now I've had a serious offer for it. However, I wished to give you first refusal.'

'Oh.' Lissa's attention sharpened and she felt that familiar buzz of excitement.

'If you really want it, I see no reason why we cannot come to terms.'

'Oh, that would be wonderful. Thank you.' Happiness shone from Lissa's face and the transformation almost took Stella's breath away. And then a cloud darkened the heart-shaped face and the brilliance instantly faded. 'Would there be much in the way of legal documentation? It's only that I've no wish to involve Philip yet . . . at this stage . . . until . . .'

Miss Stevens gave a polite cough. 'I prefer not to discuss the state of your marriage, Lissa, though as you can appreciate, I have given your problem a good deal of thought. You once saved my life. Had you not discovered me that day senseless in the stock room, who knows what might have been the outcome?'

The waitress arrived with their salads and they were both able

284

to cover their respective embarrassment with passing salt and salad cream.

'And I appreciate the fact that you did not – broadcast – the reason for my presence in such an odd place on that occasion,' Miss Stevens said. 'The hospital realised, of course, but no one else seems to have known. Which is a great relief. I'm quite well now,' she hastily added. 'Never touch the stuff. No more Milk of Magnesia bottles.' A wry smile to which Lissa responded, understanding perfectly.

'I'm so glad.'

'You gave me a second chance, so I think I owe you one. Take the shop. Do with it what you will. But make it a good business. Give it your all.'

Lissa was thrilled. 'Oh, I will, I will.' She could hardly believe it. When she had set out today on one more act of charity, she'd never guessed that someone would do the same favour for her. Now she could begin to build a future for herself and later, if life with Philip became too much of a strain, she could turn the two rooms above the shop into a small flat for herself and the girls. Lissa's head buzzed with ideas and her smile turned into one of beaming delight.

Stella Stevens, a shy woman with few friends, was nonetheless an astute judge of character and resolutely set her own misgivings aside as she watched the expressions of joy and excitement flitting across the girl's enchanting face, as if she'd been given the whole world.

'I'll never forget this. Thank you so much,' Lissa said.

Clearing her throat and paying excessive attention to her ham, Stella felt quite moved by this gratitude. But she judged it best to bring Lissa down to earth. 'I have no wish to pry, but in view of your other – um, confidences, may I point out that you will need money to set up a shop? People never realise quite how much. There's stock and new fittings, and decoration will be considerable. Then there'll presumably be wages for an assistant, electricity and advertising, rent and rates, and working capital is vital. It will take some time before you move into profit. Can you manage all of that, without your husband's assistance?'

Lissa smiled. 'As a matter of fact I do have a sum saved. It was a gift from my – my grandfather. Not a fortune by any means but enough, I believe, and I've added more to it over the years. I was told to save it for a rainy day.' The smile changed to a grin. 'It's rained quite a lot recently.'

Stella sipped quietly at her tea, then set down the cup with a decisive click. 'Taking everything into account I see no reason why you shouldn't begin your little enterprise in an unofficial sort of way. So long as the rent is paid regularly I shall be perfectly happy. Later, once you are successful, which I'm sure you will be, we can settle all the legal niceties of leases and so on. You may even prefer to take on the freehold in time. We'll see, shall we?'

'Oh, I can't tell you how grateful I am.'

Miss Stevens cleared her throat. 'As to that other matter, think of your children. Do nothing hasty. Did you see your doctor?'

'Yes.'

'Ah, no good, eh?'

'Not a lot.'

'Lawyer then. Take some advice on the matter.'

Lissa bit on her lip and promised that she would.

She ran all the way home and arrived breathless but relieved to find that Philip had rung to say he would not be home for lunch.

'Have the children eaten?'

'Of course. It is after one.' Nanny Susan sounded offended.

'Then I shall take them out. Let's get them ready. Come along, darlings, find your cardigans.'

She ignored protests that the twins had not yet taken their afternoon nap, and bubbling with happiness, Lissa grasped their small hands and marched them off. They giggled and skipped along with her, delighted to find Mummy in such a happy mood, singing and laughing all the way through Fairfield Park, past the ducks on the lake and along Fossburn Street to Nab Cottage.

'I've done it,' she announced, the moment Renee opened the door.

'What, left him?'

Lissa looked startled. 'No, not yet. Taken the shop.'

'Well, strike me down with a feather, I never thought you would.' Renee's mouth hung open as Lissa hugged her. 'I've never seen you so full of yourself. Have you told him then? Has he agreed?'

A small silence.

'Ah, like that, is it?' Renee shrugged. 'I've always been of the opinion that the less men know, the better. Time for a celebration then?' She wore strawberry pink lipstick today and the bright mouth widened into a smile. 'Shall I fetch the sherry?' She grinned at the two smiling faces below her. 'How about ice cream for you two? I just happen to have some in the freezer compartment of my fridge. So long as the door isn't gummed up with ice.' She laughed as the twins screamed their delight and galloped off into the kitchen. 'Don't stand on ceremony your two, do they?'

There was a choice between vanilla, strawberry or chocolate, and since a decision was quite impossible, a small amount of each was put in two dishes and the little girls sat happily on the back doorstep, eating.

'They'll be covered in the stuff soon.'

'I know,' laughed Lissa. 'I'll stick to Coca-Cola. Philip will smell alcohol on my breath.'

Renee brought two glasses and they sat at the small kitchen table, a plate of coconut cakes between them. Then going to the dresser Renee brought out a bottle of rum and added a dash to each fizzing glass. 'It's Jimmy's really but he won't mind us having a tot. Your husband won't smell that little bit.' She picked up a glass. 'So what do we drink to? What's this shop to be called? What are you going to sell?'

'Good Lord,' said Lissa, stunned. 'I haven't the first idea.'

Renee roared with laughter. 'Well, there's a good start. Here's to it, anyway.'

The new incumbent of the budgie cage, bright green this time, bashed his bell and sqawked joyously in the front parlour. Both girls laughed.

'I'll let him out in a bit. He likes a fly round. This one's called Mickey.'

'Hallo, Mickey. I'm glad you let him out,' Lissa said. 'I hate to think of a bird in a cage, like a prisoner.' She went oddly silent, dipping her head to her glass.

They munched their way through several cakes, drank another Coca-Cola, though Lissa positively refused any more rum. Then they chewed over several ideas and Lissa rejected them all. The germ of an idea was growing in the back of her mind, perhaps it had always been there, waiting to be picked up, but she didn't feel quite ready to bring it out into the open yet and examine it.

Renee frowned at her over the rim of her glass. 'What did you mean when you said, not yet?'

'Pardon?'

'We've finished our ice cream, Mummy. Can we play in Renee's garden?'

She said, ''Course you can, Poppet. There's a shed down there with a bed in it. You can play at house.'

Squeals of delight, and more when Renee went to the understairs cupboard and brought out scarves and hats and bags in riotous colours. 'Here you are, my pets, get dressed up and enjoy yourselves while your mum and I have a bit of a crack.'

'Ooh, bags I have the pink one,' cried Sarah. 'You can have the blue hat, Beth.'

'That Sarah, chippy little sprite. She'll organise you all one day,' laughed Renee, shaking her head as the two skipped happily away, small bottoms wriggling with self-importance.

She turned back to Lissa, eyes shrewd. 'So, when I asked if you'd left him, why did you say "not yet"?'

Silence, which grew and lengthened. Lissa chewed on her lip and Renee quietly waited.

'You'd feel better if you talked about it.'

'Would I?' Violet eyes like bruises in a pale face gazed into hers. Lissa knew, deep down, that although Renee might be right, she simply couldn't. It was too private, too personal. 'It's just that I feel such a failure. You and Jimmy seem so well matched, so happy, always laughing and kissing, making love without a thought. While I . . . How do you know when you do it right?' Lissa flushed deeply and Renee laughed.

'When it feels good. There aren't any rules. So long as you're both happy in what you do.'

Lissa looked at her. 'I see.'

'You're not?'

'I don't think either of us are.' She manufactured a laugh. 'Perhaps I was a silly romantic girl expecting too much. We're fine really. Philip is very kind to me.'

'So long as you do what he says.'

The smile trembled a little and faded. 'Philip always seems dissatisfied with my performance, and as for my feelings . . . Oh, hell, I fail in that as in everything else. I would so like to succeed in something.'

It all poured out then, her dashed hopes for a happy secure marriage, the way he controlled her every move, made all the decisions, liked to keep her at home, told her what to think even. But she could say no more about the intimate side of her marriage.

'Sometimes my brain feels quite numb.' And Renee sipped her rum and Coke and listened.

'So when?' was all she said when Lissa finally fell silent, the tears mopped up, deep breaths taken. 'And how?'

'What?'

'You can't go on like this, Lissa. You have either to leave him or make him change his ways. And I can see that wouldn't be easy. Loving a man is good. Sex is good too, smashing with the right fella. Everyone deserves to be happy.'

Lissa was calm again now. 'Oh, I couldn't really leave him. He's good to me in so many ways. And there are the children to consider. They would miss him terribly.'

'Children would rather have one happy parent than two unhappy ones. I'll vouch for that. Mine drove each other crackers then took it out on me.'

'Oh, Renee, how sad. Maybe I will leave him one day, who knows? One step at a time. I told Miss Stevens a little of my problem, no details, but she'll keep my confidence. She thought he'd walked out on me and I was about to bring shame on my head by divorcing him.' Lissa gave a bitter little laugh. 'I soon put her right on that score. Philip will never leave me.'

'More's the pity, eh?'

She squared her shoulders and looked Renee straight in the eye. 'I don't want him to know anything about this business. Not yet. Not until it's a success and I have some money coming in.' Her eyes became distant, narrowing on some future plan. 'Then we'll see.'

Renee sipped her drink, reading Lissa's faraway thoughts. 'D'you think he'd let you keep them?'

Lissa frowned, not understanding. 'Keep what?'

Renee jerked her head in the direction of the garden. 'Them two. The lively duo. Would he give them up if you did leave him?'

Lissa looked stricken. 'Oh God, I hadn't thought, I mean . . . why shouldn't he? I'm their mother?'

'No reason,' Renee put in hastily, thinking for a moment that Lissa was going to pass clean out. 'You could move in here you know, any time.' But Lissa shook her head.

'No, you have a lodger.'

'My Water Board man? He comes and goes. We have another room.'

Much as Lissa enjoyed Renee's company and was glad of her

support, the thought of sharing a house with her and the rapacious Jimmy did not appeal.

'I saw an old lady today. The one who used to have our house. Poor thing has gone quite senile.'

Renee looked sympathetic. 'My gran went that way. Loved the old so and so I did, for all she was nutty as a fruit cake in the end.' She blinked hard, batting her spiky eyelashes. 'So what about this old dear?'

'It was so sad. She kept on talking about her husband, long dead in the war, I'm afraid, whom she obviously adored and thought would arrive at any moment to carry her away. What romantics we women are.' Lissa got up to glance out of the window. 'I hope the children are all right.'

''Course they are. Made you think about how you'd feel about giving up that grand house on the Parade, did she? Or growing old with a man you don't love?'

Lissa gave a wry smile. 'I didn't say that I didn't love Philip.'

'I know.'

'You're right though. She made me think how transitory life is. What little time we have. Troubled me a bit, actually.' Lissa took a deep breath. 'Anyway, Philip doesn't ill treat me. If I can improve my life, win back some pride and self-esteem, I can cope well enough.' She turned to Renee with a grin. 'No more self-pity. It's bad for me. What about this shop then? Shall I risk it?'

'Absolutely.' Renee grinned. 'How will you manage to keep it a secret? Till you get it going, I mean. You can't work behind the counter yourself, or everyone will know and tell him.'

'I've thought about that. I shall work in the office upstairs and employ a shop girl. Why not? I can deal with the ordering and buying, while she can do the selling. It should work. I may need more than one assistant eventually, if the shop gets busy.'

Renee considered this, then set down her glass, looking unusually bashful. 'I don't suppose . . . I mean, I was wondering if . . . How would you feel about . . .?'

'About what?'

'Nah, forget it. It was a daft idea.' Renee picked up her glass again, looking flushed and embarrassed.

Lissa cleared her throat, smiling quietly to herself. 'Of course the person I really need is someone I can work with, someone I can trust. Initially to help get the place ready. Too late for this season but certainly by next, perhaps even Christmas. After that I'll need a manageress, someone reliable and honest to be in charge of the day to day running of the shop, train new seasonal staff and so on. I have the twins to take care of too, you see. Ideally I need a person who is good with people and of course likes clothes. Someone, for instance, rather like yourself. It's a pity really that you're so busy . . .'

Renee's eyes opened as wide as her mouth which formed into a perfect strawberry oval. 'Ooh, I'd kill for a job like that. All dressed up and in charge of a shop. Crikey!'

Lissa said, 'Then the job's yours, Renee. If you want it. But what about your bed and breakfast?'

'Hang the B and B! Jimmy never liked it anyway. And I have the lodger. Not that I wanted him, but the money's useful, I can't deny that.' She thought it best not to mention how she'd come by him. 'Oh, Lissa. It'd be grand to work in a lovely shop. I'd never have to serve soup to pawing old men again.' Then they were laughing and shrieking their delight, hugging each other and jumping up and down with excitement like the young girls they really were.

Later they stood at the front door, the twins looking exceedingly grubby after their afternoon's adventures. Sarah's dress was torn and Beth had lost her hair ribbon.

'Lord, look at them. Philip will kill me.'

'It's all good clean muck, isn't it, kids?' laughed Renee.

'He can't bear to see them dirty. I'll have to scrub you both in the bath before your daddy sees you,' Lissa warned and their small faces looked so doleful she couldn't help but laugh. Then Lissa turned to hug Renee again.

'I'm so glad it's all worked out. I must visit my family. And Jan, of course. Long past time I did. This plan that's growing in my head won't work without their help. We'll see what they have to say about it. If their response is positive, then we'll get cracking. You can come too, if you like? OK?'

Eyes shining. 'Oh, hecky thump. OK by me. Just say the word and I'm your girl.'

Philip was waiting for her when she got home later that afternoon and tore into her about the state of the twins' dresses.

Deeply embarrassed at Nanny's obvious satisfaction at seeing her scolded as if it were she who were a naughty child, Lissa fought to maintain her dignity.

'They are children, Philip, and must be permitted to play.'

Ignoring her he ordered them to the bathroom at once. 'And there will be no supper,' he warned.

Both little girls opened their mouths and started to cry in unison and Lissa grabbed hold of his arm as he would have walked away from her. 'How dare you? You can't do this. They're only four years old. I may put up with your bullying, but not my children. Do you hear?'

'Bullying? What nonsense. When have I ever bullied you? You are hysterical, Lissa, as usual.' Even so, her unusual vehemence had shocked him and even silenced the twins. 'I shouldn't have shouted at them perhaps, though discipline is important, Lissa. Look after them better in future.'

He still refused to let them have supper and later Lissa crept upstairs with a tray when he had gone out to the Yacht Club and Nanny wasn't looking. The twins thought an eiderdown picnic was a wonderful treat and the bad feelings were soon smoothed over and forgotten, by them at least.

To Lissa it seemed a portent for the future. Would he start to treat his children with the same mocking contempt with which he treated her, as they grew older? Dear God, please not. It sealed her determination more firmly than ever.

She spent the rest of that week secretly sketching and drawing up plans. She paid a visit to the shop, making notes as she walked through the dusty rooms, talking to herself, planning. Her mood lifted with each passing day and never had she felt so positive about life, so filled with new hope.

23

The sky was eggshell blue over Broombank, streaked by ice pink cloud, the mountain air so crystal clear that Lissa drew great healing gulps of it into her lungs. She was always surprised, and calmed, by the peaceful wilderness of the place, loving the way the humps of grey mountains blended into the blue haze. Lissa looked about her with sweet relief, glad as always to be home.

The harvest had been brought in and the lower fields were already showing flecks of fresh green between the stubble. The leaves on the wild cherry tree in the garden were beginning to change colour and drop. Soon the mellow days of autumn would be upon the dale, Meg's favourite time of year.

Lissa could see her, halfway up Dundale Knot with the dogs, moving among her sheep, checking the feet of any that were limping, making sure they stayed healthy, and probably deciding which ones must go in the backend sales.

'Do you never sit down for a minute?' Lissa called up to her, laughing as Meg waved madly, hurrying down the hill to hug her. Lissa forestalled the embrace by offering a cheek which Meg awkwardly kissed before picking up her giggling granddaughters. Ruff and the rest of the dogs smothered Lissa in a moist and joyous welcome, rolling over onto their backs so they could be tickled and petted and admired.

'How did you get here? Where's Philip?'

'He let me come without him for once. And lent me his precious car. I was so afraid of scratching it I've driven all the way at twenty miles an hour. Tea would be a life saver. This is my friend Renee, by the way.'

'Hello Renee. You must be exhausted.'

'Walking would have been quicker,' Renee agreed, grinning.

Meg chuckled. 'The kettle's already on.'

'You're going to sell woollens? Our woollens? But that's a wonderful idea. What on earth made you think of it?' They were all seated about the big pitch pine table in Broombank kitchen, Meg pouring tea from a huge brown tea pot, Tam smilingly watching her every movement, and Sally Ann stoutly content, hands appropriately busy with her knitting.

Jan and Nick sat as close together as they could get, arms full of babies. Robbie, who at fifteen months was already showing a mind of his own, one moment content to sit in his father's lap, the next wriggling free so he could chase after the twins, squealing with delight. And the new arrival, Alice, cooing happily in Jan's arms.

The remains of a ham and egg meal littered the table and cheeks were flushed, eyes sparkling, voices light and happy. It was good, Meg thought, to have her family all together again. If only she could feel they were enough for Lissa, she would be the happiest woman alive. But she could see that her darling girl was unhappy, and finding it harder to disguise the fact.

'I need to be occupied. That's why I want a business. I feel it's time for things to change.' They all stared at her, waiting, listening, while Meg nodded, her head teeming with questions, asking none of them. Except one.

'What does Philip think of all this?'

Lissa dare not meet Meg's shrewd gaze in case it should carry disapproval. And it was suddenly so very important that she gain her support. If she lost it, what would she have left? 'I haven't told him. Not yet. He's a bit – over-protective, and not in favour of my working.'

A small explosion of exasperation from Meg that made Lissa glance at her in surprise, and then laugh when she read her expression. 'Of course. You must have struggled once, so you'll perhaps understand how I feel?'

Meg gave a rueful smile. 'You could say so! I hoped things had changed. Apparently not.'

Sally Ann gave a deep chortle of pleasure. 'Ate bank managers alive, this woman did.'

Everyone was smiling, trying to disguise their concern.

'I know it's wrong to keep secrets but it would only be for a little while. Till I've proved it's possible.' Lissa paused and finished rather obscurely, 'Then I'll sort everything out.'

'I've kept secrets of my own,' Meg mused. 'It took me ages before I admitted to my father that I'd been given a dog. And as for when I got you, well . . .' She could laugh now, remembering Joe's reaction to the unexpected arrival of a baby. 'But keeping secrets from your own husband, that's another matter entirely. I couldn't fool Tam, could I now?' She glanced across at her husband who merely shook his head, his eyes on Lissa.

'Are you sure, lass, that it's a good idea?' he asked.

'Yes,' Lissa said, tight-lipped. 'For the moment it is necessary.' She looked about her at the many serious faces, all of whom wanted the best for her, she knew. 'You're far enough away from Carreckwater here for Philip not to hear about your knitting. And Renee and Jimmy are sworn to secrecy too. I'll tell him soon, I promise. As soon as the time seems right.'

'We'll not lie for you, girl,' Tam continued sternly.

'I know. I'm not asking you to. I need a little time, that's all.'

They shifted their feet, glanced at each other, then Meg spoke for them all. 'Very well. We'll ask no more questions. We want only your happiness.'

A quick smile of gratitude then Lissa became businesslike again, making it clear the subject of her personal life was closed. 'I'm not asking you to wash and card your own wool. You probably wouldn't have enough anyway. I'll supply it, ready dyed. The point is, would you enjoy knitting it up for me, do you think? I would need lots of colourful sweaters, mittens, hats and scarfs. Anything you like really.'

'They'd love it,' Nick said, indicating his wife and mother with one all encompassing nod. 'Those needles are an extension of their arms, didn't you know?'

Sally Ann finished a row and tapped him on the head with the tip of her steel needle, thereby proving his point, much to everyone's amusement. 'Less of your cheek. You're not too big to put across my knee.'

Nick burst out laughing. 'I'd like to see you try.'

Jan was smiling too, a pair of glasses now perched on her small nose. It was lovely to see her sweet face, as if in some way it made life seem normal again.

'Nick's right,' she said. 'We'd love it, Lissa. And there are other people in the dale who knit. Hetty Davies for one. Mrs Barton. How about them?'

Lissa looked pleased by the suggestion. 'The more the merrier. I could call on them tomorrow. And the other dales hereabout. There must be many women in need of work.'

'Eeh, that'd be grand. Just like the old days. But d'you think we'd be good enough?' Sally Ann wanted to know. 'For a real town shop, I mean. Would anyone want to buy what we produce? They might look a li'le bit amateur.'

'Of course you're good enough. And yes, I'm banking on the fact that people will want to buy.'

Then Renee spoke up, wanting to be a part of this warm, lovely family. 'By heck, look at you all. In lovely, hand knitted sweaters every one. Like dandies, you are. I'd give my virginity, if I still had it, for such a skill.' And they all burst out laughing.

'Renee, I like you,' Meg said, eyes suddenly growing misty as she glanced at Lissa. 'I'm glad my daughter has you for a friend. She looks sorely in need of one.'

A small silence, for no one present had missed the pride in Meg's voice as she had called Lissa 'my daughter'. But Meg filled it herself, smiling, blithely unconcerned. 'So tell us, miss. What do you want us to knit? As if we don't have enough to do.'

Lissa took a deep breath, hoisted Beth on to her knee and continued, 'I don't want you simply to produce sensible, working jerseys, though we will sell plenty of those, I hope. I want bright colours. Stripes, squares, zig-zags, interesting designs, lots of bold patterns. Perhaps Jan and I could work on some ideas together before we go back?'

Jan positively bubbled with delight at the prospect. 'Oh, that would be lovely,' she sighed. 'And we could do with the money, couldn't we, Nick?'

Then the baby started to tune up and cry and Nick went off to refill the bottle with Ostermilk. The twins trailed behind to make sure they didn't miss anything important while Meg fussed happily over the new mother, urging her not to do too much, bringing a cushion for her back. Jan appeared to be in no need of so much concern. She looked a picture of glowing health and contentment and Lissa felt a twinge of envy. It made her feel even more of an outsider. It was hard to see her friend so plainly happy with Nick, whom everyone had expected her to marry and she'd been too stuck up to consider. Yet she was delighted for them both and shook the feeling away. She had never loved Nick, only Derry. And he was gone.

As they talked, she strived to give the impression of being a happily married woman. Inside lay a still, grey pool, which did not bubble with happiness when she thought of her husband. Lissa dutifully hid it from view. Or thought she did.

She told herself that life couldn't be filled with joy every day. The lake often looked grey. It was only when the sun shone that it glistened like silver. Life was like that. So all she had to do was bring some sunshine into her own life, then she would glow again.

She mustn't permit Philip to use, even abuse her, every bit as heartlessly as the almost forgotten Kenyon Parker. The gypsy had been a stranger who had looked upon her as a foolish, rebellious young adolescent asking for trouble. For a time the experience had threatened to destroy her but she had survived, hadn't she? Derry had helped her. This time she must do it alone.

Oh, Derry, why did you leave me? Life could have been so different with you. She pushed the thought away. Concentrate on reality, the way things really were.

As his wife, Philip should treat her with more respect. And with loving care. Lissa was tired of being a victim, worn out by trying, and failing, to please him. She felt doomed constantly to fall short of his impossibly high standards. Changes had to be made. Did he have such a low opinion of her worth? Did she have such a low opinion of her own worth?

It was time to build, time to start the long fight back.

'I give you a toast,' she said, holding up her tea cup. 'To Broombank Woollens. May it grow and prosper.'

'To Broombank Woollens,' everyone cried, laughing happily as they sipped the strong brew.

'And when we get our first successful year we'll toast it again, in champagne,' she said, violet eyes glowing with fresh determination. 'And we *will* be successful, mark my words.'

'To success then,' Nick cried, pouring out more tea and dribbling it over the table cloth while Sally Ann scolded. 'Champagne might make less of a mess.'

'We won't trust you with any,' said Tam. 'Find him a job

too, Lissa. Then we don't have to put up with his idiocy round here.'

'You could drive a van, deliver all the orders,' she agreed.

'I have a farm to run. Anyway, what orders?'

'I'm sure we'll get some. Eventually.'

And the dreams came thick and fast while Meg made Nick mop up the tea, to much teasing and joking all round. Oh, but it felt good to be home, to be one with her family again, to feel human. Lissa knew this was much more than a fancy for an amusing occupation. This was a fight to regain her self-esteem, and she could not, dare not, lose.

The next day Lissa and Jan called on everyone in the dale. It felt good to visit the old places, meet old friends, gossiping, drinking endless cups of tea, explaining what she wanted. And everywhere she went she met nothing but eager enthusiasm.

'Exactly what we're needing.'

'My sister's a dab hand at knitting stockings.'

'I'd welcome anything I can do at me own fireside.'

'The woollen industry is near dead. If you can get it going again, I wouldn't say no to earning a bob or two.'

'My mother came from Dentdale, she's an expert knitter.'

Some of the older ones offered to teach the younger wives the traditional patterns. Sally Ann and Jan volunteered to check and pack the finished garments and Nick agreed to drive them over to Carreckwater in batches in his van. Meg was already planning how she could get some of her own wool involved in this budding industry. And Renee never stopped talking for two minutes together.

The rest of their stay at Broombank, Lissa spent huddled over pieces of paper with Jan, sketching, rubbing out and redrawing endless styles and patterns.

'We must do an Aran type. They're always so popular,' Jan said.

'I agree. Ours will be in a choice of Herdwick or Swaledale. Dark or light, natural and chunky. And what about a snowflake pattern? We get plenty of snow on these fells, we should represent it.'

'White against grey, yes, beautiful.'

The ideas buzzed, grew in ambition to the outrageous and downright impossible.

'In the end, of course, hand knitting will only be the beginning,' Lissa said. 'We won't be able to produce garments fast enough.'

Jan looked anxious. 'Are you saying this is all a waste of time?' And Lissa laughed, shaking her head.

'Heavens, no. I'm saying we'll have to grow, to expand. Once we get going we'll have to tackle frame knitting which will produce knitted garments so much faster, and to order if necessary. Though I hope there'll always be a good market for hand knitted goods. It will be part of my job to seek new business, make it grow and expand. But that's for the future. Oh, Jan, it has so much scope, it excites me.'

Jan smiled at her friend, glad to see a sparkle in those dull, bruised eyes. 'Something to hand on to our children, eh?'

'Something to feed them with.' And both girls laughed again.

Then Jan reached out and grasped her friend's hand. 'I have to ask. Are you all right? You aren't still worrying over being illegitimate and your mother dumping you, are you?'

'Lord, no. I never think of it these days.'

'You're not jealous of me then? Being here with your family?'

Lissa shook her head. 'It's your right to be here. They're your family too now, you and your lovely children.'

'What about you and Meg? Have you made your peace yet?' And when Lissa avoided her shrewd gaze, Jan persisted, 'It's long past time you did.'

'I know.'

'Think about it then. It would make Meg happy.'

Despite her embarrassment, Lissa felt warmed by Jan's concern. 'I will.' She gave a wry smile, then softly musing, 'It's ironic really. I've spent so much of my life fighting this feeling of rejection, wanting to belong. As a result I made hasty judgements and rash decisions, for which I must now pay the price.'

'What sort of rash decisions?'

Lissa shook her head. 'Don't ask. Not yet. I now seem to have quite the opposite sort of problem. Isn't that silly? Serves me right, I suppose.' There was a hint of bitterness in the falsely bright tone, a bleakness in the flashing eyes that Jan did not miss nor feel able to remark upon.

Somewhere deep in the house a clock struck ten, the notes chiming endlessly on, and a log fell in the great hearth. When silence fell again Jan asked, 'Have you ever heard anything from Derry?'

'You're his sister,' came the tart reply. 'He'd write to you, not me.'

'You were his friend. I did think at one time . . .'

'Don't say it, Jan. I don't think I could bear to hear you say it.' Lissa was on her feet, pushing her chair back so hard that it grated on the slate flagstones and almost fell over. 'Shall I make some coffee, then we really must get back to these patterns. Any ideas for our first colour scheme? Autumn colours, do you think, or blues and reds?'

'Blues and reds would be good.' Jan spoke to Lissa's retreating back. 'Derry is back from America. Did you know?'

Lissa's heart jumped, and she stood holding the kitchen door frame for a moment, as if needing its support. After a moment she said, 'I'll get that coffee. Please don't tell me any more. I really don't want to know.'

Oh, but she did. She wanted to know everything there was to know about him.

'Are you happy?' Meg and Lissa were seated together on the windy heaf beside Brockbarrow tarn, as if there wasn't still the prickle of past differences between them. 'I like to have you to myself for a while. But you look tired, a bit peaky. Aren't you well?' Meg cast her a sideways glance. 'You're not pregnant?'

'No.'

'Isn't little Alice a treasure?'

'Yes.'

'You wouldn't care for another?'

'Not at the moment.' High above, the small blue outline of a merlin falcon flying low and fast in a passing air stream swooped and dived, seeking a wandering mouse or vole who might have escaped Meg's harvesting. Lissa changed the subject. 'It's so lovely to be at Broombank again. I don't visit nearly often enough.'

'You don't,' Meg agreed. 'You haven't been near since your birthday in March. But I know you have your own life to lead.'

'There were – reasons.'

Meg stifled a sigh and turned her head away to stare at the horizon, not wanting to ask if it was herself who had kept Lissa away. Nor did she wish to let her daughter see the hurt in her grey eyes. The distance between them yawned as wide as ever, hurting her more than she cared to acknowledge. But it had to be bridged. One of them must make the first move. 'Do you want to talk about it?' Summoning all her courage, Meg put an arm about Lissa's shoulders. She expected her to move away or shrug it off, as she usually did, and was glad when she didn't. But the slender body seemed somehow far frailer than usual.

'There's nothing to say.' Head down, lower lip quivering. The misery etched in her daughter's profile cut her to the heart.

'I see.'

Was this man making her daughter happy? Philip Brandon had seemed so very sensible and caring, a suitable person for Lissa to marry despite his being older than they would have liked. Certainly an improvement on that young Teddy Boy she'd once taken up with. Not that Tam had agreed with that. He'd been quite taken by young Derry, but then he was a soft-hearted Irishman. Philip got on well with them all, fitted in at festive and family events. Only there was something wrong now, Meg could smell it. How could she be sure he was being good to her lovely girl? 'You'd tell me if you had a problem? If you were distressed about anything, wouldn't you?' she quietly asked and Lissa gave a half laugh, blinking away the prick of tears.

'I'm fine. Don't worry about me.' The shoulders stiffened and Meg put her hands in her lap.

'And Philip?'

'He's fine too.' A light, jocular tone. 'Overworked and underpaid he says, but otherwise fine. How very motherly you sound all of a sudden.'

'And why not? I am . . .' The sharp words faded into silence and the two gazed upon each other for a second before both looked away, awkard and embarrassed. Something inside Meg seemed to snap and she tossed back her hair in a characteristically defiant gesture. 'I'm the best mother you're ever likely to get.'

A long pause, then a reflective smile at the circling merlin. 'Yes, I dare say you are,' Lissa agreed, an edge of resignation in her tone. 'And I should make the best of that.'

Meg felt as if she'd been slapped. She stood up and glared at the ground, kicking a small pebble with the toe of her boot so that it rolled down the bank and fell with a plop into the tarn. The ripples widened and spread, just as Lissa's remarks spread within her like a canker, making her heart bleed. It was impossible to know where you were with her. Meg tried to tell herself that the young tended to make these pithy comments without thought of their effect. Yet

Lissa made too many, and too often for Meg to shrug them all off. 'Do you still write to Kath?' she asked, dreading the answer.

'Once. I never got a reply. No point, is there? She's made her position clear.' Lissa gazed out across the ruffled water. 'I used to come here when I was a child, against all your rules, to make wishes. I called it my Wishing Water. Grandfather Joe told me of a silly ritual he used to do when he was a boy. I thought it would be sure to bring Kath hurrying home to see me.' She smiled now at her own youthful folly. 'Kids have such wild notions, don't they? All fantasy and foolish fancies.'

'There's nothing wrong with a bit of fantasy. It would be a dull old life without it. I wish I could have made your dream come true, Lissa, but I couldn't. I even swallowed my pride and tackled that dragon of a grandmother to make you happy.' A rueful smile. 'But I failed you. Perhaps I should have let you go when you were seven, when you wanted to go with Kath back to Canada. I see it was selfish of me not to consult you.' She hugged her body with arms that suddenly ached. 'When you were very small, I used to ask how much you loved me. More than all the world, you'd say.'

'I remember.'

'I couldn't risk losing that, you see. I was so afraid, so afraid that you might not come back. I didn't even have Tam at that time, didn't know if he would ever come back to me. I'd no one but you.' There were tears in her eyes, in her throat, which as ever she refused to shed.

Tears glistened too in Lissa's eyes as she stared up at Meg as if seeing her for the first time, seeing her as a young woman, vulnerable and alone. When she spoke it was in a hauntingly quiet voice. 'I didn't know about Tam. I'm glad you didn't let me go. How can a seven year old choose what's right?' Her eyes pricked but she didn't want to touch them in case Meg thought she was crying. Yet the tears started and rolled down Lissa's cheeks nonetheless. 'I made you lose the baby.'

Meg looked shocked. 'Good heavens, that wasn't your fault.'

'I thought it was, because you were worried over me staying out all night.' But Meg shook her head, her face warm and alight with sympathy and love.

'That didn't make me lose the baby. It was an accident, nature's wisdom perhaps.'

'I wanted to hurt you. I was so cruel, so jealous.'

302

'You were young, rebelling against the world that had hurt you. I just got in the way of your anger.' Meg came to sit beside her again. 'I tried to explain the baby wouldn't have made any difference to us, to you and me. You weren't ready to take that in.'

'But could you ever forgive me for that? I've wasted so much time in foolish wishing. I'm sorry I ever blamed you for Kath's deficiencies. Now that I'm a mother myself, now that I can perhaps understand human nature a little better, I realise how lucky I was. It's taken me a long time to say it, but I'm so glad I had you for a mother, Meg.'

Meg looked in wonder at her daughter, grey eyes into violet blue.

'You're right. It has taken you a long time.'

Lissa swallowed. 'Have I left it too late? For us to be friends, I mean?'

Lips tilted into a smile and Meg felt her heart swell with happiness and pride. 'No, my bonny lass. Never too late. I've picked up and started again more times than I care to count. I could do it again, and gladly, with you. It's the way of the world between mothers and daughters. It's what binds us together. It's called love.'

And then Lissa was putting her arms about Meg and they were hugging and laughing and crying together, wiping each other's tears away, drawing closer than they ever had before.

'It'll be all right,' Meg said, patting Lissa's back as if she were a small child again. 'You'll see. It'll be all right. Never say die, eh?'

And somehow Lissa knew that it would be. She did have the love of a mother. She'd had it all along and never realised.

The winter following was long and cold and filled with a million pinpricks of frustration. Lissa longed to spend every spare moment in the shop. She wanted to make frequent trips home to see how the knitting was progressing but dare not go too often, as that would arouse Philip's curiosity.

Hilary's committee and voluntary work proved to be the perfect alibi. If Philip believed her to be thoroughly involved with charity, the less suspicious he would be of how she spent her time. Even so, Lissa was made constantly aware that he continued to keep a close watch on her, his dark eyes often fixed upon her with disappointment and concern.

'I may well wish to keep in Don Cheyney's good books, but you mustn't overdo it, my sweet.'

Lissa never complained, however much Hilary Cheyney asked of her. In fact she volunteered for more.

She wheeled the library trolley around the wards of the Cottage Hospital. She attended at least two coffee mornings a week for some charity or other, and her expertise at pricing bric-a-brac for a jumble sale became legendary. But the feeling that she walked a tight rope grew with each passing day.

Philip must not discover her secret until she was ready. And that couldn't happen until she had proved the business to be a success and secured independence for herself and her children.

They were her delight, her joy. It was as much for them that she worked so hard, and planned with such care. It was for their sake that she continued to climb into his bed each night.

Philip was stern and firm with the twins, but did not ill treat them. What kind of father he would be when they began to show a will of their own, however, when they in turn became rebellious adolescents, she dare not imagine. He may be all outward gloss and charm but beneath lay a determination to control and use people on a whim, with no thought for the consequences. Would there be room for them to grow in this house?

Beth and Sarah were babies still, only four years old. Philip loved to see them dressed in their pretty frocks and shiny shoes, with ribbons in well-brushed hair. He loathed sticky fingers and grubby knees, washing soaking in a pail, toys in the living room, or even to find them not in bed when he arrived home from work. He did not see them as real children, but as pretty toys to decorate his beautiful home, and prove what a fine chap he was.

The same high standards he expected to be kept in his house.

'You are learning to manage so much better,' he told Lissa, fondly patting her cheek as if she too were a pretty child.

She managed by getting up at dawn. By the time Philip had showered and come downstairs to eat the breakfast she had cooked, Lissa had cleaned through the ground-floor rooms. After breakfast she played with the twins for a while, then hurried to meet Renee at the shop where they were in the process of scouring, scrubbing, cleaning and redecorating. At the end of each session she had to make sure that she left not a scrap of paint on herself. Lissa had not taken into account how exhausting subterfuge could be.

In the afternoons she fulfilled her voluntary work obligations and later, after she got home, worn out and ready to drop, she would smile at her darling babies, freshen herself with a quick sip of tea and then take them for a walk by the lake or to play in the park. It was the best part of her day. The only time she dared relax. Then it was back to the house and the strain of continuous deceit.

'You bath us tonight, Mummy.'

'Make French toast for tea.'

'No, pancakes, Mummy.'

'Read us another story.'

'Play jig-saws, Mummy.'

'Want a drink of water.'

And even when she had handed them over to stiff-backed Nanny Sue, Lissa must rush about giving the bedrooms a sketchy dust, and twice a week run round with the vaccuum cleaner. And there was still the evening meal to prepare, herself to make ready and beautiful with Philip's bath run and his drink poured, as if she had been there all day, waiting for him to come home to her.

It was all too much and the strain began to tell. She forgot to eat, lost weight, got too tired to sleep, fell prone to constant colds and infections. And was sure that Philip watched her with his keen, inscrutable gaze.

Sometimes she took risks, cut corners by hiding dirty laundry in cupboards, resorted to tinned soups and sliced bread though she knew he hated both and would give her a long lecture on good housekeeping. But Lissa scented freedom and had no intention of letting anything stand in her way. This was the sixties, for God's sake, time for women to make a stand. And one day she would summon the courage to face him with her plans, she really would.

Her one relief was that he made surprisingly few demands on her sexually. Lissa decided it must be pressure of work as he often seemed preoccupied with concerns of his own. Sometimes he sat up for hours in his study, working at his desk. Such nights were bliss for she could stretch out in the wide bed and catch up on some much needed sleep, undisturbed.

But one evening she felt so ill from the tension and exhaustion that she tried one more appeal to improve her situation.

'I did wonder, Philip, about employing a cleaner? It's such a big house and I don't seem to have the same time for it.'

'I believe you have forgotten my gin and tonic.'

'Oh, goodness,' rushing to pour it out, afraid of any little slip that would make him investigate her life too closely. 'The twins are so much more demanding these days and then there is my charity work. I thought perhaps if I had a little more help? Not a whole battery of servants as Mrs Fraser had, but one woman would be a help.'

'What do you know of Mrs Fraser?'

'Oh, I met her once. Didn't I tell you? At the Birches nursing home when I was standing in for Hilary.'

'She told you about her servants?' He sounded so startled that Lissa had to laugh.

'She told me about her darling papa and her beloved Charles. Poor old lady, mind quite gone.'

He was frowning at her again, dark eyes narrowed with displeasure. 'You do too much.' The telephone rang and he went to answer it. 'It's for you.' He sounded surprised, as if she had no right to have telephone calls.

'Who was it?' he asked when she returned, flushed and trying not to look as if she wanted to rush off and solve this latest problem which had arisen.

'Only Renee – asking how I am.'

'You're not still seeing that foolish girl?'

'Haven't seen her for ages,' Lissa lied. 'That's probably why she rang. To see how I was.' All business calls were directed to Nab Cottage but there were times when Renee felt the need to call her at home if some emergency had cropped up. As now, with a firm having difficulties with a particular shade of dye. Even so, Lissa decided she must speak to Renee, ask her not to take the risk again.

Dark eyes considered her, and in the silence Lissa could hear her heartbeat, loud and hard against her breastbone.

'Ice?' Philip asked, making her jump.

'What?'

He waved his glass at her. 'Will you fetch it or shall I?'

She did not raise the subject of a cleaner again.

306

1964

24

Life wasn't running too smoothly at Nab Cottage either. Renee's two menfolk were not hitting it off at all well and she was beginning to feel more like a referee at a banty cock fight than a wife and landlady.

'I can't stop here arguing with you two,' she said. 'I'll be late for work.'

'I'm waiting for him to tell me if it's true,' Jimmy roared, waving the newspaper in Andrew Spencer's face. 'Does the Water Board mean to flood Winster or not?'

The Manchester man dabbed at his mouth, buttered a second slice of bread to accompany his last slice of bacon and seemed to consider whether or not to answer the question. 'Perhaps I'm not the person to ask,' he said at last. 'Most folk seem to know more about what's going on than I do, certainly the local paper thinks so.'

'Then it's just another rumour?'

'There've been so many.' He waved the bread about, almost apologetically. 'We must have more water, that's true. You can't ignore the fact. And Manchester Water Board aren't all bad. Look how they built a school for the children of the workers on Thirlmere.' He laid the bacon on the slice of bread and bit into it.

Jimmy looked stunned, his face becoming a dark purple. 'That was last century. What's it got to do with things as they are now?'

'I'm pointing out that the Board do try to be reasonable and considerate.'

'Like hell they do!'

Renee touched her husband's arm. 'Calm down, Jimmy lad. Don't get so worked up.'

'Worked up? Manchester Water Board is God's gift to hear this chap talk. They threaten to ruin the boating and the tourist industry, put a reservoir in one of Lakeland's loveliest little valleys, right in the middle of the National Park, and you tell me to *calm down*?'

'The engineers are very skilled. They've already built underground aqueducts from Haweswater by way of the Marsdale tunnel to the Stockdale syphon in Longsleddale and then on to Garnett Bridge. As well as the Winster reservoir, they hope to build a brand new conduit right through Longsleddale till they can carry all the Lakeland water they need, by gravity I might add, right to the Manchester taps. A wonderful feat of engineering,' Andrew Spencer announced, with as much pride as if he were responsible for building it with his own hands.

'And ruin another dale in the process?'

'Nonsense. It's called progress. The Electricity Board have put many of their cables underground to reach the farms in those dales, haven't they? There'll be few signs of the aqueduct, once it's built, though admittedly it'll take a few years and there'll be pumping stations, that sort of thing, but all the concrete will be underground.'

'Ruining the land,' growled Jimmy. 'If you think we believe you can hide all your mess, then you must think we're daft.'

'You'd imagine, wouldn't you,' Renee said, 'that if man can fly to the moon, he could make better pumps on the tunnels you do have? To make more water come through, I mean.'

They both looked at her in surprise. 'Aye,' said Jimmy. 'She's got a point there.'

'I really couldn't say.'

'Well, is it Winster or somewhere else you're after? Hellifield, for instance? Good farming land. And all so industry can take hundreds of millions of gallons of water that's too good for 'em in the first place!'

Andrew Spencer wagged his sandwich. 'Now you are quoting rumour again.'

'Well, why don't you tell us what you're really up to, and put an end to rumour?'

'Because decisions have not yet been made,' he said, looking more clerical and pompous than ever, lifting the sandwich to his mouth as if that were an end of the matter.

308

Jimmy reached over and snatched it from his fist, leaving his mouth hanging open in mid-bite. If Jimmy hadn't been so fired up, Renee might have roared with laughter at the man's shocked expression. Instead she chewed on her lip and worried, deciding it best to keep out of this.

'You'll have to come to my next meeting. You'll hear more then.' And the water consultant closed his mouth, eyes still riveted on the sandwich.

'Happen I will,' said Jimmy. 'There are other ways. Desalination of sea water for one, the Morecambe Barrage scheme for another.'

'Ah, but are they economic? Are they viable? It's my job to consider all sides of the case.'

'Oh, aye, and money is more important than land, I suppose, and people?'

'It must all be taken into account. I do listen to your point of view, Mr Colwith, to everyone's point of view. But it is only my job to suggest a suitable site. I leave arguing on policy to the politicians. I haven't put my final report in yet, but when I do, it will be when all relevant factors have been considered. We all have our jobs to worry over, and our own personal problems. I for one have a sick mother to consider, requiring day long care. It's human nature to want to do what's in our own interests in the end,' he said, then retrieving the sandwich, filled his mouth with bacon and bread, as if afraid he might have said too much.

Lissa was polishing the mahogany knobs on the tops of some new stands, singing loudly to the strains of 'Please, Please Me' on her transistor radio, when Renee arrived, breathless from running.

'I'm sorry I'm late. Ooh, what a picnic this morning!'

They had disposed of the dreary mannequins as too silly and old fashioned for jerseys, hoping their customers would agree. Lissa stood back and admired the result of her efforts.

'Look good, don't they? Be even better when the stock arrives.'

Renee did a little jig of happiness to the music then collapsed on to a chair to get her breath back. 'Oh, now what was it I had to tell you? Oh, yes, the new shipment of cobalt blue will be dispatched from Keswick next Wednesday. Mrs Barton has made up a new design for a skinny jumper using crochet for you to see, and Jan rang to say Nick's bringing the first batch of stock this afternoon.'

Lissa switched off the radio. She felt too tingling with impatience to listen to it any more. 'Oh, that's great. I hope he brings plenty. We need to have the shop looking beautiful for our long awaited opening.'

The months of effort were beginning to bear fruit. The decorating was complete, a new green carpet covered the floor, and there were curtained cubicles in which customers would try on garments. The two glass counters shone and the wall of mahogany drawers had been given a new coat of yacht varnish by Jimmy, who had been a tower of strength. Lissa said as much now.

'I'd never have done it without you two. You don't know how grateful I am.'

'The feeling's mutual. I'm going to enjoy this job. Mind you, it's a wonder Jimmy had time to help, since he's so busy fighting this latest scare.'

'What scare?'

Renee leaned on the counter and folded her arms, ready for a gossip. 'That's why I'm late. They've been at it for hours this morning, our Jimmy and this water consultant chappy. You know, the one who's lodging at our place? Cocky little chap. Sending my Jimmy wild he is. Tramps about the fells and dales all day, treading his muck into the house every night, and all he ever talks about is how wonderful it is that so much rain falls here. Wonderful my eye! Jimmy'll have apoplexy before he's done. They argue all the time. I'm sick of it.'

'Jimmy can hold his own corner,' Lissa said, chuckling as she set out the stands in the window.

'The latest rumour is that they're going to flood Winster. We're going to another meeting, to talk it through. Are you coming?'

Lissa sighed. 'I daren't. I'm defying Philip enough. I daren't take any more risks.'

'You still haven't told him then? About the shop?' And Lissa shook her head.

'I will, soon.'

Renee returned to her own problems with a heavy sigh. 'If we could just get rid of him and his tin pot schemes we'd be on cloud nine. And he cramps our style, sitting with us every evening like a great sour gooseberry. I wish he'd go jump in the lake himself.'

She looked so mournful and sounded so vehement, that Lissa burst out laughing. 'Bit extreme. Why not simply ask him to find alternative accommodation? Tell him he's upsetting Jimmy.' As you did with Derry, she might have added, but that would have been too unkind.

Renee looked surprisingly nonplussed for someone who was rarely lost for words. 'Oh, well, he's no trouble really, bless him. And I tell Jimmy he'll have to put up with it 'cause the money comes in handy.' And snatching up a cloth she took out her frustration on the glass counter, round bottom in skin tight black jeans wobbling alarmingly, wishing she'd never opened her silly mouth, telling herself to think in future before she mentioned Andrew Spencer again, or Lissa might start asking more awkward questions.

'Invite your Mr Spencer to our opening. That might cheer him up and give him something different to talk about for a change.'

'Oh, no, he wouldn't be interested. Heavens, I'm that scared.' Renee sank on to a stool and wrapped her arms about her knees. 'I've never been so scared in all me life. Aren't you?'

'Scared rigid. I must make sure I order enough sherry. Or should we stick to wine, do you think?'

Lissa walked briskly to the office where she had a pile of paperwork that needed attention, and several telephone calls to make. She'd had the phone installed only the other day and used it for the slightest reason. She could ring Jan or Meg from the shop now and talk business or pleasure to her heart's content, without worrying over Philip finding out. It was really quite wonderful. Jan had sounded a bit cool the other day when she last spoke to her, and Lissa frowned as she recalled this now, making a mental note to tackle Nick on the subject when he came this afternoon.

'Not that I intend to let anyone else know how scared I am,' she called over her shoulder as she went off to her office. 'I mean to make this work.'

'Right,' Renee agreed and there was admiration, and something not quite so easily identified upon her face. You had to hand it to this lass, she thought. She's changing. And once she gets going, who knows where it'll all lead?

Nick arrived shortly after two. He came alone and insisted Jan was fine, if a bit taken up with the new baby. 'And Robbie's being a bit jealous.' He was plainly anxious to get back so Lissa said no more and helped him quickly to unload several large boxes from the old Ford van.

311

'That should keep you two busy for the afternoon,' he said. 'But then it's kept half the dale busy for months so why shouldn't it?'

'Thanks. You are all coming tomorrow?' Lissa asked as she brought his mug of tea, unable to avoid revealing how anxious she was for their support.

'Try keeping us away. Everyone's titivating like mad. What about – you know who? You have told him?'

Lissa felt herself flushing bright scarlet. 'Oh, don't you start.'

He said, 'For God's sake, Lissa, you're sailing a bit close to the wind, aren't you? There'll be all hell to pay if Philip finds out from someone else.'

'I know.' She looked from one condemning face to the other. 'I *know*. I've been waiting for the right moment, that's all.'

'Happen it's come,' said Renee. 'Judgement day is nigh.'

'I could always leave telling him for a few weeks, or months.'

'Hide in the office, you mean?'

'Till I'm sure the business is going to work and be a success. I could at least see if we have a good Easter. What do you think?'

They both stared at her in silence then Nick came and put his arms about her shoulders, his round face unusually serious. He held her close for a moment then spoke very quietly against her ear. 'Whatever you want to do, Lissa, is all right by us. But take care. The longer you leave it, the worse it'll be. Philip won't take kindly to being kept in the dark.'

'I-I know.'

He held her from him and smiled reassuringly into her troubled eyes. 'And then there's the lease. That'll have to be sorted soon. Why not surprise him with this opening thing? Invite him, and ask for his help with the lease. That should soften the blow and make him feel important. He might surprise you and be really pleased. In any case, what can he do? He won't eat you, will he?' He laughed. 'You're probably making a mountain out of a molehill.'

'Mr Brandon likes to feel important,' Renee agreed, then flushed with embarrassment as she saw Lissa's face, pinched with anxiety. Poor kid, she thought. What a mess.

'I'll think about it,' Lissa agreed. 'I will, really I will,' and they had to be satisfied with that.

Lissa stood on the pavement, a chill east wind blowing her hair about her face, as Nick climbed back into the cab. She always wore it flying free at the shop. A bit impractical perhaps but it was the way

312

she liked it best. 'Tell Jan to bring the baby, won't you? I'm longing to see little Alice again. And Robbie of course.'

'Try stopping her. Changing the subject,' he said, in his airy, I'm-not-really-worried sort of tone, 'there seems to be some discrepancy over my mortgage payments.'

Lissa glanced up at him, surprised. 'Oh? I hadn't heard anything. Though to be honest, Nick, I know nothing about it. I leave all of that to Philip and never give it a thought. Where do you pay the money?'

'I take in a sum every time I've had a good auction mart, same as all the farmers do, paying a bit extra when I can. We like to deal in cash, you know that.'

She couldn't help but smile, remembering Joe's wily ways with money. 'I know,' she said. 'So what's the problem?'

And now he looked embarrassed, the tips of his ears showing pink, looking anywhere but at her face. 'To be honest with you, Lissa, things've been a bit tight lately, what with the new baby and all. And prices for the sheep aren't what they might be. We've missed a couple of months. Mebbe three at most. But we'll catch up, I promise.' He sounded so fervent and worried that Lissa laughed. Reaching up she kissed the stubble on his cheek.

'I'm sure you will. Don't worry, I'm not going to throw you out. Get some sleep, you look hollow-eyed.'

He grinned, sighing with relief. 'Chance would be a fine thing with that little howler. You'd never believe how expensive bairns are. Jan's given me a shopping list as long as your arm. See you tomorrow then.' He grinned, winked at Renee, told her he liked her skin tight jeans and did she use a shoe horn to get them on? He just managed to get the van into gear and drive away before she ran at him with her sweeping brush.

'Cheeky bugger!' she shouted after him, coral pink lips wide and laughing.

They spent a happy afternoon unpacking jerseys, hats, mittens, scarves and socks and stockings by the score, for every size of feet, and every need and taste.

Most of the garments were in the natural colours of cream Swaledale and grey Herdwick, but Lissa had provided her knitters with specially dyed wool in bright jewel colours of blue and red and green. They filled the shop in a kaleidoscope of patterns and designs.

'Look at these,' she cried. 'Traditionally patterned gloves in black and red. Each one has the date knitted into the wrist. Aren't they marvellous?'

'These have names on,' Renee said. 'Sarah. John. David. Mary. We could take special orders. Provide gloves for folk with their own name on the welt and in their own choice of colour.'

'Oh, yes. Brilliant idea, Renee. I'm sure they'll be popular.' She was growing excited. The future stretched before her, glittering like the crystal waters of the lake, as if her youth had been returned to her, like a gift.

There were high-necked navy jerseys for the fishermen to wear, thick warm Herdwicks to keep the walkers warm. Cream cardigans, jerseys with low necks, vee necks, round necks, fancy patterns and plain. Garments in purl or plain, stocking stitch or cable, with neat ribbed welts or bright rows of circular bands at wrist and neck.

And then there were the hats. Thick and warm to pull well down over the ears, ideal for mountain walking. Berets in bright primary colours to wear with a certain panache, and Scottish tam o'shanters with flirty pom-poms on top.

A selection was artistically displayed in the window and on racks inside the shop. The rest were folded and placed in the mahogany drawers or underneath the counters. A multitude of talent to delight the folk of Carreckwater and the visitors who came to enjoy the Lakes.

When they had done, Renee and Lissa stood and beamed at each other, well pleased, wanting to open the shop door that instant for the window was already creating interest, and have everyone come in and admire their new stock. 'It's going to be all right,' Renee said. 'I can feel it, like magic in the air.'

Lissa could only nod, too choked with emotion to speak. She pushed back a lock of hair and polished away a fingermark with the sleeve of her cardigan from the corner of one counter. 'It's such a relief to have got this far. I know we've plenty of space for more stock that we can't as yet afford, and people will ask for all sorts of sizes and styles that we don't have. But it's a start, isn't it? We've managed this far. Now we can go on and on, up and up. Nothing can stop us.'

And then they were laughing and giggling and hugging each other. For it was true. The air was filled with hope and a sense of achievement and what else was that but magic?

*   *   *

314

'I can't. Not tomorrow.' Lissa gazed at her husband horrorstruck, begging him to accept her word and not question her further. It was too much to hope for.

'I would have thought you'd be delighted to entertain the Cheyneys? Hilary has been very good to you of late and we owe them a dinner.'

'I've already made plans for tomorrow. It will have to be next week.' Lissa couldn't believe her bad luck. How could she desert everyone? How could she abandon her own business on its opening day? It simply wasn't possible. But how to explain all of this to Philip without telling him the truth? She couldn't lose her fight now, not when she was so close to winning.

'Cancel them.'

'I can't, Philip. Really, I'm sorry.' He started to rub the bridge of his nose with one finger, a gesture he always made when he was keeping a tight hold on his temper. Something at which he was adept. 'Perhaps next Friday?' Lissa suggested, her face, her whole body, pleading for him to agree.

Philip let his gaze wander over the slender lines of her youthful figure, still disappointingly showing no sign of pregnancy. And why was she turning awkward when lately she had been so very agreeable? Something was wrong. Could she be meeting a lover? Was that the urgent matter she had planned?

'Tomorrow at seven I've told them,' he said, settling the matter.

But Lissa was determined to hold firm. She smiled sweetly at him. 'It's all right. I'll ring Hilary and make other arrangements,' ignoring his frown, worrying over whether she had the courage to tell him about the shop now. She had to tell him sometime. She'd already spent hundreds of Jeffrey Ellis's inheritance on new shop fittings, wages for Renee, wool, and a multitude of other expenses. Stella Stevens had not exaggerated. Broomdale residents had been knitting all winter and now her lovely new stock had been delivered. There could be no question of failure. She daren't even consider the possibility.

All she had to do was keep Philip happy. Was that so difficult? And not appear too tired, or disagree too firmly with him or he might start probing into her daily routine more closely, perhaps even regret agreeing to the voluntary work. Then she would be in real trouble. Housebound again, alibi gone. The prospect terrified her. Not that she could depend upon this ruse indefinitely. Hilary might discover the truth about the shop and blab about it to Philip. She was the greatest gossip in Carreckwater. Oh dear, Nick and Renee were right. She really ought to get the matter cleared up.

'Philip,' she began, 'I quite enjoy helping Hilary in her endeavours.'

'Of course you do, and it is good that you should be so occupied. I like people to look upon you with respect. It reflects well upon our status.' He swelled out his chest as he sipped his drink, and Lissa's courage almost failed.

'Only, the Lady Bountiful bit doesn't exactly suit me. I'm not sure I'm terribly good at it and don't find it nearly so all absorbing as Hilary does.'

'Not long ago it was your greatest desire to get out and about with this charity thing. Now you've grown bored of that, have you?'

'No, that's not the way of it at all.'

'Then what is troubling you, my precious?' His eyes were caressing her, shrewdly speculating, and Lissa hastily stood up.

'Nothing,' she said. 'Nothing at all. I'll go and fetch the supper.'

The party was a great success. Meg and Sally Ann brought far too much food and everyone drank to the success of the new business, congratulating each other on how splendid everything looked. Miss Stevens was there too, of course, wishing them all well. The shop refurbishments were generally admired and ideas flew for the future.

A warehouse at Broombank, or a workshop for frame knitting? A woollen mill perhaps? Sheepskin slippers? Nationwide sales? Export?

'We'll all be rich,' Nick said.

'We'll all be exhausted,' Renee drily pointed out.

'I think we'll take one step at a time,' Lissa laughed, but she felt well pleased. 'Where's that champagne, Nick? My glass is empty.'

'Coming right over.'

Everyone was happy and she felt so good. For a moment she wished she could share this achievement with Philip. Lissa thought she would have liked him to be proud of her instead of always seeming to put her down. If only he'd give her a chance. She wished too that she could have brought the twins to share this party and celebrate her success, but knew they could never keep a secret. They would go right back and chatter excitedly to Daddy all about Mummy's party.

She would have to tell him soon, of course. Lissa knew she couldn't put it off for ever, and hated herself for her own cowardice and deceit. Why hadn't she told him yesterday? He'd given her the perfect opportunity. Probably because she preferred a time of her own choosing, to plan exactly what she needed to say before she began.

Now if she had been married to Derry, the thought came unbidden, and she wished suddenly that he could be here, to see this one moment of glory at least.

She half glanced across at the door, wanting so much to see him, she almost thought for a moment that he stood in the open doorway, but then laughed at her own foolish imagination. This man was tall, broad-shouldered, smartly dressed in a crisp grey suit and a very conventional silk tie. Handsome. Strong. Certainly not a boy. But then Derry wouldn't be a boy, not now. He was looking across at her, walking towards her. Smiling, the same lopsided grin.

'Hello, Lissa.'

'Dear God!'

Lissa stared up into his face in wonder. Could it really be him? So different and yet . . . And yet the same. And so very beloved. She was half aware of Renee giggling somewhere in the background. Could it be true? Or was this his double? Heart thumping like a hammer, she tried out his name. 'Derry?'

Then he was kissing her cheek, very properly of course but it felt delicious. Her heart was melting and her mind had become quite empty of all thought and sound and sensation but the fact that he was here, holding her hands, smiling into her eyes.

'So, I was right.' The voice from the door rang out across the shop so that voices instantly hushed, faces turned in that direction. 'No wonder you couldn't spare the time to carry out my wishes today. Derry Colwith is back in town, making trouble again. And you can't keep your hands off him.'

Lissa dragged her bemused gaze from Derry to stare at Philip, horrified. 'No, no. You've got it all wrong. I didn't know Derry was home.' Even to say his name out loud was a delight.

'What Lissa says is right,' Derry put in. 'She didn't know I was here. I didn't know I was coming myself until a day or two ago. Renee invited . . .' But Philip silenced him with a few clipped words.

317

'This is between myself and my wife.'

'I'm sorry, only I don't want her blamed for . . .'

Lissa put out a hand. 'It's all right, I wanted to tell you, Philip, about the shop – but I couldn't find the words.'

'Shop? What are you talking about?'

Lissa drew in a deep breath and took a step towards him. 'Miss Stevens has agreed to let this shop to me.'

'I beg your pardon?'

Very quietly she explained, aware as she did so of Meg gently ushering Derry, and the rest of the family, out of the main shop and into the stock room beyond.

'So this is our launching party. I would have told you before, as I said, but either you never wanted to listen or I was too afraid to. Isn't that silly?' She was gabbling now, reaching for a bottle of champagne. 'Would you care for a glass?' She thought for a moment he would knock the bottle from her hands as he had once swept the pie dish from the table. Instead he took her arm in a punishing grip and thrust her towards the door.

'We agreed, I think, that there would be no business, no career for you.'

'It's true that you expressed that wish, yes,' Lissa said, in her most reasonable voice. 'I didn't agree, that's all.'

'You didn't agree?'

'No. There's no need for you to worry, Philip. You won't be neglected in any way. Why, you'll never notice the difference.'

'We'll discuss this later,' he said, in freezing tones. 'The car is at the door. Get in.'

Lissa glanced anxiously behind her. 'I can't leave my guests.'

'*Get in!*'

Meg appeared at this moment and walking up to Philip, kissed him on the cheek, as if he were not trying to frogmarch her daughter off her own shop premises.

'Philip,' she said, in her sweetest tones, 'how glad I am that you could come. Isn't she a clever girl? You must be so very proud of her. I certainly am.' Meg swept a hand to indicate the room. 'She's done all this herself, you know.'

'I had some assistance,' Lissa butted in, rather breathless and bemused but grateful for Meg's intervention.

'Of course you did, sweetheart, but the idea was all yours. And she's breathed new life into Broomdale.' Meg beamed up at Philip.

'She'll go far, this girl. Oh dear, she hasn't even got you any champagne. Come along, before Tam and Nick drink it all.' And taking her son-in-law's arm she led him back into the bosom of her family. 'Chicken vol-au-vent or a sausage roll?' she offered with a smile. 'Oh, have both.' And Philip accepted a plate and a glass with the best grace he could manage.

25

The month was April and the lake water was as clear as crystal. Chips of grey slate and shale shimmered beneath the surface like pale jewels.

As Lissa walked along the lakeshore to Nab Cottage she watched with delight as the mute swans upended, their long necks diving deep as they sought some tasty morsel. Teal, coot and mallard crowded the shoreline and not far away in a copse of birch and oak could be seen a party of cormorants roosting high on the branches. The Lakeland air was pure and fresh, sharp with the promise of spring in its breath, and like Lissa the ring of mountains all around seemed to lift up their faces to the smiling sun. It felt good to be alive.

It had been a whole month since their launch day when Philip had discovered her secret. For Lissa, it had been the worst month of her life.

To begin with Philip would hardly speak to her for days. Then he called Hilary Cheyney and put an end to her charity work. That didn't particularly worry her but his final thrust did. He spoke to Miss Stevens and made the poor woman agree to refuse Lissa the lease.

'I'm sorry, Lissa,' she'd said. 'But I really can't become involved in marital disputes. And Mr Brandon has all my affairs in his office. It's rather difficult. Best, I think, if you find other premises.'

'Yes, I do understand,' she had replied, swallowing her bitter disappointment. 'But the season is only just beginning, all the shops are taken and we have hundreds of pounds worth of stock. Will you give me some time at least, to find an alternative?'

'But what of your husband? I'm sure he meant you to close down altogether. He won't be pleased by such an arrangement.' Miss Stevens had poured tea from a pretty little porcelain teapot in her pretty little conservatory. A safe, well-ordered life, and Lissa had felt again that nudge of envy. She had neither security nor freedom.

And to make matters worse she was haunted by the thought of Derry's being back in town. Why did he have to come now? Of all times to choose, he came when she was at her most vulnerable.

Lissa had not seen him since that dreadful day, nor did she wish to. Perhaps she had dreamt him and he had not been there at all. It was only her longing which had conjured him out of the air.

Yet the knowledge that he might appear at the turn of a corner, that she might see him by the lake when she was out with her children, or hear his voice when she lifted the phone, left her jumpy and sleepless. She had lost Derry years ago. Now she was trapped in a loveless marriage with a husband determined to destroy every part of her life which did not include him.

And here she was risking more of Philip's displeasure, seated on a hard chair in Carreckwater Town Hall, listening to the speaker express his concern over the latest plans for acquiring water from Lakeland.

'I'll not have my wife wandering about the town in the evening,' Philip always sternly told her whenever she expressed an interest in going out anywhere. So on this occasion, fearing he would refuse his permission, she hadn't even asked. But Lissa felt that as a part of this community, she had every right to know what was going on. She'd broken the chain that had kept her fastened to the kitchen sink and had no intention of putting it on again.

Jimmy was loudly agreeing with everything the speaker said.

'Hush,' Renee warned him, grasping hold of her husband's jacket as he bounced up and down on his chair, his bristly brown hair seeming to stand on end. 'Sit still, Jimmy lad, I can't hear for your noise.'

'Sorry.' He gave her an abstracted kiss and Renee rolled her eyes at Lissa, 'He gets so worked up,' she said.

Lissa felt heady with the relief of being out of the house, away from Philip's increasing coldness. She was determined to enjoy it, feeling young and reckless at her daring. 'It's a powerful problem,' Lissa shouted above the din.

'They're trying to get water on the cheap,' the voice declared. 'So they can sell it to industry at a vast profit.' Lissa thought this sounded economic sense but didn't say as much as there were general murmurs of agreement all round.

'Winster is one of the finest, most beautiful valleys in Lakeland,' stormed the speaker. 'It would be appalling if it were to be flooded. It would be a national outrage to ruin this lovely scenery.'

Lissa leaned over to whisper in Renee's ear, 'Is this a scare or for real?'

'It looks more than a rumour this time.'

'But Winster is beautiful, close to Windermere and in the National Park.'

'*Ssh!*' Jimmy hissed fiercely at them both and Lissa apologised and began to concentrate on what the speaker had to say, her attention held now. A feeling of outrage grew inside her as the speaker continued his long explanation of Manchester's needs and how they meant to satisfy them. She thought of the beautiful landscape which she loved; the wild life, the flowers and hedgerows and butterflies, pretty woodlands and character cottages, destroyed. All to be swamped by water for the needs of faceless industry?

'We're aware that the country needs more water.' Another man was having his say now. 'But why should our countryside be ruined, *raped*, in order to get it? They talk of digging tunnels under Longsleddale. Scarring virginal land for all time. Sacrilege! They talk of damming scenically beautiful valleys as if it were of no account. Outrageous!'

Loud cries of agreement.

The speaker continued: 'The threat to this area is very real but there is also a view held by some that Winster is no more than a stalking horse. We should take care. Manchester Water Board are not fools. They will guess public reaction if they choose to put their reservoir in such a pretty spot. This may be a blind. While we're all protesting against Winster, they'll suddenly come up with somewhere else, outside the National Park, which we'll gladly accept as an alternative.'

There was silence in the hall as this new fear was digested. Lissa glanced about at the troubled, caring faces and suffered with them. You couldn't trust anyone in this world. She'd learned that much herself, hadn't she?

'They may take good farmland instead, for instance,' the speaker pointed out. 'How would we feel about that? We all know what a precious commodity good farmland is in this area.'

Rousing if troubled applause as the speaker sat down.

The next put the case for the Morecambe Barrage scheme, where water could be held in the estuary. Yet another wanted to drill bore holes and another talked at length of how new pumps could be installed at strategic points along the pipe lines to speed up and increase the flow. There were suggestions for flooding disused mines, of piping water from other areas such as the Pennines or Scotland. On one thing only was there complete agreement. It should not be the beautiful Winster valley, or any other in the district. Storage reservoirs were out.

And then it became the dubious privilege of the Water Board representative to stand up and face the meeting with calming words and promises to listen to every argument. A small man in a spanking grey suit who kept pushing his spectacles higher on his nose, treating with disdain any repartee from the audience.

'Is this your Water Board man?' Lissa whispered and Renee nodded.

'Pompous twit!'

Though to be fair he was listened to, if disagreed with. He explained how they needed an average of 25 million gallons extra a day from Ullswater and about 20 million from Windermere to meet future demand. This was greeted with roars of disapproval. He talked of sympathetic treatment, more meetings, even public enquiries, finally pointing out that no matter what decision they reached, it could take two or three years or more before it was acted upon.

Jimmy suddenly stood up and waved a fist at him. 'Don't matter how long you take, we won't have you spoiling any of our dales, nor our meres, not now nor in the future. Lakeland is precious.'

'And we'll bloody make sure you don't!' a voice cried from a rowdy group sitting behind.

Cries of 'hear hear', and 'you tell 'em, Bill', as the group grew noisier by the minute. Lissa glanced worriedly over her shoulder, troubled by the sudden shift in the atmosphere.

Bill shouted, 'Take it from the lake, that's what I say. At least until they get the national grid going.'

'If they ever do,' another voice yelled.

Shouts of disapproval from the boating lobby, Jimmy amongst them, arguing that if they concreted the shoreline it would make it too high and dangerous for swimmers and boaters.

324

Andrew Spencer assured them Manchester Water Board would not make that mistake but no one was listening to him now.

'Let 'em use the rivers,' another cry went up.

'What about the fish? It'd ruin the angling.'

The water consultant tried to draw the proceedings to a civilised close, saying it had been a 'useful meeting', he was always available to calm people's fears, nothing would be done without Ministerial approval . . .

'What about our approval?' shouted Bill, from behind Jimmy's chair. 'Do we have no say then?'

'You'll be given your chance at the Public Enquiry.'

'And when will that be?'

'I really couldn't say.'

'Well, you'd better bloody listen, or you can watch for me one dark night. To hell with the boats and the fish. Leave the dales alone. Use the bloody lake!'

'Sit down and shut up,' Jimmy shouted. 'Swearing does no good. You don't know what you're talking about.'

'And who'll make me? You and whose army?' The red-faced Bill clenched his fist and waved it threateningly at Jimmy, his friends noisily joining in, and the atmosphere suddenly became charged with real violence.

'Leave it, lad,' Renee warned, nervously plucking at Jimmy's jacket.

He put up a hand, though whether he meant to calm the rowdy group or continue with his own point of view no one ever found out. A fist came out, connected with Jimmy's jaw, sending him flying backwards, right into the next row of chairs.

Renee jumped to her feet in terror. 'Oh my God! You *bastards*,' she screamed, and turned on his assailant with flying fists and sharp nails. Pandemonium broke out. Feet and fists and chairs flew everywhere. If Lissa hoped to escape she was soon disillusioned. A whole wave of people swept them forward in their rush to get out of the hall, treading underfoot those not quick enough to keep up.

'Renee!' Lissa cried, seeing the top of her friend's red head swallowed up in the crowd.

'I'm OK. See to yourself.'

Miraculously Lissa found herself out on the pavement, held up by a crush of bodies.

'We'll have a sit-down protest,' someone yelled. 'That'll show 'em.'

Lissa couldn't have resisted if she'd wanted to. She found herself thrust down on to the pavement with the rest of the crowd, bumping her shin and elbow in the process, bringing tears to her eyes and blinding her for a moment. Then there were whistles, and more screams and shouting. A hand gripping her collar.

'You can come with me,' said a grim voice. Then a chair struck her on the head and blessed blackness closed in.

'How could you disgrace me in this way?'

After an uncomfortable hour in the police station Lissa, Renee and Jimmy, along with a large group of protesters, had been charged and bailed to appear before the magistrates the following morning where they would be bound over to keep the peace. Lissa had rung home and given the bare details to Nanny Susan, declaring her intention of spending the night at Renee's. Philip had arrived just as they were released from court.

'Hecky thump,' Renee had said. 'Look out, his lordship is here.'

Lissa hadn't needed to ask who she meant. She'd put on a brave smile and kissed her husband's cold cheek. It was plain from the thin white line of tightly suppressed anger around his mouth how he felt about finding her in such a situation.

Now she was sitting in his office, the green blind drawn demurely down over the glass so that Miss Henshaw might not peer in and witness his wrath or her misery.

'I wasn't thinking of you at the time,' she very reasonably explained. 'I was thinking of the issues at hand. Besides, I had little choice in the matter. Have you any idea of the crush I was in?'

'I can guess. What possessed you to go in the first place?'

'I'd promised Jimmy and Renee that I would.' Violet eyes flashed fire. 'Where and how they get the water concerns us all. It is important.'

He paced jerkily back and forth in the small dusty office, increasing Lissa's sense of claustrophobia. 'You should have been at home, looking after your children. Is that asking too much from my wife?'

'I'm sorry, Philip.'

He came and stood before her, eyes condemning. 'I rang to tell you that your grandmother was ill and you weren't even there to receive the news. And for all your words about wanting to feel part of a family, you had abandoned them.'

She stood up quickly, shaken by what he had told her. 'That's not fair. The girls were quite safe with Nanny. And how was I to know Rosemary would choose this particular evening to be ill?'

'It's typical of you deliberately to hurt the old lady, even on the brink of death.'

Lissa gasped. 'That's not true. I don't wish her any harm. Anyway, I'm sure she isn't on the brink of anything. Rosemary Ellis is a consummate actress.'

'And you are a useless mother.'

She slapped him. Without a pause she lifted up her hand and slapped him right across the face. It was hard to tell for a moment which of them was the more startled.

'Don't ever say anything like that again,' she said, voice so low and dangerous he almost backed away. 'As for Rosemary Ellis, she's never done anything for me in my life. Never.' Tears glimmered on her lower lashes.

A terrible, awesome silence. Then he put his arms about her and drew her close, smoothing her hair and patting her back as if she were a small child. 'There, there. Perhaps I did get a little carried away but I was upset and concerned about you. You see how you so easily get involved with the wrong sort of people. And with this silly passion for protests.'

She wanted to protest, to say that Renee and Jimmy were not the wrong sort of people, that they weren't to blame, it was some bully called Bill. But he wouldn't be interested in her excuses and in a way he was right. Hadn't she been led astray in the past?

'Perhaps I've been too soft with you,' he mourned. 'Given you your head in too many things.'

Lissa gasped. 'When? For heaven's sake, how can you say that? You hate any sign of independence.'

He smiled affectionately at her. 'You don't need any, you silly girl. You are my wife.'

'I'm not a child bride, Philip. I'm a woman, with a mind of my own.' Heedlessly she ploughed on, 'I can't go on like this. You must listen to me. I need my own life.' But he wasn't listening. He was wagging a finger at her, issuing a stern reprimand.

'You should have stayed home where you belong. Haven't I said so a million times? Don't I always know what is best for you?'

His voice was so coaxing, and his smile so kind, Lissa was almost tempted to agree. It was easier. 'Perhaps,' she said.

'No perhaps about it. I shall have to exercise more discipline, not less with you, my dear. What would people think if they saw my wife in a protest march?'

'It was hardly that.'

He kissed her nose, such a delightful small nose. He could feel his arousal starting at her increasing submission as he gently scolded her for her naughtiness all the while busy with the buttons on her blouse.

His actions filled Lissa with alarm. How could she make any preparations to protect herself here, in his office? And if she got pregnant, how could she ever be free of him then? And she must be free. Somehow. 'Philip, please. Not here. Miss Henshaw might come in at any moment.'

'Not if I lock the door.'

She glanced about her, desperately seeking escape. There was none. How to distract him?

'Philip, there's something you should know. Something I've been meaning to tell you for a long time . . .'

The sound of the key turning in the lock made her jump and as he came back to her, slipping off his jacket, hanging it carefully on a coat rack as he did so, he smiled. 'What is that, my precious?'

The words were almost on her lips when the reality of her situation hit home. She couldn't tell him now, like this. She couldn't say, 'I've been secretly using contraception.' Not while standing in his office, with the door locked.

She swallowed, lost for words, all her courage evaporating. Laughing softly, he slid up her skirt with the palms of his hands and curled his fingers into her crotch, massaging the soft mound of flesh. Lissa gasped, stifling the sound in her throat. She pushed him away with a light laugh. 'Really, Philip! Not here in your office.'

'You are so beautiful I can't keep my hands off you. I've neglected you recently. I'm sorry, my sweet. Business worries. Grim bank managers. We seem to go through money like the proverbial water. I've had my mind on other things.' His breath was shortening, his eyes clouding over. 'It seems so long since I had you. But everything will be fine now.' He kissed her throat, pushed open her blouse and slid his lips down to her nipple. 'But you must be kinder to your grandmother, my darling. We need Larkrigg to be truly secure.'

328

She pushed him away with all her strength and faced him with narrowed, incredulous eyes. 'What are you saying? Is that what you've wanted all along? Larkrigg. Is that why you married me?'

He chuckled, reaching for her again. 'You were a delightful child. How could I resist you? And I was patient, wasn't I?'

'But would you have been so keen if I hadn't had a wealthy grandmother in the background?' Her eyes opened wide now as she saw it all. 'That's why you've tried so hard to bring us together. Not for my benefit at all, but your own. Oh dear God! Philip, I trusted you. I thought you truly loved me.' She felt sick, and a terrible weariness came over her. How naïve she had been, how very young and foolish.

'I do love you, my darling. What is so wrong with wanting you to have your just desserts? That family owes it to you.'

Lissa moved away from him, a sound of disgust on her lips. 'I can't take any more of this. I'm going home, Philip.'

She unlocked the door and let herself out of the office, politely declining Miss Henshaw's offer of coffee. When she arrived home the twins were perfectly well and probably hadn't even noticed her absence. A telephone call to Broombank proved that Rosemary Ellis was indeed on her death bed and Meg agreed that it would be respectful to go and see her.

Lissa took a shower, brushed her hair and her teeth, which helped dissolve her temper and made her feel better after all that vigorous scrubbing and brushing. When Philip came home he insisted that they take the twins with them and they set out on a cold April night to face the final interview with her grandmother.

The stale smell in the bedroom was so overwhelming it made Lissa feel sick. In the great bed lay a figure, white as wax and just as still. She wanted to feel compassion, wanted to experience grief. This was her grandmother, after all. Her own mother's mother. She felt nothing.

'Have you brought them?' The voice sounded uncannily strong.

'We are all here, Rosemary,' Philip said, in a voice Lissa recognised as the one he reserved for old and valued clients. Unctuous, grasping. Like Uriah Heep, she thought, feeling a nervous spurt of laughter in her throat.

The eyes opened, regarding her with cold dispassion, and Lissa wondered why she became such a bag of nerves whenever she was confronted by this woman? And riddled with guilt, even when Rosemary Ellis was quite plainly in the last throes of life. And why must the twins be subjected to this misery?

'I'll take the children out, shall I, Philip?' she whispered.

'Leave them.'

'But this is no place . . .' She could feel Beth's small hand creeping into hers. Even Sarah was shivering, her small mouth turning down in comical self-pity.

A voice from the bed. 'Let me see them.'

There was nothing for it but to bring the children forward. Stern black eyes peered fiercely over the hump of blankets. 'Why are they whimpering? Are they stupid?'

'No, Grandmother,' Lissa said, a new firmness in her tone. 'They are sensitive, and a little overawed.'

'Don't call me that. I've told you before, I'm not your grand-mother.'

Lissa hung her head. 'I'm sorry.'

'Humph.' A hand came from beneath the bedclothes, like a claw. One yellowed finger nail touched Sarah's cheek. 'That one, she's very like . . .' The old woman's gaze slid away to fix upon the ceiling and the hand dropped. In the silence a clock ticked and Sarah gave a half-strangled sob of fear.

'Do you have everything you require?' Philip asked, and Lissa watched in amazement as he poured out a glass of water, tucked in the covers, held the glass to thin dry lips.

'Thank you,' Rosemary said, and returned accusing eyes to Lissa.

'I brought you here for a purpose. Now I have seen your children, you can send them away. They tire me.'

With relief Lissa sent the twins scampering to Nanny Susan. Straightening her spine, she faced Rosemary Ellis with resignation. There was nothing she could do to hurt her now.

'My energy is limited,' Rosemary said, and a long pause followed before she continued, 'Don't interrupt.'

'Yes, Gr . . . Mrs Ellis.' It seemed ridiculous to address her so formally. The old woman's lips twisted into a wry smile.

'Katherine has expressed a wish to compensate you for her defection. Says she should have stayed and tried to keep you. I don't agree but there it is. The young have their own ideas.' Rosemary paused, though whether to take a breath or give her the

330

opportunity to comment, Lissa couldn't rightly say. She was aware of Philip at the other side of the bed, hovering anxiously. Rosemary Ellis gathered her breath and spoke again.

'Larkrigg Hall would naturally go to her in the normal course of events. I'm not going to live much longer.'

'Oh, I'm sure you'll recover and be up and about in no time,' Philip put in, smiling condescendingly. Blackcurrant eyes turned to his.

'Don't pretend, or I might change my assessment of you. Which would be a pity since I am never wrong.' The old woman's breathing was growing harsher, rasping in her throat and Lissa became anxious. She had no wish to be responsible for Rosemary Ellis's last breath.

'Don't tire yourself, Grandmother. Not on my account.'

'It's Katherine's wish, not mine you understand. Katherine's request – that Larkrigg Hall be left to you. She doesn't need it. Says she owes you that at least.'

Lissa took a step backwards, away from the high bed. 'No, no. I don't want it.'

She sensed Philip twitch as Rosemary turned astonished eyes to hers.

'Of course you want it, you silly girl. You've wanted it all along. I know that.'

The sickly sweet smell of death seemed to clog her nostrils, the room swam before her eyes and Lissa grew light-headed, as if she might faint. 'I n-never – never wanted anything of the sort. Larkrigg Hall is yours. Nothing at all to do with me.' She became aware that her voice was rising, sounding close to hysteria. 'How dare you accuse me of being so mercenary?'

'Toffee!' said Rosemary Ellis in scathing tones. 'All you have to do to win it is agree not to pursue your claim to being Katherine's daughter.'

And now Lissa stared at her grandmother in total shock. 'What did you say?'

'I said, you must give up this foolish demand to be acknowledged as an Ellis. We can't do it. Not possible. Have Larkrigg Hall by all means, since Katherine seems to want you to have it, but don't expect anything else. No money, no recognition.' She scrabbled her withered hand across the bedclothes and Lissa saw Philip put a paper into it. 'Sign this,' she said, and the voice was weakening, growing tired, though rasping just as harshly.

It was Philip who took the paper from the shaking hand and

331

brought it to her. Lissa stared down at it, bemused. He offered her a pen.

'Sign here, along the bottom,' he said, crisp and businesslike. Lissa did not, could not move. She looked from one to the other of them in wonder.

'Don't either of you understand?' She dropped the paper on to the eiderdown as if it had scalded her. 'I don't want your house or your money. I never wanted those things. I wanted to belong to you. I wanted to know that you cared about me. That Kath cared. It wasn't my fault that I was born illegitimate. Why couldn't you have forgiven me? Do you realise how that dreadful feeling of rejection messed me up when I was an adolescent? All those broken promises. It made me seek out unsuitable friendships, anyone who would show some interest in me. God knows what might have happened . . .' She paused, trying to keep a grip on herself. 'I took it out on Meg and Tam, the two people I should have cared most about in all the world. And you offer me your *house*, like a *bribe*?'

Philip's hand closed tightly upon her wrist. He was forcing the pen between her fingers, his voice furiously calm in her ear. 'Take the pen, Lissa. Sign. It's what your mother wants for you. You deserve it. She owes you that at least.'

'*No*.' Lissa threw the pen to the other side of the room. 'She owes me *nothing*.' And turning on her heel, she ran from the room.

There was snow on the roads as Philip drove furiously home, slipping and sliding on black ice. The mountains frowned at her, at their most forbidding at this time of day with darkness already closing in, though it was but late afternoon. The air was piercing cold, almost as cold as the ice forming about Lissa's heart.

'How could you?' she kept saying. 'How could you do this to me?'

The twins sat silent in the back seat, one on either side of their precious Nanny Sue who had long since learned to give the impression of closed ears while drinking in every titbit to relay to her dear mother whom she visited each month. The old lady could hardly wait for the next instalment, so intrigued was she by the goings on of the rebellious Mrs Brandon and her handsome husband.

Philip changed gear with a furious hand, grating it loudly. 'How dare you upbraid me for wanting the best for us all, when it is you, with your foolish dreams, your determination to disobey me and

332

show me up before everyone who is at fault. You have no sense of what is right, Lissa. I quite despair of you.'

'I know it is not right for that woman to treat me with such contempt.' Or you either, she thought, not quite daring to say it.

The car skidded on a corner and the twins screamed. It must have shaken Philip too for he slowed right down and seemed to draw a steadying breath, getting his temper back under control as it more usually was. 'All right, my precious ones. Daddy is sorry.' He turned to Lissa. 'You see how you make me behave? Couldn't you for once consider someone besides yourself. The girls, for instance, and me, even if you don't care about Larkrigg for yourself.'

'Why don't *you* care how I feel?'

'I'm not made of money. To ignore such a valuable gift would be lunacy. Fortunately I was able to put it right.'

'What? How?'

He glanced up in the driving mirror at two white faces and one pink one, avid with curiosity. 'We'll discuss this later.'

And over a dinner which Lissa could not eat, he explained how he had persuaded Rosemary Ellis to leave Larkrigg Hall to the twins instead.

'You may not want it but it's certainly not right to deprive the children of their heritage. Larkrigg Hall will stay in the family, after all.'

Lissa gazed at him, stunned by this new twist, furious that he had gone against her wishes. 'I hate you for this.'

He smiled. 'Hate away. It is done. In these uncertain times we may well be glad of it in the future.'

'You surely weren't thinking of going to live there? Expecting me to . . .?'

'I might. Why not?'

'I couldn't. I hate it.'

'Nonsense.' He kissed her tiny nose, so pretty, so alluring. 'You'll love it. You'll be near your family, and you know how much you like to please me.' I've succeeded, he thought. Now I have tied you to me for all time. He smiled at Lissa, well pleased. 'She'll be dead within the week.'

But she was not dead within the month. Rosemary Ellis stubbornly clung to life, determined to be as difficult in dying as she had been in living.

26

Lissa put on a blue kilted skirt, not too short, a lemon turtle neck sweater and a soft ginger suede jacket. She brushed her hair into a tight knot on top of her head and in her ears wore very proper pearl earrings. Quite the right outfit, she decided, to suit a staid lawyer.

She kissed the twins goodbye, promising to be home as usual for lunch, but instead of going to the shop, caught the bus into Kendal. She'd chosen this particular practice, hidden away down one of the yards, because it was far enough from Carreckwater not to have any involvement with Philip Brandon. She needed an independent opinion, not one influenced by that of friend-ship.

All through the long journey she had rehearsed what she wanted to say. But by the time Lissa was sitting in the solicitor's office, her hands clasped together in her lap, breathing in the familiar smell of dusty law books in an unfamiliar setting, every word had gone from her mind.

Perhaps it was because the solicitor was younger than she had expected, and carried a slightly bored expression on his pale flat face. Surely he was too inexperienced to be of any use to her?

Lissa told her tale haltingly, with embarrassment pinking her cheeks. It did not come naturally to her to reveal her most intimate secrets to a stranger. He asked a few questions, made notes on a pad, then leaned back in his chair, steepled his fingers and stared at her over the tips of them.

'So there is no question of his desertion?'

'No.'

'You realise, I am sure, Mrs Brandon, that there are three grounds only for divorce. One is desertion, a long and tiring method which I prefer not to recommend. Should your husband wish to return within the three-year period, and you refuse to accept him back, then you lose your grounds.'

'He would never desert me.' Lissa swallowed and slackened her hands as she realised she'd been pressing them together so hard they were hurting her.

'The second is adultery.' The solicitor raised querying brows and Lissa shook her head.

'Not that I'm aware of.'

'Pity. He wouldn't, I suppose, do the decent thing? We could set up a hotel room, a woman . . .?'

'No, I'm sure he would not consent to that.' She felt unclean discussing her life and hopes of freedom in this unsavoury way.

The solicitor sighed. 'Pity. He would only need to go through the motions. Still . . .' He gave a resigned little sigh. 'It leaves us with cruelty, and I have to say I see little sign of it. He has not beaten you?'

'No.'

'Locked you up? Twisted an arm perhaps? Thrown anything at you?'

'No.'

'Not a single bruise to show me?'

She flushed dark red. 'None. But I have explained – about his – his lovemaking. If you can call it that. He's completely selfish, never waits for me and . . .'

The solicitor politely coughed. 'Were we to use inadequacy as a lover as grounds for divorce the courtrooms would be full to overflowing.' He gave an embarrassed little smirk. 'Perhaps a little discussion between the two of you before . . .'

'But it's very nearly *rape*.'

He looked surprised by her sudden aggression and then covered it with a professional mask of sympathy. 'No such thing in marriage. Not in law.' He stared at his notepad. 'How long did you say you've been married, Mrs Brandon?'

She abandoned that line of discussion, despair starting to close in. 'He totally controls my life. I have no say, no freedom. He keeps me like a bird in a cage, watches my every move, tells me what to wear, decides when I may be allowed out, which is never alone. He almost

336

tells me what to think, and now he means to put an end to my new business venture.'

'Curb your bolt for freedom as it were?'

'I-I suppose so, yes.'

'Quite.' The expression on the solicitor's face told her he was sympathetic but thought she exaggerated. His next words confirmed it. 'Few men take such good care of their wives. And even fewer like the idea of their wives working. It reflects upon their own ability as a provider, d'you see?'

Lissa felt close to tears. How could she make anyone understand? But the prospect of a lifetime's penance for one mistake was more than she could bear. She tried again, her patience straining. 'I know he has never actually struck me, but there is violence in him, I can sense it. I feel he is barely holding it under control. I was very young when I married. It's proved to be a mistake and I would like out of it. Is that too much to ask?'

She lifted violet eyes, dulled by pain but still achingly beautiful, and for a moment the young solicitor very nearly, and against his better judgement, agreed to take the case. He had seen few women as lovely. He could quite easily understand any man's obsession with her. Unfortunately this husband appeared to have been particularly crass about the matter.

'I'm sorry to say that you have no grounds for divorce, Mrs Brandon. You could wait until the children are grown up but even then there is no guarantee a judge would grant you a divorce. You may still find yourself unable to break completely free.'

She couldn't believe what she was hearing. 'And if I were to take a lover?'

His head snapped up and horror registered in every muscle of his face, every line of his erect frame. 'You must *never* consider doing such a thing. Not only would you then be the guilty party and completely at your husband's mercy, but most judges would deem you to be an unfit mother. You would lose your children, Mrs Brandon, without doubt.'

Carreckwater was a small town and Lissa knew it would be difficult, if not impossible, to avoid Derry altogether. So when she caught her first glimpse of him she turned and hurried in the opposite direction.

She'd agonised over the solicitor's words but had known all along

337

what her decision must be. The children must come first. They were everything to her and no risks must be taken with their happiness, bad marriage or no.

Whatever she and Derry had once shared was finished long since. Forget him, she sternly told herself. He would go back to America and she would stay with Philip, and do her best to make what she could of her life.

But Renee told her that he was at Nab Cottage still, and it took every atom of her will power not to seek him out, not to run into his arms and ask him how he was. Not to kiss his beloved face and feel the hard strength of his body against hers. She shuddered with longing at the memory of their loving.

If she passed through St Margaret's Walk by the churchyard she expected to hear him clattering down the steps behind her. If she walked by the shore, her eyes scanned the silvered water for a sign of his boat, or sought out the woodland that bordered the shingle, as if he might emerge, grinning, at any moment.

Not trusting herself, Lissa took every care. She checked every shop, every bus, every street before she entered or walked along it. Sometimes she thought she heard him call her name and would turn to look for him, expecting to see him coming towards her, arms outstretched.

She could guess now why Jan had come to sound so odd on the telephone, worried over Lissa's reaction to the arrival of her brother, no doubt.

Yet her mind buzzed with questions. Would he be leaving soon? To go where? Had he made a success of his life? Was he happy? And would he ever tell her why he had left Carreckwater so abruptly? She stubbornly asked none of them.

Best if I don't know, she told herself.

Best if I don't think of him.

But if the days were difficult, the nights were worse. Lissa was haunted by him: the smile upon his beloved face, the touch of his lips, the caress of his hand as if he were really there beside her in her bed. Then she would wake and find that it was Philip and would turn her face into her pillow and cry silent tears of despair.

She was in Fairfield Park, rolling on the grass with the twins who were climbing all over her, when he finally came, and Lissa could do nothing but sit and stare at him, her mind empty of words, of every sensation but the glory of his nearness. And as she sat in this small, silent capsule of time, she felt her body come alive, as if every nerve crackled with a new awareness, every part of her reaching out to the boy she had once known and loved. But he wasn't a boy any longer. He was a man. The Teddy Boy image had quite gone, so had the quiff and the brilliantine. The hair had grown fair now, and thicker, flopping casually over a wide brow. He was smart and assured, a new confidence emanating from him. And successful, if the cut and style of his pale grey suit were any guide.

'I rather think you've been avoiding me,' he said very softly, and smiled. That smile wrenched her heart for it was exactly the same, lopsided and funny, making him look rather like a mischievous boy again. And his brown eyes were as warm and merry as ever, laughing at life.

Her own must have flashed some sort of warning for she saw his expression change, growing oddly serious as their gaze held and locked.

Lissa lifted a disdainful brow. 'I really don't see any reason for us to meet, do you?' She felt oddly rumpled and grubby, hastily brushing the grass from her skirt and all too aware of the twins' avid interest. If she'd been able to read inside his heart and see the uncertainty there, well disguised by the show of confidence, she might have spoken more kindly. As it was she remained cool and distant.

He picked a stalk of grass from her hair and laughed, gently teasing. 'No pony tail now, I see.' The touch of his hand against her hair set her on fire.

'No.'

'Yours?'

'Yes.' She gathered the two children to her, as if for protection.

'They take after you. Lovely children.'

'Thank you,' she said, very coolly, not missing the implied compliment.

A silence grew and lengthened and Lissa got to her feet, trying not to look as if she hurried. She gathered two sticky, grass-stained hands in her own. 'We must be going. Time for tea.'

'Of course.'

She started to walk away. Would he let her go like this, without saying any more?

'Lissa?' he called, and she instinctively paused, feeling her heart leap as she half turned to him. She desperately quenched the joy soaring in her heart, determined to hide the effect he had on her.

Derry hesitated, as if not quite knowing what to say next, and she saw him draw in a quavering breath. 'I can see you are busy today,' he said, and his voice was not quite steady as his eyes devoured her.

'Yes,' she said.

'I would like a moment of your time, just to talk. There's something I need to say.'

She stood on the sweet green grass in the park, her children tugging at her hands and skirt, asking for their tea or one more play on the swings, and she could find no words to answer him. How could they meet? Where? For what purpose?

She shook her head. 'We have nothing to say.' Then dipping her chin as she saw the pain come into his eyes, Lissa turned quickly away, wanting only to hurry from him.

'Why are you crying, Mummy?' Sarah asked.

'I'm not. I think I have some dust in my eye, that's all, sweetheart.'

'The Cobweb,' he called, his voice fading as she broke into a run, trying to make a game of it as she hurried the twins along. 'Lunchtime on Friday.'

She couldn't go, of course. When Friday came she pleaded a migraine and stayed in her room all day. How could she trust her feet not to take her to the small café if she let them out of the door?

Lissa knew that she must stand by her decision to stay. She had considered every avenue, taken advice, and come to realise that there was to be no escape. Her duty was to stay with her husband until her children no longer needed her. She must make the best of it. Hadn't everyone told her so?

Yet she could not deny that she wanted Derry. How could she not? She loved him still after all these years, and longed for him till her body ached with the pain of it.

'You may tell your friend, Nick, to come and collect all that stock back again,' Philip said. They were taking the twins out for a walk, any ordinary family on any ordinary Sunday. The girls were scampering ahead in their blue jeans and pink tops, exclaiming over tiny wild violets and golden cowslips with the kind of wonder only found in the very young. 'I think it best if you do not continue,' he announced, as if settling the matter.

They were walking to Elterwater, through the valley where Lissa had first been kissed by Derry. Beyond, in the distance, was the Band which they'd climbed together and the Old Dungeon Ghyll where they'd enjoyed tea, pretending to be sophisticated and grown up. And beyond that lay Bow Fell, where she had promised to walk with him and never had. Their youth had flown by, over in a moment. If only she'd been able to hold on to it.

Lissa blinked and brought herself back to the present. 'It's too late, Philip.' If she didn't hold fast to her courage now, she would have no life left. 'Renee says we're doing well. I mean to continue, for all you may force me to seek alternative premises. I mean to be a success.'

'I beg your pardon?' He stopped and stared at her, a stiff, incongruous figure in neat grey slacks and matching sweater. Philip at his most casual looked like a man unused to himself. Unlike Derry, who had seemed to come into his own up here, among the crisp green and white mountains. 'Are you defying me yet again?'

She gazed imploringly at him, begging him to be kind, to understand. 'Can't you see, Philip? I must have something of my own. I can't become a mindless dolly bird, devoting myself to you and the children. It would only make me grow bitter and resentful.'

'It's enough for most women.'

'Is it? I'm not so sure. Has anyone asked them if they are happy?' Her rebellion was growing. Lissa felt like a reckless teenager. It was most exhilarating. And possibly dangerous. 'I'm beginning to feel respect for myself again. It's a good feeling.'

Then he used his usual tactic of laughing at her, diffusing the tension, treating her like a foolish infant. 'Even if you had the skill to run a business, which you don't since you make such a mess of everything you do, how can you possibly continue? You have no money. Pray don't ask me for a loan.'

She smiled at him then and went on walking, forcing him to follow, a sensation of power flowing through her veins, warming her blood. 'I have money of my own, as a matter of fact. My grandfather, Jeffrey Ellis, invested a small sum for me as a gift when I was a child. He loved me, you see. Unreservedly, though he was kept from me in his later years. I shall continue with the shop, Philip, no matter what you say. I've employed Renee and I'm finding work for the women in the dale. I can't simply abandon them. You ask too much. I won't do it.'

341

'Gift?' Philip looked stunned for a moment, then pulled her to a halt and made her face him. 'How very naughty of you not to tell me of this before. Nor did you mention the shop until it was too late.' His anger now was palpable, his flintlike gaze boring into her. 'I do not care for secrets, my sweet. I do not care for them at all. I'll have no more, do you understand? Or I may have to take stronger measures with you. And I don't think you'd care for that at all, would you?'

But she only smiled and walked on, hiding the unease growing within. 'It'll be all right, Philip. You'll see. Neither you nor the children will suffer. I can fit everything in. You could save some money by getting rid of Nanny Sue if you wish. I'll take the children to the shop with me. They'll be old enough for school soon in any case.'

'I will not have my children brought up in the back of a shop.'

Lissa sighed. 'Very well. Then don't complain about being short of money.'

'And what of Derek Colwith?' The question was quietly asked in his most soft, enquiring tone. Lissa felt the energy drain from her body and put out a hand to steady herself as they reached a stile over a dry stone wall, willing herself to be strong.

'H-he came with Jan, probably on a visit. I didn't even know he was back. What of it? I'm a married woman now.'

He came to her and slid his hands over her neck and shoulders, curling over her bosom and hips, down to the flatness of her stomach. Lissa willed herself not to move or reveal the revulsion she felt at his touch.

'You belong to me. Remember that. You might have found a form of young love with Derry Colwith once, but you couldn't keep it, could you, my darling? He left. That's the hard part, isn't it, keeping love?'

Lissa felt herself flinch as she heard the cruel taunt in his words. 'Yes,' she agreed. 'I suppose it is.' Philip knew how to inflict the most hurt.

'As for the shop . . .' He was brisk again, calling the twins to heel as if they were dogs. 'Sarah, Beth, come here at once. I'll concede that you have made promises so I will permit you to finish the season. You need to get your money back from the stock in any case. Then you must devote yourself to me and our family.'

Lissa flicked back her hair and the sunlight glossed it like the blue-black wing of the ravens who inhabited the high crags. 'And if

I leave you?' It was the most reckless thing she had ever said. Lissa held her breath, refusing to wish the words unspoken.

He raised one quizzical dark brow then gave a loud snort of laughter, as if she had made a joke. 'You will never leave me, Lissa. I won't let you.'

'I had a baby kingfisher once,' she suddenly told him. 'Abandoned by its parents or fallen from its home in the river bank. It depended upon me utterly for a while. I reared it and loved it, then I let it fly free.'

'And you think I should do the same? Don't be foolish, Lissa. You have the story all wrong. For one thing I am not some adopted parent, I am your husband, so we belong together for life.'

'And for another?'

'I expect the kingfisher was unable to cope alone. It probably died.'

A chill washed through her, rippling down her spine, but Philip did not notice, he seemed too amused by her little tale. He was still smiling when the twins came running up, Beth climbing up into his arms, Sarah leaping about her mother, making demands.

'We're hungry, Daddy, Mummy. When are we going to eat?'

'The moment we reach the lake,' Philip announced, and set off at a gallop with Beth bouncing on his shoulders, screaming her fear and delight while Sarah scampered after them.

Lissa clenched her fist and drove it into her mouth.

She seemed to see Derry everywhere. If she turned a corner he bumped into her, coming the other way. If she took the children down to the shore he would be sitting on the benches. If she took them to the swings in the park he would be leaning against the bandstand, watching her. She saw him striding down St Margaret Steps, on the path to the woods, seemingly at every turn she made. She even found him in the shop talking to Renee on one occasion but obstinately refused to acknowledge his presence, walking past him to her office with her face set and her chin held high.

'Sorry about that,' Renee said afterwards. 'He just popped in to take a look at the place, for old times' sake. He won't be staying long, he says.'

Won't be staying long. Lissa wished he'd never come in the first place. Oh dear God, when Derry left, that would be the end. Lissa's instincts told her she would never see him again, never know any of the answers to the questions that haunted her.

Yet how dare she allow herself to ask them? She alone knew how much she needed him. All she could do was bury that need in work.

She helped Renee in the shop despite Philip's protests.

'I'll not have you demeaning yourself,' he told her, face flushed with fury.

'I love it,' she said. 'And don't feel at all demeaned.'

She daringly bought herself a small Morris van so she could drive back and forth to Broombank and Ashlea to collect more stock or chat with Jan and her workers about new designs and styles and the progress of work. The business was beginning to do well and it gave Lissa a wonderful new sense of freedom. It made her feel capable of building a life for herself after all. She even recklessly hired a woman to come in and clean for her, though that didn't work for long as Nanny Sue complained and Philip sacked her on the spot.

Undeterred, Lissa battled on. She felt a real person again with a mind of her own, able to make decisions and answer queries, ring up suppliers and issue complaints, instructions or warm praise with equal confidence. It really felt quite wonderful.

But each night she must return home to Philip's criticisms, his lists of rules and requirements, his glowering disapproval. And his bed. Faced with this reality her strength would sometimes falter. Could she survive this task she had set herself? Could she remain with him as his wife? Even as she vowed to do so, her heart desperately sought a way to be free and yet keep her children.

She was twenty-four years old and had nothing to look forward to for the rest of her life but a bleak future with a man she could not love. But Lissa realised now how much he had chipped away at her self-confidence. Her victory would lie in reclaiming her mind and sense of purpose. Otherwise Philip would have won completely.

He was sitting in the wide hearth, his feet in thick woollen walking socks steaming gently before the basket grate, laughing at something Tam had said. Lissa saw him the moment she walked into the room and the shock of it made a pain hit her flat in the chest, quite robbing her of breath. He seemed a reincarnation of that other Derry, the one who had fascinated her most, the one who had kissed her on their walk to the Langdales.

'Hello.' She couldn't say his name. It was astonishing really, how normal she sounded.

Derry was on his feet in an instant and Lissa saw the tell-tale flush creep up his neck. This was dreadful. He hadn't expected her to walk in, unannounced, any more than she had expected to find him here.

'Lissa. Hello. I've been staying with Jan. Doing some walking on the fells. Thought I'd call in for a chat and a cuppa.'

She wanted to say there was no need for him to explain. It was really none of her business if he felt he had the right to make himself at home at Broombank.

'He's a different person, is he not?' Tam said, unaware of the undercurrents. 'Not a Teddy Boy now. Grown up fine he has. A successful businessman, would you believe?'

Lissa tried to force her stiff lips into a smile. 'I can see,' she said. 'What is it you do, Derry?' Politely enquiring, obeying the social niceties. Why? Why stand here and talk to him when she wanted to turn and run?

'I work for a management agency. We represent and protect young people who wish to enter the music business. There are a lot of sharks out there, waiting to bite.'

'Lucky you came,' Tam butted in. 'Derry was wondering how to get back to Carreckwater. You could give him a lift, could you not?'

Panic swamped her. 'I'm surprised he doesn't have a flash American car if he's so successful.'

Derry grinned. 'I do. In the States. Nick brought me over, but his van is broken down. It's OK, I can wait for him to fix it.'

'Good. That's all right then,' Lissa said with a cool smile, feeling nothing but relief.

He set down his mug, rubbed his hands on his cord trousers in a familiar gesture and she knew then that his palms sweated, that he was as uncomfortable about this meeting as she.

Perhaps Meg saw something too for she took Lissa's arm in a comforting gesture. 'Shall we go into the barn? I want to talk business, if these men will excuse us.' They went off, talking woollens, Lissa struggling to concentrate on Meg's bright chatter.

'I could clear this barn of rubbish. I don't really need it. If you wanted to expand into frame knitting, this would be the ideal place.'

Lissa fought to focus her mind. 'Ideal,' she agreed, in a faint voice that she struggled to strengthen. 'Not this year perhaps, but maybe next. If we do well and I can find alternative premises.'

'What do you mean, alternative premises?' Meg sounded puzzled. 'Haven't you just spent all last winter doing up the old drapery?'

Lissa found it difficult to explain why Miss Stevens had changed her mind about letting her have the lease, yet there seemed little point in pretending. 'Philip still isn't keen and Miss Stevens has no wish to become involved in a matrimonial dispute.' She gave a wry smile. 'Fair enough. It's her shop.'

But Meg was frowning. 'Is that what you are involved in? A matrimonial dispute?'

'No, no, of course not,' Lissa lied, not meeting Meg's shrewd gaze.

'Is there something you'd like to talk about?'

'Everything's fine. I have two lovely children, why wouldn't it be?' She turned from Meg to walk through the barn, judging how many machines they would need, where they could store the boxes of unworked wool, where they would put the tables for the cutting out. 'We'd need lots of shelving to store the finished products. And machines to sew the pieces together. I'd have to find new markets. Travel further afield. We couldn't sell everything in Carreckwater.'

'Of course not. You would be our representative and take samples of our products to other shops, other districts. Bring back lots of orders.'

Lissa recognised an enthusiasm in Meg's voice as keen as her own. 'I'd enjoy that,' she agreed, feeling the kernel of excitement grow. Lissa knew she should explain that this season would be Broombank Woollens first and last. She should go round and tell all her hand knitters not to make any more garments. Tell them that she was tired of fighting and her husband had won. 'How much would frame knitting machines cost?' she wondered aloud. 'I might run out of money.'

Meg shrugged. 'Find out. Cost everything out that you'd need, then go and see the bank. I did. Surprising what you can do when you set your mind to it.' She regarded her foster daughter with quiet grey eyes. 'It all depends how badly you want something, whether or not it's worth fighting for.'

'Yes,' Lissa agreed, meeting her gaze at last. 'I suppose it does. You know, Meg, you seem to be the only person on my side.' And they both knew she wasn't simply talking about knitting.

346

'And where else would I be? Whatever you decide to do with your life, Lissa, I'm right behind you. Remember that.'

A smile of appreciation, and love. 'I know. Thanks.'

She had to fight on, with all the strength she could muster. If she gave up now, what kind of life would she have?

27

'Tam had no right to insist on my taking you.'

'He doesn't know about us.'

'Then you should have insisted on going with Nick.'

'I wanted to talk to you, Lissa, and I know you've been avoiding me. All right, I'll admit I engineered this meeting by hanging around Broombank and Ashlea. It was my last hope.'

She threw a glare at him, trying to freeze him with her anger. Even the wet wool smell of him was familiar, sending her senses racing.

'Watch the road,' he smiled, as the small van bumped against a rock and lurched alarmingly. Then he reached out and touched her hand where it gripped the steering wheel, white knuckles standing out like bare bones. 'Or better still stop, so we can talk for a few moments without risk to life and limb.'

'No.' But she did. She had to. She simply couldn't focus on the winding lane ahead. Lissa drew the van to a halt and yanked on the handbrake, sulking at the view. The day appeared to match the confusion of her mood. A cornflower blue sky marred by streaks of grey. Dark shadows melding the mountains into greyness one moment, highlighting them into brilliant sunlight the next.

'Whatever it is you want to say, get it over with quickly,' she said, tartness in her tone. 'I have children waiting for me at home.'

'And a husband.'

'Yes,' she said, with stubborn haste. 'And a husband.'

'Why did you marry him, Lissa?'

She was filled instantly with a flush of hot temper and turned to him, violet eyes flashing with anger. 'Why did you leave, without even a proper goodbye or explanation? Why did you promise to come home, in that pathetic little scrap of a letter, and then not keep that promise? You made a fool out of me, Derry Colwith. Don't think I'll ever forget it or forgive you for that.'

'I'm surprised it still matters so much to you,' he said, his voice soft, like a caress, and she realised at once her mistake.

'Don't kid yourself. I'm very happy, thank you very much.'

'Are you?'

'Yes.'

'You don't look like the picture of a fulfilled happy woman. You look like someone who's made a bad mistake and is spending the rest of her life paying for it. Rather like me, in fact.'

She glared at him as the fury bubbling inside her slowly subsided and the crackling tension between them changed imperceptibly to another sensation, far more compelling, far more dangerous. Dear God, how she loved him. She sensed him move towards her even before he'd put thought into action.

'Don't,' she said, holding up her hands in a defensive gesture. 'Please, Derry. Don't touch me. I can cope with anything but that.'

'OK. Can I tell you then, what happened? Will you listen without jumping down my throat?'

She turned the key, making the engine spurt into life. 'I don't want to know.'

'Yes, you do.' He reached over and turned the engine off again. Then he got out of the van and stood, hands in pockets, staring out over the panorama of dale and fell, lifting his face to a fitful sun. Lissa was forced to follow him.

'What can I say?' he said. 'I was young. Obsessed with the hope of fame and fortune. Like a lot of other kids I've met since, I was sure I was the one with the special gift, the one who would take the music world by storm.' He gave a light laugh, mature honesty in it, with no hint of bitterness.

'And I came second, probably even last in your calculations?' Lissa guessed.

He gave a rueful smile. 'Like I said, we all make mistakes. I'm no exception. A part of me was arrogant enough to believe I'd return in no time with money in my pocket, a record contract, and you'd be eating out of my hand.'

'I was already,' she admitted. 'I didn't want your money, only you.'

350

He was silent, putting back his head and staring up into the sky as if by watching the movement of the clouds he could make time run backwards, give them a second chance.

'I realised my mistake a bit earlier than you though. I came back, remember, hoping to make amends. But it was too late. You were already engaged to Philip Brandon.'

'I know.' She would never forget that night. The awful sight of Derry's face had haunted her for months afterwards, trying to understand what she had read there. Lissa recognised it now as the final acknowledgement of lost hope, hastily smothered in pride.

They stood now side by side, not looking at each other, not touching. The wind lifted the curls she'd left loose about her neck and slapped them against her face.

'I could tell you that it wasn't entirely my fault, that your husband had a hand in my decision to leave, but you'd only say I was making excuses.'

She half glanced at him then bit down on her lip, feeling a hard knot growing in her throat. 'Not necessarily. Philip has a way of making things go his way. I could have stopped our engagement but I let it happen. I went ahead and married him. I thought I'd be safe with him, older man, not too many demands. He would never reject me as you had done, as – as others before you had done.'

Derry groaned, realising more than ever the effect of his actions. 'Lissa, if I'd come back sooner, would you have forgiven me?'

There was a plea in his voice that cut deep into her heart. She could almost feel the blood running from it. 'Don't – don't ask. Who knows? It's gone, done with. All over.' She turned from him to go back to the van but he caught her arm, held her by him.

'It isn't,' he said. 'You know it isn't.' She could feel the heat of his fingers the length of her arm, his gaze warming her face, and her head jerked round of its own accord. As their eyes finally met and held it was as if her soul was drawn from her body, leaving it weak and shaking with need.

'It has to be,' she managed, on half a breath. 'I'm married now, a wife and mother.'

His eyes were soft and warm, compelling and powerful, telling her things she didn't want to know, reminding her of feelings she'd much rather not remember.

'It never will be over. Not for me. I've learned that much about myself at least.'

351

She must have made a small sound for he told her not to cry, even so the tears were raining down her cheeks.

'I never cry,' she sobbed. 'Never.'

'I know,' he said, stroking the tears away with the gentle tips of his fingers. 'Crying is dangerous. It makes you weak and vulnerable.' Then his arms were around her, his mouth on hers, and he was kissing her as never before. And Lissa was gasping for more, holding his head, opening her mouth to receive his tongue, his love, as if by that method he could give her life.

He was holding her so tightly she could hardly breathe. She didn't want to breathe, not if it meant living on for ever without him.

His hand was cupping her cheek, her throat, her breast.

Dear God, *what was she doing*? Dangerous emotions, dangerous actions. She broke from him and ran to the van. Then she drove away and left him standing there, alone on the empty fells.

Yet Lissa could no more prevent herself from seeing him again than she could stop the rain falling on the fells or the tarn freezing over in winter. Just one more time, she'd told herself. She owed him that. Settle the matter properly between them without emotion this time. Though it had taken her a while to pluck up sufficient courage.

Renee had acted as intermediary by giving her a note, a knowing grin on her bright face.

'I won't see him,' Lissa had said.

'Please yourself,' Renee had shrugged. 'No skin off my nose. He only wants a cup of coffee at The Cobweb, not a necking session behind the bike sheds.'

'Oh, do stop it,' and Lissa had laughed, feeling faintly foolish and wishing she could view life as lightheartedly as Renee did.

So despite all the promises to herself, despite the risk she ran were Philip to discover her deceit, she was going.

'Why are you sad, Mummy? Are you cross with us?'

'Of course not, my darlings. You are my world, my life, my little treasures.' Lissa, cuddling both children on her lap, warm and fragrant after their bath, kissed them each in turn and explained how they must be very good for Nanny Sue this evening.

'Where are you going, Mummy?' Beth wanted to know, pillowing her head against her mother's warm breast.

'Why can't we come?' put in Sarah, outrage on her small heart-shaped face, and Lissa laughed, kissing them both again, brushing

352

their soft curls with a pink baby brush. Beth with hair the colour of pale chestnut leaves and eyes grown more grey than blue as the baby years had passed; Sarah's hair black as her own, the eyes as deep a blue except for flecks of pale grey which altered the light in them, almost to suit her mood. Unusual, bewitching. She smoothed their perfect limbs with a gentle hand, tucked frilled cotton nighties over dimpled knees.

'How I do love you both. Do you love Mummy?'

'Yes, yes, *yes*.' Soft warm kisses, tight hugs, joyful giggles and laughter. With her children, Lissa felt completely relaxed and happy. She must do nothing to risk that happiness, or their future, no matter what the cost to her own life. How would they ever forgive her when they grew older if they realised she had put her needs before theirs? As her own mother, Kath had done. However much Lissa might long to leave Philip, she could never risk that. Never.

'Now, my darlings, here is Nanny Sue. Will you put them to bed for me, Susan? I must go out to – to a meeting.' Lissa felt sure the woman would guess she was lying.

'As you wish, Madam,' said Nanny in her usual frosty tones. Though for all her unfriendliness with adults, Lissa could not fault the girl's care of the twins. She adored them to a point of fierce possessiveness. An emotion Lissa was familiar with in this household.

'Is Mr Brandon aware you are going out?' she asked, meaning 'Has he given his permission?'

Lissa smiled, lifting Beth into Nanny's arms. 'He is out at a meeting himself. If he rings, I'm sure you will tell him. I promised my friends that I would go but I know the children will be quite safe with you.'

'And what time shall I say you will be back?'

Lissa stifled an irritated response with a sigh, and smiled sunnily. 'You know, if you should ever lose your job here, apply for one as a prison warden. You'd be perfect. 'Bye, my darlings. Be good. I'll come in to kiss you good night when I get home.'

They sat at a table in a corner of The Cobweb Coffee Bar and sipped their coffee without tasting it, without speaking, without even looking at each other. It was Lissa, in the end, who broke the silence.

'I don't know why I came,' she said, in a pitifully small voice.

353

'If Philip were to find out . . . What was it you wanted, Derry? I can't stay long and I thought we'd said all there was to be said between us.'

His eyes held an appeal she dare not read and could not ignore. 'I can't begin to say all I feel,' he said. 'I'm sorry if I went too far the other night. I lost control. It won't happen again.'

'I'm sorry I abandoned you on the fells. It was childish of me.'

Then suddenly he was on his feet, tossing coins on the table as he'd probably learned to do in America and taking her by the arm. 'Come on, I need air. Let's get out of this place.'

Walking by the lake, the breeze in her hair, Lissa felt herself start to tremble. 'Someone might see us,' she said, glancing back over her shoulder.

'Meaning your husband?'

'Meaning anyone. Plenty of people would love to spread gossip. I'm well known here, even if you no longer are.'

Derry dug his hands in his trouser pockets, shoulders hunched. 'Come away with me. Leave him, Lissa. I know you don't love him. You still love me, I can tell. Come back to the States with me.'

Lissa stifled a gasp. 'I-I can't do that. You know that I can't.'

'Bring the kids, I don't mind.'

'Philip is their father. He wouldn't let them go so far away.'

They had reached the dark clump of oak and beech that crowded the shoreline and Lissa halted, shaking her head in distress. 'If this is all you wanted to say then it'd better stop here. I must get back.' She half turned from him but he caught her hand, a whole aching world of emotion in his touch, and in his voice when he said her name.

Then she was in his arms, willingly surrendering her lips for his kisses, bringing his arms tight about her waist, pressing herself as close as she could get. 'Hold me, oh hold me, my darling. Never let me go.'

They were two young lovers again, absorbed in each other, their love, their kisses, the sensations that soared through their young bodies. He cradled her head against his breast, kissing her brow, stroking back the riot of ebony curls.

'I won't ask you for more than you can give. It's enough to have you here, to hold you and kiss you.' But as he stared over her head, out to the moon – silvered water, Derry knew it wouldn't always be that way.

*   *   *

354

He said as much to Lissa when they met in the same place the following week at exactly the same time, falling into each other's arms with a hunger that could no longer be assuaged by kisses. Streaks of early-evening sunlight shafted through the branches of the tall oaks, highlighting her beauty so that his stomach went weak as water inside.

For a long time they clung together, not speaking, hardly daring to breathe as they held each other tight in a close embrace.

The lake shore was thick with laurel, holly and rowan, and there was the whisper of willow skimming the water. A cheeky robin hopped upon a twig and cocked his head to one side, considering them, making them both laugh while a family of moorhens, disturbed by their presence, swam away in a huff.

'Do you really still love me?' she asked, shyly, softly, not daring to hear his answer.

He lifted her chin with one finger and grinned at her, kissing her forehead, her nose, then finding her lips. 'Shall I prove it?' he murmured.

But before he could steal a second kiss, a flippant breeze whipped her hair across her mouth, robbing him of its sweetness, and she laughed out loud at the look of disappointment on his face.

'I love the softness of your skin,' he said, trailing his lips over the curve of her throat, sending a quiver of fierce passion through her as he found the sensitive hollows beneath her ears. 'And you always smell so good, as if you had just shampooed your hair.'

More often than not she had. Lissa had spent an hour in the bathroom this very evening, preparing herself with trembling fingers, shampooing, brushing, styling, applying 'Outdoor Girl' pearl pink lipstick and blue mascara which set off her black hair so well. She was very tentative with her make-up, aiming to enhance rather than overwhelm her features, but she dared not ask herself why she was taking so much trouble. One moment with Derry and she could deny it no longer.

By the time he had finished kissing her on this occasion there wasn't a scrap of lipstick left, and she looked decidedly rosy all about her mouth and chin. 'Don't,' she said, far too late, as she reluctantly disentangled herself from his arms, feeling dazed and warm with love. 'You really mustn't.'

'Yes, I must,' he said, applying himself to the task of starting over again.

She remembered as a girl at school the biology mistress urging them to keep control of their emotions by thinking of other things. Letters to write, errands that needed running. That way they wouldn't be tempted into indiscretion. As her lips throbbed from Derry's kisses and her body burned with desire, Lissa tidied out two cupboards and a book shelf in her mind. Yet she wanted him more than ever. The biology mistress, she decided, had got it all wrong.

So had Philip. Lissa had never felt such an overpowering emotion with her own husband.

As the muscles in Derry's arms tensed about her she felt certain it must be possible to die of delight. She put up her hands to caress his face, to push back the strands of hair from his forehead. Oh, if this was love it was wonderful, perfect. Why hadn't she trusted it before? Derry made her feel so wanted, so loveable.

It was as if they were young lovers again, slipping back in time, trying to brush aside the years of exile from each other's arms.

After a while she had to make him stop kissing her so she could catch her breath.

'I shall certainly have to wash my hair after tonight,' she teased, as he pushed his fingers through the wayward curls, pulling her close. 'And make my face again before I go home.'

He put one finger to her lips. 'Don't talk about going home. Not yet.' His eyes were burning with his need. 'Let's sit under the trees.'

'The grass will be wet.'

'No, it won't,' he lied. 'Trust me.'

'I do. I love you very much. I love you to kiss me,' she encouraged, not considering how she might stretch his self-discipline too far by the taunting expression in her violet eyes and the pressure of her bewitching body against his. 'It makes my heart pound and my head spin. Does it you, Derry? I can't get enough of you.'

It was some moments before Derry felt quite up to answering, and then it was not to answer her question at all.

'Let me unbutton your blouse,' he murmured, the excitement tight in his voice. Edging her gently backwards under the trees, his warm breath against her mouth was sending her wild with fresh desire. Lissa could feel him trembling. Or was it her own limbs that were shaking? 'Only a little way,' he pleaded, making a start on the pearl buttons and kissing her hard at the same time so she wouldn't realise he'd undone them all.

356

'Oh,' she gasped, straining against him.

'I won't hurt you, or go too far.' And to do him justice, he didn't. But there was no doubt in Lissa's mind that she wanted him to. The feel of his hands on her bare breasts made her whimper with pleasure and her heart soar with joy at this proof that she had banished one demon at least. She wasn't frigid at all. Philip was wrong. There was nothing she wouldn't agree to do for Derry. She loved him so much.

Rosemary Ellis finally succumbed one day at the end of May. Lissa was staring out of her bedroom window when the call came, watching malicious little waves scurry across the lake, the whooper swans trumpeting their desire to leave Carreckwater for their summer breeding grounds on the Arctic tundra, or a few carefully selected moorland tarns. Normally she loved to watch the coming and going of birds on the lake; today she felt sad, as if in some way they carried with them the remnants of her childhood dream. She packed two protesting children and Nanny Sue into the old van and drove off to Broombank without waiting for Philip.

It felt like a wonderful release to be driving free through the open countryside. Lissa left the wooded slopes of Carreckwater without a backward glance and headed for home. She passed Troutbeck bridge and unbidden her lips curved into a smile at the memory of her day on the high fells with Derry. She made a detour through Winster valley and wept as she thought of its possible loss.

'Mummy is crying again,' said Beth in her sad voice. 'Why is she always crying?'

'Perhaps she has a problem,' said Nanny Sue tartly, and Lissa glanced hastily at her in the driving mirror and tried to cover up her lapse by explaining about the reservoir. She didn't think Nanny was entirely convinced even if the children were enthralled.

They drove past several old white-walled cottages, a small tarn that was popular for skating in winter, then she was heading north and her home fells were in sight. It was good to experience again the peace of Broombank and hear Meg and Tam's cheerful banter. She breathed deeply, letting normal life wash over her, letting the timelessness of the fells work their old magic.

'The funeral is tomorrow, at the local fellside church,' Meg said. 'You could stay for a few days.'

'Love to.'

'Then let's not think of funerals today.' And Lissa was more than happy to agree.

They spent a happy afternoon clearing out the old barn, the twins helping, getting covered in dust and cobwebs, giggling and squabbling by turn.

'I've spoken with the bank manager and he's happy to help,' Lissa told Meg and Jan, as they sat in the kitchen over a much needed cup of tea, Robbie bounding noisily about while the twins played with baby Alice on the rug.

'Good for you.'

'Once he saw what I was putting in. I've ordered two frame knitting machines to get us started this winter. Three sewing machines and a special sort of ring knitter which does the welts on the necks. A couple of tables, some metal shelving and various small tools. I've got a list somewhere. They'll be delivered within the next few weeks. I shall need an expert to set it all up of course. Do you know of anyone?'

'I'll ask around,' Meg said. 'Or you could advertise.'

Then Philip would know what she was doing. He would realise that she was ignoring his instructions to close the business down. Dare she risk it? She had to risk it, she supposed, if she was to survive.

As if reading her thoughts Jan asked, 'Does Philip approve of Broombank Woollens now?' Lissa offered a vague sort of smile that might have been taken for agreement. She wanted to pretend everything in her life was normal.

When Meg went off to investigate a lame ewe, Jan took the opportunity to divulge something of her own troubles.

'Do you remember Nick once telling you about our worries with the mortgage?'

Lissa showed her surprise. 'That was ages ago, when Alice was born. He told me money was tight but that you'd catch up.'

'Well, we haven't.'

'I'm sure you will, Jan. Don't worry about it.' Jan hesitated, tucking her hair behind the ear while she wondered if she should continue, then deciding she must. 'It's just that we've had a letter. From your husband, in his official capacity as solicitor.'

Lissa became very still. 'What kind of letter?'

'It listed what we owe and Nick hit the roof. He didn't agree with the reckoning. Said we didn't owe half as much. Never seen him in such a fury.'

'There must be some mistake. I'll talk to Philip. Put it right. You can have as much time as you need.'

Derry came in as they were talking and Lissa's heart skipped a beat. She hadn't realised he was here. Every time she saw him it was like the twist of a knife in her heart, making her think of what might have been, if only they hadn't both been so young, so foolish, so quick to make decisions about the rest of their lives. And she knew she must never allow her eyes to meet his, in case anyone could tell how they felt about each other. 'I thought you'd have gone by now?' she said, sounding perfectly composed, just as if she hadn't seen him since that day at Broombank when she'd been coerced into giving him a lift, and had instead abandoned him on the fell.

He gave her a wry smile. 'I missed my lift, remember, so I'm taking a later flight.'

Lissa stared at him in surprise then dissolved into laughter. How wicked of him to read her mind so well and play her at her own game. 'Perhaps you deserved to lose your lift,' she said.

He came and sat at the table with them. His sleeves were rolled up and Lissa found herself staring at tanned arms, muscles round and strong, that her fingers itched to touch. He smiled at her. 'I hear you've been attending protest meetings and even got yourself arrested after a sit-in? How did Philip feel about that?'

'As a matter of fact . . .' Should she lie? Pretend Philip wasn't concerned? Lissa screwed up her nose with wry good humour. 'He didn't speak to me for hours.'

'Some benefit came out of it then?'

And they all laughed, as if it were the funniest joke in the world.

At that moment the kitchen door burst open and two giggling little girls came staggering in, Alice's chubby baby body lugged between them like a sack of potatoes, though she seemed content enough with their ministrations.

'She's wet and wants her pants changing,' Beth said, quite seriously, and Lissa's heart turned over yet again. She would be mad even to consider walking out on her husband, How could she face the whole terrifying process of law and risk losing this precious pair? But Derry would have her without the benefit of law. He'd take the children too. No, no, the risk was too great.

'Right,' said Jan. 'We'd best see to her then. Find the nappies, Sarah. Bring the powder, Beth.' The twins did her bidding with delight. They much preferred a real baby to their plastic dolls at home. Alice was much more fun and surprisingly amenable.

'I'll help too,' said Lissa, jumping up, desperate not to be left alone with Derry.

'My word, I am the lucky one today,' Jan laughed.

28

It was a cold, brisk spring day for the funeral. The snows still lingered on the tops but lambs were bleating, cherry blossom and daffodils bloomed. Maytime had come belatedly to Broombank. Along the track by the little church the leaves of the whitebeam flashed with silver as they turned their undersides to the wind, and there were tiny clusters of white flowers on each stem. But the golden broom, which gave the farm its name, was more cautious, waiting for any sign of frost to be gone before it deigned to bloom.

The family stood about, dressed in sober colours, Joe fidgeting in his best setting-off suit, cap pulled well down, and Sally Ann unusually smart in a black hat with a tiny veil she probably hadn't worn since the war. Nick stood alone as Jan had stayed home with the children. Lissa wished she could do the same but braced herself against the wind, and the resolution to do the proper thing by her grandmother, whether she deserved it or not.

Philip came, of course, declaring it was his duty to pay his last respects, taking Lissa's arm in his as if they were the best of friends. But it was a poor, miserable affair since there was no one but themselves and Mrs Stanton, the housekeeper, to mourn.

'Poor old soul,' Tam said, and Meg rolled her eyes, giving a sad smile.

'She can keep the holy angels in their place now.'

'You'd have thought Kath would've come to her own mother's funeral, wouldn't you?' Lissa remarked, as they stood in the small churchyard, the helm wind whipping roses into their cold cheeks, and bringing the predicted shower of rain.

361

Meg made no reply and the painful subject was pursued no further.

For Lissa at least the rest of the day passed slowly. Philip, aided by the unsuspecting children, gave every appearance of a happy family with not a care in the world. Only Lissa knew it to be all a sham. And he resolutely ignored Derry, barely speaking to him or acknowledging his presence.

'You could at least try to be civil,' Lissa told him. 'He is Jan's brother, and since she is married to Nick you could almost call him family.'

'Not my family. Nor yours,' he coldly reminded her, and she didn't ask for his co-operation again. Life was difficult enough without deliberately picking a fight with her husband just because she felt at odds with the world.

Without even looking up she knew the instant Derry walked into a room; the hairs at the back of her neck would prickle with keen awareness as if they had a perception all their own.

Lissa could feel Philip's eyes upon her as Meg served up the meal. And despite her own best efforts, Derry only had to brush past, or accidentally touch her hand for her heart to scud into rapid beats. If he needed something passing at lunch she instinctively handed it to him before he had asked for it. If he spoke, she had to bite her tongue not to finish his sentence for him. And she avoided his gaze with such studied attention she felt sure everyone in the house must guess how she felt. Including Philip.

But she could feel no guilt.

She loved Derry. Lissa knew she had done her best with her marriage but that it was a failure. Now she could only do her duty to Philip, but never love him, if indeed she ever had.

Philip went up to Larkrigg Hall later, to issue instructions to the housekeeper who had agreed to stay on for a while until he could find someone to replace her. Then Mrs Stanton meant to retire to the West Country, with her great niece and a small legacy left by Rosemary Ellis.

Lissa spent those hours with the twins and Jan, trying her best to ignore Derry though it proved difficult if not well-nigh impossible. Her eyes naturally followed his every movement and a part of her longed for a moment alone with him. She wanted to know when she could see him again, if he was thinking of returning to America soon. She wanted to talk to him of her hopes and plans for the future, to hold

362

him and touch his lips with her own, and offer him all the love that lay unused within her. The desire to put thought into action became so overwhelming that she got up from the table, somewhat abruptly, and took herself off for a long walk. She would go down to Allenbeck and her favourite childhood haunts.

Lissa loved the feel of the wind whipping through her hair. She ignored Philip's instructions these days and always let it fly free instead of screwing it up into neat little French pleats. She loved the wind scouring her cheeks to a polished brightness, wishing she could cleanse her life as thoroughly.

She sat by the humped bridge and called to mind a picture of a laughing girl in her best frock waiting to meet her mother and grandmother for the first time. Now that grandmother was buried and the dream with her. The regrets Lissa felt in this moment were not entirely selfish. Surely Rosemary Ellis had suffered more than anyone from her self-imposed bitterness? How sad that Lissa had been denied the opportunity to make her grandmother happy and proud.

Over a matter of principle and family honour, Rosemary Ellis had banished love from her life. Was that what would happen to Lissa?

Was it really for the sake of her children that she stayed with Philip, or because she wasn't quite brave enough to risk the scandal of leaving him? Could she start a new life, even without the benefit of divorce? Could she earn enough from her new business to keep herself and the children? Could she face the gossip and the snide remarks if she took Derry for a lover and lived with him unwed? And would Derry want her under such conditions?

And if she lacked the courage to do any of these things, would she then end up as a bitter and lonely old woman, as Rosemary Ellis had been? The prospect made her shudder.

She met Philip on his way back from Larkrigg.

'Are you still thinking of moving us in there?' she asked, eyes troubled.

He looked at her, dark eyebrows raised. 'That depends,' he said. 'On what?'

'On you. Don't think I haven't seen the way you look at Derry Colwith. I won't let you go, Lissa. Not now, not ever.' He sounded so reasonable.

'What if I say I prefer any man but you?' The pain in her breast must be because she was holding her breath.

He took hold of the front of her jacket and pulled her gently towards him, pushing his face close in to hers. And still he smiled. 'If you leave me, or take a lover, my dear wife, you can kiss goodbye to your beloved dale. And your new little business.'

'What?' She tried to laugh, sound amused and incredulous, anxious to disguise the sudden spurt of fear. 'What are you talking about?'

'I know you've been making plans with Meg. Nanny overheard you talking. Let me make it quite plain that Broomdale is only safe so long as I permit it to remain so.'

'I don't believe you. You don't have that kind of power.'

'Oh, yes, I do,' he said, sweet as you please. 'One word from me and Winster would be forgotten. It would be Broomdale you'd be fighting for then. All that lovely fresh water would be washing over your old home, swamping Broombank and Ashlea, flooding your burgeoning woollen business. Waste of time and money that is, in any case, my sweet.'

Lissa gasped. 'Is this why you're hounding Nick about the mortgage on Ashlea? I'd rather you didn't. He'll catch up with any late payments, given time.'

'*You'd* rather?'

'Yes, me. Ashlea does belong to me, if you recall.'

He stared at her, then laughed. 'Soft-hearted as ever, I see, and you think you can make yourself into a businesswoman? Close your silly little shop, dear wife, sack your lady knitters. I can get much more money by letting them flood the whole damn' valley. We'd get compensation for Ashlea, and I have a buyer already lined up for Larkrigg who would dearly like to turn it into an on site hotel, high on the ridge there. Water sports are the coming thing.'

'You wouldn't dare!'

'I might. Don't test me. Or I could be satisfied just with selling Larkrigg as a hotel, though we'd get less for it. It's really entirely up to you.' He smoothed down the collar of her jacket with a caressing hand, enjoying the satisfaction of seeing her face grow pale, the awful realisation of his power dawn in her beautiful eyes. But then he had always loved power, hadn't he? Over Felicity, over his own mother because his father had been so useless, and now over Lissa. It had to be this way. She must learn that.

Lissa tossed her head. 'You can't do it. Larkrigg belongs to the twins.'

'Rosemary left me in charge, as their guardian. If I decide it would be a good investment to sell, so be it, I'll sell.'

Lissa couldn't care less what he did with Larkrigg Hall. Hadn't she always hated it? Broombank and Ashlea were another matter.

'How can you influence Manchester Water Board?'

'One greedy little consultant with sticky fingers and a demanding mother who will do anything for money. He thinks the project sounds feasible and is looking into it. A dam could easily be built across the head of the dale.' Philip's lips curled into a smile though it did not radiate any further as he took her arm and hooked it in to his. 'You know how I like to be in control.'

Withdrawing the arm with a grimace of repugnance, Lissa stepped back and faced him, her expression as cold and hard as his own. 'You can't control me, Philip. Not any longer. I've broken free. You might as well know I intend to build this business up, create my own independence and a new future for myself.'

'And take Derry Colwith for a lover despite my warning?'

'I never said so.' Lissa could feel the trap closing in upon her. It tightened her rib cage and made her breath ball into a hard pain in her breast. She was silent for a long moment then she met his assessing gaze with her own steady one. 'If I remain, as your wife, for the sake of the twins, you must promise to drop this idea.'

'Ah, promises.'

'You must, Philip. If you do not, I'll fight you, every inch of the way.'

He smiled at her. 'And if I make this promise to leave your precious dale alone?'

She swallowed. 'Then – then in return, as I say, I'll stay. Only on my terms. After we leave here I shall want a bedroom of my own. A separate life. Keeping up appearances, isn't that the phrase?'

He looked vaguely nonplussed by her defiance and new air of assurance, as if she had caught him off balance for once. Then the skin about his mouth tightened and the lip curled in a snarl of distaste. 'Sounds very like an ultimatum.'

'Call it what you wish.'

'Then remember mine. Or the price might be more than you are willing to pay. Certainly more than your precious family and dale knitters would be prepared for. You are exclusively mine, Lissa, and I intend to keep you that way.'

They stood on the quiet hillside and stared into each other's eyes while Lissa felt the joy of victory slip from her heart and the trap snap shut.

'Checkmate, I think?' he said, smiling his satisfaction, and Lissa knew she was as much a captive now as ever, despite her brave show of defiance. Yet even in this bleakest of moments her mind turned at once to Derry. She must give him up. There was no help for it. Something inside of her shuddered and sank. But she could at least see him one more time, to explain this new turn of events.

It was when she was collecting cups at teatime that he whispered desperately in her ear.

'I can't bear this. I must see you.'

'By the tarn, this evening,' she said, without glancing up from her task.

It was reckless to risk it. Perhaps a madness had come over her but as darkness fell, Lissa pleaded a headache and went early to bed. Philip followed soon after, as she guessed he might, but she kept very firmly to her side of the bed as he climbed in beside her.

'Are you tired, my sweet?'

'I think I'm starting with a cold.'

She lay, not daring to move, for what seemed like hours, telling herself this was the last time she would ever share a bed with him. Tomorrow she would move all her things into the spare bedroom. Or better still, all his things.

Only when she was certain of Philip's deep breathing and gentle snores, did she slip from the bed. Pulling on a wrap, Lissa quietly let herself out of the house.

There was no moon but she could have found her way blindfold. The night enfolded her like soft black velvet and she moved surely up the sheep trods, through the stand of trees at Brockbarrow woods and on to the tarn beyond. Excitement beat hard and sure in her breast, and the awareness of danger was strong in her. Yet she could no more have denied herself from taking this risk than her next breath.

He was waiting for her by the glittering black and silver water and she went straight into his arms.

Later, when they were breathless from kissing, they sat with their backs against the warm trunk of a rowan and Derry stroked her brow, her cheek, her throat, with his lips and fingers, not able to get enough of her.

'Darling Lissa, how I love you.' He kissed her again, his mouth soft and sweetly compelling. 'I always will.'

'You know that it is not enough simply to love each other, don't you? I have the twins to think of.' She explained then, carefully and in a matter-of-fact sort of voice, how she had taken advice from her doctor, a lawyer, even Miss Stevens. She looked at him with tired resignation in her lovely eyes. 'There's no help for it. If I leave Philip for you, they would call me an unfit mother and I could lose the children. I daren't risk that. You know I daren't.'

Derry was silent. Only the sound of water lapping softly against stones disturbed their thoughts.

'What if I promise to be as good a father to them as he would be?'

Lissa gazed into Derry's beloved face. 'You'd probably make a better and he'd hate you more than ever.' She didn't feel she could mention Philip's blackmail concerning the dale. Derry might react badly to the threatened loss of his sister's home and make matters worse. Besides, if she had to sacrifice Derry in any case, for her children, why trouble him with it? The problem needn't arise. 'Philip is a very difficult man. He would always win. I have to make the best of things as they are. He and I have agreed terms. There's nothing more I can do.'

'Terms? What kind of terms?' Anger etched with despair came over his young face. 'A farce of a marriage, you mean? What kind of life is that? You love me, as I love you.'

'You must go back to America, Derry. Forget you ever saw me again. As I must you.'

'Come with me. We can start a new life, take on a new identity if you wish. Philip Brandon would never find us.'

'No, no. I can't do that. Looking over my shoulder for the rest of my life? Afraid for the twins every time they're late home from school? No, Derry. I must accept what cannot be altered.' His eyes glittered in the darkness, though whether with anger or tears Lissa couldn't have said. 'I'm sorry, Derry.'

'So am I. How shall I ever live without you after this? I need you, Lissa.' His mouth came down hard upon her own and for a moment she gave herself up to the savage joy of his loving.

'Please don't,' she moaned, leaning against him, lifting her lips for more kisses, loving the hardness of his body against hers. 'Don't ask for too much, Derry. I can't break my marriage vows.'

They were both breathless and tousled with wanting, afire with need, afraid of going too far and unable to break apart. His lips trailed over her throat and down to her breast, and Lissa arched her body while he kissed her some more, a burning ache in her stomach making her shiver with unspent emotion. Oh, how she wanted to give herself to him completely, for now and for all time, but how could she? She was married. Philip would be sure to find out and use it against her. And against her family.

She pulled herself away, ineffectually tidying her hair and trying not to see the dark need in his eyes. 'We must cheer up. It's not the end of the world. We'll make a wish,' she said, half laughing at the childhood memory. 'Come with me.'

Lissa took him to the edge of the tarn and, cupping her hands, filled them with water. 'Quickly! You must drink from my hands and make a wish before the water soaks away. Nick and I used to do it when we were children. Quick. Close your eyes.'

Laughing, Derry did so. 'Shall I tell you what I wished?'

'No, no, or it won't come true. Now my turn.'

She drank deeply from his hands and wished for happiness, pure and simple, for herself and her babies. Impossible. And hadn't she given up wishing long since?

They dried their hands on the grass and lay together, not touching now, staring up into a midnight blue sky, counting stars.

'You do intend to leave him eventually though?'

Lissa was silent for a long time, then uttered a deep sigh. 'I don't know. How can I say what the future holds? I would like to. Perhaps one day, if I could make a home and provide for my children without risk of losing them, then I would do so. But I have no grounds for divorce. None that the law will recognise. I've been into all of that. He would never hurt or leave them, or me. He needs us. We are his life. He won't let me go.'

'And you won't fight him?' His voice sounded harsh, so uncharacteristically unkind that Lissa turned her face away to hide the spasm of pain it caused.

'Don't blame me too harshly, Derry. I cope as best I can but what is the point of fighting if I can never win?'

'So you want me simply to pack up and go?'

'No.' She sat up, her heart breaking with the agony of it all. 'I can't bear to think of never seeing you again. But this is how it must be.'

Derry clenched his teeth. 'Yes, I dare say it must. I couldn't

368

bear to watch you with him, day after day. I'd kill him, I swear it.'

'I won't – you understand, sleep with him. That's all finished,' she said, wrapping her arms about Derry's neck, kissing him lingeringly on the mouth. 'I can only offer Philip duty now. That's part of the terms.'

They were silent for a long time after that, holding each other, happy simply to be together and think through the reality of her decision. Then of one accord their gazes locked, saying everything that they could not.

'I won't go right away. I'll leave in a week or two,' Derry said. 'A month at most. As soon as I can see that you are all right and if we haven't thought of any other solution in the meantime. Then I'll leave for America and that'll be the end.' He pulled her close, capturing the memory of this moment for all time, coming to terms with the harsh reality of a life without love.

'Oh, Derry,' she said, and surrendered herself for one last time to his fevered kisses. But it was he who kept their emotions in check that night, he who held her in his arms until she slept, then gently woke her as a cold pink dawn streaked the sky.

He led her silently back to the house, steadying her when her feet slipped on the stones, both jumping with alarm when somewhere an owl hooted, then falling into each other's arms on a spurt of nervous laughter at their foolish fear.

Their parting kisses were painfully poignant for all they promised each other to meet one last time, like this, before he left England for good.

'I love you, Lissa.'

'And I you, Derry.'

She waited until he was quite out of sight down the lane, on his way back to Ashlea before she pushed open the kitchen door and slipped inside.

Lissa crept silently up the stairs, pulled open the creaking bedroom door with a shaking hand and slid beneath the bed clothes, certain that Philip had not missed her.

She was wrong.

'I know where you've been,' he said, his voice splintering the darkness like chips of ice. 'I warned you, didn't I? What has he done to you?'

369

Lissa started to tremble. 'He has done nothing. I don't know what you mean.'

'You know well enough.' She made to get out of bed but he threw back the covers and straddled her, holding back her arms when she would have pushed him away. 'Did you use any protection? The kind you've been using with me.'

'Oh dear God. How did you find out?'

'Doc Robson.'

'He shouldn't have told you. It was confidential.'

'It was easy to persuade the silly old goat. You've made a fool out of me, Lissa, promising babies and then using a diaphragm to stop them. I don't like that. I don't like that one bit. And all this pretence of being too tired and feeling unwell. All lies. Absolute poppycock. Well, you'll not cuckold me as well as cheat me. It's long past time I re-established my rights, don't you think? I'll show Derry Colwith whose wife you are.'

Then he pushed one hand flat across her mouth, laughing into her terrified eyes, and pulled up her nightgown with the other. As he took her that night, he unleashed all the pent up frustration and ferocious anger he usually kept so tightly buttoned. And when she cried out in her agony, despite his restraining hand and her efforts not to wake Meg, he told her she must be learning to show appreciation of his attentions at last. He shouted his triumph as he climaxed, saying if this didn't do the trick and bring them babies, nothing would. And later he took her again, with no hint of consideration.

Only when he was quite sated did he finally let her turn on her side and rest, though sleep was beyond her. Silent tears slid down Lissa's cheeks, dampening her pillow and running into her ear. This would be the last time, she promised herself. The very last. She fell into a troubled doze, her body bruised and her heart breaking, wishing it had been Derry who had made love to her this night, and not Philip. Wishing it had been done with love and not hate. How different life could have been then.

Yet as morning finally came Lissa found herself wide-eyed and staring, wondering if it had been the children who had cried out. Then a pain pierced her belly and she realised it had been her own cry that had awakened her. He was on top and inside of her again, grunting noisily in a sound that curdled her stomach.

And when she protested, he wrapped her wrists in his pyjama cord and tied them to the bed head.

'I warned you,' he said, very kindly. 'You should have listened. Now you must learn by discipline.' Then he plunged into her, on and on, continuing to use her for his own pleasure whether she wanted him or not. As he had done even when she was asleep. It seemed, somehow, to be the final humiliation.

29

White pointed sails bobbing on blue water beneath a sunlit blue sky. The sounds of happy laughter ringing across the lake, bounced back by the circling mountains. The hooting of the steamer taking a group of early-season trippers to a lakeside inn for lunch. Ducks quacking and squabbling over pieces of crust thrown to them by toddlers with an unsteady aim, the tramp of boots crunching on the shingle. Any normal day by the lake. But not a normal day for Lissa.

She flew about her bedroom emptying drawers and cupboards, fingers fumbling with coat hangers. From the moment Philip had dropped them at the door and gone back to his office this morning, Lissa had been in a fever of activity. She had rung Renee to tell her she would not be into the shop this morning but now, with her suitcases finally packed, stared at them in some distress. How to get them out of the house? And there were still the twins to get ready and Nanny Sue to deal with.

Thrusting the cases back into her wardrobe she decided she would have to risk collecting them later. Perhaps she could ask Jimmy. All that mattered was that she get away.

Now she stood and gazed down at the happy scene, the blue and white image blurring in her tears. What a mess. Why couldn't she be happy as these people were happy? But this wasn't the moment for self-pity. She refused to be a victim any longer. The terms, so far as Lissa was concerned, had been broken. Now she must take her chances alone.

'I've decided to take the children out this morning,' she told Nanny Sue who at once frowned in disapproval.

'But it's very nearly their lunchtime.'

Lissa panicked, feeling the sweat start up between her breasts. Philip would be home for lunch. He would ring first, to check she was back from the shop. It had taken far too long to get ready but she couldn't stop now. She drew in a steadying breath. 'I'm taking them out to lunch. Miss Stevens is expecting us at twelve sharp. Come along, my darlings, wash your hands and find your favourite doll or teddy to come with us. We are going to have a picnic.'

Squeals of excitement and much running about and demands to change clothes, choose another toy or take a bicycle. Lissa refused all requests, keenly aware, beneath Nanny's gimlet gaze, that time was of the essence.

'Say bye bye to Nanny,' she called cheerily, trying not to appear in a hurry as she piled them into the old van. Where could she take them? Certainly not to Miss Stevens. It wouldn't be right to involve her in 'matrimonial disputes'. Nab Cottage perhaps? No, Renee would not be there. Besides, that would be the first place Philip would look. The shop then. There was nothing else for it but the rooms over the shop. Stella Stevens would have to be placated about that too, in the end.

But first the promised picnic. Lissa stopped at a bakery and bought doughnuts and tiny sausage rolls, a stick of bread, a packet of cream cheese portions, and some Grasmere gingerbread. Far too much in her panic. The twins were delighted.

'Can we have Coca-Cola?' A special treat, reminding Lissa of her teenage years.

They ate the picnic by the lake. At least the twins did, Lissa's throat refusing to swallow a morsel. And then they must play the twins' favourite games. Hide and Seek among the trees, The Big Ship Sails through the Alley-Alley-Oh. Going through the motions of normality when inside she was falling apart.

Derry was waiting on the doorstep of Nab Cottage when Renee arrived home to lunch. He seemed strangely silent, unlike his usual self, so she chatted on, saying how it made a nice break to have lunch at home in her otherwise busy day. They sat in the small parlour sipping tea and eating the potted beef sandwiches she had prepared, cut into triangles and spaced out neatly on a blue and white striped plate.

'Do you like the new style? You never said, when you called before.'

374

Derry glanced vaguely about him, trying to sound interested. 'It looks very smart.'

'I'm a girl of the sixties now,' Renee said proudly. 'With a career. But I spend my money on our home. Jimmy likes it to be comfortable.'

Gone was the brown-tiled fireplace, replaced by a neat electric fire in a teak surround. The old orange-spattered walls were now a pale cream, one of them decked out with black glass and chrome fittings on which reposed a record player, a battery of speakers, and a stack of records. Above hung a picture of a pretty Chinese girl and a photograph of Jimmy with his boat on the lake.

'I'm glad you're doing well, Renee,' Derry said and was surprised to find that he meant it. She looked different too. The orange lipstick had been replaced by palest pink against a flawless, cream-tinted skin. The red hair was puffed out on top in the new bouffant style, tucked up at the nape of her neck with a tortoiseshell comb. She looked attractive, and surprisingly smart and tidy in a neat trouser suit of pale green linen. 'Dad looks well too, happier than I've ever seen him.' He gave her a wry grin. 'I can see I was wrong about you two.'

Renee's eyes glimmered. 'Odd couple we may be, but well suited, eh?' she said drily.

'Something like that. It all seems to have worked out right for you.'

Renee recognised the haunting sadness in his voice. 'You haven't done so badly yourself. Got a good job in a top Jack agency. Making loads of money by the looks of you. Swanky car back home, eh? Fancy house, I shouldn't wonder.'

Derry's eyes were bleak as they looked anywhere but into hers. 'I've done all right. I was near starvation at one time, then one guy took pity on me and gave me a job as a gofer.'

'Gofer?'

'Go for this, go for that. It's an American term.'

Renee chortled with glee. 'I like it. And the rest is history, eh?'

'I worked my way up, with hard graft and lots of boot licking. Now I'm a partner in the business. I even enjoy the work, feel like I'm doing some good helping the poor over-optimistic souls to get going in the music trade on the right terms. The contract is all, you see. Or gently letting down those who'll never make it.'

'So your training as a lawyer's clerk has come in handy after all?'

'I suppose it has.' He set aside a half eaten sandwich and flopped back in the chair, clenching his fists on a spurt of anger. 'But for what purpose? What's the good of being successful when you can't buy the one thing you need most in all the world?'

'Lissa?'

'Lissa.'

They were both silent for a long moment, even the loquacious Renee lost for words. He stood up. 'I have to go. I wanted to ask you . . .'

Renee looked up at him with a smile, her eyes kind. 'Ask away, lad.'

'Look after her for me, that's all. I'll be staying at Ashlea for a week or two yet, till I'm sure she's OK. Then I'd like to spend a day or two here, with Dad, before I leave.'

'Yes to both requests. You're always welcome here, it's your second home. No more garden sheds, I promise.'

He laughed fondly at the memory but then saw that she wasn't joining in. 'It's all right,' he said, grinning. 'I bear no grudges. I probably deserved to be turfed out, behaving with typical teenage arrogance and total lack of consideration at the time.'

'No, it's not that.' Renee got up and started to tidy and smooth the blue and yellow scatter cushions on an already immaculate sofa. She spoke quickly as if to get it done with. 'I haven't told your dad but I went to see Philip Brandon. I told him I wanted you out from under my feet. That Jimmy and me wanted to be on us own. It was Philip Brandon's idea to put you in the shed. And he said he'd encourage you to find a place of your own.' She slanted a glance across at Derry, saw his frozen expression.

'I only wanted him to give you a raise,' she explained. 'So's you'd have enough to pay the rent. And to ask his advice on bed and breakfast and that.'

'Instead of which he cut off my home base then made up a tale about my damaging his yacht and sacked me on the spot.'

Renee looked horrified. 'Oh, my giddy aunt! It's as bad as I thought then. Worse. Why didn't you tell us? Did he threaten you with the police?'

'Yep.'

'And that's why you left?'

'That's why I left. That and my own arrogant ambition.'

Renee gazed at him, stricken, realising how they'd both been manipulated. 'He wanted Lissa. That's what it was all about. He'd fancied her for a long while. By heck, it's obvious now, isn't it?'

'I was all too aware of his interest. Jealous as hell I was. Only I was too wrapped up in my own ambitions, silly dreams really, to do anything about it. I stupidly thought she'd wait for me. But then it didn't work out and I couldn't come back to her a failure, could I? And when I did it was too late. Philip Brandon had won.'

He sank back into his chair and Renee went to him and patted his shoulder, feeling helpless in his despair. 'Nay, lad, what could you have done? You'd no money to fight him. Lissa chose to wed him. A mistake she now regrets and can't get out of. I've known there was summat up for ages, though it took her a while to admit to it. And it's mebbe all my fault. Oh dear God!'

'It would still have happened, Renee, with or without your complicity. And, no, I won't tell Dad you had anything to do with it, if that's what's worrying you. You don't need to blame yourself.'

Renee blinked away the prick of tears. 'That's the nicest thing you've ever said to me. It took me ages to pacify him after your last visit.'

They both gave an embarrassed laugh at the memory of their impromptu kiss.

'You're all right, Renee, you know that?'

'And you don't have to worry. I'll keep an eye out for her. It'll all come to an head soon enough, you'll see if it don't.'

'If he treats her badly, I'll . . .'

'Don't say it, lad,' Renee interrupted. 'It'll do no good. Don't even think it. Now I'd best get back to work or I'll be given my cards.'

'I've done it, Renee. I've left him.'

'Crikey, I never thought you would!' She stared at Lissa in disbelief and some concern, and at the two children beside her, faces daubed with jam, innocent of their new status in life.

'We had a lovely picnic, Renee.'

'And Mummy says we can sleep at the shop tonight.'

'Well, well. Orphans in the storm, eh?'

'There's so much I have to arrange. My luggage, for one thing. Two suitcases in my wardrobe. Do you think Jimmy would . . .? He'd have to go this afternoon, while Philip is in the office and Nanny is out on her walk.'

'I'll see to it.'

'Is it clean upstairs, do you think?'

'Clean enough but . . .'

'Oh, I have so many plans, Renee. I'm going to live up there, if Miss Stevens is agreeable. And develop the business, and . . .'

Alarmed by the feverish brightness of Lissa's chatter, Renee put out a gentle hand. 'Aye, well let's get these bairns cleaned up and seen to first, shall we?'

By half-past five the shop was locked up for the day. The children had been fed and put early to bed, unprotesting for once, because of the novelty of being in sleeping bags on the floor of a tiny room above the shop.

'Is this a real 'venture, Mummy?' they asked.

'Yes, my darlings. A real adventure.'

'Will Daddy be coming to share it?' Beth wanted to know.

'Not tonight. Now close your eyes. You've had a busy few days. Far too much excitement.' She kissed each soft round cheek, left a small night lamp lit and crept downstairs with a sigh of relief.

'I'll count up the takings tonight, Renee. You must be worn out.'

'Not too bad. That new girl is shaping up pretty well. Been busy though. Sold three of those new hooded jackets.'

'That's good.' Lissa struggled to find the necessary enthusiasm as she clasped and unclasped her hands, unable to resist glancing at the door.

'Do you think he'll come?' Renee asked.

'I-I don't know. I hope not. I don't think I could take any more just now.'

'Did you leave a note?'

Lissa swallowed and managed a brief nod.

'I'll stay with you,' Renee decided.

'No, no, there's no need. I'll be fine.'

'Nevertheless I'm staying. I'll go and explain to our Jimmy, then I'll be back.' She grinned. 'Have you had any supper?'

Lissa shook her head.

'Then I'll fetch some fish and chips and a couple of beers. We'll have a party to celebrate your freedom. Why not?'

'Why not?' Lissa grinned back, trying to recapture her earlier mood of optimism.

They drank the bottled beer and ate the fish and chips, licking salt

378

and vinegar from their fingers like giggling children. Renee insisted on staying until it was quite late before finally being persuaded to go home to Jimmy. Then Lissa climbed the stairs on weary feet, putting out the lights as she went. She was glad to be alone at last, wanting to think and work out what was best to be done, but her mind was too tired to function.

She scrubbed her face and teeth, dragged a brush through her long hair and softly kissed each sleeping twin. Then she climbed into her own improvised sleeping bag with a sigh of relief. It felt strange, and oddly exhilarating. Whatever the future brought, she would face it.

It was five past midnight when she heard the hammering on the door. Lissa struggled from her bed, rubbing the sleep from her eyes and went to the landing window.

Philip stood below, standing at the door of the shop. She pushed open the tiny window and called down, as quietly as she could so as not to wake the twins.

'What are you doing here at this time?'

'I need to talk to you. Open the door, Lissa.'

'No, Philip. I can't talk now. I *won't* talk now,' she said. 'Perhaps in the morning. Or when I feel ready.' She started to close the window when he thumped his fist against the door. The noise echoed in the empty street.

'Don't you walk away from me when I'm talking to you. You are my *wife*, and will obey me. Come home at once.'

'It's no good shouting, Philip, I'm not coming home.'

'I never shout.'

'No, you don't, do you? But you give plenty of orders. Unfortunately I'm not prepared to obey them any more.'

He raised two clenched fists, looking for a moment like a man ready to beat in the door if he had to. 'Where are my children? I insist on seeing my children.'

She told him, with surprising calm, that they were asleep. 'I need my sleep too. We'll talk tomorrow, Philip. There are a number of things we ought to discuss, including a divorce.' Whereupon she closed the window firmly on his silent rage.

He did not come in the morning, nor the next day. In those first few weeks, Lissa began to worry over what he was up to and her feeling of victory quite evaporated, almost to the extent of wishing the reckless words unsaid. She knew it would not be easy to start again from scratch, to face the gossip and snide remarks. A strange malaise came over her. Lissa felt too ashamed even to go out. Her marriage had failed and she could not bring herself to walk down the street. She felt sure that everyone would see her shame and remark upon it. They would say that it was her fault, that she was never able to keep anyone's love, that there must be something wrong with her.

Derry came but she sent him away. 'It wouldn't be safe,' she told him. 'Don't come here again. My case is weak enough. If Philip were to find you . . . I must think of the children.'

Renee proved to be a tower of strength. Together they scrubbed and cleaned, tidied and decorated, turning two rooms and a small washroom into a presentable home. The twins joined in with exuberance, not understanding anything that was going on. Renee lent Lissa pieces of furniture and carpet she'd borrowed from friends and neighbours. Then she and Jimmy carried up a table and three chairs from the stock room.

'They're not exactly polished mahogany but they'll happen do for now.'

'Everything's wonderful, Renee. I'm so grateful.'

'Are we going to live here?' Sarah demanded, her small heart-shaped face a mask of affronted dignity, as if she should have been consulted on the subject. 'Where will Nanny Sue sleep?'

'And Daddy?' put in Beth.

'I'll explain later,' Lissa said, wondering how these matters could ever be satisfactorily explained to a four year old. She pushed back an untidy lock of hair, thinking how dreadful she must look since she'd hardly had time to attend to herself recently. She spread out her hands and frowned at the nails, broken and chipped, the pink varnish peeling. Philip would not approve, she thought, and then her heart flooded with relief. It didn't matter what Philip thought. He didn't control her any more. She found a pair of scissors and began to cut them.

'What are you doing?' Sarah, ever curious, wanted to know.

'Cutting my nails, darling. They get in the way when I'm working. And I must work very hard in future.' She would tell them soon, she thought, when she'd worked it all out.

And all this on top of what was proving to be a busier season than they'd ever hoped for. But at least Lissa no longer had to hide herself away in the office. She could take a full and active part in the day to day running of the business.

The first time she walked down Carndale Road she felt certain everyone was looking at her.

'Stick your chin up lass, and smile,' said Renee, at her elbow as usual. 'Everyone has some cross to bear, this is yours. Let them see you aren't bending under it.'

And so Lissa lifted her chin, straightened her spine and held fast to her courage. At least Philip was leaving her alone. Perhaps at last, she thought, I am free.

It was well into August before she found time to make an appointment to see her solicitor and tell him the news. He seemed less than enchanted by it and kept plucking at his lower lip, making worried little noises. 'Such a pity that you walked out on him, Mrs Brandon. Dear, dear. So difficult.'

'I've asked Philip for a divorce and he has gone away to consider the matter.' He had yet to acknowledge her request but Lissa was determined to think positive. He had simply stormed off in the middle of that first night, in the closest to a temper she had ever seen him. But he would be forced to consider it, wouldn't he, in the end?

'Hmm,' said the young solicitor and proceeded to repeat his warning that the divorce law, as it stood at present, was not favourable to an easy divorce. 'There must be no sign of complicity between you. It was misguided of you to leave. Much better had it been the other way around.'

She told him what Philip had done on their last night together. The solicitor seemed remarkably unimpressed.

'As I tried to explain to you before, Mrs Brandon, deficiencies in the bedchamber are hardly grounds. Many people indulge in such games. Consenting adults and all that.'

'But that's the whole point. It wasn't a game, and I didn't consent.'

'Did he hit you?'

'No.'

'No bruises then.' He seemed disappointed, then shook his head and tugged on his lip again. 'You are his wife, you see. Most judges would consider that complicity enough. They simply would refuse to grant a divorce on those grounds.'

'But the marriage is *over*.' Lissa felt as if she were battering her head against a brick wall yet knew the fault was not with the solicitor, who was only doing his job. 'He rules my life, my thinking, he suffocates me and I can't stand it any more.'

The solicitor offered his sympathies but declared himself unable to change the law. 'It is government policy not to make divorce too easy or the courts would be full of women wanting their freedom, claiming their rights.' He laughed with slight embarrassment and Lissa could only grit her teeth with vexation.

'Then what can I do?'

'Leave it with me for a while. I'll give the matter some thought, perhaps take counsel's opinion. We'll do what we can.' He spread his hands then quietly clasped them, concluding the matter. 'And I'll write to your husband, sound out his feelings.'

She offered her thanks and got up to go.

'He will, of course, be entitled to access.'

'Access?'

'To the children. Perhaps every Saturday or Sunday. That is the usual method.'

Dear God, of course, access. 'Oh no, I couldn't possibly have him take them away.' How did she know that he would bring them back?

The solicitor looked surprised. 'I'm afraid you must. It is his right.'

Lissa was almost choking with fear now. Couldn't the man see what Philip was like? He would take the twins simply to spite her, to use them as a pawn to control her, as he so liked to do. 'He'll only leave them with the nanny. What about my rights as a mother? Can't it wait until this divorce question is settled?'

He took her elbow and led her to the door. 'Don't worry, Mrs Brandon. He's a man of honour. You surely don't imagine he would hurt them, do you?'

'No. No, of course not.'

A smile and a pat on her hand. 'There we are then. I'll be in touch. Good day.'

The bus took for ever on her journey back from Kendal to Carreckwater. It crawled through every village, stopping frequently, the bus conductor chatting with everyone who got on and off as if there were all the time in the world. But there wasn't. She'd foolishly left her children behind, and though Lissa trusted Renee implicitly, how would she cope if Philip took it into his head to come for them? Lissa decided never to let them out of her sight again.

'They're in the stock room trying on hats, I shouldn't wonder,' said Renee, in some surprise at Lissa's high state of anxiety. 'Don't fret, lass. They'll come to no harm with Aunty Renee. I'd soon see that one off, should he turn up again.'

'Oh, I'm so sorry for doubting you.'

'There now, I'm almost forgetting. Jan rang, seemed in a bit of a lather. Will you ring the moment you get in? she says.'

Lissa pulled off her coat and smiled at Renee, shamefaced. 'Any tea going?'

'That's more like it. I'll go and see if I can find the kettle. Look after the shop, Julie, and call me if you've any problems. And try not to get in a muddle with that new till.'

'Yes, Mrs Colwith,' said the young girl, trying to look important.

Lissa dialled the number for Ashlea, wondering if perhaps there was some problem over the latest batch of woollens. Had they run out of wool? Or got confused over the sizes and patterns she wanted? She hadn't been giving her proper attention to the business these last weeks and tomorrow she must go and see Miss Stevens. It was vitally important that they should feel secure now.

'Hello?' Jan's voice, frail and anxious, came on the phone and Lissa proceeded to ask about everyone's health, in particular little Robbie and Alice, but Jan was not in the mood for small talk and quickly interrupted: 'Is Nick there? Has he come to see you?'

'Nick? No. Why should he be here?'

'We've had another letter,' she said, almost shouting down the line. 'He's foreclosed on us, Lissa. He's evicting us, turning us out. Sally Ann is nearly having a heart attack here, and Nick has stormed off threatening blue murder.'

'Evicted? What are you talking about?'

'I'm talking about your husband turning us out on the streets. Well, the open fell.'

Lissa could hardly believe what she was hearing and managed, at last, to say as much.

'Why? That's what we want to know.' Jan's voice was growing hysterical. 'You promised to give us time and we've made some payments recently. We were catching up nicely, only he says we're further behind than we think and he won't give us any more time. Why, Lissa? What have we ever done to you?'

Lissa's heart was beating twenty to the dozen and she felt suddenly sick. It was perfectly plain how Philip's mind was working. 'You haven't done anything, Jan. I'm the one who has upset him and he's taking his revenge out on you. Only he won't succeed. I won't let him. I'll fight him over this, I promise.'

'You'd better. God knows where we'll go, what we'll do, if we lose the farm. Things were just starting to improve and . . .' Tears drowned her next words and it took some time for Lissa to calm her down before she could ring off.

Lissa rang her new solicitor right away and told him to get the eviction order quashed and to take all her financial affairs away from her husband. She wondered why she hadn't thought to do it in the first place.

'He can do nothing without my signature,' she said. And the solicitor saw no reason why the matter couldn't be satisfactorily settled.

Lissa immediately rang Jan and told her the good news but when she'd rung off this time wished with all her heart that her own affairs could be so easily settled.

Philip had very efficiently proved that he still held the power. He'd demonstrated that he could, and would, carry out his threats. First Ashlea, next Broombank? Would he also manage to persuade Manchester Water Board to choose Broomdale as a site for their reservoir, just so he could take pleasure in destroying all their lives and lining his own pocket in the process?

And almost worse than all of that was his most dire threat of all. He would never let her go. Never.

30

Autumn had passed and winter was approaching. There was a nip in the air that bit at small fingers and toes but the twins were not short of warm woollens to keep them warm. Sarah had a red knitted coat and hat with a tasselled scarf that wound round and round her neck, and Beth a blue set, exactly the same. The twins wore them every day with pride, and to show off to their friends at the infant school they attended. They were learning to read and do sums, which made them feel very grown up. But it was still difficult sometimes to understand about adult things, like why a mummy and daddy lived in two different places.

Sarah had asked once or twice but got no answer that quite made sense. She missed Nanny Sue and the clean starchy smell of her apron but Beth missed Daddy most of all. Beth was Daddy's pet. Sometimes, on a Sunday, he would come and take them for a walk or to play in the park. But only for a short while. Then he would leave them with Nanny Sue and go back to his office to work. He was a very busy and important man, as all Daddys were, he said.

The first time had been the worst. Mummy's lip had trembled like when Beth fell down and didn't want to show how it hurt. Sarah knew she hadn't wanted to let them go but Daddy had insisted. So Sarah hadn't enjoyed herself that day, thinking that Mummy might be at home, crying. She'd refused to speak to Daddy or anyone, just to show she could please herself who she wished to be friends with.

But it was better now. Mummy said she knew that the twins were safe and would always come back, which had puzzled Sarah for a long time. How could they not be safe with Daddy?

'It will soon be all over,' Daddy promised them. 'Then we can be together for always.' But it wasn't over. New beds had been bought for them, their bedroom walls decorated with Magic Roundabout pictures and there was no talk of going back to their house on the Parade.

Sarah didn't really mind. She quite liked living above the shop and Renee was fun. She let them play with the till sometimes and help wrap things in tissue paper for the customers.

But they both missed their big garden at home, their sand pit and swing. It seemed mean of Mummy not to let them go there more often. But she was much happier these days, always laughing and singing as she worked in the shop, playing games with them all the time, and so much more fun. She would let them sit up sometimes and watch Mr Pastry on television or eat dinner with a candle on the table as if it were a real dinner party and they were grown ups.

At other times she was too tired to be bothered and then Sarah worried. Why did she work so hard? Why was she always on the telephone or buzzing about in the van just when they needed her? It wasn't fair that both Mummy and Daddy should work so hard. But whenever Sarah complained, Mummy would only smile and tell her that she had to earn a living, didn't she, to buy them all the bread and jam and cake they ate.

Perhaps it was something they had done? Did they cost a lot of money to keep? And what would happen if they grew and got too expensive to keep? Sarah worried. Perhaps if they gave up cakes for tea or saved up their pocket money to pay for the Magic Roundabout pictures? Perhaps then Mummy could afford to keep them. Or they could ask Daddy for more help.

'Is it my fault Daddy doesn't want us to live with him any more?' she ventured to ask one night. Mummy had just finished telling them the tale of the Three Little Pigs and was tucking Beth up and tickling her, so was in a jolly mood. It seemed a good moment to risk it.

She looked surprised and troubled by the question. 'Darling, no, of course not. And he does still want us. He does love you. It's simply that we don't love each other. We can't be happy together. Sometimes that happens with a Mummy and a Daddy. But it has nothing to do with you two. It isn't your fault, my darlings.' And she kissed them both again which made Sarah feel better.

'You love Derry, don't you?' Beth calmly said and Lissa started. Could the child be quite so astute or was she only repeating what she

386

had heard? Her next words confirmed it. 'Daddy told us. He says Derry Colwith has spoiled our lives and will be the death of us all.'

'Oh, Beth, what a dreadful thing for Daddy to say!' Lissa burst out, aghast. 'That simply isn't true. I've known Derry for a long time, since I was a young girl in fact. He's an old friend, that's all.' Two pairs of questioning eyes, one grey, one blue, regarded her with uncanny shrewdness.

'Are you going to marry him instead of Daddy?' Sarah asked, frowning and feeling that odd, uncertain feeling again somewhere in her tummy.

'No, no, of course not,' Lissa hastily assured them and inside felt suddenly and intensely cold, and rather sick. What had Philip been doing? Was he deliberately trying to poison the twins' minds against Derry? 'Anyway,' she laughed, 'would it be so very terrible? Derry is nice and very good fun. You'd like him.'

'We like Daddy,' Beth said, pursing her small mouth.

'Of course you do, darling. I love you both, that's all that matters, isn't it?'

Twin smiles, heads nodding, eyes wide and dark from tiredness.

'Then leave these matters to Mummy and Daddy to worry over. Now go to sleep both of you, it's very late.'

Despite her natural worries about the twins, and the inevitable confusion they suffered, Lissa was certain they would settle in the end. And she was happy. 'It's working fine,' she told Renee. 'He's accepted the separation better than I could ever have hoped for.'

Even if there never is a divorce, Lissa thought, I'm happier here, in my private world above the shop, than in the awful pretence of marriage with him. I have my children, my lovely twins, and the excitement of a developing business. What more could I want?

Now that she was free of Philip's critical restrictions, Lissa felt as if she had emerged from a long dark tunnel and found life shining and new at the end of it.

The frame knitting machines were delivered to Broombank and two women found who understood how to set up and operate them. A thriving industry was quickly developing with a third woman entirely occupied cutting the rectangles and squares of machine knitting into the sleeves, fronts and backs for jerseys. These were then sewn together on machines by a group of young girls who came every day from Kendal. The welts of the neckline were then knitted up by a special machine and the finished garment checked for any mistakes, dropped stitches, flaws or changes of dye colour in the wool.

Lissa was rarely still for a moment. She took every opportunity to drive up to Broombank and check on the work in progress. Not that she really had any need, for Jan was responsible for managing this side of the business and performed it with great flair and skill. But Lissa loved to take the twins with her, see Meg and Tam and make a family day of it. It was fun. Life was fun.

The moment she'd been sure all was going well at Broombank, she'd set out on the road in search of orders. She was racked with nerves at first, and approached the proprietors of shops with diffidence and some embarrassment. They proved reluctant to commit themselves despite being impressed with the samples she showed them.

'I'll think about it,' they'd say. Or, 'Well, I'm not buying at the moment. Maybe next season, if it's a good one. I'll let you know.'

Gritting her teeth and promising to call again, just in case, Lissa pressed on to the next shop, and the one after that.

She drove from town to town all over Lakeland, Lancashire and parts of Yorkshire, trying every means of persuasion she could think of. She offered discounts for bulk purchase, personal service, a wide selection of colours, and of course whatever delivery date they required.

'Christmas is coming. How about some lovely snowflake sweaters? They went well in our own shop this summer.' Trying not to show the desperate need for an order in her calm voice.

'Well, I'd try mebbe half a dozen. See how they go.'

'Wonderful.' She wrote the order in the book, trying not to let her customer see that he was her first. And went back on the road with a marvellous boost to her confidence.

Bit by bit the order book for next season was growing nicely, and a few orders for Christmas were looked upon as a bonus.

'It's going to work.' Lissa squealed in delight to Renee when she came home with her first orders. And they celebrated with a bottle of wine and cream cakes, which the twins loved of course, getting much of it in their hair.

Once, she had the idea to visit some local council offices where after several frustrating hours of being kept waiting and passed from department to department she talked with the right person and gained an order for two dozen working jerseys, in green, with leather patches on shoulders and elbows, for the town refuse collectors. It was her largest order to date and so filled her with optimism she went off to other towns seeking similar contracts.

'Slow down,' Jan laughed. 'Don't over-stretch us.'

'I intend to try councils in Lancashire, Yorkshire and the Midlands next year,' she said, her enthusiasm growing. 'Then perhaps we'll tap the export market after that. Holland perhaps, they have cold winters. We could design some skating sweaters, Jan.'

'Good idea, but not all at once, right?'

'The ever practical Jan.' But it was good advice which Lissa took note of. The excitement of developing her own business thrilled and engrossed her far more than she would ever have thought possible. Gone was the hesitant, over-anxious woman she had been during her marriage and in her place grew one who was strong and confident of her own abilities. It was a good feeling.

Even the water consultant was no longer in residence at Nab Cottage and Lissa hoped that Philip had forgotten all about his dreadful threat. He certainly seemed to have accepted the situation and was not a problem to her these days. She scarcely had time to think about him anyway, as each day seemed filled with activity, and always different. No two days were the same.

The twins had settled into school well, she'd improved their little flat, even persuaded Miss Stevens to let them have the lease on a secure tenure after all. And as she built up security in her life, for the children and with her business, Lissa began to feel safe herself, for the first time in years.

The one flaw, and one which yawned wide and dark and empty within, was her longing for Derry, which never for a moment eased. He was still staying with Jimmy and Renee, seemingly reluctant to leave. Lissa took care never to mention him to Renee, nor did he ever call at the flat or ring her up. But it was, of course, quite impossible entirely to ignore him.

They continued to meet, infrequently and in secret, and never by the lake in case Philip should see them. But it would have been easier to deny herself breath than not to see Derry, however rare or brief the occasion.

He provided yet another pressing reason for her to visit the quiet fells of Broomdale and Larkrigg, where they could walk together without fear of being disturbed. It was the one place she felt safe. On these days, as today, she told no one of her

389

visit, not even Meg. And she chose a time when the twins were in school.

'We really shouldn't meet like this,' she told him now, slipping her arms about his neck and laying her cheek against his chest so she could breathe in the crisp, clean scent of him. 'If Philip were to find out . . .'

'He won't. I've missed you Lissa. It must be a whole week since I held you like this.' He held her fast in his arms, one hand gently cupping her breast and fire shot through her, making her gasp with pleasure and fierce need. How could she bear not to love him totally when she wanted him so much? Why did she stick so stubbornly to her worn out marriage vows? She worried that he would grow tired of her and leave, and how could she bear to lose him?

'I used to think I was frigid,' she told him, lifting her mouth to his, and blushed as she saw his eyes kindle with excitement, his arms tightening instinctively about her. For a long while they had no breath left for talking.

'Frigid my giddy aunt! Don't I prove otherwise every time we're together? I want you so much, Lissa, I'm not sure I can bear not to take you, here and now upon the heather.' He slipped his hand beneath her sweater so he could smooth the silken skin of her back and then beneath her bra to caress the luscious softness of her breast. It peaked hard and wanting beneath his fingers and he felt he would go mad with desire.

Lissa didn't help much either. She never resisted his caresses, rather encouraged them, giving a soft groan, pressing closer, her body begging for more. 'You know I can't, Derry. Don't ask. Please.' And, as usual, they would break apart, tense and troubled, to walk in silence and try not to think, not to touch each other. It was always this way, but after a few yards their fingers would interlock, their bodies sway close together again and moments later his arm would creep about her waist and she would lean her head on his shoulder with a sigh.

'When you go away will you forget me?' she asked, breathless with pain as she waited for his reply.

'Yes,' he said, 'instantly.'

Lissa jerked her head up to meet his serious gaze, then saw the anguish lurking there and playfully buffeted him with her fist. 'Don't tease me, I'm serious.'

'So am I. Desperately. How can I bear to let myself think of you when I can't have you? Will he ever let you go?'

Lissa turned her head away, her face tightening. 'He's said nothing for ages. I don't honestly know. Perhaps, when the twins are grown. For now I've given up hope. What grounds do I have? He hasn't been cruel or unfaithful or anything, and would take me back tomorrow like a shot. Everyone thinks him charming and handsome and well mannered, and that I must be mad to leave him. Which he is, that's the pity of it.'

'And a bastard.'

'Derry.'

'Isn't he?'

She stared at the ground and kicked at a stone. 'Let's not talk about him, you know it only upsets me.' Silence again, more strained this time.

After a time they stopped and leaned on a stile to gaze out at the mountains. Coppergill Pass and its neighbours. Dundale Knot, her favourite, its bowed head wreathed in grey mist, like a vicar's collar. The escarpment below the summit was pock-marked with old mine workings, grooved by shifting ice, and plunged downward to the valley floor below and a patchwork of green fields and grey stone walls. Sheep stood about, peacefully chewing or resting in the sweet grass, undisturbed by the two lover's quiet presence.

'I love this place,' she said.

Lissa hadn't told Derry of Philip's threat to persuade the water consultant to choose this dale for the reservoir. She hadn't told anyone, hoping that it would never ever happen, though it haunted her sometimes, at night, when she couldn't sleep. She had hurt Meg once before, she couldn't bear to do it again. It would be too dreadful. She risked so much by continuing to see Derry. Too much perhaps.

'Meg and her family have worked this land for generations. Her brother, Grandfather Joe and his father before him, and Meg's old friend Lanky, who left Broombank to her. And she scraped and saved, working all through the war to buy it and enough sheep to get her farm going. Sally Ann too had her struggles. How would they bear it if they lost it?' But she didn't say, 'Because of me. Because of us.'

'Why should they? It won't ever happen.'

'I hope not.' Silence for a moment. 'Philip has been surprisingly good about all this, better than I expected, but I don't entirely trust him. Look what he tried to do to Nick and Jan. He keeps his word. If he ever found out about us . . .' A shiver ran through her body and Derry felt it. It gave him the strength to tell her what he must.

He rubbed his finger on a fringe of lichen that clothed the rough wooden post with its coating of velvet. 'I've been thinking that too. I don't want you to suffer. And also I'm human enough not to be able to bear to be around you without – without wanting you too much.' He took a deep breath. 'I've decided. I leave next Monday, on the morning train from Windermere.' He didn't look at her now, though he sensed her whole body stiffen at his words. 'Long past time I did, eh?'

Lissa did not reply. She couldn't. Her throat seemed locked fast in pain.

'Then we must both get on with our new lives,' he said, and there was such bitterness in his voice that she was forced to find her voice, trying to soothe him.

'Yes,' she said. 'I see that would be for the best.' And she turned away, knowing that if she stayed with him another moment she would beg him never to leave her, and she dared not succumb to such wanton emotion. The risks were too high.

Derry stayed by the stile, watching her lithe figure walk away over Larkrigg Fell, her dark cloud of hair lifting in the breeze. When she reached the standing stones by the lane she turned and shielded her eyes to gaze back up at him and lift an arm in a single wave, then she climbed into her car and drove home to her twins while Derry looked back at the mountains, no longer able to see the beauty of the scene.

The next few days Lissa walked about in a daze. She had known, of course, that their idyll could not last. Hadn't they accepted long since that he must leave? What then had she expected or hoped for? That Derry's departure could be delayed indefinitely? Why? For what purpose? There was no solution to her problem, no escape from her marriage. How foolish. How naïve of her to think she could keep him. Soon Derry would be gone and she would be alone.

Lissa was at her lowest ebb when Philip called to see her that following Sunday afternoon. The shop was closed, Renee was at Nab Cottage making something delicious, no doubt, for Jimmy's lunch. And the twins were in their beds having a short afternoon nap.

'Wake them in a moment,' he said. 'There's something I wish to discuss with you first.'

She was at once on her guard, feeling alone and vulnerable. He usually sent Nanny Sue to collect them, as he knew it made her feel more comfortable. She supposed it was the only reason he kept the woman on, and felt oddly grateful. 'I don't want any trouble, Philip. Please don't start any.'

'Have I caused any problems so far?'

'N-no.' Lissa hated herself for trembling, and drew in a deep breath, steadying her nerve. She had nothing to fear from Philip any more. No longer could he bully her or demolish her with a well-chosen piece of criticism. She was free of his cutting tongue at least.

'Then let us continue to be civilised about all of this, shall we?'

'I'm sorry. Would you like coffee, a cup of tea?'

He smiled at her. 'I would like you to simply sign this paper and I will go away and leave you in peace. For ever.'

'What?' She stared at it, white and rustling in his hand. 'What is it?'

'What is it you've been asking for all these weeks? A divorce. To be free of me. I have come to the realisation that there is little point in continuing with this sham of a marriage. I dislike bitterness and rancour. Surely we can be two modern-thinking adults and accept the inevitable?'

Excitement leapt in her breast. 'Oh, Philip, do you really mean it?'

'You only have to sign.'

Caution reasserted itself as she recalled how he had so carefully controlled her. 'But why? I realise you've treated me with more consideration recently but why this sudden decision to let me go?'

'Perhaps I don't like soiled goods.'

Lissa flushed deeply and at once protested. 'That's not true. Derry and I never – never . . . I swear I've kept my marriage vows to you, Philip.'

'And in your mind?' He held out the paper, a frown of irritation on his handsome face as she took it from him. 'I think not. I deserve a wife who gives herself whole-heartedly to me, not grudgingly, as you have done. I am not made of stone, Lissa. You have hurt me.'

She looked at him properly then and saw the sadness in his eyes, the etched lines of worry about his mouth and shame flooded through

her. She rested her hand for a brief moment on his arm. 'I'm sorry.'
She should never have married him of course. Lissa knew now that
she had never loved him. No wonder their marriage had failed. Now
she held the key to her freedom in her hand. She only had to sign and
she would get her divorce. Derry wouldn't have to leave tomorrow
and they could start a new life together. Hope started up deep inside,
conflicting with the strange new pity she now felt for her husband.
'I realise I've been an inadequate wife from the first. You're right.
You do deserve better. We simply aren't suited, Philip, that's all.'

'And you think Derry Colwith will suit you better? He'll let you
down of course, in the end, as he did before.' Philip's voice was
filled with a quiet bitterness but Lissa shook her head, her eyes soft
with love.

'Stop it, Philip. You don't know him as I do. I am sorry that I've
hurt you by leaving. But you know there is no future for us together.
I must be free.'

'Then let us not prolong the agony further.' He held out the pen.

Somewhere in her head a voice spoke to her. *He's a solicitor and
knows the law and you know nothing*. She paused. 'Perhaps I should
speak to my solicitor first.'

'I've sent him a copy. Let's make this as painless as possible,
shall we? You may doubt my ability as a husband but surely not
as a professional man? Either you want your freedom or you don't
but my time and patience are limited, as you well know.'

Her confidence evaporated in a cloud of confusion as it always
did when he spoke to her in that condescending way. Lissa recalled
how his clients always changed into their best suit before keeping an
appointment with him, and never questioned his word or honour. On
matters concerning his profession he was surely entirely honourable.
And if she hurried she could catch Derry before he left. She signed
the paper and handed him back the pen with a smile of relief.

'At least we have the twins,' she said. 'We made a good job
of them.'

'Yes,' he said, folding the paper and slipping it into his briefcase.
'We have the twins. Nanny will be along to collect them as usual.
Make sure they are dressed warmly. We thought a little trip to
Grasmere this afternoon.' And as she unlocked the shop door to
let him out he took her hand gently in his.

'You know that if you change your mind I'd take you back. These
papers could be torn up. I'd never let you down, Lissa. Never.'

The urge to remove her hand from his grasp was compelling but Lissa felt she couldn't do so without seeming cruel and rude. She managed a smile. 'You've no need to worry over me. I'll be fine, thanks. Let's leave it at that, shall we?'

'As you wish. Two-thirty then for the twins, on the dot.'

'Two-thirty.'

She was all eagerness to please and had the twins ready in their new hooded jackets when Nanny called. Lissa kissed each in turn, making sure their mittens, hanging on a tape threaded through their knitted coat, were fitted on each small hand. 'No taking them off now,' she warned. 'It's quite cold out.' Lissa smiled at Nanny Sue. 'Watch Beth, she might be starting with a cold. Perhaps she shouldn't come with you.'

'Fresh air never did a cold any harm,' said the starchy nanny, well wrapped up in her grey overcoat and hat. 'Come along girls, Daddy is waiting.' And with a wave and a kiss, they left.

That Sunday afternoon Derry was saying goodbye to his sister. They'd enjoyed a substantial roast lunch and she had issued her usual list of instructions, just as if he were still a young boy.

'Don't leave it so long before you visit us next time,' Jan warned. 'We are your family, remember.' And hugging her, Derry made his promises.

'I'll walk up to Broombank and say goodbye to Meg and Tam before I go. Then I'll stay with Dad tonight and be off first thing in the morning.'

Jan looked sorrowful. 'You'll say goodbye to Lissa before you go?'

Derry drew in a quick breath and briefly shook his head. 'We've said all there is to say. Stop your bossing, sister dear. Produce lots more nephews and nieces for me.' And dodging her slap he went off, laughing. If he hadn't, he might well have cried.

Meg was far more blunt and to the point. 'I was wrong about you, lad,' she said as she met him at the door and kissed his cheek. 'I'm sorry. If I hadn't interfered that day perhaps things might have been different for you two.'

Derry shook his head. 'I doubt it. There were mistakes made, and complications. Still are.'

Meg stood with him in the old porch at Broombank, her grey eyes troubled. 'Lissa isn't happy about your leaving though, is she?'

Derry gave her a quizzical look. 'She's told you that her marriage is over?'

Meg gave an exasperated sigh. 'Eventually she did. She's so proud, bottles everything up. Always has been so. Oh, but I grieve for her, I really do. Not that I was surprised. The cracks have been showing for a while. Only this will make her feel even more unwanted and rejected.'

'She left him, not the other way about.'

'I know. Even so . . .'

'Philip won't give her grounds for divorce, not yet, so . . .'

'So you have to go or you'll complicate matters?' Derry nodded and a small sad silence fell as Meg nodded her understanding. 'We've made up our difference now, Lissa and me, but I often think she'd have been so much happier if she had at least met Kath, if only once. A girl likes to know what her own natural mother looks like at least, and have the chance to get to know her a little. I can see now that it would have helped her to understand herself a bit better perhaps.'

'It wouldn't bother you?'

Meg shook her head. 'Not now.'

'Why did Kath never come to see her?'

Meg wrapped her arms about her body, rubbing them with workworn hands as a chill breeze rattled around the porch. 'I don't know. Perhaps she thought it was for the best. She wasn't a bad girl, you know.' Meg gave a wry smile. 'Funny, I still think of her as a girl. We were great friends once but life played a few tricks on us too.'

'Doesn't she keep in touch?'

Meg shook her head. 'Nothing beyond a Christmas and birthday card each year. But what are we doing standing out here in the cold? We can at least give you a cup of tea before you go.'

Derry had meant to keep away, but he couldn't. He had to see her one more time, for all his determination not to. An hour after leaving Broombank, he called at the shop and found Lissa jubilant.

'Oh, I'm so glad you came. I've been frantically ringing everyone, trying to locate you. Come in, come in. You won't believe what I have to tell you.'

It was plain she was bubbling over with excitement and they sat together on the old sofa, holding hands while she told him her news.

'So you see, you don't have to go at all. You can stay for ever.

Philip has agreed to give me my divorce and then . . .' Blushing now, dropping her gaze in a sudden rush of shyness. 'Then I'll be free.'

He lifted her chin with a caressing hand that very faintly shook, brown eyes ablaze with his love. 'And what would you do with this new freedom, do you reckon?'

Lissa felt transfixed by him, held a willing captive by his gaze. 'I really couldn't say. Have you any suggestions?'

Derry chuckled softly. 'How long will the children be out? Two hours?'

She pretended to consider as she got up and drew the curtains, unbuttoning her blouse as she moved quietly back to him. 'At least three.'

They were both far too eager to worry about going to bed. Derry took her there and then, on the rug, with only half her clothes off. Later they bathed together and made love again, teasing and loving for the rest of the afternoon. Lissa discovered in those two glorious hours what it was to be truly loved by a man. Not for Derry a selfish, cruel coupling. He stroked and kissed, loved and caressed her till it was she crying out for fulfilment, she who begged him to take her, her whole body screaming her need of him. They made love with joy and complete generosity, quenching a long held thirst.

31

They wrapped themselves together in a sheet and talked by the light of the fire.

'I've waited so long for you, I never thought this would ever happen,' Derry said, his arms sheltering her nakedness beneath the sheet while he kissed her hair, her face, her eyes and ears, making her giggle with delight.

'Darling, darling Derry. Don't ever leave me. I'd die if you left me now.'

They talked of everything and nothing, as lovers do, and every touch set them on fire for more, breathless with fresh desire. And they talked of a future together.

'I'd give this all up for you,' she said. 'If your work is more important. Or you could take a share in the business. I don't mind, the decision is yours. So long as we're together, I don't really care where we live or what we do. I shall be yours, completely.' Violet eyes shining, translucent with love. 'Mrs Derry Colwith. Doesn't that sound wonderful?'

Derry pretended to frown. 'Did I ask you to marry me? When was that? I must have missed it.' And she playfully slapped him, straddling him so she could beat him on his chest with her fists.

'Don't tease me, Derry. I love you too much. I need you too much. If you don't want me, so be it. You can leave now, this minute. You aren't the only man in the world.'

'OK.' He started to unwrap the sheet.

'No, no. I didn't mean it.'

Then he wrapped his arms about her and rolled her over, taking her again in a paroxysm of passion that left her gasping and spent. 'What was that about other men?'

'Oh, nothing,' she murmured, weakly compliant. 'Nothing at all.'

Only slowly did Lissa drag herself back to the present, as if coming from a distant country, her mind drugged with love, her senses aware of nothing but the warmth of his body against hers, the sweetness of his mouth, the slick of his sweat mingling with her own.

She made tea and they forgot to drink it, still endlessly talking and planning. In the distance the church clock began to strike and they lost count of the chimes. But Lissa started to worry. 'You ought to go. Nanny Sue will be back soon with the twins. They mustn't see you here. It would ruin everything. I know,' she said, seeing his quick frown. 'But we must be patient and keep away from each other for a little while longer. It will be worth it in the end, my darling, when we can be together at last. For ever.' And she gently nibbled at his lip, then laughed as his arms crushed her to him again and she had to wriggle, laughing, from his grasp. 'We must be good and not see each other until the divorce is safely through. It would be dreadful to mess it up now.'

Lissa helped him to dress which took an uncommonly long time, then hastily pulled on a skirt and blouse, trying to tidy her hair. 'I must try to look normal, as if I've spent the afternoon knitting or doing my accounts.'

'You look as if you've been happily tumbled in the hay,' he grinned. 'I'd splash some cold water on those hot little cheeks if I were you.'

Giggling and concerned, she hurried off to the bathroom as the church clock chimed six.

'Heavens, they'll be walking through that door at any minute. You must hurry.' She was desperate now to persuade him to leave. 'Oh, do go,' kissing him, clinging to him a moment longer as she pushed him through the door into the cold, empty street. 'Any second and they'll be here. Hurry.'

When she was finally alone Lissa flew about the small flat tidying and titivating, making it look neat and calm, as if she had spent a quiet and lonely day instead of one that had changed her life for ever.

By seven o'clock there was still no sign of the twins and she was growing anxious, reaching for the phone. Where were they? Why didn't someone answer? Fear grew like cold molten lead in her stomach. Philip couldn't have taken them, could he? She had done everything right, everything proper to keep them safe. *Apart from this afternoon.*

But surely Philip couldn't know that Derry had been here with her? Could he?

Oh God, what if he did? What if he had seen Derry leave? She should never have let him in, never have let him make love to her. Only she had wanted him so much how could she help herself? And she'd been so thrilled by Philip's agreement to a separation. No, no, he wouldn't be so cruel, not now. Would he?

Fear overwhelmed her and Lissa felt suddenly, desperately alone. If she lost the twins her life wouldn't be worth living. Hadn't she always put them first? Why on earth had she taken such a stupid risk this afternoon? Now she might have ruined everything.

For some reason it made her think of her own mother. Perhaps she too had tried to put her child first, and failed. Perhaps Kath had wanted to keep her, and in the end couldn't. Dare she be so quick to judge others when she was capable of mistakes and selfishness herself?

The door bell rang and Lissa jumped as if she'd been stabbed. She was there in seconds, flinging open the door.

'I'm so sorry they are late, Mrs Brandon,' said Nanny Sue, looking unusually breathless and rumpled. 'The car broke down and we had to wait for the garage to come out and rescue us.'

Lissa dredged up a smile as her arms greedily gathered her children to her breast. 'That's all right, I wasn't worried.'

But as she lay in bed that night, curled up and weeping, Lissa recognised that she was still vulnerable after all. Perhaps she always would be.

A figure stepped out of the shadows on Fossburn Street as Derry approached Nab Cottage. His skin could still feel the imprint of Lissa's touch, his mouth was still curved into a smile and he had even started to whistle an old favourite melody, 'Young Love, First Love,' as if he were a boy again. Now he stood and stared, his whole body on alert.

'Whistle away,' said the voice. 'This is your last night in Carreckwater.' Philip Brandon blocked his path, mouth twisted in malice.

'Who says so?'

Philip smiled and Derry was at once filled with foreboding. This man never looked happy without good reason. 'You're taking the train tomorrow. For Manchester, London, America or Timbuctoo. I don't care which,' said the mild, good-mannered voice. 'Just make sure you catch it.'

'I'm in no hurry to leave.'

Philip slipped his hands into his pockets, as if to point out that he had no need to resort to fisticuffs. Physical violence was not his style. 'I think you are. If you have been with my wife this evening as I suspect, and I'll remind you that she is still my wife, then you'll know she was very anxious over the fact that the twins were late home.'

'I know no such thing.' What game was this that Brandon was playing? Had he deliberately brought the twins back late just to prove a point? 'I've been to the Marina Hotel as a matter of fact, for a drink.' It was true, only he'd gone there after he left Lissa.

Brandon gave a shrug of contempt. 'As you wish. I thought it prudent to demonstrate to my wife that I still hold the power. She may keep the twins only so long as I am prepared to allow it. And there are rules. One of which is she is not to have anything to do with other men, particularly you.'

'That's only until the divorce is finalised,' Derry said, gritting his teeth on his fast disappearing patience.

Philip Brandon looked mildly surprised, dark brows lifted in polite enquiry. 'What divorce? I have said nothing about divorce.'

'Yes, you did. You took a paper to her to sign.' Derry groaned as he saw Philip's smile broaden, for he had carelessly given away the fact that he had seen or at least spoken to Lissa today. 'She rang and told me,' he tried with little conviction, but Philip only laughed.

'Then she must be confused. She often is. Haven't you noticed yet how very incompetent she is? Sweet and charming but rather stupid, don't you think?'

'No, I don't see her that way at all.'

'Then perhaps you would like to see the paper to which she refers?' Brandon held it out and Derry found himself scanning the small print with growing horror.

'These aren't divorce papers.'

'I never, exactly, said that they were. I merely acknowledged that Lissa wanted a divorce and perhaps we should be mature, modern people and end this sham of a marriage. But in my own time, if all else fails, and on my terms. Perhaps I forgot to add that small rider.'

402

Derry was tearing up the paper and throwing it all over the pavement. Philip laughed again, a bitter, hollow sound in the empty street. 'That's only a copy, of course. I have the confession of her adultery with you, for that, as you see, is what it is, safely locked in my safe. If you want her to keep her beloved children, and you know how precious they are to her, Lissa herself being only a foster child, then you will leave Carreckwater without delay.'

Derry could feel his stomach shaking with rage. He had never felt so helpless in all his life. 'And if I refuse?'

Philip shrugged. 'Then I will remove them at once from her care. A married woman with a lover is not considered a fit person to have care of young children.'

Derry took a half step towards him but Brandon didn't even flinch. 'I wouldn't if I were you. I am within my rights. As their father.'

'You've never been a father to them. Lissa has told me how you simply issue orders, expect them to be neat and perfect to gratify your ego. You don't even love them, not as Lissa loves them. You leave them with the nanny all the damn' time.'

'Hardly unusual. Half the aristocracy was brought up that way.'

Derry was clenching his fists in fury, desperately peventing himself from smashing one in Brandon's face. 'A child needs a loving family. You are twisted and sly and yes, damn' it, for all your charm you are evil and cruel.'

Brandon burst out laughing. 'How very melodramatic you sound. The point is, I will choose their future, not Lissa. And what I decide depends very much upon you, Mr Colwith. When Lissa finds that you have gone, without a word, she will see that you are as unreliable as I warned her you would be. She'll be more than ready to return home.'

'*Never*!'

'As you see, I have ways of making people do as I wish. Good evening, Mr Colwith. I can't say it has been pleasant knowing you, but it is certainly a pleasure to say goodbye. First train of the day, remember.'

Meg rang Lissa on Monday morning to ask her to come up to Broombank. 'I think you and I should talk.'

Lissa arranged for Renee to take the twins to school and pick them up at lunchtime if she wasn't back in time.

'I'm sorry to dump them on you but there seems to be some sort of emergency at Broombank.'

She was smiling as she asked, untroubled now as her mind replayed those hours with Derry. Yes, she had broken her marriage vows, and the twins being late had given her a scare. But Philip had agreed to a divorce and soon she and Derry could be together for always. Then they could lie together and love every night, without restraint or fear. Lissa's stomach clenched with excitement at the prospect. How long would the divorce take? she wondered. She could hardly wait, making a mental note to ring her solicitor and ask him.

'Don't worry,' Renee was saying. 'We can manage fine. I welcome any excuse to play with those little terrors, sorry – treasures.'

'Thanks.' Laughing, Lissa kissed the twins and went on her way.

There was a lingering tang of autumn still in the air as she drove through the wooded valleys, replaced by the bite of winter coming rapidly on its heel as she climbed higher. The mountains looked paler than usual against the blue sky, as if already glazed by a coating of hoar frost. Meg met her at the farm gate and Lissa saw at once that something was wrong. She looked weary, older somehow.

'You should have talked to me. I'm your mother,' Meg scolded, putting her arms about Lissa and drawing her close.

'I know, I know, only I wanted to get it all sorted first and decide what I was going to do. And it is sorted now. Everything is going to be fine.'

They walked together over the heaf as they so loved to do and Lissa struggled to open her heart. For such an instinctively private person it wasn't easy. She told Meg of the papers she had signed and how she would soon be free.

'Philip has agreed to a divorce and though I know everyone will point the finger and talk, at least I'll be free then to start again.'

'With Derry?'

Lissa smiled. 'I hope so.'

Meg sighed. 'I'm sorry this marriage has turned out wrong for you, and for Philip. But I've told Derry that I was wrong about him and that Tam was right. He'll do, will Derry Colwith.' She grinned at Lissa and then as quickly sobered. 'However, your marital problems are not, in fact, the only reason I asked you to call this morning.' Meg handed Lissa a letter. 'Take a look at that. I think we have real problems here too.'

They sat on the drystone wall of the old pack horse bridge while Lissa read, and as she did so her heart sank. Philip had kept his word, in this respect at least. 'I never thought he really meant it,' she said.

Meg turned startled eyes upon her. 'What are you talking about? Never thought who really meant what?'

'Philip. He threatened to bribe the water consultant into choosing Broombank as a suitable site for the reservoir, if I refused to stop seeing Derry.'

A small, awful silence. 'And you did refuse?'

'No, I-I promised nothing. I didn't really believe he'd do it.'

Meg's grey eyes seemed to pale and grow bleak, for all her tone was still sparkling with spirit and determination. 'Look at this land.' She lifted one hand in a gesture partly possessive and partly indicating despair. 'It's mine, and has been these last twenty years and more.'

'I am aware of that, I never meant . . .'

'Most of this dale is good, sound land, productive enough to grow a little corn during the war. Admittedly my sheep spend most of their time high on the fells but the intake land is important to keep them in good heart at lambing times. And I could never leave here, Lissa. It is a part of me now. The house, the land, everything.'

'I know, Meg, I never . . .'

'I drained some of the wet parts,' she continued as if Lissa had not spoken. 'It was back-breaking work. But there are still patches of bog where no bracken or good grass grows. In the spring and summer you'll find pale mauve marsh orchids, kingcups and bog myrtle. There are the troublesome sedge rushes, yes, but even they have their uses, building up the silt, holding it together.' Her voice took on a dreamy quality, filled with love and affection. 'And you'll find forget-me-not, ragged robin and a variety of ferns you can only wonder at. I love this land, wet or dry, high and low, every blade of grass and chip of stone. As the larks and meadow pipits love it, as the thrushes and merlins, the deer and the stoats. As the tiny fritillary butterflies who depend on the sweet violets for their survival, so I too depend on this land. And no one, *no one*, must be allowed to harm it.'

Humbled by the passion in her foster mother's voice and shamed by her own negligence in not warning her, Lissa grabbed Meg's hand and clung to it. 'Don't Meg. Please don't blame me for this. I tried. I really tried. I meant never to see Derry again but I couldn't help myself, and nor could he. I prayed it was all a meaningless threat, no more than Philip's hurt pride.'

'But it is real. This letter tells me Manchester Water Board are sending some geologists to inspect the land and take samples, whatever that might mean.'

'I can't believe it.' Lissa felt panic rise in her throat. 'It must be a mistake. He's agreed to a divorce. Why should he do this?'

Meg's face was white and grim. 'He's set it in motion so how can he stop it? Broombank has been chosen as a possible alternative to Winster Valley, and if the samples are good, then our dale will be flooded. Your business, and my beloved home, Ashlea and all the other farms, will be flooded and destroyed for ever.'

'Oh dear God, no, we can't let that happen. We have to fight,' Lissa cried. 'As we've never fought before.'

Derry did not catch the train from Windermere that Monday morning. After a sleepless night tossing and turning in a bed that felt harder with each passing hour, dawn found him walking by the lake, desperately seeking a solution. He sat on a log, head in his hands, and glumly watched the swirl of mist roll over the water, swallowing up a troop of ducks waddling out for their first paddle. The tips of the far mountains seemed to be suspended in space, like lavender fairy mountains.

Never had he felt so low in all his life. He loved Lissa and she loved him. They wanted to be together, was that so wrong? Derry refused to feel guilty about their lovemaking last evening. Hadn't her marriage been over for months, if not years? And hadn't Brandon tricked her into it in the first place? But how to get her out of it? There must be something he could do. Brandon was the slippiest customer he'd ever met.

'Slimy toad,' he shouted across the still water, but only disturbed the ducks and set them beating their wings in a flurry of alarm, which did no good at all.

He remembered Lissa's kisses by Brockbarrow tarn. He'd managed to hold back on that occasion, but no longer. Last night they'd made love and he could never return to being content with kisses ever again. If he continued to see her, he must possess her. And if he could not possess her, then . . . His mind balked at the thought, but resolutely continued. He would have to leave. Infuriating as it might be, Brandon was right. Derry knew that given a choice between himself and her children, he would lose out every time, and quite right too.

'But it's not fair to ask it of her in the first place,' he shouted, flustering the ducks again.

He'd wished for Lissa, that night by the tarn when they'd drunk the wishing water together. For her to be by his side for the rest of his life. But it had been no more than a desperate, childish game. He couldn't rely on wishes, he had to find the answer for himself. And for Lissa.

At ten to eight he was waiting at the office door, knowing that Miss Henshaw always arrived early. She was surprised to see him but delighted to offer coffee in her inner sanctum, a minuscule kitchen little bigger than a cupboard.

'I still love my morning cup before everyone comes,' she confessed, smiling flirtatiously at him. 'Gives me just the right lift for the day ahead.'

'So, how're things?' Derry asked, leaning against the wooden draining board and giving the best imitation of his usual grin that he could manage.

'It's been very dull since you left, Derry. Not at all the same.'

'And Mr Brandon?'

Miss Henshaw fiddled with her glasses as they bounced against her flat bosom on their long cord, her lips pursing slightly as she picked up her cup, small finger extended. 'Much as usual, I suppose. I really couldn't say.'

Did he detect a slight slackening of devotion in her stiff-lipped reply? Derry wondered. His mind was whirling. What exactly was he looking for? He had this idea that if he learned more about Brandon's life and professional matters, it might help Lissa in her fight. But what and how, he couldn't imagine. Miss Henshaw had seemed the obvious person to try, now he hadn't the first idea where to start. Hope slid away, and his depression must have showed in his face for Miss Henshaw leaned forward and patted his hand.

'There, there, don't look so sad. You weren't wanting your old job back, were you? I'd heard you were doing well.' She looked suddenly troubled.

'Good lord, no. I have a job, a much neglected one back in the States. I hope it's still waiting for me when I get back.' If I go back, he thought. There was no real reason why he shouldn't do the same

407

thing here, if he wanted. He'd had to conduct some of his business by telephone since he came anyway.

She sighed with relief. 'That's all right then. It wouldn't do at all for you to come back here.' She glanced about her, as if half expecting her employer to appear like a genii from behind her shoulder. 'Business is slack at the moment. Bank putting on pressure, I believe. Not that he ever tells me anything, or lets me look at the accounts but I know money is tight. He always gets slightly tetchy, you know?'

'I remember,' Derry grinned, glad that he was no longer under Philip Brandon's edict. 'It's an ill wind, as they say. Did me a favour sacking me, as it's turned out.'

''Course he did.' She set down her cup. 'Well, I can't sit about here gossiping all day. I must get on. I've a funeral to attend later this morning.'

'Oh, I'm sorry. Anyone close?'

'Not really,' she said. 'A client.'

Derry lifted one brow, almost his old cheeky self. 'My, my. I thought Brandon usually did those, enjoying the kudos and the funeral teas. Not like him to let you out of the office. How will he manage without you? Even for an hour.'

Miss Henshaw clattered the cups as she washed them up, handing them to Derry to dry. 'I insisted, as a matter of fact, though it really shouldn't be my place,' she said, tight-lipped. 'Mr Brandon had declined.'

Derry's eyes narrowed with speculation. There was something not quite right here. Brandon never missed the funeral of a valued client. It was part of the deal. He read the hatched, matched and dispatched columns every day in the local paper to check if an esteemed client would be requiring his probate services. And he always liked to be seen to be doing the right thing. 'Anyone I know?' he asked.

Miss Henshaw set the cups and saucers back in the tiny cupboard and slammed the door with a firm click. 'A dear old lady. Elvira Fraser. Utterly senile by the end and not a penny to her name, but it wouldn't have hurt him to go anyway. I don't understand him these days, I really don't.'

'Elvira Fraser? I seem to recall the name.'

'Lived on the Parade. Had a falling out with her son-in-law and came to us for cherishing and support.' Miss Henshaw half glanced about her again, then leaned forward and whispered in Derry's ear.

'Philip bought her house from her in point of fact, after she'd had a stroke and ended up in The Birches nursing home.'

'I see,' said Derry slowly, not quite seeing at all but feeling a quickening of interest. 'I remember her now. I once took some papers for her to sign, didn't I?'

Some papers to sign. It was like an echo in his head. Lissa had signed some papers. So had Elvira Fraser. But then Philip Brandon dealt with forms and papers every day, he was a solicitor for God's sake, so where was the significance in that? The significance was that Lissa had not signed what she'd thought. Not divorce papers at all, but a confession to adultery. He still had to break that awful news to her.

Had Elvira Fraser signed what she expected?

Miss Henshaw was still talking and he hadn't heard a word. 'Where is this funeral?' he interrupted, and she looked surprised. 'I do remember her, you see. Quite a sparky old thing, reminded me of my gran.'

'Oh, really? How lovely of you to want to come. I was so disappointed in Philip,' Miss Henshaw admitted, and told him the time and place, then on hearing a sound from the inner office, gripped Derry's hand. 'Go quickly. He's arrived.' And giving a wicked wink, Derry wrapped his arms about Miss Henshaw's birdlike figure and kissed her soundly, full upon the mouth.

'Bless you, Vera, I knew I could depend on you.' And then he was gone, leaving the back door swinging open as he'd always used to and Miss Henshaw blushing furiously.

'Oh dear,' she said, touching her lips. 'Nothing has been at all the same without him. Nor will be again.'

The lady at The Birches remembered Elvira quite well.

'Though she hasn't lived here for quite some time. Ran out of funds, poor thing, and had to move into council care. A not uncommon occurrence, I'm afraid.'

'But how did she lose her money? I always thought Mrs Fraser had plenty. That house must have been worth quite a bit for one thing, and then she had shares, money in the bank and so on.'

The matron shook her head. 'Property is often mortgaged and they've usually been living above their means for years, poor dears. Still living in the style they were used to back in the good old days of Empire and servants. Edwardian affluence, a world gone by. I know nothing about her investments of course, but prices rise and their income shrinks.' She sighed and gave a resigned shrug, moving away, her mind already on the next task. 'It's a changing world.'

Not if it's invested properly, Derry mused to himself as he bade her goodbye and took his leave. 'Thanks for your help anyway. I'll try the council home.'

Whatever it was he wanted from them, and he wasn't entirely sure himself, they could tell him nothing more. Yes, they said, Elvira Fraser had lived with them, old, confused, still expecting her young husband to call and collect her. Now she was dead. End of story.

But Derry felt certain that this wasn't the end of the story. There was more to this than he'd yet discovered. He'd go to the funeral. Just in case. Then he would go and see Lissa.

Lissa rang Renee to say she would not be home as early as she'd hoped, and would Renee collect the twins from school at the end of the afternoon session as well as the morning, and look after them till she got there?

'It could be early evening. I can't explain on the phone but I wouldn't ask if it wasn't important.'

'No problem. They can have lunch at the shop here with me. And Jimmy'll love having 'em home for tea,' Renee said.

'Thanks.'

Lissa spent the next several hours hanging around waiting rooms and chatting up secretaries, hoping for a chance to have a word with various important people who might help them in their fight.

Meg went to talk with the local newspaper and enlist their support but Lissa insisted that she did most of the donkeywork. She felt it was her fault that Meg was in this mess in the first place, so it was up to her to get her out of it.

She gained five precious minutes to speak with a National Park authority spokesman, who was very sympathetic but admitted they could do little since Broombank was not quite in the National Park and many people would be agreeable to the pressure coming off Winster.

The Friends of the Lakes took a similar line but offered their support, so long as it didn't prejudice their own efforts.

Lissa was worn out when she returned to Broombank, but her frustration and lack of success made her all the more determined.

'I called at Lord Carndale's place but he wouldn't see me,' she said. 'I'll try again this afternoon. He is a neighbour after all, and may be able to put the right word in the right ear.'

'Good idea,' Tam agreed. 'I'll come with you. I worked for the old boy once. He's fair and I'm sure he'll do all he can, but a bit deaf and doesn't readily take to strangers these days. He has a son though, who may be willing to help. Let's hope so.'

'Great,' Lissa said. 'And then we must have a word with all the local councillors.'

'Who?'

'All of them if need be. We'll start with the mayor and the town council and work our way through the District and up to County.'

'Why stop there?' Tam grinned. 'How about Westminster and the Lords?'

Lissa stiffened her spine, jutting her chin almost as Meg did. 'I'd willingly go there and try.'

'You've got a lot more spunk than you used to have,' Tam said, admiringly. 'It's good to see it, lass.'

'I've had to learn how to fight and stand up for myself. Perhaps it's being a mother,' and she caught Meg's smile and laughed.

Meg suggested they also go and talk to the National Farmers' Union representative, and so it went on for some time as they worked out their plan of campaign, and time flew by without her realising.

'Mustn't keep the treasures waiting.' Renee handed the order sheet to the young shop assistant. 'Get on with this, Julie, while I'm out, will you?'

'Sure. Who's it for?'

'Mrs Hughes. She wants six pairs of mitts for her grandchildren. Names, dates, colours she wants and all the other details are on the sheet. Check they're correct, will you? She's a good customer and Lissa will never forgive us if we make a mistake. Then gift wrap each one individually and you can take them round in your lunch hour.'

'Right you are.'

Renee reached under the counter as she pulled on her coat at the same time, feeling very slightly harrassed as a result of a hectic morning. 'Use the new gift wrap, blue and silver, with our name on. And some pretty ribbon.'

'I know.' Julie was pushing her to the door. 'Don't worry. I can cope. Go away, boss lady.' And laughing, Renee did so, almost running up Carndale Road.

32

The funeral took place at the local parish church. A small knot of people whom Derry did not know gathered about the open grave. Miss Henshaw stood by his side and next to her was Miss Stevens, who had been an old friend of Elvira Fraser's apparently. Derry felt uncomfortable at first, as if he were an intruder, but then remembered the old lady's essential dignity, her kindness to him when he, young and green, had no answers to her many questions. How sad that she should lose the ability even to think of the right questions to ask in the end, let alone understand the answers. Anyone could take advantage of such a situation.

A young man approached and thanked Miss Henshaw for coming. 'Glad to,' she said. 'I liked her enormously.' And they exchanged small talk about the weather being fine for once, though the skies were darkening now, and how he appreciated the fact that a representative from The Birches had also attended.

'She did at least find a modicum of happiness there for a while. My grandmother once had the reputation of being a tartar. Made my late father's life a misery, I'm afraid. He never quite came up to scratch in her opinion.' The young man, named David, smiled. 'But she was simply sad in the end.'

'Sad that she lost her money, despite careful investments,' Derry put in.

The young man glanced sharply at him and Miss Henshaw hastily intervened to introduce Derry.

'Mr Colwith used to be a clerk in Mr Brandon's office many years ago. He's quite important in a music agency business now

413

but he still remembers visiting your grandmother, taking papers for her to sign.'

'Ah.' The young man nodded then glanced about him and continued in a cool voice, 'Mr Brandon didn't find time to come himself then?'

Miss Henshaw flushed. 'He's very busy at the moment, I'm afraid.'

'I see.' A slight awkward pause then someone came and spoke to him and he started to move away. 'You'll come to the Marina Hotel for a spot of lunch, both of you? You are very welcome,' he said politely.

'Fine,' said Derry quickly. 'Can I give you a lift?'

The young man looked surprised, almost as if he'd not expected them to accept. He was about to refuse the offer when he met Derry's gaze and changed his mind. 'That would be good. Thanks.'

It was raining by the time Renee darted between the traffic at Benthwaite Cross and on up the hill to Hazelwood Crescent where the small infant school was situated. The twins loved it and of course adored their teacher.

Not like when I was at school, Renee thought, recalling being made to stand in a corner on more than one occasion.

She glanced at her watch. Almost ten past twelve. She was late after all, but Miss Swift, their teacher, was very understanding and any child not collected on time was kept with her. Lissa had told her this, so Renee wasn't worried that the twins would wander. It was considered almost a treat to help teacher clear away and make ready for the afternoon lessons.

After lunch, and if the rain stopped, Renee thought she might take them for a short walk by the shore. Sneak a half hour off work until it was time to take them back. Lissa wouldn't mind. Nor would the ducks. The twins liked to see and feed them every day of course, and she could do with a bit of fresh air herself.

Renee turned the corner into Hazelwood Crescent and hurried through the main swing doors of the small school, quite out of breath from running. Miss Swift was in the classroom, painting clowns on the windows in poster paint.

'Hello, Renee. I didn't expect to see you today. Is Mrs Brandon feeling any better? I heard she was unwell.'

'Unwell? She's fine, only she got held up at Broombank so I'm deputy today.' She glanced about the classroom. 'Are they hiding? Come out, you two terrors.'

'No, of course not,' laughed the teacher. 'They aren't here.'

'What do you mean, they aren't here?' A small, terrible dawning of fear.

The infant teacher smiled reassuringly. 'No need to panic. They're quite safe. Mr Brandon collected them, not twenty minutes since. They'll be home by now I should think. Quite safe, you see.'

Renee went straight to number 22, The Parade, and hammered on the door. Her guilt at being too late to prevent Brandon collecting the twins was almost overwhelming. Lissa would never forgive her.

It was opened at once by Philip Brandon, as if he'd been expecting her, or Lissa.

'Where are they?' Renee demanded, in a voice like thunder.

Dark brows rose in mild surprise. 'I'm afraid I don't quite . . .'

'Don't act the innocent with me.' Renee brushed past him, marching down the long passage and straight in to the kitchen. 'You aren't supposed to collect them.'

'Nor are you.'

'Lissa asked me to, as a favour, since she was a bit tied up at Broombank.'

Philip smiled grimly, as if at some private joke. 'Seems she's more and more tied up these days. She should put the children first for once.'

Renee opened her mouth to dispute this but thought the better of it. You couldn't win an argument with a lawyer, particularly this one. She'd tried it in the past. 'Well, where are they?' she insisted.

'Nanny has taken them for a dental check up, if it is any concern of yours. They are my children and you may remind Lissa that, as yet, no court has given her custody.'

'Or you access,' Renee hit back but inside felt a flutter of nervousness. Dental check my eye, she thought, worrying more than ever.

'As you say. Which can easily be rectified.' He took Renee's elbow in a firm grip and started to lead her to the door, Renee protesting all the while as she struggled to free herself. 'And tell her, while you're at it, that I wouldn't have been forced to take the action I have if she'd left Derry Colwith alone. If children will play with fire, they'll get their fingers burnt. Tell her that.'

415

'What the hell are you talking about?'

'I think you know well enough.'

Renee was beside herself with fury. 'I know I shouldn't have tried to put her off our Derry in the first place. And I shouldn't have told you that she thought herself a bit too grand for him. I was wrong, and look what a mess I've made of everything by interfering.'

This seemed to amuse him and he laughed all the more. 'Don't blame yourself. Nothing happens in my life that hasn't been carefully planned out beforehand.'

'No, I can believe it,' she said. 'And get your hands off me or I'll set my Jimmy on you.' Renee wrenched her elbow free and stood facing him, blue eyes blazing, red hair standing out like flames about her head, but much to her discomfiture, Philip Brandon did not seem at all put out by this threat, he only laughed again, his handsome face as mildly composed as ever. Then almost as suddenly the laughter died and he was advancing on her, forcing Renee to retreat backwards up the passage.

'Tell your employer that she may come and see the children at any time. That they are safely at home, where they belong, and where she belongs. The solution lies in her hands. Tell her that.'

'You expect Lissa to come back to you?' Renee was astounded, giving a false little laugh, determined not to let him see how her heart was pounding.

'She'll be back all right, once she realises what is best for her, and for the twins. Once Lissa realises she could lose them, and her precious Broombank, if she doesn't. She's confessed to adultery in her futile efforts to gain a divorce, and compounded her sin by permitting your precious stepson to visit her yesterday afternoon while sending the children off with nanny.'

Renee gasped. 'What are you talking about? Were you spying on her?'

'Not at all. It was quite by accident that I saw him. The courts will take a very dim view of such loose behaviour. She's quite unfit to be given custody of the children under those conditions. While I have done nothing wrong. Nothing at all. Fortunately there is no question of my being so cruel as to divorce her and deprive her of her beloved children. Tell Lissa I will forgive her for all her indiscretions and she may return at any time.'

'You dirty, blackmailing . . . You'll get no help from me. You can deliver your own damned messages.' Renee was stopped by one finger pressed against her lips, silencing her most effectively.

'I dislike people who disagree with me,' he said, so pleasantly they might have been discussing the weather, except for the feverish glitter in his dark eyes.

My God, he's up the pole, Renee thought. Mad as hell.

'I won't have it. Not from Felicity, not from Lissa, and certainly not from you. Do you understand?'

The finger slid from her lips and trailed down her throat, tracing a path to the cleft between her full breasts. 'Ere, gerroff,' Renee choked, knocking his hand away. No wonder Lissa had left him. He was creepy. 'I'm taking them nippers back wi'me. Soon as I can lay my hands on 'em,' she said, with more bravado than conviction in the weakening voice. He had beaten her, as he did them all, in the end.

Derry was waiting at the door when Lissa got home early that evening. She wanted to fling her arms about his neck and kiss him but he led her into the little living room and turned her to him, his face serious.

'You must listen, Lissa.' He made her sit down and fold her hands on her lap instead of about his neck and concentrate very carefully on what he had to say. 'Philip cheated Elvira Fraser of most, if not all, of her money. I believe he took it, bit by bit, from her accounts, assuring her that he was investing it safely when all the time he was feeding it into accounts of his own.'

Lissa stared at him, bemused. 'What are you saying? What is all this?'

'I even remember acting as errand boy for him, only I was too young and green to understand what he was up to. And who is there to check on him?' He explained about attending Elvira Fraser's funeral, and of his visits to The Birches and the council home.

'I spoke to her grandson, David, and he's going to do some investigating of his own.'

'Elvira Fraser's troubles happened so long ago. I met her once. She was old, and sick. We bought her house, which is all very sad, but how does that affect me, or Philip?'

'I'm not sure she was aware at the time that she was selling it. Philip had her sign so many papers, her mind was probably spinning with it all. She was old, vulnerable, and at odds with her family. A

417

perfect candidate for an unscrupulous solicitor. Perhaps there were other clients, equally vulnerable.'

Lissa stared at Derry as if she had never seen him before. 'Are you saying that my husband is a fraud?'

He put out his hands, stroked her arms, urging her to remain calm. 'I have more news for you, Lissa. And it isn't good.'

He gathered her hands warmly into his own, and her smile, so full of trust and love, almost made him change his mind. But no, she must be told, and he was the only one to do it.

He revealed what Philip had told him about the paper. That she had signed a confession of guilt and not for a divorce at all. Lissa sat in stunned silence, her confidence crumbling before his eyes.

'I signed a confession?' Her voice barely had the strength to reach her lips. 'It wasn't the divorce papers?'

Derry shook his head as he knelt before her, stroking her hands, wishing he could do anything to take this pain from her. 'A confession of adultery – with me of course. Philip intends to use it to blackmail you to return to him.'

Lissa started, as if he had slapped her. 'Return to him? Never, never, never. What if I have admitted to adultery?' she went on, in a wild moment of bravery. 'What of it? I've seen today how he means to wreck the lives of a dozen families in my dale and I've spent all day fighting him. I shall spend my life fighting him if I have to.' Tears were shining in her eyes, spilling over on to pale cheeks. 'He thinks he can ruin Broombank, destroy my family's home and my independence. Well, he can't. We won't let them flood the valley, we won't.'

Her voice was rising, growing close to hysteria and Derry put his mouth to her cheek, hushing and soothing her. 'Tell me slowly what else has happened.'

Lissa gulped and swallowed her tears and explained about Meg's letter from the Water Board and of Philip's involvement. 'I won't let them do it, I won't. I thought it was simply an empty threat. I never imagined he had the power, not really.'

'I'm sure you didn't, my darling. It's not power he uses in any case. He simply cheats.'

'Oh, Derry, but it's the same thing in the end.' Her mind was in turmoil, her heart plummeting in despair.

'Not really. Let's go and see this water consultant. He's at Nab Cottage still?'

Violet eyes lit up and she was at once on her feet. 'Of course, that's the answer. I have to collect the twins from Renee in any case. I shall tackle him on the subject at the same time. Philip won't beat us, Derry. We won't let him.'

'No,' he agreed, holding her close and not letting her see the concern on his face. 'We won't let him beat us.'

'I don't believe you. I *won't* believe you!' Lissa cried.

The water consultant was not at Nab Cottage but Renee was, sitting in her chair by the new teak effect electric fire, her face a white mask of anguish. Even her lips were white, with not a trace of lipstick.

'Oh, Lissa, what can I say? I was barely ten minutes late. I was so busy doing the orders that I forgot the time. But I knew the teacher would keep them safe, only I never expected Philip Brandon to . . . I went round of course, right away.' She was gabbling now, trying to assuage her pain and the terrible shame of her failure.

'What did he say? What happened? Where *are* they?' Lissa was distraught but desperately struggling to keep a hold upon her fast disappearing control.

Renee hugged her arms about herself, struggling to speak through the lump as big as a brick in her throat. 'Dental check-up, he said. With Nanny. But they've gone back home and will stay there.'

'Oh, dear God.' Lissa's cry of anguish cut Renee's heart in two.

'Don't,' she gasped, reaching out to clutch at her friend, voice and heart broken. 'I'll get them back for you, Lissa, I promise.'

'Did he hurt you?' Jimmy wanted to know, bouncing to his feet. 'I'll kill him if he did.'

'No, no,' Renee lied, touching her throat. 'Why should he hurt me?' She'd thought for a minute that he might snuff her out with his finger and thumb, like a candle.

Derry put his hand on Renee's shoulder, trying to console her. 'It wasn't your fault, Renee. Don't torment yourself, but you'd best tell it all. What exactly did he say?'

When Renee had finished her tale, the tears raining down and washing mascara in black streaks down her death pale face, nobody could find any words of consolation or hope. He had won. It was as simple as that.

Then Lissa turned on Derry like a lash.

'It's all your fault,' she screamed, flying at him with her fists flailing. 'If you'd gone back to America, like I asked you to long since, as Philip asked you to, this would never have happened. You've lost me my children. I'll never forgive you for that, *never!*'

It was the most unfair and bitter attack and Derry stood like a man felled. Then, very quietly, he nodded. 'Yes, I suppose you're right. It is my fault. It's been my fault all along really, just because I love you.'

'Lissa.' Renee stepped forward but Lissa shook off her hand, tears of anger and pain and grieving loss running in scalding rivers down her cheeks. When she spoke again her voice was calm, but hard as iron.

'Get out. Go. Philip has won. If I'm to keep my children I must return to him. Just as he always planned I would.'

'And what about us?'

'We're finished, Derry. It's all over.'

Lissa went back to the house on the Parade the very next day, but on very different terms. She insisted on her own room, that they be man and wife in name only.

'I will not share your bed,' she said, violet eyes holding a new resolution that even her husband could not ignore. 'Also, Nanny Sue must go. The children have no need of a nanny now they are at school. The rest of the time they can spend with me, either at home or at the shop. And before you say it, no, I will not be giving up my business. I shall employ a cleaner, or whatever help I need so that your life is not disturbed too much, but my work will continue.

'I'll host your dinner parties and otherwise be a wife to you until the children are grown. Nothing more. Is that quite clear? Those are my terms for returning, take them or leave them.'

Philip smiled at her, lounging against the door frame of the room she had selected as her own, watching her unpack the few belongings she had taken with her. He'd celebrated her return with half a bottle of scotch and felt particularly mellow. 'I accept them,' he said. 'This is where you belong, Lissa, with me to care for you.'

'I need no one to care for me, thank you very much,' she said, tone sharp as spears of ice. 'In future I'll look after my own affairs.' She glanced at him then, trying to ignore the triumph in his eyes.

'Is it true that you took that old woman's money?'

'What tale is this you've been listening to?' His face was instantly so bland and inscrutable, Lissa's doubts returned. Could he really be capable of such professional mischief?

'It has been suggested to me, by a friend, that Elvira Fraser's grandson is not happy about the way her affairs were conducted. Is that true?'

Philip stretched his eyes wide in a shocked innocence so genuine, Lissa found it hard not to believe in him. 'I can guess who that friend is, and it seems to me it's in his interests to malign my good name, since he is sleeping with my wife.'

Lissa jerked, the spiteful words hitting home. 'Is it *true*?'

'You must believe what you wish to believe. Elvira Fraser was an old and valued client. Were she still with us today she would, I am sure, vouch for me.'

Lissa struggled to recall some of the old woman's words on the day she had met her in the home, but they were so jumbled as to be incomprehensible. She slammed shut her wardrobe door and tilted her chin high.

'I want you to realise, Philip, that you won't win over Broombank. Nor will I permit you to sell Larkrigg. If it belongs to the twins, then it must be kept for them. I'll fight you on those issues till my last breath. Do you understand.'

'Yes,' he said. 'I understand perfectly.'

It was Renee who gently broke the news to her that Derry had finally gone.

'He caught the train to London this morning. Said he had some business to do there before he went back to the States.'

'I really don't want to hear,' Lissa said, heart breaking.

It made the hurt worse to think that her last words with Derry had been harsh, unforgiving ones, but then perhaps it was for the best. It might help her to keep the reality of her situation in mind and forget about the romance and the love. Look where her quest for love had led her. None from her real mother, none from her husband, and that which she had found with Derry had constantly been denied her.

She must think of her children now. And though Philip may have won the battle of their marriage and broken her heart in the process there was other work left for her to do. A business to develop for one thing. And Broombank for another. She was determined not to let him beat her on that score too.

The business suffered from some neglect in the weeks following while Lissa returned with renewed vigour to the campaign to save Broomdale, though with more sense of desperation than design. It was hard to know how best to fight it since all the arguments had already been made by every association in Lakeland and beyond.

Lissa spoke to all of the local councillors and succeeded in enlisting the support of many. She visited every house in the area with leaflets she'd had printed, gave endless interviews to the press and held meetings in the old school hall. Time after time she hounded the National Parks Committee, the Planning Board and every other body she could think of, to give her their support. They were always sympathetic but continued to put their main resources into saving Winster. Reasonable as this was, it left Lissa feeling isolated.

She even tackled the water consultant and though she managed finally to force an admission out of him of accepting Philip's bribe, he said it was out of his hands now.

'They'll send in the geologists and the engineers and that'll be that. Then the Board will make the decision, not me,' he said.

'The National Farmers' Union is right behind us,' Meg said. 'And the District and County Councils. They want water extraction from the lakes rather than a reservoir. With suitable conditions attached, of course.'

'But how to win our case?' Lissa groaned. 'We need some evidence, some good reason to put forward for not using Broomdale.'

'You mean beyond the fact that it'll destroy top grade farming land and wild life habitats?' said Meg drily.

Lissa acknowledged these words with a sad shake of her head. 'But it doesn't seem to be enough, does it? Having right on your side is never enough.' It hadn't been enough to win her freedom from Philip. And in their cold, sterile life together Lissa despaired of knowing the joy of love ever again.

It was perfectly legal for him virtually to rape her within the sanctity of marriage, just as the Water Board was permitted to rape their land.

'You look done in,' Meg told her softly. 'You need to get more sleep.'

'Of course I need more sleep,' Lissa snapped, then apologised when she saw Meg's face. 'Sorry. Not your fault. But what can we do? Everyone is sympathetic, or supportive but more concerned over the possible loss of Winster. Jimmy and the other boatmen are worried that the extraction of water from the lake will lower the water level too much, ruin the shoreline and prove a hazard to the tourist industry. Others are concerned about the rivers, or tunnels under Longsleddale. How can we all win? It isn't possible.'

And how could she find the strength to continue with her fight for much longer? She was tired of fighting. Her own future looked bleak whatever happened, and all her energy was used up.

Lissa sat by the big hearth at Broombank and held her head in her hands, despair and failure eating into her soul. In this mood she almost believed Philip's judgement of her to be correct. She was incompetent. A useless mother, wife, and even daughter to Meg. She could feel the tears standing proud in her eyes but refused to shed them. The time for crying was done.

'Thoo'll git nae wark done by laiking theer,' said Joe, coming in on an icy blast of wind and settling himself with his pipe in the opposite corner.

Meg gave a hollow laugh. 'It's good to see you're so busy, Father.'

'A chap can tek a spell to put oop his feet I dare swear, when he's visiting his family.' He adjusted his cap upon his head, without removing it, and looked from his daughter to his granddaughter as he sucked on his pipe and waited for his pint pot of tea to be brought to him. 'Well, you two's a cheerful pair, I must say. Lost a shilling and found an 'appeny, hev thee?'

'Don't start, Father,' Meg warned.

'Is it this watter business?'

'Yes, Father, it is.'

'Dun't say they've getten you licked?'

Lissa sank back in her chair and tried to smile. 'Yes, Grandad, I think they have. But then, when do I ever win?' she added, with an uncharacteristic tinge of self-pity.

'I dun't know what you're both worrying over. It'll niver happen. Niver.'

Lissa sighed, unable to find the energy to bring one old man into the present. 'It might,' was all she could manage.

'Huh. Over my dead body. Cost 'em a bob or two. Dun't carry water well, dun't limestone,' he said, his tone scornful. 'This dale ain't Mardale with half a lake in it already. And the dam'll have to be twice as wide. Bankrupt the Watter Board, it would. Won't be done in my lifetime, that's for sure. Never find the money.'

Lissa leaned forward in her chair and stared at her grandfather. 'What did you say?'

Joe was always happy to repeat himself when he had an attentive audience, so he said it all again, at leisure.

Lissa was on her feet in a second. 'I have to go.' Then she was running out of the house, getting in the van and driving with the wind in her tail all the way back to Carreckwater.

At Nab Cottage the water consultant had just sunk his knife into a steak and kidney pudding, his favourite repast, when Lissa burst in through the front door without even a knock.

'When are the geologists coming?' she demanded, and he, Jimm·· and Renee all sat and stared at her, mouths agape as if she had dropped through the roof.

'Er . . . it's on their rota of visits,' said the Manchester man in pompous tones. 'I can't say exactly when. Why?' He lifted a forkful of succulent steak and steaming pastry to his mouth but Lissa stopped him.

'You know that any dam they build will have to be wider than Mardale's, and more expensive?'

'We've taken that into account,' said Andrew Spencer loftily, irritated by the way she was holding on to his wrist while the tantalising drift of steam from the rich meat and gravy tickled his nostrils. 'But the reservoir would also be twice the size and therefore more profitable.'

'And have you taken into account the quality of the stone?'

'That is for the geologists to investigate but I see no problem there.' Again he attempted to lift his fork but Lissa was having none of it. She held fast.

'There's a limestone pavement runs right under the dale, did you know that? Full of cracks and crevices, nooks and crannies that would never hold water in a million years. Never has so far, apart from one boggy bit that we leave to nature. Have you taken that into account, Mr Water Consultant?'

He looked very faintly stunned and tried, ineffectually, to disguise his concern.

Lissa shook his arm. 'Well, have you?'

The portion of steak pudding fell from his fork to the floor and he grieved for it. 'Broomdale is gritstone and granite, like Shap Fell,' he said.

'Some of it is, yes, but the limestone is hidden. My grandfather has lived in that dale all his life and if he says it exists, believe me, it exists.' She offered up this information with triumph in her voice, a toss of silken curls and a wide smile. 'Wouldn't that make a big difference to your Board's plans?'

'The limestone could be sealed.'

'At what cost?'

Too high, said the expression on his pale face and he set down his fork with a trembling hand. Really, much as he had enjoyed his continual visits to the Lake District these last years, and there was no doubt that he had benefited financially, as had his dear mother who now had her own personal attendant to save him the bother of fetching and carrying for her, nothing at all had gone right for him here. Manchester Water Board had grown irritated with his frequent alterations of plan and gone so far as to appoint other consultants to check out the area. Nor had they expected such opposition, so well planned and orchestrated. It was developing rapidly into a nationwide affair being talked about on radio and TV. Barristers, members of parliament, poets and every man and woman in the street deemed themselves fit to express an opinion on the matter. It was really most disconcerting.

Lissa could see that she had won this battle at least. It was written plain in his eyes. And so it proved. By Christmas, Meg had word that the Water Board would not be pursuing their decision to create a holding reservoir in Broomdale. The land had proved unsuitable for their purpose. The family were jubilant.

'Bless you, Grandfather,' Lissa cheered, hugging the old man.

'Nice to know we old 'uns still have some use,' said Joe, pink-cheeked and smiling for once.

33

Victory was sweet. Lissa's achievement turned her into a local heroine, at least for a time. Even Grandfather Joe was quoted in every paper, and there was a picture of him in one, standing on Broombank land, the neb of his cap set straight on his round head, looking as proud as if he'd done it all single-handed.

Their success seemed to add further fuel to the ongoing contest with the Water Board but everyone knew that it was only a matter of time now before they admitted defeat over the question of another reservoir. The debate would continue, the battle rage on for a while yet, and a major public enquiry was planned, but the people of Lakeland had the bit between their teeth and did not intend to lose. The land was too precious, the loss to the nation would be too great.

And victory over Broombank meant that Philip lost his prospective buyer for Larkrigg Hall.

All the fight seemed to go out of him after that. He spent more and more time locked in his study with a bottle of whisky at his side. Correspondence came regularly from the bank manager, and frequent telephone calls were taken behind closed doors.

Lissa found herself consoling him, almost forcing him out of the womb of his study, but he showed little interest in attending either the Golf or the Yacht Club. Each evening he downed several gin and tonics, barely picked at his food and then started on the whisky. It was Lissa who made the decisions now.

'It's for the best, Philip. Larkrigg must either remain empty until the twins are old enough to decide for themselves or we could

427

perhaps find a tenant. In the meantime I'll have the water turned off and see the windows are properly boarded up.'

'We should still sell it. It could save us. Do you realise we could lose our home?' He told her, eyes bleary with drink and worry. 'I owe the bank more than I can pay and as a solicitor I'm not permitted to go bankrupt. I'd be struck off.'

This news jolted Lissa but she knew better than to show it. 'Then let them have it. It's only a house. We could live in the flat over the shop.'

She might very well have suggested they camp in a cave, so horrified was his response. 'Never. I refuse to live in a flat. I have my status to keep up.'

'Perhaps if you'd been satisfied with less status we wouldn't be in this mess now. What has happened to all your money? Why are we in such dire straits?'

'Nannies, cars, houses, entertaining. And that damned Manchester man, greedy little tyke!'

Lissa wanted to say that the source of the greed was closer to home but managed to hold her tongue. A small frown creased her brow. 'You did pay Elvira Fraser a proper sum for the house, didn't you, Philip?'

He made a sound of disgust and reached for the whisky bottle again. 'Questions, questions, questions. Do you never stop?'

Watching him, Lissa thought that if he really had got the house cheap or, if Derry was right, perhaps paid nothing at all for it, then to lose it to the bank would be fitting retribution for Elvira's penniless death. But not for the world would she say as much.

Business continued to thrive and Lissa was happy and relieved for Meg and Jan since farming wasn't doing too well right now. She was pleased for the new handknitters in and around Broomdale, and for herself. But how she wished she could solve her personal problems as easily. She had created as good a life for herself as she could but Philip still had no intention of letting her go. He had merely lengthened, and not cut the chain.

She once spent an afternoon, when she knew that Philip was safely out of town, going through the desk in his private study at home. She wasn't sure what she searched for but found nothing of interest, nothing that she understood. There was probably nothing to find.

'Why don't you search his office?' Renee suggested when Lissa confessed to this piece of snooping. Their friendship had been bruised but not ended by Renee's failing to collect the twins that day, and in a way Renee had suffered the greater loss because Lissa had always held the sneaking feeling that Philip would win, in the end. He was far too clever not to. And she should not have been so trusting as to sign a piece of paper unread. Lissa knew now that she should have realised it wasn't what it seemed. But then it was easy to be wise after the event. He had tricked them all.

Now there would be no divorce. Derry was gone, and she was back with her husband and children, where she should be. All right and proper like a good little wife. So be it.

'I did hope he might take a mistress,' Lissa told Renee, with a wry smile. 'But he's taken to drink instead.'

'That's men all over. Never do what you want 'em to.' And they both had to laugh.

Sarah came skipping into the shop, plump cheeks glowing. 'It's snowing again, Mummy, and it's freezing cold. Can we go skating on the lake?'

'No.'

'*Please.*'

'There isn't enough ice on this lake. No.'

Beth came in and added her pleas to her sister's, tugging at Lissa's hands, one on each side.

'By heck,' said Renee. 'At least you have these two to keep you going.'

'Yes,' Lissa agreed, eyes shining with love and laughter. 'I'm happy to say that I do. I'll take you to play snowballs. Will that do?'

She wrapped them up warmly and off they went, hand in hand along Carndale Road, through St Margaret's Churchyard, past the Marina Hotel and down to the benches by the shore. She never thought of those youthful summers now. It was too dangerous, and much too painful.

'Let's build a snowman,' Beth shouted, grey eyes bright.

They were searching for bits of stick to mark his nose and eyes when Renee came hurrying up, holding her side and panting for breath. 'It's Miss Henshaw. She says you are to come at once to the office.'

'What is it?'

'I don't know. Go on, I'll look after these two.'

Lissa turned and ran back up the church steps and across the busy crossroads of Benthwaite Cross. She did not stop even to think, or hope, what this summons might be about. Miss Henshaw was waiting for her at the door, a rather shabby but flustered woman in a navy suit with her glasses dangling on a chain about her neck.

'We have visitors,' she said, half under her breath as she pulled Lissa in to the little kitchen and closed the door. Lissa's heart leapt, robbing her of the ability to speak for a whole half minute.

'Who? Who is it?' Could it be . . .?

But Miss Henshaw was wearing her professional expression, though there was some other emotion behind it too. Disbelief, uncertainty, fear? 'It's two accountants, sent by the Law Society. They're going through all of Mr Brandon's papers. Taking the place apart they are. They arrived just after lunch and Mr Brandon, well . . .' Miss Henshaw paused, drawing in a shaky breath. 'I can't say where he is now. He lost his temper when he saw them, blew up he did. Never, in all my life, have I seen him lose his temper but he did today. A shocking rage he was in, throwing books everywhere. Now he's taken himself off, I don't know where. In a huff I shouldn't wonder. He's not a happy man. Not at all.'

Lissa felt numb. Whatever was going on? 'Why are they here? Who brought them in?'

'Elvira Fraser's grandson. He says he's not satisfied about what happened to all her money.'

'Is he the one Derry talked to at the funeral?'

'Derry?' Miss Henshaw nodded, fingers twitching on her chain. 'Yes, he did, now I come to think of it. And this grandson said he would look into the matter. Now he claims to have found letters in his late father's desk proving that Mr Brandon had made himself entirely responsible for the investment of Mrs Fraser's funds. He wants to know where every penny has gone and has put in an official complaint to the Law Society. I must say, Mrs Brandon, that it doesn't look good.'

'No,' Lissa agreed. 'I don't suppose it does.' Then why was her heart beating, almost with delight? As if at last her wishes were about to come true?

Moments later her mood changed as Jimmy burst through the door, bristly hair standing even more on end than usual.

'He's done it again,' Jimmy cried. 'Came up whilst me and Renee

430

were helping the twins finish the snowman and just took them off. Only this time she's gone with him, says she's not letting them whippersnappers out of her sight.'

Lissa felt herself grow quite cold, yet her voice was oddly quiet. 'Where has he taken them?'

'Don't you fear, Lissa, he seems very calm and them two is happy as gnats. He's taken 'em up to Larkrigg.'

'Oh dear God.'

The trees by the tarn were feathered with snow, hanging as heavy as lace over the white-encrusted surface. A dry, freezing cold bit through Lissa's thick woollens and her breath froze into puffballs of ice on her cheeks. She struggled through the thick snow, frustrated by its cloying softness in her anxiety to reach the colourful figures out on the ice. Renee crouched beneath the rowans, shivering and making tiny keening sounds in her throat.

Lissa pressed a hand to her shoulder. 'Don't fret, Renee. I'll soon have them home and safe. Where is he?'

'He wouldn't listen,' she mourned. 'Oh, hecky thump.' Renee slid her eyes round to where Brockbarrow wood stood, black and forbidding against the stark white of the snow. 'He's over there, brooding.'

'Beth! Sarah!' Lissa called, waving to her excited children.

'We're skating, Mummy. Watch.'

The twins, both dressed in their red and blue hooded jackets and thick trousers, ice skates clamped to their small boots, slid about in the middle of the ice, wobbling madly. Lissa's heartbeat quickened, as any mother's would but she smiled reassuringly at them. 'I must speak to Daddy, then I'll watch you skate. Take care now. Come away from the middle now. Keep to the edges where the ice is thicker.'

'Yes, Mummy,' they said, in sing-song, happy voices.

Lissa found him at the opposite edge of the small copse, seated on a rock above Whinstone force. Below him shafts of water split and cascaded over jagged stones, the brilliant spray crisp as diamonds in the sharp air.

'Hello, Philip.' The gushing sound of the water hammered in her head. It made her feel giddy. The falls here, high on the fells, made Skelwith force look like a toy. 'Can we sit somewhere else, please?' she asked.

431

He did not respond. He sat unmoving for so long that she gently touched his arm, in case he had not heard. Then he turned towards her and she saw his face, empty and bleak as the landscape. 'Hello Philip,' she said again, trying to put some warmth into her voice. 'I thought I might find you here.'

'Why have you followed me?' His voice was bitter yet rich with self-pity. 'Why aren't you working, as you always seem to be these days.'

'I was concerned about you.' Very gently Lissa propped herself on a rock beside him. 'Miss Henshaw told me about the Law Society's visit. Why did you do it, Philip?'

'Necessary,' he said vaguely, and the eyes he turned to hers looked odd, as if they looked into some other place.

'Did you really embezzle Mrs Fraser's money?' And when he chuckled she could only stare at him, appalled. 'But why? Why couldn't you earn your money honestly, as other people do?'

'I am not other people. I deserve more. My mother told me how special I was when I was quite small. We were very poor then, you know,' he said, as if it were some sort of crime. 'My father was useless, an ineffectual idiot who was besotted with books and fishing and points of law. He let my mother down, showed her up before everyone by being so totally lacking in ambition. Once I had control of my own life, I vowed never to let that happen to me or any wife of mine.'

'But to cheat an old woman . . .'

He glared at her then, eyes burning with unexpressed fury. 'What did it matter? People like her have plenty of money in their fancy houses, why shouldn't I have some of it?'

'You mean there were others?'

'And she loathed her family. They never visited her so why should they inherit what they don't deserve?'

'Even so . . .'

'You don't understand,' he snapped, grasping her arm and wrenching her suddenly towards him. 'You *never* understand, do you?' The gushing drops of water spun before her eyes and Lissa instinctively shrank away, her finger nails scrabbling for purchase on the slippery rock beneath her. Surely he wouldn't toss her down the waterfall? The dark anger in his charcoal eyes told her he was capable of any horror in his present mood.

'Philip, please be calm. Why don't we go home? It's cold here and the twins will be wanting their tea.'

'I never had this trouble with Felicity.'

The sudden reference to his former fiancée took Lissa by surprise. 'I beg your pardon? What has Felicity to do with all of this?'

'She did as she was told. You never did, not once. Felicity was humble and sweet and obedient.'

Out on the ice came a loud squeal and Lissa turned her attention at once to her children. She could just make out Sarah pulling Beth about by her coat tails as if she were a sled and they were both squealing with delight. Then she was brought sharply back to her predicament by the sting of icy water upon her face. One wrong move and both of them would plunge thirty feet into the abyss, beautiful in spring and summer, lethal in winter, as now.

'You aren't well,' Lissa gently reasoned. 'It must have been a shock seeing the Law Society move in. But we can face it.' She swallowed. 'Together.'

It would be the end of his career and they both knew it. His laughter rang out, bouncing back off black rocks and Lissa shuddered, fear crawling up her spine.

'Felicity was considered delicate,' Philip said, conversationally. 'She was an only daughter. Spoiled, of course.' He smiled at the memory. 'Her father knew I wanted to marry her but he did everything he could to stop us. He didn't consider me quite suitable.' Philip patted his pocket. 'Not enough in here to match his own fortune.'

Lissa struggled to take in what he was saying, hoping that if she kept him talking she could gradually ease him back from the brink of the gorge. 'Did Felicity want to marry you?'

'Of course, but in the end she wouldn't because of Daddy. He'd convinced her she was too delicate for marriage.' His lips curled at the corner into a parody of a smile. 'Even got a doctor to agree, would you believe? Utter nonsense. It didn't matter to me if she was. I loved her and would have looked after her.'

'Oh, Philip.' Lissa felt her blood start to freeze and as she shifted a foot to more solid ground, accidentally loosed a stone which fell and bounced from rock to rock till it disappeared, swallowed up by frothing foam. 'So what happened?' She really didn't want to know. All Lissa wanted was to get off this icy rock and take her children home to her warm fireside.

'My darling Felicity simply could not disobey her beloved father and that, she said, was the end of it. I took my revenge, of course. I had every right to do so. They ruined my life. Instead of being a member of a well-respected family, with a rich and beautiful wife, I was to be deserted, jilted, cast aside. I couldn't let that happen, d'you see? Not when I'd worked so hard. You can see how that would have ruined my reputation.'

Lissa was scarcely daring to breathe.

'I did explain to her how it had to be,' he said, sounding perfectly reasonable as he turned a smiling face to Lissa. 'I suggested it would be far less painful than living a life without love, under the thumb of her father. She did agree, in the end, really she did. Compliant to the end, my sweet Felicity. It was all so very simple, and everyone was most sympathetic. How tragic, they said, to lose a fiancée by drowning, mere days before the wedding. For one so young to take her own life in such a way was so very sad.'

Oh dear Lord, what was he saying? Lissa found she was shaking uncontrollably by this time, her eyes flickering from the hard planes of his face to the rushing water below.

'What future did she have, without me?'

She gazed at him in horror. 'But why, Philip? Why? You gained nothing from her death, nothing at all.'

He looked puzzled. 'Of course I did. I kept my good name, the respect and status that was due to me. And I gained my revenge. Her father deserved to suffer as I had.'

Lissa could find nothing else to say. Her silence was over-whelmed by the roar of the water below, muted only slightly by the icicles forming at its edges. Lissa had no wish to repeat Felicity's mistake. The poor girl must have lost all will to resist. But Lissa had fought for her freedom and gained it. She was her own person now and must cling on to that with all her strength. She looked down at his fingers, curled possessively about her arm. 'Let me go, Philip.' Cold panic threatened but Lissa knew it was vital to keep calm, to stay in control. 'We have to take the twins home for their tea. We mustn't have them catching a chill now, must we?'

But he was shaking his head. 'There's nothing left for me, Lissa. Nothing left for either of us. If I can't have you, nobody will. I explained all of that to Felicity. I can't let it happen again.'

It happened so quickly she knew afterwards that she could have done nothing to prevent it. One moment she was desperately clinging to the rock, the spray of iced water stinging her eyes and nose as she battled to free her arm from his menacing grip, the next a cry rang out. Renee's voice calling her name. A great cracking sound ripped through the air like a gun shot, only half swallowed up by the screams of her children.

Then she was somehow free of his hold and they were both running through the sticky snow, breath a hard ball in her frozen breast as instinctively they both leapt forward, out on to the ice. It was quite the wrong thing to do. Philip was taller and faster and was halfway across before Lissa had thought of it.

'No, no,' she cried. 'That's not the way. A tree branch. We need a branch. *Renee.*' The ice was breaking up even as she frantically searched and her children were huddled precariously together on one ridiculously small ice floe, arms about each other, in danger of slipping into the water at any moment. Then Renee was beside her, thrusting a branch into her hand.

'I'll hold it, go on.'

Sarah and Beth, too stunned to cry or move, clung to their small island of ice.

'Come to Mummy, my darlings. Be brave. You can do it.' Lissa was lying on her stomach on the ice, urging them, filling them with her energy and confidence till first Beth and then Sarah finally found the courage to let go of their island and reach across the black water to grasp her hand and the branch that Renee held. Then they were in her arms and they were all crying and sobbing together. Her wishes had been answered and her lovely children had been saved.

Philip's body was not found until the thaw came. Then he was buried with due ceremony in the small churchyard at Carreckwater.

The Law Society found all manner of problems in his practice. Any number of bank accounts in various names had once held the money which should rightly have belonged to Elvira Fraser and several other clients. Philip's mistake with Mrs Fraser was to imagine that she would stay at odds with her family. Her grandson, David, had proved him wrong and could at least be satisfied that justice, of a sort, had been done. Even sad Felicity's fate had been given restitution in a way. He had died much as he had caused her to die.

The house on the Parade was taken by the bank, in lieu of debts, and Lissa moved into the flat above the shop with the twins.

But it didn't trouble her. She felt she had been given a new life, a new beginning. And if there was sadness still, no one would have guessed. Or so she imagined.

But she reckoned without Renee.

She it was who insisted they visit Broombank one particular spring day, going on at length about problems with a design on the frame knitting machine upon which Lissa's opinion was vital.

But after an hour's thorough investigation, she could find nothing wrong.

'Jan must have sorted it, bless her,' Renee suggested. 'She's pregnant again, did you know?'

'Really? Oh, that's lovely. When is it due? I must go and see her.'

'She's down by Allenbeck, having a picnic with Nick and the children. I said I'd send you down to see them once you'd sorted this out.'

'I'll go now. Come on twins.'

'Leave them with me,' Renee said. 'We're going to play Shipwrecks and Pirates in the barn.'

Loud whoops of excitement from Beth and Sarah, so, laughing, Lissa left them to play, not unwilling to enjoy a half hour on her own. There seemed little enough time for that these days. The walk would do her good and she looked forward to congratulating Jan on her news.

Spring was well advanced now and the broom was a blaze of gold as she followed the sheep trods over the fells. Lissa saw a couple of hares boxing and crept by on tiptoe so as not to disturb them. Overhead a lark soared, singing its joyous song, and as she reached the little pack horse bridge her mind turned back to her girlhood days. She couldn't help but smile. Nick would tease her again, as he always did, about falling in. No doubt Robbie and little Alice were giving him heart failure in this respect now. Lissa sincerely hoped that the twins would never fall into anything. Trust them to choose the tarn when they almost did. If they had gone in to the water and slid beneath the ice, that would have been the end. But her wishing water had kept them safe, hadn't it? Only Philip had been lost.

'Nick? Jan?' She mustn't think of it. She mustn't remember. Lissa had suffered nightmares for weeks afterwards remembering the accident, remembering what Philip had told her just before it and how her own life had seemed to be in danger. Perhaps, in time, she might find it in her heart to forgive him, and forget.

Lissa turned her attention to how pretty the tiny forget-me-nots looked, to the tang of garlic flowers and the first heady scent of bluebells. And over by the drystone wall grew a clump of hart's tongue ferns, unfolding their shiny green fronds like miniature shepherd's crooks.

Lissa saw his legs first. Sensible boots with green woollen socks tucked over cord trousers. She'd know those legs anywhere for all they were no longer in crêpe soles and tight blue jeans. He was sitting with his back against the drystone wall of the bridge and Lissa leaned over to look down upon him, at his fair hair falling across his brow, at shoulders broad and strong in a thick Herdwick sweater.

'This is a long way from the States,' she said, a lightness to her tone which belied the heavy thump of her heartbeat.

'I missed my lift again,' he said, without even glancing up. 'You can't rely on anyone these days.'

Lissa came down from the bridge and glanced quickly about her, though she had to drag her eyes from his beloved face. 'Where are Jan and Nick? I was told I'd find them here.'

'That's Renee for you. Just loves to tell a tale. Even when it isn't true.' Derry grinned and Lissa's lips curled upwards into an answering smile.

'Why didn't she tell me the truth?' A rush of shyness made her feel suddenly awkward though her whole body was tingling as if it had been set alight like a fire cracker. Lissa longed to touch him, to make sure that he was real. But her mind rushed ahead. Could he possibly have forgiven her for blaming him for everything on that last day together. Should she apologise? How?

Then he got up and came towards her, still the same swaggering arrogant walk, and she loved it. 'You and I have a lot of talking to do, Lissa. For one thing . . .'

'Oh, I'm so sorry,' she blurted out, interrupting him. 'I shouldn't have blamed you because of what Philip did. And you were absolutely right. He *was* a fraud. And how were you to know that he'd steal my children and use blackmail? I was upset, that's all. I didn't really mean it. Can you ever forgive me?' She did not

437

doubt that he would but when she moved towards him he held up a hand to stay her, looking very stern.

'You must learn, Lissa, not to make hasty assumptions. You once accused me of not loving you enough. That hurt. And you should have known it wasn't true.'

Lissa was flushing, embarrassed and concerned by his teasing, for she was almost sure that's all it was. Almost. 'I wasn't thinking clearly. I'd lost the twins. I was worried.'

'I'm not simply talking about Philip and the children. I mean the time I went to Manchester and promised to come back for you. Then, through no fault of my own but that of arrogant pride, I came rather later than expected. When it was too late.'

Lissa swallowed the hard lump which had come into her throat. 'Don't bring all that up now. Please. Anyway, did you expect me to wait for ever? You let me down, remember, not the other way around.'

'I'm simply pointing out that sometimes a person has to wait a little longer for things.'

She reached for him then, her whole body refusing to be denied for another second. 'I do understand, really I do. I'm free now, Derry. Did Renee tell you?' Why didn't he come to her? Why didn't he take her in his arms and kiss her, as she so longed for him to do? What was holding him back?

'Life doesn't always behave exactly as one would wish it to.'

She was contrite now, reaching up to his face, touching his lips, his brow, his cheeks. 'I know, and I promise I have learned to be more patient, more trusting. At least, I hope I have. I've grown up, Derry. I don't throw tantrums or go off into sulks any more.'

'I'm glad to hear it. So if someone else were to say that they were sorry for letting you down, long ago in the past, you'd forgive them too, wouldn't you?'

Lissa was laughing, eager for his kisses. 'Yes, of course I would. Oh, do stop your teasing, Derry. I've waited and waited this long, haven't I? A whole six months at least. I thought you'd never come. I can't bear to wait another moment for you to kiss me and tell me you've wanted it too.'

But instead of taking her in his arms Derry did a little side-step. There was a rustling from beside the bridge as another figure emerged. A woman's. She was tall and beautiful with brown hair that swung in a page boy bob about her face, as smooth as a thrush's wing.

'Hello, Lissa.' She moved towards her with a graceful, swaying movement and even before Lissa looked into her eyes the prickling in her spine told her that this was her mother.

'Kath?'

A rueful smile. 'I've missed your birthday again, haven't I? Sorry. Rather too many in fact. I dare say I've a lot of explaining to do, huh?'

Lissa remained silent. For the life of her she could think of nothing to say.

'Better late than never?' Kath smiled and her hazel eyes held an appeal. Listen to me, they said. Give me a chance. Then laughing softly, as if embarrassed by Lissa's steady gaze, she glanced, half teasingly at Derry. 'I'm not surprised you're so anxious to kiss this young fella. And I think he'd be ready enough to oblige. What if I were to walk on ahead, then you two could set that little matter to rights? He put my case rather well, so I guess I owe him a favour. Maybe then we can talk, and you'll let me give my excuses in person so we can catch up?'

Lissa stared at Kath, bemused, struggling to put her thoughts into order. 'All right,' she managed.

'Good.'

Lissa watched as Kath turned and started to walk up the hill to Broombank. Then she ran after her and put a hand on her arm.

'Meg is up there.'

'I know.'

'Meg is my mother. I want you to understand how it is. And Tam is my father. They are my family now.'

'I do understand, honey. But you and I could perhaps be friends. At last. How about it?' She looked oddly uncertain, as if she half expected Lissa to tell her she wasn't wanted, that it was all much too late.

Lissa's smile lit her face, bringing an indrawn breath in response. 'I'd like that,' she said.

When Kath had gone, Lissa turned to Derry and held out both hands to him. 'This was your doing, wasn't it?'

'By way of a peace offering,' he said, giving his lop-sided grin. 'To make up for past neglect.'

'Thanks,' she said, violet eyes shimmering with tears and

happiness. 'Now I seem to have two mothers, and more love than a woman deserves.'

Derry took her in his arms at last, his mouth seeking hers. 'So long as you're content with only one husband, I can live with that.'